PATRICK PARKER'S PROGRESS

1940, Coventry burns but Patrick Parker, miracle baby, is born away from his home town, safe in London, saved by Fate, and clearly a Man of Destiny. Florence Parker, mother of Man of Destiny, glories in his progress and waits upon his pleasure. George Parker, father of Man of Destiny, would, if he could, do likewise, but he scarcely gets a look in. Patrick, born out of rubble, will be a great builder. He will admire Brunel, he will build great bridges, nothing will stand in his way and the world—and its women—will adore him. Audrey Wapshott will adore Patrick, too. But he abandons her for a useful marriage and she follows her own random path to Paris. It takes thirty years but in the end Audrey triumphs, and Patrick—though as grandly esteemed as the builders of the great ziggurats of Babylon—is humbled by the marvel of enduring love.

PATRICK PARKER'S PROGRESS

Mavis Cheek

WINDSOR
PARAGON

First published 2004
by
Faber and Faber Limited
This Large Print edition published 2004
by
BBC Audiobooks Ltd
by arrangement with
Faber and Faber Limited

ISBN 0 7540 9511 8   (Windsor Hardcover)
ISBN 0 7540 9402 2   (Paragon Softcover)

British Library Cataloguing in Publication Data available

Printed and bound in Great Britain by
Antony Rowe Ltd., Chippenham, Wiltshire

Sixteen years on—for Bella again, with love.

'. . . so from
this bridge, a geologist of the centuries
will succeed in recreating our contemporary
world.'

Mayakovsky

Begin, small boy, to know your mother with a
    smile
(Ten lunar months have brought your mother
    long discomfort)
Begin, small boy: him who for this parent has not
    smiled
No god invites to table, nor goddess to bed.
  Virgil, Eclogue IV

According to Isambard, Ellen (Hulme) appears
to have been a lively young lady . . . who indulged
in the 'shocking habit of . . . quizzing . . .' him.
  Angus Buchanan, *Brunel*

. . . He evidently considered himself sufficiently
well supplied against disaster to ask Mary Horsley
to marry him . . . without talents, she constituted
no threat to his ego . . .
  Adrian Vaughan, *Isambard Kingdom Brunel:
  Knight Errant*

. . . I wish you were my obedient servant. I should
begin with a little flogging.
  Isambard Kingdom Brunel's reply to John
  Scott Russell, naval architect and shipbuilder,
  September 1855

The reputation of Isambard Kingdom Brunel is unassailable.

Observer, 10 March 2002

The Clifton Suspension Bridge (Egyptian in style) is my first love,
my darling . . .

Isambard Kingdom Brunel

Postcard of Brunel's Royal Albert Bridge over the Tamar sent by Patrick Parker to Florence Parker and dated 11 April 1954.

Now here's a beauty, Mother! Aud liked it. But she called it 'lacy looking'. I ask you!
P. x

Postcard of Brunel's Royal Albert Bridge over the Tamar sent by Patrick Parker to Audrey Wapshott, 12 November 1961.

Here's one for your album Aud! I wish I could show it to you. What do you think of it?
Yours, Patrick.

ONE

PATRICK

Patrick is Born

It was Han engineers who advanced the suspension bridge into the form we recognise today . . . More than a third of the Empire's economic output was made up of luxury goods to be transported west. As a result, canals were developed and fibre towropes refined to consistent qualities and strengths. These cables could, in turn, be used in suspension bridges: lightweight, economic, and without the large foundation forces associated with the arched alternatives . . .

Matthew Wells, *30 Bridges*

November 1940. Coventry burns. The hospital in which Florence and George Parker's baby might have been born is no more than melted rubble. The house to which Florence and George Parker would have returned with their baby sits in the row of smoking artisans' dwellings, like a blackened tooth stump. The railway station where George Parker (excused service duties, flat feet) collects tickets is twisted like a handful of grotesque barleysugars. If you wish to travel north after the night of the fourteenth of November, you must travel from Tile Hill. If you want to travel south you must go from Brandon Street.

Miraculously on the night of the fourteenth of November the Parkers have no need of this information for they have already done their travelling. On that dreadful, scorching night, the fourteenth of November 1940, the Parkers—miraculously—are not there. At the exact moment that the devastation of Coventry takes place, Florence, after nearly twelve hours of labour—is brought to bed of a fine baby boy in her friend Dolly's house in south-west London. He is a little early, it is true. But he is nevertheless perfect, perfect.

Florence Parker and Dorothy Wapshott were in service together before their marriages and are close as sisters. Closer, some might say, though Dorothy, at thirty-five, is seven years younger than her friend. The visit to London was a little pre-Christmas treat for Florence, who is somewhat dazed to find herself expecting at all, given her age, and not a little embarrassed, but it is wartime and strange things are happening everywhere. Now she is even more dazed to find herself far from home with a new and perfect, perfect baby in her arms.

Long, long after this day they will talk in awed tones about the strangeness of fate. Why should Florence choose that day to visit and not another? Why did the baby choose that afternoon to arrive early? If he had come the day before, then . . . They speak of this in whispers and they shudder down the years. One more quirk of fate bringeth forth a miracle. Florence feels that God has not let her down, despite her shame in front of Him for her obvious dip into carnal sin. The baby is destined, quite clearly, for greatness.

George, father of the baby, though left behind in Coventry has also escaped the inferno. He is surprised, and pleased, to be summoned. It is not customary for his wife to want him for anything

4

much. But summoned he is by Florence's shrieking to Dolly and Dolly haring off up the road clutching her pinny about her to the undertaker's on Brokesley Street (the nearest telephone) and ringing the station. George is therefore halfway between Coventry and King's Cross when the sirens wail and the terror starts and he knows nothing of it. He has swapped his ticket duties with Arthur Crow, his friend. Something about which Molly Crow might have had something to say now that her husband lies a crisp corpse on the bumpy, bubbling asphalt of Station Road. Only Molly, too, is dead. Five orphans, five more orphans, to add to the toll of that night. But the baby born of Florence Parker is quite, quite safe and has both parents alive and sound in wind and limb.

There is rare black humour when George finally returns to Coventry after a twenty-four-hour visit to London. He slipped and slid and did very little sleeping on the unyielding Rexine-covered settee provided for him by Dorothy overnight and he is not up to much excitement as a result—but he gets some anyway. For as he turns the corner of Lamb Street, Lilly Willis of the little General Stores passes out when she sees him. One minute George is walking along and smiling at her, the next she is stretched out cold and white on the cobbles. When she is brought round she says, faintly, that she thought he was dead, the ticket booth having caught it. To which, with unaccustomed humour, George replies that he certainly came close to thinking death was preferable once or twice in the night because of that dratted settee—but though weak, he points out, he is alive . . . 'Very much so,' he says, which makes Lilly regain her colour, and

5

add a little more to it. Blushing becomes Lilly though she does it seldom. She has an old head on her young shoulders.

To Lilly's questions about mother and baby, George is positive. Both are doing well, he says, and Florence seems to be in her element. Lilly sniffs. Not like George's wife to be in her element over anything, she thinks. But Florence, to Lilly's grim amusement, has apparently forgiven the carnal act that brought about the child, taken to motherhood like a duck to water, and the baby has taken to its mother like a—like a—duckling. Lilly asks who the baby favours and George says, somewhat mournfully Lilly thinks, that the baby—apparently—takes after Florence's side of the family. Entirely. The baby is Florence to the spit was what Dolly said. Women always stick together, was what George thought, and he could only nod, look at his child, and agree. All the same, he thought he saw something of himself in there. The long, sensitive fingers, if nothing else. George may collect tickets for a living but he is good with his hands, too. Creative.

'It's a miracle—' Lilly shudders—'that Flo was off out of it.' What she really thinks is that the real miracle is how *George* was off out of it.

According to George, the miracle of being off out of it is what Florence does nothing but repeat to the baby in her arms. That he is a little miracle. That he will go far. That he was destined. That he is her little angel risen from the ashes. That he will really *be* someone—do something—one day. He'll probably end up making cars like the rest of them, thinks Lilly, but she wouldn't say so. It has not been her happiness to have children and she is aware

6

that she can sometimes sound sour. The old head on young shoulders is quite a wise one.

'Oh,' says Lilly, 'It's a he, then?' And George agrees that it is.

'And what colour hair has he got?'

But George shakes his head. He hasn't actually held the baby, or got very close, buried as the infant remained in his wife's pillows and bedjacket and bosom and armpits.

'There doesn't seem to be a lot of it,' he says cautiously. 'Yet.'

'And a name?'

'We have called him Patrick,' he says. 'Not Pat and not Paddy—but Patrick.'

'That's nice,' says Lilly.

'Can't stand the name myself,' says George. 'I wanted William.'

'He'd be called Willy then and you wouldn't like that,' says Lilly, who likes to look on the bright side and cheer people up.

'Nothing wrong with Willy, is there?' asks George, gone sly all of a sudden.

Lilly simpers. The colour has returned even more strongly to her cheeks. She may be an old head on a young body but she still knows how to colour up fetchingly like a girl. She turns back towards her shop. George follows. They go in and Lilly snags the lock and turns the card at the window to 'Closed'. George runs his hands through his hair as prelude to pushing open the door that divides the shop from Lilly's living quarters. 'Go on then,' she says. And he does.

Now that Lilly has recovered from her faint, George and she go up the stairs to Lilly's bedroom, as they have been doing every Wednesday half-day closing for several years. Ever since, in fact, George and Florence were wed. After the wedding night Florence said that once was quite enough for her. And she turned a blind eye. Around the same time, Lilly's new young husband Alfred Willis lost his bits in a weaving accident, and she had already got the taste for it was how she put it to George. It is a suitable arrangement all round. If the community knows, the community says nothing and does not condemn. It is a friendly part of Coventry. Or it was. The General Stores, Willis's, round the corner from Chapel Street, has been saved, along with a couple of houses either side—while, all around, the rest of the street stands smouldering and blistered. George refers to this as he follows Lilly up the now oddly sloping stairs.

'It's a miracle,' he says, looking lugubriously at her ascending bottom.

'Swings and roundabouts,' says Lilly the pragmatist.

George puts his hand out to pat the bottom, thinks better of it and removes it. He is still not quite sure how to approach touching a woman in broad daylight and with her clothes on. Somehow the body takes over once the lights are out, the curtains are drawn and the sheets are pulled over their heads.

Lilly is brisk and friendly and sweet-smelling of Parma violets during the experience. She keeps herself, as George says to himself, nice. Not too fancy but nicely turned out. She paints her nails, even her toenails, and she unashamedly wears lipstick. He likes that sort of thing though he feels slightly bashful about it. And she is cheerful afterwards. When it is over she smiles and sings as

8

she dresses and smiles at him as if they have shared a good joke and her voice is softer, sweeter somehow. The change in her voice reflects how his body feels. Kind and gentle and good.

He would like to ask Lilly what she thinks about it all—the act, the afterwards—but he never does. He wouldn't know how to begin the sentence and he is afraid she will laugh. He can hear her saying in response 'Oh George, what *do* you mean?' if he should say, 'Now then, Lilly—don't you feel this is unsatisfactory?' But he knows what she would say. 'What can we do?' And he would not have an answer.

Once he just went on lying there and said, half dreaming, 'Be good to go away somewhere together, Lil. How about Paris? We could go up the Eiffel Tower. I'd like to see it. I'd make you a model of it afterwards. Paris is the place for lovers.' The word lovers is heavy in the room. Lilly just stood there in front of him, hands on her hips, shockingly naked and carelessly amused, and smiling crookedly, all lipstick gone.

'Now then, George,' she said. 'Don't get all sentimental.' Then she touched his face in a different way from usual—and somewhere inside of him he felt as if a plug had been pulled out— everything was running away to nothing. He said, moving into the murky waters of taboo—'If I had stuck with you we'd be together like this all the time.' For a moment she had looked down at him with the sweetest look on her face. And then— snap! The look was gone. 'Come on now,' she said, back to her usual self, 'gee-up. You've got a baby on the way . . . And there's a war on.' She pulled him up, aware that he did not look too happy about

9

it. Probably, she thought, as she dressed, he was worried about the baby's future in this death-filled world. She tried not to think the other thought which hurt, surprisingly: that he and Florence made that baby, together. Unless bloody Florence was going for the Immaculate Conception. Which Lilly Willis would not put past the woman.

But it was not that then, and it is not that now. George already has an inkling that this son of his will never be his at all really. Already he feels the exclusion. Another possibility has let him down. His life all round has not been what he once thought it would be. In short, George is a disappointed man and a once-a-week pleasuring has not fulfilled him at all. Always, as soon as he has left the shop, George wonders why he bothers. Lilly is so cheerful, he is sure that she forgets him as soon as the door swings shut. He tries to be like that too. But by Monday he is running his hands through his hair and back to waiting for the following Wednesday session with a pleasurable need. If he hadn't got flat feet he might have seen something of the world, expanded his horizons, even if it did end up putting a bullet into his chest. As it is, his horizons are narrow and getting narrower. A model of the Eiffel Tower is about as far as he will get, he knows. He makes models like some men have dreams. He hopes his son will do better. He certainly hopes his son will do better in the matter of marriage and happiness and all that. He couldn't do much worse.

The little diversion from George's sensible sexual arrangement with Lilly, and from which baby Patrick occurred, happened the previous Easter when Florence ate a considerable number of

10

liqueur chocolates. She was keeping them, two boxes, winnings from the church tombola, to give away as gifts herself, being teetotal, but since the Germans were very likely due to land at any moment, it seemed an act of Patriotic Duty to swallow the lot. Fortunately she could remember nothing of the ensuing conjugal act, except the room going round and George above her looking very surprised.

Now, down in South London, tucked up in Dolly's bed with a pink bedjacket around her shoulders, her once harsh mouth bears the soft curve of contentment. 'I never knew I wanted you until you came,' she whispers to the bald, pink head. And she kisses its pulsing tip. Like many a mother before and since, the act of maternal union took her quite by surprise, rendered her weak, and made her ready to rip the world apart with her jaws should any element in it try to hurt the babe at her breast. It surprised her all over again that such perfection should be borne out of such an ugly act, such a painful sequel. No wonder, she thought, that it was considered original sin.

*   *   *

After a few weeks, Florence reluctantly made the train journey back to ravaged Coventry, with George at her side. 'Ah, the proud father,' said a hearty lady in the carriage, after cooing over Florence's bundle. Florence looked up as if she were about to say something sharp and all George, who had come to accompany his wife and son, managed was a sheepish smile. He knew it embarrassed his wife. If he felt any atavistic

11

stirrings of masculine pride, he kept them to himself. If you were a woman and you sat with a man in a railway carriage, and you held that man's baby, then it meant you had been doing unmentionable things with him. It was all George could do to stop himself leaning across the carriage and saying to the hearty lady, 'It's all right you know, we only did it twice—ever.'

The council found them the three-roomed ground floor of a house to the south of the town—with a small scullery, shared bathroom above, but its own privy out the back. Florence, though she moaned about it, realised that they were lucky compared with some. Her previous neighbours, a childless couple, were now living in one room and a kitchen and the WC was down two flights of stairs. She stroked little Patrick's head as he nuzzled at her breast—another blessing, another miracle—if it hadn't been for him who knew what kind of a tip they'd be rehoused in. He was, in every sense, his mother's salvation. In the midst of ruin and chaos, he will bring light, she thinks. She also thinks he will bring glory for her. Before her marriage Florence looked after her three brothers and her father—Mother having departed when she was in service in London and little Flo recalled to take her place. George had seemed like a miracle then. A man with a future, she thought, in the railways, a safe job throughout the Depression—only he never got further than collecting tickets and making his models and looking miserable about it.

With miracles and blessings in mind, the baby was draped in white lace and fine, handknitted woollens (this latter a present from dexterous Dolly) and taken into town to the Methodist

12

Church where he shrieked and yelled a blue fit at the coldness of the water. Indeed, he pummelled and cried and held his breath and made the Reverend Pincher so irritated and tight-lipped with all his kickings and wrigglings that Florence was convinced the Man of God had lived up to his name. She very nearly took her baby back off him, but the Reverend Pincher held on tight (thus increasing the outraged volume of those little lungs) saying that it was necessary in the sight of God that he hold on to the little perisher to complete the job. With Florence shadow-close and snorting and flapping like a mother seal the baptism took place. Plain Patrick became Patrick Nigel and was handed back as such. The Reverend Pincher mopped his brow and called him a determined little lad. George, shaking the man's damp hand, could not quite hide a little smirk, feeling that if the ruddy church didn't know how to deal with the boy, it was no wonder that he, George, his own father could not. Florence strode off calming the angry child and was overheard to murmur all the way down the chapel path, 'There, there—didn't you like the nasty man with the horrid water, then?' Which the Reverend Pincher thought was somewhat against the grain of the baptismal ritual.

George's daft sister Ada stood godmother, upsetting his other sister Bertha—which pleased Florence who did not care for Bertha's outspoken ways. Although Ada lived in Coventry she was not one of those women who knew, to the nearest number, how many beans made five and she would leave well alone. The godfathers were distant relatives—one no more than a lad himself,

13

the least godly and not at all likely to interfere. Florence was not having anyone come between her and her son.

George's daft sister Ada soon found herself under a burnt-out bus, not much more than a pile of ashes herself. The war did terrible, terrible things to communities, it was true, thought Florence, as she sat holding baby Patrick at the funeral—but there was always a bright side to everything . . . For instance, she was able to nurse baby Patrick for the first two and a half years of his life without anyone taking exception. And that kept him close to her. You might almost say, tied. Before the war it was becoming fashionable to use bottles for babies but not now. A good mother was a production unit like everything else. The war was useful in respect of this. Nobody bothered to tell you what to do and what not to do when the sirens sounded. Florence could pretend to the world, perhaps to herself, that she was still nursing him beyond his second birthday because it was convenient and best for him and natural. Nobody remarked on it. Only Dolly Wapshott's visit changed things. Dolly, whose baby girl Little Audrey arrived nine months after Patrick (the juxtaposition of two bodies, one male, one female, sharing a small single bed for several nights while Florence and son reposed in their double one awoke a surprising urge in Dolly and her husband). Little Audrey had already been weaned by the time she was one year old.

'And that,' Dolly told Florence firmly, 'was considered late . . . Who knows what's waiting for us at the end of this war?' she said firmly. 'It doesn't do to make a milksop. They need to be a bit independent in this day and age. My little Audrey

14

can chew on anything nowadays.'

Very reluctantly, Florence yielded up her last two pleasurable moments with him—first thing in the morning and last thing at night—and it should be said that Patrick did not object very strongly. On the first night of the withdrawal of the maternal tit, when Auntie Dolly put a sweetened dummy in his mouth at the moment the tears began to well, he sucked on it and became quite cheerful again. Mother or sugary rubber teat, it was all the same to him. It was, after all, something new and therefore interesting. Patrick might not know the word but he knew the sensation: the world was an interesting place and he was ready to enjoy each new experience.

'There you are, you see—' said Dolly in triumph. 'He doesn't need it at all.'

She playfully chucked her own chubby daughter beneath the chin and the child chomped on a bickey-peg and smiled through its fat red cheeks. 'Quite the independent Little Audrey, aren't you?' she proudly said. Florence sniffed, looking at her own little angel as he lay in his cot, eyes closed, dummy moving rhythmically. Despite his having arrived early he was a perfect shape—neither fat, nor thin—and he was elegant, cautious—not one to do anything unforeseen—a thinking child, and quick on the uptake. From his earliest days, when the merest movement in his cot, the lightest change in his breath, the slightest flicker of his eyes brought his mother to his side to see what was required, Patrick had a way of looking out at the world that said he knew he was very important. Florence stroked his long, artistically shaped fingers and then looked at her friend's daughter's plump digits. 'Little Audrey?'

15

she said suddenly, and acidly. 'Nothing little about it.'

'Got George's fingers, I see,' said Dolly, by way of a counter. She knew where Flo's bodies were buried if she'd a mind to.

Florence was not one to find anything appealing apart from her son, even baby girls. Girls had a way of looking at you that went straight through and out the other side. Patrick just looked up at her, and trusted. That was what counted. To her Patrick she was everything, or almost everything. Not quite, because for some irritating reason, when they visited London, Patrick seemed to find Little Audrey fascinating—he liked to push at her and see her topple and then watch, smiling, as she righted herself, laughing and scarlet from the exertion among the cushions. He liked to pull her bottle in and out of her mouth and hear the sucking sound of the air and bubbles rushing back into the teat. Throughout it all, Little Audrey was entirely good-humoured. Florence did not like these games at all. But if she ever tried to change the mood—with a clapping song or 'Come to Mother . . .' Patrick paid no attention. Until he was ready. And then he would say so, loudly. 'Patrick stop now,' he would say, nodding sagely. And that would brook no nonsense. Florence would reclaim her prize. She swung him up in the air telling him he should go higher than the highest he had ever been before. 'You'll be something, my boy,' she would mutter. 'Not like the likes of Little Audrey. You'll look down on them all—'

Coventry remained a wasteland. On one of her visits Dolly said, 'You'd have thought they'd start rebuilding this place, Flo—it's no setting for

16

bringing up a kiddie.'

'Oh,' said Florence. 'They keep talking about doing this and that but nothing ever happens. If anyone does produce an idea then the Council can't make up its mind.'

'Your George should go along with some of his models.'

Florence just sniffed.

Dolly whispered the question. 'Still Lilly, then?' To which Florence just sniffed the louder.

Little Audrey liked to watch as Florence bathed and caressed and spoke to her baby boy. She watched the games and the rituals as Patrick meticulously put brick upon brick without knocking them down. 'Mother's little builder,' Florence would say, or 'Who's Mummy's clever boy, then?' Little Audrey saw that George looked on but said nothing. And that he built the boy things that Florence brushed aside. The general view of Patrick's great talent with the bricks was that he would one day grow up to rebuild Coventry, probably single-handedly, and be the wonder of the world. Little Audrey smiled and clapped as the bricks went higher but she was never allowed to touch. Once, overcome at the great height of the tower of coloured wood Patrick had made, she tottered over and gave it a mighty, satisfying punch and the bricks went everywhere. Patrick looked at her coldly and rebuilt his tower. He ignored her for the rest of the afternoon. She did not do it again.

But Little Audrey showed she had some tricks of her own. As soon as Patrick saw how she sat up at the table and made use of a spoon all on her own—with a few spillages which Florence made quite a bustling fuss about—Patrick followed suit.

17

Perfectly. He also asked for another cushion. Little Audrey sat on one, he would sit on two. When his mother tried to help him guide his spoon, he pushed away her hand. His first act of extreme independence and Florence was saddened to the core.

When Dolly came to stay, or when Florence visited London, the children were given their baths together. Florence did not like it and objected. 'There's a war on,' said Dolly firmly. 'Economy is important.' So here it was, in that warm, soap-scented water, that Florence told Patrick—and Little Audrey—all over again about the night of his birth and how he had escaped, that he was a miracle baby, that out of destruction he had been born. 'How clever you are,' said his mother, over and over again, as she watched his dexterous play with sponge and nailbrush and flannel. 'Clever, clever, clever boy.' When he had done with the play he drew steeples and roofs and chimney stacks in the steam on the mirror. It was all she could do to persuade him that he could not take his beloved wooden bricks into the bath.

Little Audrey watched. She was fascinated and repelled at this sweet talk. But she saw how it pleased Patrick. She also came to recognise the moment just before Patrick decided that he had had enough and required lifting out of the water— because before saying so he ran his little hands through his fluffy baby hair from forehead to back . . . As soon as she saw it she pulled out the plug and the splendid rushing gurgle always coincided with Patrick holding up his arms and saying, 'Out, Mummy, out.' Both Florence and Patrick would look at Audrey in astonishment. How did she

18

always know? Or did she? Or was it always a coincidence? It was never—quite—distinguished. Florence Parker refused to consider the possibility that Little Audrey was bright.

On one occasion George suggested that he might bath baby Patrick for a change and Florence had looked so shocked—so defensive—it was as if he had suggested that he would quite like to brain his son with an axe. 'That's for a mother to do,' said the mother in question. 'You'd probably drown him.' Audrey lifted her hands to George and offered herself, but of course there was no question of that.

Fortunately it was not considered odd if a father had nothing to do with his children until they misbehaved and needed attention. But George felt it. He could very likely count on the fingers of one hand, as he told Lilly, the number of times he had held his child. One of those was in church during the baptism. Florence watched him so sharply that he felt sure he would drop the little body. He liked holding Patrick, he liked the way the baby looked up into his eyes and struggled to make sense of what he saw—he liked the way, now that he was older, the boy tottered towards him and held up his arms. But he let Florence have her way. 'Well,' said Lilly, 'that's the way of it. Mother knows best.' Lilly had made a vow that she would never say anything bad to George about his wife. Sometimes she felt she could choke on the undertaking.

Lilly did not like to dwell on George's domestic arrangements because it always made him so mournful. And her. When he was mournful it reminded her that she had nothing much to look forward to, either. Neither of them spoke of the past. Too long ago and best forgotten were those days when they were both young and free and went for walks together by the canals because they had no money to do anything else. They held hands and spent their dreams instead. George would build himself a castle to live in and Lilly would make a garden. And then he married Florence and she married Alfred. Now he lived in three rooms and her bedroom looked out over a small back yard, a shed full of sweet boxes, and a patch of earth that never got the sun. All Lilly wanted, needed, now was a bit of fun and bugger the garden. 'I'm sure Flo knows what she's doing,' she said sourly. 'She's devoted.'

He longed to talk to her, really talk to her, but if she said it was all just a bit of fun between them, then that is all it could be. He would rather have it than not. A little bit of Lilly at any price was worth it. 'She is,' he said positively in return. 'Devoted. As you say.'

When George suggested that he and Patrick pack up a picnic one day and go for a bit of a hike, something that George had once done with his own father and enjoyed, Florence said it was out of the question because of the biting cold. When George waited until the sun shone and suggested it again, Florence said that Patrick could not walk far in any case because he had weak ankles. It was the first anyone had heard of it but Patrick rather liked the idea. It meant that whenever he did not want to do anything, he had merely to flick his little foot over on its side and a big, purple bruise would arrive. 'I'll carry him on my shoulders,' said George, as defiantly as he dared.

Patrick perked up at this but Florence said,

'You'll do no such thing. He might fall and crack his head open.'

An image of Humpty-Dumpty came to mind, and Patrick wailed. George decided to bide his time and wait until the boy was a bit older and a bit stronger. Meanwhile he left his son's welfare entirely in the arms of his wife and went on making his models of great buildings of the world. The war was coming to an end, the capitals of Europe would be free again, but he would never get to them now. He pinned up photographs as compensation and went on clipping tickets instead.

Bathtime continued as mother and son's special time. Even during the war years, when soap was hard to come by, and oils and lotions almost non-existent, most of the time Florence managed to get something to use on the fine, soft skin of her boy at bathtime. She even crushed rosemary leaves or lavender in season to make cod-liver oil smell agreeable, and she would rub it over her son's cheeks and lips, his legs and back and arms to keep him soft and protected. The chill winds of Midlands weather could blast his baby skin into flaky redness. When she took him out in the pram, or later toddling in the park, he was startlingly beautiful compared with the other children who had wet, sore, reddened noses and chilblained cheeks and hands. Towards the end of the war it had to be either the boilings from fish or Vaseline that Florence used. Something which the boy, even though he was under five, noticed and objected to. He was used to the best. He would have it. He ran his hands through his hair in a gesture that Florence now knew to prelude a tantrum. 'Don't want horrible smelly stuff—' he screamed. 'Want

21

nice stuff.' Florence managed to find some glycerine on the black market. 'Better,' said Patrick, mollified. Later he marched up to his father and handed him the horrible fishy concoction that Florence had tried to use. 'For you, Father,' he said. And George, who knew nothing of the incident, was touched. At first. But from that moment Patrick developed a curious way of dealing with anything that he did not like, including spinach, which was to insist that his mother gave it to George, which she did. Florence said this was the boy's caring response to hard rations and not wanting to waste things, but George saw it as something quite different. More like contempt.

In his shed at the bottom of the garden George indulged himself. He moved on from wood and glue to buying bits and pieces of old Meccano and—his first project in the new medium—he replicated the station signal box. Patrick sidled down there, though his mother forbade it—V2 raids, the cold, the dark, his health, the mess—as he liked to watch unseen through the little window while his father made structures that looked infinitely complex and beautiful. If ever Florence caught him lingering there she brought him straight back indoors. She was torn between forbidding George his shed activities and enjoying the house and Patrick without the nuisance of his father. The former won. Just. And Patrick went on looking. George, absorbed in his task, never saw how rapt his son was by the intricacies of his handiwork.

Patrick at School

The first examples of masonry arch bridges date
from as early as 1000 BC and were first built in
Persia where mud-plastered, bent reeds produced
small vaulted huts. The free profile of bent stems
tied across the top approximates to the ideal
parabolic profile for a free-standing arch . . .
Matthew Wells, *30 Bridges*

A month or two after D-Day the Parker family was
finally and permanently rehoused in a three-up two-
down on the edge of the town where the air was said
to be purer. This would eventually mean the end of
Lilly and the Wednesday afternoons. Not only
because the journey across town was long, but
because Florence decided it was time for the liaison
to cease. She made it clear—though not in so many
words—that now George was a father and his son
was so knowing, *It* (unspecified) was no longer
seemly. 'Halfway across Coventry,' she would say to
the boy—just as if he was an adult—'And for what, I
ask you? For what?' And she would cross her arms
and appear to juggle her swelling bosom. Her chest
was formidable and she used it to advantage. It was
as if, on finding itself no longer required, Florence's
embonpoint was determined to maintain a high
profile and palpable dudgeon.

Patrick was intrigued. Both by the juggled bosom
and by the question. Neither was forthcoming. If he
reached out to touch her bosom Florence always

tapped his hand away calling him a naughty boy, but smiling all the same so that it was like a little game between them. If Patrick then asked, in his piping little voice, 'What does my father go halfway across Coventry for?' his mother's smile would fade. 'Never you mind.' And she would busy herself with something. 'It's not the sort of thing you'll want to know about . . .' And out would come a biscuit, or his drawing things, or a scarf to tuck around him before they set off for a walk. He always liked his drawing things best. His mother would smile a particular smile, pat his arm, prop him up at the table on a cushion and tiptoe out of the room leaving him alone with his ideas and his thoughts. He was special, what he drew and imagined was special, and his mother kept his drawings, every one. When Little Audrey came to stay she did almost nothing you could possibly recognise on her paper. Patrick was contemptuous. He was also the tiniest, weeniest bit envious of the way she held her pencil in her fist and just seemed to throw the colours at the page. When he pointed out it was a mess she merely beamed at him and made some more. At the end of the session there would be polite maternal praise for her work and then it would be screwed up and thrown away. Little Audrey did not seem to mind. Later, though, when she drew pictures of Queens and Princesses, she liked to keep them, even though Patrick always liked to explain how the arms were too long or she had only put three fingers on a hand.

Patrick noticed that Little Audrey's mother was very different with her daughter from the way Patrick's mother was with him. Dolly quite often told her little girl not to bother her, to go and play in the yard and to find something to do. Patrick's mother never said any of those things. If he was ever at a loss, she was always there to talk or amuse or suggest. And she still liked to sit him on her lap, which Little Audrey's mother very seldom accommodated, calling her daughter—though she smiled as she said it—a big fat lump and too big to be carried. Unless she was that universally invoked word 'tired'—she had a scream on her if she wanted to—she toddled off quite unconcerned. Dolly also said quite often, 'You're a big girl now and I'm busy.' Patrick—when he was called a big boy—knew it was always an invitation to stay and be praised. There were, it seemed, different ways to be and different degrees of importance. Some children were not as important as he was and this fitted in with his experience quite perfectly.

The other difference he noticed was the difference in attitude between his mother and himself, and his mother and his father. They never touched, hardly spoke unless it was a question: Do you want tea, fish for supper, an egg? Is the rubbish out? Have you seen the paper? And sometimes Florence would listen to her husband and then, behind his back, turn to Patrick and roll her eyes and grimace. It seemed to him it was the way things were when you got older. 'I will never grow up,' he said to Florence, putting his arms around her neck one night after a particularly exhilarating, if confusing, eye rolling. She hugged him back as if that were the right answer to some silent question.

If he was lucky, if the crossness that Florence felt on account of this '*It*' thing that his father went across town for made her truly irate, he might wheedle the odd hint or image of what it was. He imagined a place made of cotton wool in which a creature called Lilly-Her-That-One, gave presents to his father and offered him pleasure with no thought for anyone else . . . To Patrick this was really intriguing. Like Santa's Grotto at Webb's.

'Perhaps if you gave my dad some presents with no thought for anyone else he wouldn't go halfway across town to Lilly-Her-That-One for them?' he said.

Florence looked at him with a new expression on her face, which was a mixture of anger and fear, and it was then she decided that enough was enough.

When his father came home on that Wednesday evening, Patrick was waiting for him.

'Where is your present?' he asked.

George stared at him.

'From Lilly-Her-That-One?'

'You see,' hissed Florence. 'You see?'

George never went for a Wednesday afternoon again. He told Lilly, by letter, that it was for the boy's sake, and for the respectability of his wife and the community. Lilly tore it up into tiny little pieces and did not reply. She knew that it was not what he wanted, that the sanctimonious tone was not his but his wife's. What she did not know was that what he really wanted to write but which was buried somewhere beneath the priggish, stilted phrases, was 'Come away with me . . .' But you could not say that to someone who only wanted a bit of fun. And whose husband was impaired.

Without those afternoons there was little in life that pleased George and nothing to relish and he became more and more morose. Once more he tried to assert himself in the matter of his son. He showed him the Meccano model of the station signal box in the shed and watched, pleased, as the boy ran his fingers over it with a gentle reverence. Emboldened, George then took him for a tour of the station, letting him collect and issue tickets, and stand with one of the drivers right up next to him in the engine. He also took him down to meet Joe Mundy in the signal box. But while the levers and switches quite interested the boy, they did not thrill him and he showed more interest in being high up, which he considered grand, and in the still damaged footbridge over the rails, replaced by a temporary structure. He stood staring at it from the signal box for a long time. Eventually he said to his father, 'You could mend that, couldn't you, Dad?' And George thought he probably could if they ever asked him. He nodded. 'So could I,' said Patrick firmly.

George felt a momentary flicker of excitement and fear. 'When we get home,' he offered, 'we could go into the shed and see how I made one. A model. A little one.'

Patrick nodded. 'And then I can make a big one later,' he said. George—without thinking too much about it—held his son's hand. It felt warm and soft and as he held it, it was as if the muscles in his body were suddenly released. They sang songs like 'Ten Green Bottles' for the rest of the journey and Patrick looked at his father with a new admiration.

When they arrived home, Florence, who was standing at the front-room net curtains as if she had never stirred from the spot, watched them coming down the road. Saw them holding hands and how brightly Patrick chattered up at his father. Saw how their hands swung as if they hadn't a care in the world. Patrick came rushing in, words jumbling over themselves as he described the afternoon and how high up they were. Florence said, 'Yes, yes,' and sat him down at the table in front a plate of fresh-baked biscuits and said that his father shouldn't have taken him all the way up the box. 'Why?' asked Patrick, still quite happily. George sat down opposite him and knew what was coming. When Florence had finished describing to Patrick what might have happened to him (you might have missed your step and plunged onto the rails below. You could have been splattered all over the line) the boy burst into tears and looked at his father with reproving eyes. George said nothing and they did not mention the shed. No doubt Florence could have drummed up a major catastrophe for that too—the roof falling in or spider bites or a screwdriver piercing his heart. He gave up.

But Patrick was still intrigued. On the day that he knew his mother went into town on the bus to do her shopping he feigned an earache. Very occasionally, Mrs Glaister from next door was requested (or given the privilege, as Mr Glaister would say with high irony) of looking after Patrick for a couple of hours if Florence had something to do in town that could not be delayed and Patrick was not quite up to it. As usual, Mrs Glaister tucked him up on her front-room settee. Florence told him to be a good boy, and left. Patrick told Mrs Glaister that he felt tired and thought he would have a sleep. She covered him with a blanket and tiptoed out. He waited until he could hear the radio in her kitchen and then he slid off the settee, slipped out of the front door, closing it behind him, and went around to his own garden.

No one was about—Father was at work, Mother was on her errands, and he knew where the key was hidden. He let himself in at the front door, replaced the key carefully (being methodical even at that age, as many had already remarked) and went through to the back. He also knew where the key to the shed was kept and he let himself in. He pulled the door closed, stood on an old potato box, gazed about him at the pictures on the walls, at the neat lines of tools and the mug, kettle and primus stove—thought it was just the kind of place he would like to live in when he grew up—and then, turning to the workbench, he dismantled, very carefully, the entire Meccano structure of his father's newly completed signal box.

An hysterical Florence, with a distraught Mrs Glaister in tow, found him, nearly two hours later, with half the Meccano pieces laid out neatly on the bench and a look of complete concentration on his face. She gasped with emotion when she found him and pulled him into her pillowy chest, nearly suffocating him. He pushed her away, ran his hands through his hair, and began to holler. Mrs Glaister bent down and stuck her nose almost into his and wagged her finger and said, 'Never, never, never again, you naughty boy . . . you need a good smacking, you do . . .' and flounced out when Florence told her off for it. Florence then wept, Patrick wept. He was attempting to reach the workbench. Florence barred his way. 'I want to finish it,' he yelled. 'I want to finish it . . .' He crossed his little arms beneath his chest as he had seen his mother do and he stuck out his lower lip which was a feature entirely his own. 'I won't, I

29

shan't . . .' he said, and stamped his foot, thereby slipping off the potato box and cutting his knee.

Florence scooped him up. He held his breath and nearly went purple before the piercing yell arrived. 'You must never, ever do such a thing again,' sobbed Florence, still holding him fast. 'Look how cold you are. You will be ill yourself and you will make me ill with the worry of it.' And she dragged him back indoors, by which time he had a temperature and was wheezing.

That evening, when his father came home, Patrick, unusually, went into the hallway to greet him. Florence had left him tucked up on the settee with a book telling him not to move. But as soon as he heard his father's key in the latch he hopped down and ran out to the hall. Florence was in the kitchen with the door closed so that the smell of stewing onions did not invade the house. By the time George had closed the door behind him the boy was standing right in his path.

'I was in your shed,' he said. 'I like the pictures you have pinned up, Father. And the signal box you made.'

And George, who knew nothing of the megaton bomb that his wife was about to drop into his life, smiled and patted his son's head and said that he had already made up the Eiffel Tower and Tower Bridge from those photos, and now the signal box was done—a present for his boy—he was going to work on the Clifton Suspension Bridge. He might take Patrick to see it. It was built by someone called Isambard Kingdom Brunel and it was a wonder.

Patrick could not get his tongue around the name. He tried to say it, got in a muddle, and they both ended up laughing at the attempt. It was this uniquely cheery scene between father and son that Florence walked into when she came out of the kitchen. Instinctively, she pulled the laughing boy to her and looked up accusingly at George. He looked back at her wondering what he could possibly have done wrong now. Was it, he wanted to shout, a crime to laugh with your own son? He opened his mouth to speak, but he had no chance. Florence immediately began to tell him what had happened that day, how afraid she was, and that he must get rid of the horrible stuff in the shed at once. He refused. She asked him what kind of father he thought he was. George laughed at her, a sneering, bitter laugh, and went out to his beloved shed. He might stand up to his wife. He might tell her that he, too, wanted a share in the pleasures of their son, he might, he might—and then he saw the pieces of Meccano and the half-dismantled signal box. It was as if his son had kicked him in the stomach.

He returned to the house. Now that Lilly was out of the picture, the constructions he made in his shed were his only private pleasure. The only physical and mental place that he could say was his. And now his own son had defiled it. He was angry. Cold with rage. It was as if the last vestiges of him as a man, as anything, were wiped out. A small boy, one who held him in contempt, had shattered the last bastion that was George alive. For the first and only time he gave Patrick a good telling off. Just for once, Florence allowed him to do so.

'You must never, ever go out there again,' he said sternly. 'And you must never, ever be so destructive of something that doesn't belong to you ever again.

You must, must, must respect other people's things.' He paused. 'Even your father's,' he added, in a sudden burst of sour irony. No one noticed.

'But . . .' said Patrick.

His father wagged his finger. 'Never. Understood?'

And Florence said, meek as a lamb, 'There now, Patrick. Do as your father says . . .'

Patrick, unused to such unity and such sternness, was silent.

What he wanted to tell them was that he had dismantled the thing once and put it back together, and that when his mother found him he was doing it for the second time and thinking of ways to improve it. If they had only left him alone it would all have been good as ninepence and no one any the wiser. From that day on he held not only his father but *both* of them in his child's version of contempt. What did they know?

George bought a large padlock for the shed and on the few occasions Patrick tried to follow him out and spy through the window, his mother, now on her guard, stopped him. If Patrick tried to talk to his father about what went on out there, whether the unpronounceable name's bridge would be finished soon, George merely went on reading the paper. He was under Florence's watchful eye. One false move and it could be the shed's last. But though he worked away on Brunel's wonder, the relish had gone, he felt under threat, observed, about to be punished for this little bit of freedom. And he was.

*　　　*　　　*

32

In the end, catching Patrick sneaking down the garden path with a torch in a freezing wind, Florence declared that enough was enough. She could not stand the stress. George must get rid of his hobby. George, accepting the inevitable, did so. He ripped down the pictures and threw them away. He packed everything else into tea chests, covered them with sacking, locked the shed and pretended to forget about the whole wretched thing. As he pretended to forget about Lilly and the Wednesday afternoons. This, he thought, was what you got if you didn't look out. What you got if you married the wrong woman. What you got for being weak and cowardly.

It was the weak and cowardly that had him marry Florence—that and her cooking. George was friendly with her youngest brother and the two of them used to sit at the table of a Sunday tea time and stuff themselves with her cakes and biscuits. While Florence looked on smiling, neat as a pin. It was the highlight of the week in gastronomic terms. Then Raymond—so quickly—died of a burst appendix. It was over before you knew it and a dreadful shock. At the funeral George put his arm around the weeping Florence and—well—she did not object. The next thing he knew he was engaged to her. It seemed the right thing to do. And Lilly was all but forgotten. Then it was wedding bells. After that nothing was what it had seemed. Even the sweetness of those cakes carried its own destruction. His teeth, as Lilly used to point out to him when they resumed their connection, were in a terrible condition. Fatherhood might have made up for most of what he had lost but he wasn't even allowed that. And this, he thought, is my life . . .

33

He made a few half-hearted attempts in the future. He showed Patrick how a screw went into wood and how to make a dove-tail joint. Which wood was good for what use, how a nut and bolt could hold more than two pieces of metal together, and the best way to grasp a ratchet wrench. And indeed, Patrick liked doing these things. But he was too good at them. The rudiments were not enough. George attempted to show him more sophisticated methods. He suggested that they make a swing together. Patrick asked if it could be a rope bridge instead. He drew one in firm but childish outline. George altered the drawing a little here and there but in essence—in essence—it was correct. He felt pleased to be doing something with the boy at last—almost he felt restored—but it came to nothing. Florence was not having it. Patrick was too weak (the boy coughed on cue), the rope was too flimsy—he might fall and hurt himself. George might have fathered a son but it was no more relevant than the bee stumbling out of the flower. If he had been made of mightier stuff, he knew, he might have drowned his sorrows in drink, might even have died of it. He wanted Lilly and he wanted her badly. But Florence kept a watchful eye. 'If I can see you up to your tricks,' she seemed to be saying, 'then so will everyone else.' Nothing, of course, was actually said.

Dolly came to visit and Florence shared her fears with her. How did you let boys be boys without them killing themselves? Dolly commiserated, but she had a girl. Girls were different. They did not go out risking life and limb and wanting to screw things into wood and what not (little known to both women as they sat sipping their tea, at the end of the garden Patrick was showing Little Audrey exactly that—and she was fascinated). It was Florence's contention to Dolly that Patrick was different from other boys—more sensitive, more delicate, more thoughtful—and it was Dolly's contention to Florence that Little Audrey was no different from other girls at all. She liked pretty dresses, dolls and copying her mother and Dolly was thankful for it. Florence nodded in an understanding but superior way. Patrick was out of the ordinary. He would be somebody someday. Dolly thought to herself that he would be somebody spoilt someday, but she did not say so, valuing her long friendship. 'Unlike his father,' Florence said, 'Patrick will achieve something in this life. Whereas George just sits there in his chair and stares at the fire or the wall. Never does a thing.'

They talked about school. Little Audrey just could not wait to go and she could already read a bit and knew her numbers up to ten. Patrick really ought to have started last year. Florence sniffed. School was a dreadful business as far as she was concerned and she did not like to think about it. She wanted Patrick to go to the smart private seminary. But there was nothing in the kitty for school fees. 'My poor little boy,' she said, stroking his head, 'you'll never manage it. Not that horrid, rough council school.' But Patrick had no choice. Another failure on George's part. In the caves of Neanderthals George would have been thrown out for the poor quality of his fresh-killed offerings.

'If my Little Audrey can do it, so can he,' said Dolly firmly.

'Your Audrey,' said Florence, choosing her words carefully, but they both knew what she meant, 'is—

well—very—accepting.'

'Nothing wrong with that,' said Dolly. 'Being accepting. Getting on with it. You can go a long way before you find something better than being ordinary. Think of Hitler.'

Florence was silent for a moment. Normally when she was discussing her son there was no room to think about anyone else—but *Hitler*? 'And just what do you mean by that?'

'Well,' said Dolly, 'we'd have all been a great deal better off if he'd stayed ordinary, now wouldn't we?' The logic was faultless. Florence ignored it.

'My Patrick is different,' she said. 'He's got a Destiny.'

'Destiny is as Destiny does,' said Dolly good-naturedly (she was now thinking of *Gone With the Wind* and *Forever Amber*).

Both mothers stole a quick glance down the garden at their respective offspring. Patrick was lying on his stomach drawing something meticulous, a frown of concentration on his tender brow. Little Audrey was lying on her back, staring at the sky humming something in a low voice and playing cat's cradle with confident, unseen fingers. Both mothers wore an expression of profound certainty.

'Ah,' said Dolly. 'But will it bring him happiness?'

'What?'

'Destiny?'

Florence sipped from her cup of tea and said no more.

*   *   *

Florence kept Patrick at home as much as she

could but what the Attendance Officer found difficult to implement, Little Audrey did all on her own just by coming to visit and describing the jolly things she was going to do at school. Patrick suddenly wanted to go, and very much. Despite Florence's reminding him over and over again about the big hard playground and the rough, dirty boys, and how ill it would make him, Little Audrey's picture of it painted every day as a little adventure. Florence might baulk at the distance that Patrick would travel, but Little Audrey had to go to a school ever so far from where she lived, on account of the local one being bombed. Now the war was over and it was no longer in danger from air raids, Dolly sent her off on the bus with some of her friends, all holding hands so as not to lose anybody, and she managed very well. Patrick was enraptured at the idea of doing something entirely alone—free of parental restraint. He stamped his foot, he would go, he would, he would. And on a bus, too. Florence was horrified. That woman, she said to George, whose face did not flicker, that woman will be sorry one day . . .

*   *   *

'He's a very delicate little boy,' she told the Headmaster.

The Headmaster smiled. 'Then he will have to toughen up,' he said. 'They always do.'

'But my son is different.'

The Headmaster, who had heard it all before, said he knew that. But the boy must attend every day because it was the law.

'You'll never be able to cope,' said his mother,

37

clucking over him and tucking in his scarf and his shirt and his pullover. He was both thrilled and frightened to be going. Florence wrapped him up so closely that, despite the mildness of the September day, he began sweating. 'Oh my goodness look at that,' said his mother before they were halfway across the first field. 'You're starting a fever.' And she brought him straight back again. Patrick howled which made him all the hotter. 'There you are,' said Florence with much satisfaction. 'I knew it, I knew it.'

But the Attendance officer called again. And that was that.

Patrick was excited when Jimmy two doors down told him that they gave you a gold star if you were good—and he wanted one. He was special and he would tell them so, which he did. The teacher, a round, grey-haired woman who was far too firm for Florence's liking, told him that he would have one when he had done something worthwhile. He immediately went away and drew from memory the most elegant picture he could of his father's model signal box. The gold star was his. And it was a great disappointment. He held his breath, he stamped his feet, he kicked the desk and said it was *rotten*. The gold star was made out of gummed paper and the size of a sixpence and went into your writing book. The teacher said that if he ever behaved like that again she would send him to the Headmaster. 'See if I care,' he said. So the teacher said that if he ever behaved like that again she would make him do sums instead of painting and drawing. Out came his lower lip, but he stayed silent.

When Audrey told him how difficult she found

school now that she had to do real lessons, and rolled her eyes and said that she just could *not* do sums, Patrick said that he found everything easy.

'Lumme,' said Audrey. It was less in admiration than in pity. Why go to school then? she wondered. Was life supposed to be easy? She didn't think so. Whenever her father or mother said phrases concerning Easy, they were said with contempt:

'Oh they've got it easy.'

Or 'Easy come, easy go.'

Or (of the Duchess of Windsor, a continuing thorn in her mother's side living it up in Paris) 'She's just an easy woman.'

So it couldn't be right. Much as Audrey liked the sound of it. An easy woman, after all, sounded much nicer than a hard one.

'Go on with you,' she said to Patrick, 'you can't only do everything you like.'

'Yes I can,' he said. 'And what I don't like doing,' he added, 'I don't.'

Patrick, she decided, obviously had no idea. Something stirred in her Little Girl's heart. If you only did the things you wanted to do, and left undone the things you ought to do, the things they told you, repeatedly, you ought to do, you wouldn't get very far in this life. She was sure of that. She had been told it often enough. She said 'Lumme' again, a little more softly, and then, 'You be careful, Patrick,' and gave him a gentle push. He pushed her back, and she fell over. Easily.

3

A Lesson in Bridge Building

Several types of bridge structure have come down to us from ancient civilisations, including timber-corbelled bridges formed from inverted stacks of logs, which still exist in China and eastern Asia and have no modern counterpart . . . These types are unequivocally similar to Roman examples providing evidence of communication and trade, or perhaps correspondences, between opposite ends of the ancient world.
  Matthew Wells, *30 Bridges*

We crossed (to Rome) on the Ponte Molle, formerly called the Ponte Milvius . . . This bridge was built by Aemelious Censor . . . it was the road by which so many heroes returned with conquest to their country; by which so many kings were led captive to Rome; and by which so many ambassadors of so many kingdoms approached the seat of empire . . . to sue for the protection of Rome . . . Nothing of the ancient bridge remains but the piles; nor is there anything in the structure of this, or of the other five bridges over the Tyber, that deserves attention.
  Tobias Smollett, Letter XXIX, *Travels through France and Italy*, 1766

At Dolly's insistence, Florence took Patrick to London to visit Audrey for her eighth birthday. Audrey was the same height as Patrick now, and nothing chubby about her. She was a romping, cheery little girl, whose baby brother was in awe of her. 'She's an independent little miss,' said her mother very proudly, as she scooped up her baby son and held him close. 'This one's much whinier.' The baby boy in question might, thought Florence, half with envy and half with contempt, be a bit less whiny if his mother wasn't always picking him up and carrying him. Just as well she did not say so, for Dolly would have applied her favourite cutting retort: Pot calling the Kettle, I think . . .

Florence was not altogether pleased with the way the friendship between little girl and little boy was developing. Already Dolly had suggested that Patrick might come down to London to stay on his own with them. Florence watched Little Audrey's vest and knickers flicker quick and sure in amongst the branches of the apple tree while Patrick stood below looking up. The rain, or perhaps the dew, had left droplets on the spiders' webs that hung and trembled beneath Little Audrey's surefooted climb. Patrick stared, apparently entranced. Little Audrey thought his rapture was for her and showed off even more. 'Come on up, Patrick,' she called to the boy. 'It's very easy.' She dabbled her fingers in one of the spiders' webs that hung there sparkling with watery brilliants. 'See how strong it is,' she said, almost to herself with the wonder of the sudden discovery. 'And beautiful.' She touched it again, more roughly. 'It looks like lace but it is so strong. My dad says that if you put it on a sore place it stops bleeding.'

'Don't be daft,' he said, but he moved forward. For a moment it looked as if he might begin to climb. Audrey dabbled her fingers more provocatively and the spider's web shed its drops

41

but held its anchorage. 'See,' she said, 'it looks really delicate. I can't break it, though. Or not easily anyway.' She pulled it around some more. 'What's interesting about this,' she said, in a voice very similar to her class teacher's and peering at it even more closely, 'is that it does a good job and it looks nice. Like a bridge of lace.'

Below her Patrick exploded with laughter. 'Bridges are made of wood and iron and brick and steel, silly,' he said. 'They are big and strong and last for ever. Not like that stuff.' And he reached up for one of the branches to shake it. 'Come down,' he said. 'Show me how you come down.'

Audrey wiggled her fingers in her ears and stuck out her tongue and pretended to wobble about. 'Help,' she said, but she was laughing. 'Come and get me,' she said. 'Come on . . .'

He laughed, too, reaching upwards.

She held out her hand, stretching so that with just a little effort he could clasp it and be helped to climb. The spider's web dangled from her fingers, still catching the light with its beads of water. He moved further towards the tree and raised his hand as far as he could to reach Audrey's—she stretched further—their fingers nearly touched. She smiled encouragingly. 'Come on,' she said. 'You can see the whole world up here. Hold my hand.' Patrick, staring up at her, seeing the sunlit halo around her head, the bright smile, the laughing eyes, thought she looked pretty and would have said so but just at that moment, just at the very moment when Audrey could almost feel the heat from his fingertips, his mother called a warning. 'Don't you go up there, Patrick,' she said. 'You'll fall.'

Patrick immediately stepped back. He made no

further move. Slowly Audrey pulled her hand away and looked down at him sadly. He remained firmly on the grass below, staring up at her. He was no longer interested in climbing; looking was sufficient. He could see all he wanted to see from the ground. He was not interested in the spider's web or its sparkling beauty, or Audrey's sunny prettiness any more.

'Climb down for me,' he called. What interested him as he screwed up his eyes against the glare was watching Audrey as she stepped about the branches. 'Cowardy-custard,' called Audrey but he did not care. She wiped the broken spider's web off her fingers. Below her Patrick picked up his paper and pencil and sat cross-legged on the grass and made a picture of the tree above him, with the pattern of the branches crudely simplified. What he had drawn were the relevant branches to Little Audrey's climb. The ones she used. The others he had discarded.

Later, when Audrey sat on the grass beside him, and showed him the bits of spider's web on her hands—'It took some breaking . . . I think it's stronger than all those other things . . . wood and iron and stuff—' he looked up. 'Don't be daft,' he said.

She held the broken web close to her face and studied it. 'It had millions of dead insects in it. You just think,' she said. 'It held them all up, as well as the spider. Think of a piece of lace holding you and your mum and dad, even just me—it couldn't do it.'

'Don't be daft,' he repeated, but a little less certainly.

She picked up his drawing and stared at it for a moment before asking why he had only put in a few branches and he told her.

'That is very clever,' she said.

'It's the economics of structure,' he said.

Audrey blinked. 'Economical,' she said, 'is what my mother calls Sunlight. She says she prefers it because it's very ec-on-o-mical.'

Patrick was not altogether sure he liked this. 'That's washing soap,' he said with assumed disgust. 'Stupid.'

'And my skirt. She said my school skirt was economical. It meant I couldn't have a frill. I like frills . . .' she added mournfully. Patrick drew some for her, like the ruff around Harlequin's neck.

She laughed. 'That's lovely,' she said. 'Oh, Patrick, you are clever.'

They both chewed a piece of grass and looked at the drawing. Audrey sighed. Then Patrick, who felt he was losing ground, tapped the bridge drawing again.

'Now you'll know how to do it for ever.'

'Do what?' asked Audrey.

'Climb the tree safely. Follow the lines. See?' he said. 'I've drawn the way up for you.' He laughed, excited by his success.

She did not say what she was about to say, which was—more or less—that she knew the way up, stupid yourself, and that anyway the whole point about the climbing of trees was that you didn't know everything. With knobs on, thank you . . . But she said none of this. Instead she turned to look at Patrick and opened and shut her large brown eyes and smiled him a sweet, sickly smile. Patrick liked this. She was aware of it. 'I'd never have thought of it without you,' she said. 'Thanks ever so.'

'No,' he said. 'No—I don't believe you would.'

44

Patrick felt a little glow of warmth towards her. She was all right. 'You looked very pretty up there,' he said.

She smiled that same sweet smile. 'Can I keep this, then?' The smile, which he liked, stayed put.

'Oh yes,' he said airily. 'I suppose so.'

'Oh *thank you*, Patrick.'

She put the piece of paper down carefully on the grass and kissed his cheek. Then she went back to the tree and tried to climb on a different set of branches (she knew, really, that they were not the right ones to risk) but one cracked and she only just saved herself from tumbling. Dusting herself off she took Patrick's piece of paper and climbed again, making it clear to him as he gazed up at her that she was following his every line. She went very swiftly, using only the branches he had drawn. Of course it worked. She looked back over her shoulder as she climbed and gave him another, even more dazzling smile. For a moment they were both caught in a pleasure of enchantment. Dangling above her head, caught in the sunlight, was another spider's web. She ignored it and followed the drawing to her sitting place. Then she turned and waved. Patrick waved back, carelessly, with a look on his face that almost said he was not, actually, waving at all.

Back down on the ground, she asked for a paper and pencil and she made her own drawing of the way up—including the spider's web—but she linked each branch she drew with a line. At each meeting of line and branch she drew a little bobble. When he asked her what the little bobbles were, she said, 'Knots. The steps are made from ropes. It's what they call a zigzag. It's what you have to do

45

if a crocodile chases you because they can't . . . zigzag. And that—' she pointed—'is the spider's own bridge between the branches.'

They both looked at each other with a newfound respect. Patrick, on being offered Audrey's drawing, pocketed it with a thoughtful face. 'I suppose,' he said, 'crocodiles can't zigzag because it's complicated.'

'Or because they're stupid,' she said. 'After all, it's not hard to do, now is it?'

And she was up and off, zigzagging her way towards the table and the jug of lemonade.

When it was time for Patrick and his mother to return home, he and Little Audrey solemnly shook hands at the station. And then, impulsively, she kissed his cheek again and he blushed. Florence's heart tightened to see it. Dolly noticed nothing except for two children being friendly, which was nice. 'Come again soon,' she said.

'No,' said Florence firmly. 'Next time you must come up to us.'

On the train back Florence sat staring out of the window. Every time she attempted conversation with her son, he asked her to be quiet because he was working on something. He drew nearly all the way to Coventry.

'What are those?' she asked, eventually.

'Bobbles,' he said under his breath, and smiled as he drew. 'Audrey's idea,' he said, obviously amused by it.

She tried to sound as casual as she could. 'And how do you like Audrey nowadays? Bit more grown up, isn't she?'

'She's OK,' he said, resuming his drawing. 'For a girl. But she has some daft ideas.'

'Yes,' said Florence, pleased. 'She does.' She touched his bent head gently. 'Nearly home. Better pack up now.'

They stared out of the train window. War damage was still shockingly evident all the way into the station. 'There'll still be plenty for you to do here when you're grown up,' said Florence happily. 'That lot will take some shifting. You'll be the making of Coventry, Patrick. I really believe you will.'

Audrey and her mother returned home from the station on the bus. Audrey breathed on windows and in the breathy vapour she drew the climbing tree and its pared-down variations, then the sky, then the stars, and then a ladder made of rope leading from the topmost branches of the tree to the furthest star. 'Patrick is clever,' she said to her mother.

'They say,' said Dolly.

'Am I?' she asked.

'Clever is, as clever does,' said Dolly, delivered in her Somebody's Being Silly Again voice.

'I like school,' said Audrey.

Dolly's voice softened a little. 'That's because you are a good girl,' she said.

47

4

Sweets from a Stranger

London Bridge is falling down
Falling down
Falling down
London Bridge is falling down
My fair lady

Take a key and lock her up
Lock her up
Lock her up
Take a key and lock her up
My fair lady

Patrick did not enjoy Senior School. It was Preparing You To Be A Man. No matter how much Florence argued with the authorities that her son needed to be warm and indoors, the answer was always that her son was a big boy now and the world was not made of cotton wool. The playground might be cold, but there he must stay. It was, apparently, a microcosm of life.

On hearing this Florence thought the Headmaster was referring to germs. She, who had spent her life protecting her son, was horrified. 'If you think,' she said, puffing out her chest which had grown even more redoubtable over the years, 'that any son of mine is going to be exposed to microcosms, you can think again. I keep a clean house, free of anything like that and I expect you to do the same.' She sailed away with her arm around her son's shoulders (though he was now as tall as she was) and took him straight home.

Patrick was torn between pleasure at being tucked up indoors before a roaring coal fire, and the humiliation of hearing his mother's ignorance. In the end he decided to keep quiet about the mistake, favouring the roaring coal fire and hot Horlicks over the filial triumph of sarcasm, attendant draughty classrooms and freezing asphalt.

That evening Florence told George what had taken place in the Headmaster's office. 'Microcosms,' she said, shaking with indignation again. 'He admitted it. Freely. In the playground. Crawling with them, he said. Microcosms.'

George, taken completely by surprise at this shared, if erroneous, confidence, burst out laughing. 'It's not germs,' he told her. 'It's little worlds.'

Florence had never let her ignorance disturb her. 'Little worlds doesn't sound much better to me,' she said. 'I don't want him mixing in any of those things either.'

George contained his laughter. He winked at his son, and was surprised that he winked back. A moment of accord. There was a depth to that son of his that he had not—could not—plumb, but it was there. George was pleased and was quite perky about the house that night. Florence grumbled and told him to stop his humming. So he whistled very softly instead.

He went up to his son and awkwardly patting the top of his arm said, 'You know the easiest way is to do what you're told. The more you make a fuss, the more you'll make it difficult for yourself.'

'Like you, you mean?' said Patrick under his

49

breath. 'Bugger that.'

*　　*　　*

School work was hard and he was not excused doing it. Indeed, he was made to stay in until it had been achieved. His class teacher, Mr Murdoch, who also taught maths, used the famous and chilling lines, 'I'm not going anywhere. I've got all night if necessary . . .' Which Patrick was inclined to believe. It wasn't that maths wasn't interesting, or that he couldn't do it—it was being told to do it that riled him. Then the teachers began disciplining him in earnest—even to slapping his head when he pinched a smaller boy—which he took very badly. It made him ill and he went home and he told his mother. Florence, this time with George in tow, since both parents had been requested, set off for the school and the Headmaster.

'Tell him, George,' she said, as they stood facing Mr Henning across his desk. 'Tell him about hitting Patrick.'

But George was privately rather in favour of it.

'It seems to me,' he said, 'that if it is true and Patrick has hurt someone, then he must learn how it feels by being hurt back.'

It was one of the longest sentences Florence had ever heard him utter. The Headmaster shook his hand, nodded sternly at Florence. And they left.

Back at home she told Patrick, 'Your father said to Mr Henning that it was all right to hit you any time they like.'

Patrick glared at his father. George returned to his armchair on one side of the range like a dog sent back to its basket. He could never win. Well, not in

50

this life anyway. And he hoped to God there was nothing of the same going when you passed over to the other side. He was counting on Heaven being a Florence-free zone. Perhaps even with Lilly in it. He had begun to think about her again, even to dream of her. He missed her very much. He had given her up for the sake of his fatherhood, and his fatherhood had not made it worth his while.

*   *   *

On Fireworks Night Jimmy knocked on the door (bold as brass, as Florence put it) and asked Patrick out. 'I knew you'd want to help with the guy,' said Jimmy, rubbing his hands and ignoring Florence's angry face.

'Oh no,' said Patrick, 'not that. It's because they're building a bonfire.'

*   *   *

Down in London, Little Audrey (who now requested, with dignity, that they should not call her Little any more) asked if she could help with the bonfire they were building on the bomb-site at the end of the street. Despite the Dawning of the New Elizabethan Age, as her mother and the neighbours were wont to remark sardonically, they still had a fair few such places round their way. Audrey rather liked these patches of wildness in among all the dull, new buildings.

'Bonfire?' said her father. 'Don't be daft.'

But she went up there anyway and stood at the edge of the space and watched the boys and the men throwing on old chairs and orange crates and rotten floorboards. It looked fun and dangerous but very haphazard. 'Keep back,' she and the Bamber girls were told. 'Right back, now.'

She watched as flaming objects, having been hurled on willy-nilly, tumbled off again. 'Wouldn't it be better if they made up the bonfire properly before they lit it?' she asked the night air, since no one else was listening.

*   *   *

In Coventry, with his mother wringing her hands and when she wasn't wringing them adjusting his scarf and cap and buttons, Patrick Parker stood on the sidelines and told the teachers and the handyman where to put the planks and chairs and sticks just so. 'I'll give him where to put the sticks . . .' muttered Cheffy, the school caretaker. But he was only halfhearted in his irritation since the boy's suggestions worked. Even Mr Murdoch smiled at him but Patrick only gave him a haughty look back and went on pointing an imperious, absolutely confident, finger at the growing structure. He wanted it to be the best, and it would be.

There was such an air of certainty about him that pretty and dapper Peggy Boxer, in her perfect little felt jacket (made by her mother) and her spot-on little pixie hood of fluffy angora (made by her mother) and her bunny-ears gloves with bobbles (bobbles made by Peggy, the rest by her mother) came and held his hand. Just slid up slyly beside him and wriggled her hand into his.

'Get back at once,' said Florence. 'It's dangerous.' And she pulled the girl away and put her back with the other assorted pixie hoods and berets and plaits. Patrick, much interested at the warmth and softness of the very small hand, turned and waved at her. She waved back and beamed with pleasure, putting her chin on her gloved hands, much as she had seen Shirley Temple's pose in *Animal Crackers*.

The helpers built the bonfire higher than had ever been achieved before. Cheffy took the praise for it, squinting at Patrick to see how the land lay, but everyone knew it was really down to the boy. Patrick let it pass for he was now absorbed elsewhere. Between two women. Twelve-year-old Peggy eyed middle-aged Florence, and was eyed back in turn. Well over thirty years' difference in their ages but they both knew what was going on in that little scene.

*　　*　　*

Mr Murdoch persisted with Patrick. Maths was important and Patrick was good at it when he concentrated. It was a boy's school and it prided itself on its good results in the Sciences. Patrick was again to be kept in. 'But it's my birthday tomorrow,' he said.

'And how old will you be, boy?'

'Thirteen. Sir.'

'You'll be a little Euclid by your fourteenth birthday,' said Mr Murdoch sarcastically. 'Or one of us will be six feet under. And it won't be me . . .'

What Florence called Spirit—and the school called the Devil in Him—made him perverse. Sometimes he refused to do his work, stuck out his lower lip, folded his arms, sat back in his desk and stared at the ceiling. Mr Murdoch, having warned him that he would be treated like an infant if it happened again, duly shut him in the stationery cupboard. Fortunately it had two glass panels. When the doors were opened at the end of the lesson, they found him sitting cross-legged on the floor with a construction made up of large and small paint brushes and ink bottles, rulers and pencils. 'What is it?' asked the teacher, amazed at its complexity. But Patrick was in no mood to be civil. In any case, anyone could see perfectly well that it was a bridge.

'When I leave school,' said Patrick, in a voice that had the teacher's fingertips tingling, 'I shall become the greatest builder of bridges since Brunel.'

'In that case,' said Mr Murdoch, swiping at the back of his head, 'you will first need to cross the *Pons Asinorum* . . .'

Patrick looked at him blankly.

'*Pons*—bridge, *Asinorum*—of asses: in other words, Parker—know your Euclid: the bridge of donkeys, the bridge of the ignorant, the bridge of learning which you must cross over in order to achieve building your Brunellian wonders . . .'

Patrick looked up, smiling. 'Oh no, sir,' he said. 'The bridges will be mine—they'll be known as Parkerian wonders . . .'

Mr Murdoch said nothing, but he thought that they probably would be.

*　　*　　*

Audrey sent him a cake she had made at school. It was not a very good cake, as Florence pointed out, but he was impressed. When he telephoned her to thank her and they started to talk about the whole horrible business of class work, he said that he'd begun to see the sense of numbers. At least with sums you were right or wrong and that was that. Audrey laughed. That was the problem with sums. There was only ever one answer and if you didn't know it you could go hang. You had to be clever for them and she certainly wasn't *that*. She much preferred Poetry and English—you had a bit of leeway there. Even her little brother was better at numbers than she was. Oh no. She just couldn't make sense of them beyond adding and subtracting and even then she got confused with putting one on the doorstep and carry ten . . . She knew her pounds and ounces, how to check her change in shops, how to measure fabrics and the like, and that seemed to be about all she needed. Patrick said he thought she was probably right. That was the way of it. His mother was the same.

While Audrey idled away her fourteenth summer in London, lying on a rug in the sun and reading books or filmgoer magazines, or splashing about in the Lido, or giggling about the streets with some of her friends, Patrick was busy. In their garden in Coventry, where others might grow vegetables or keep pigeons, Patrick began to build constructions —of wood, of metal, of steel, or anything he could get his hands on. He lusted after Meccano as others lusted after cider and girls. His father, wishing for no further trouble, did not remind his son of what was hidden away in the now overgrown shed at the bottom of the garden. As far as Florence could remember, the stuff had been thrown out. Patrick got everything new. Shiny and new. And his father watched with quiet pleasure as his son worked away at his creations. Perhaps he had given the boy something, after all.

He bought Patrick a book on Great Victorian Builders, with a picture of Isambard Kingdom Brunel on the cover. Patrick stared at it reverently. There was his hero in a cocky stance, with cigar and tall hat, standing like a king against the vast links made for his Heroic Ship (as the book called it) the *Great Eastern*. Inside were pictures of everything he had ever created—and, crowning them all, the Clifton Suspension Bridge.

'You made a model of that once,' he said to his father.

George nodded. 'Once,' he said. 'And now you can. But you'll have to see it first.'

Hope rising from the ashes, George suggested that they visit Brunel's great bridge together, just the two of them. He emphasised Just The Two Of Them, and Patrick nodded. This was a man's adventure. While George and Patrick pored happily over maps, Florence ate her heart out. But she cheered up, for with ten days to go, George was told he had to cover for a fellow worker—the chap had broken his leg. It was too near the end of the school holidays to hope it was only postponement—suddenly the trip was not going to happen. Father and son were miserable. And then Patrick had a wonderful idea. Abandoning all thoughts that it was a man's adventure, he remembered Audrey. He telephoned her straight away and suggested that she come instead. They could set off by train, with their bicycles in the guard's van, and Youth Hostel the rest of it. Dolly, called to the telephone by an excited Audrey, agreed, providing little brother Sandy went too. And providing they looked after him. Florence was half furious, half frightened. 'I just don't think it's

56

on, Dolly,' she said, as calmly as she could. 'They're far too—' she searched for the right word—'inexperienced.'

'They'll love it,' said Dolly.

'How could you let your boy go away so young?' Florence asked, meaning, of course, her own.

'Oh, Aud's a sensible girl,' said her mother. 'She'll look after them both.'

And then, without so much as a by-your-leave, George stood behind his wife, took the telephone from her hand, looked her straight in the eye and, speaking very slowly and clearly into the mouthpiece, said, 'It's a grand idea, Doll. And they'll be fine. We've got it all mapped out, Patrick and me. He knows where to go and what to do.'

When the telephone was replaced both father and son stood foursquare in front of a speechless Florence. And that—was that. Audrey and her brother arrived.

'Thanks Dad,' said Patrick, later.

George nodded. 'You have a good look at those piers. Beautiful they are. Beautiful.'

There was nothing for Florence to fault except the unlikely possibility of a plunge in the temperature to minus several degrees. They had thermos flasks, puncture outfits, cycling capes in bright yellow, torches, rucksacks and water bottles. It was late August and the weather, if damp, was warm. They'd be fine. Audrey had money in her pocket from a summer job helping out at the local cinema, and Sandy had money that he had saved from his pocket money (and a little added by his dad.) Patrick also had money but he had been given it. Audrey gave him a smile that she had been practising ever since seeing an advertisement for toothpaste that according to the poster, went 'ping!' and called itself the Ring of Confidence. The smile was part of the plan. She'd turn her shorts up, too, once they were on the train tomorrow and out of sight. All the older girls at school did it, noticing that the football-playing boys next to the hockey pitch became noticeably more appreciative when they did.

The two older children waited until Florence was busy getting tea (proper tea with cakes and scones and home-made jam—Florence was determined to remind Patrick of what he would be missing with his bottles of pop and dried-out sandwiches) and slipped off into the town with their new bicycles. They went up Greyfriars Road, along Queen Victoria Road and into Corporation Street. Much of the area they passed still bore the scars of the bombing but Patrick no longer thought about being the person to rebuild the place. Coventry bored him. Buildings bored him. Just by looking at picture books and seeing what was being built in the rest of the country, in the rest of the world, he knew that he would leave the city one day. Head south.

'Boring isn't it?' he called to Audrey over his shoulder.

'Yes,' she agreed. 'You should come to London.'

'I know,' he said, trying not to think of his mother.

'Where are we going?' asked Audrey. 'Not that I care,' she added, shrugging as she pedalled. 'I'm enjoying this.'

'Just stick with me,' he said.

His plan was to cycle in a circle all around the city and end up back at home, just for the sheer glorious freedom of it, but suddenly Audrey, looking to her left, started laughing and pedalling off down a side road in a dingy area he didn't know. Chapel Street. He called to her, irritated, but she paid no heed, so he followed. Then, at the corner of Lamb Street, he saw why. A sweet shop. Well, a shop that sold sweets as well as everything else. Called 'Willis's Stores'. Audrey pointed and then flapped her hand in an approximate gesture for slowing down. He pulled up behind her, cross that she had taken the lead, and let his wheel ride into hers as they coasted to a halt. As if to say he was in control of the situation really.

They were still not used to sweets being off-ration. Both Dolly and Florence, whose children's teeth had been cared for and nurtured, now did sweet rationing of their own (they themselves had false teeth already, Dolly's being pulled out without so much as a by-your-leave just before she gave birth to Audrey; she never did find out why)— so this was freedom indeed. They parked their bikes at the kerb, peered into the greasy windows and pointed at a few things, and feeling very grown up, in they went. The door rattled. They stood in the dingy, cream-painted interior, with its vaguely fusty smell of sweetness and bacon and cheese, and waited. Patrick tapped his shilling on the counter, Audrey took out a sixpence and copied him. Next to the boring tins and the mundane packets of tea and cough drops and cigarettes on the shelf behind the counter, stood several rows of large jars containing various wonderfully coloured sweets. Gobstoppers, bullseyes, toffees in bright wrappings, liquorice allsorts, gooseberry eyes, lemon drops . . .

'What are you going to have?' he asked Audrey

59

eventually.

'Everything,' she replied. 'Four—from each jar.'

'Oh no you won't, young lady,' said a voice from the other end of the counter, 'That'd take all blessed night.'

The woman wore a loose fawn cardigan over a faded print dress and would have melted into the background of the shop perfectly, except that she had very yellow hair, pinned back with dark grips, and a brilliant, brilliant red mouth. Audrey gazed at the mouth with great envy as it moved its lips and called to someone in the back. It called, 'Won't be a minute Alf, just got some kids to serve.' Through the two glass panels of the door behind the woman, they saw Alf in the room beyond. He was sitting in an upright chair, awkwardly, and he was as thin and pale and white as a ghost. 'Now be quick,' said the woman. 'I've got to get his tea.'

While she weighed out the lemon drops chosen by Patrick, Audrey said, 'Your mum would kill us if she knew where we were . . . What are you going to say?'

Patrick thought. 'Don't know,' he mused. 'Might say we went to see Dad at the station. Check he's got our train tickets for tomorrow.'

'Ooh, Patrick,' she said. 'That's a good idea. We'll go to the station and see Uncle George. Then your mother won't know any different.'

The woman with the red mouth made a little noise and clattered the lemon drops on to the counter. They looked up. She was staring at Patrick very hard, still holding the large jar at an angle to the scales. He felt uncomfortable.

'My mum doesn't like me eating too many sweets,' he said, very nicely. 'But it's OK. I clean my teeth. Can I have two ounces of the toffees after that?'

The woman continued to stare. Then, very slowly, she put down the jar and leaned across the counter and looked at his face in such a way that he wanted to run. 'It's all right,' he said. 'We won't tell her where we got them.'

The woman with the red mouth looked amused, or excited. 'That might be a very good idea, young man,' she said sardonically. 'Now tell me. What's your name?'

'David,' said Patrick.

Audrey laughed. 'Oh go on,' she said. 'It's Patrick, Patrick Parker, and his Mum's a real—'

The woman put up her hand. It had red nails, to match the red mouth, and they were slightly chipped. 'Is your dad George Parker?' she asked.

Patrick nodded.

'How is he?' she said in a soft voice, looking over her shoulder at the closed door. 'Is he all right?'

'He's very well thank you,' said Patrick. 'Do you know him?'

There was a pause and the woman said, even more softly, 'In a way. I used to play with him when I was a girl.' She took a step back and looked at him with her head on one side. 'You look like him,' she said. 'The dead spit.'

'My mum says I look like her side of the family. Nothing of my dad at all.'

'She would,' said the woman sharply. And screwed the cap back onto the jar as if she was killing it.

They stood staring at each other across the counter. Audrey eventually said could they please have the sweets, in a hesitant voice, as if she knew

61

something out of the ordinary was taking place but didn't know what.

'Clarnico toffees?' asked the woman, suddenly matter-of-fact again. She turned and picked the jar off the shelf. 'What are your favourites, Patrick?'

'The nut ones,' he said.

She turned back and smiled at him. 'Your dad used to like those best, too.'

'Don't think my dad likes anything much nowadays,' said Patrick.

'Well, he used to,' said the woman, with spirit. 'He used to like a lot of things when I knew him.' She stopped herself. And more gently she said, 'And what do you want to be when you grow up, Patrick?'

'I like building things,' he said.

'He'd be proud of that. He was good with his hands, too,' said the woman, and she winked. 'In all sorts of ways.'

'My mum says he's useless,' said Patrick, putting a gobstopper into his mouth.

The woman with the jar flashed him such a look that he quickly said, 'But nobody's useless, are they? Not even girls.'

Audrey squealed and slapped his hand which eased the moment.

And the woman clamped her red lips tight shut. She poured the lemon drops into a bag, scooped up the spilled ones from the counter and put those into the bag as well, and handed it to Patrick with a smile. 'For old times' sake,' she said. Patrick, aware that something was not altogether right about this, said uncertainly, 'Shall I tell him?'

'No,' said the woman, slinging the last little bag around to twist it closed. 'He'll have forgotten . . .

But he's well, though?'

Patrick shrugged. 'He gets lumbago and he doesn't do much.'

'Poor George,' she said. 'Poor, poor George.'

When all the purchases were completed and before they had paid, the woman brightened. 'Wait a moment,' she said, 'I want you to give something to your dad. A message. A bit of a secret. Will you?'

Patrick nodded. She went to the end of the counter and wrote something in a pencil which she licked from time to time. Then she put it in a brown envelope, taken from the shelf at the back, took one toffee out of the jar, popped it into the envelope with the bit of paper, sealed it with much lick and lipstick, and wrote George Parker on the front. She handed it to Patrick. 'Make sure you do give it to him, now,' she said. 'And you can have the sweets free.'

He smiled at her. 'OK,' he said enthusiastically, and put it into his blazer top pocket.

Just as they were leaving the woman winked and said to Audrey, 'Are you his girlfriend?'

Audrey blushed.

They both did.

'No,' said Patrick, confused.

'Oh I see,' she said, smiling at Audrey. 'It's like that is it?' She stabbed her finger in Patrick's direction. 'Never trust a chap who doesn't stick up for you,' she said.

Audrey giggled.

Patrick couldn't wait to get out of the place and rattled the door until it opened.

The woman called after them, cheerily now, 'It's a good idea to marry the right person, young man. You remember that. Marry the right one. Or repent at leisure. And that goes for you, too, young lady . . .'

The door closed behind them with a bang.

'Cripes,' he said to Audrey. 'I'm glad to get out of there.'

'What's in the letter?' she asked breathlessly. Her heart was beating at the very thought of marrying Patrick, it was such a dream.

'A toffee,' he said.

'You know what I mean. The note.'

'Who knows?' He put a sherbet lemon into his mouth as if that closed the matter. 'I got hundreds more than I asked for.' He patted his lower pockets that were crammed with the assorted bagfuls. But even as he rustled them to illustrate the beauty of the feast his hand went up to his breast pocket and the note crackled. He could feel the lump of that lone toffee and something told him that the sweets he had been given were not—really and truly—free at all.

'I wonder what she wrote,' said Audrey, and before he could do anything about it she pulled the envelope from his breast pocket. She smoothed it and fingered it and held it up to the light. 'And I wonder what it was all about. It was mysterious, didn't you think? Maybe she loved him once. Maybe she loved him and never dared to tell him . . .' She said all this quite hopefully. 'Or maybe they loved each other but they could not tell the world . . . ?'

Patrick did not want to think about any of it. He grabbed the note and stuffed it into his saddlebag where it settled down to moulder among all the other detritus. 'Who cares?' he said. 'Come on, I'll race you.'

'To the station?' she called.

'No,' he said. 'Home.'

5

Towards the Pantheon of the Gods.

O'Connell Bridge was once Carlisle Bridge. 'POPULACE APPLAUDS AS QUEEN VICTORIA PASSES OVER CARLISLE BRIDGE': but the *Irish Times* mischief-makers changed the 'A' in 'PASSES' to 'I'.

It took ten years to build Carlisle Bridge and its scaffolding was used as gallows to hang renegade soldiers, with their coats turned inside out.'

Frank Delaney, *James Joyce's Odyssey: A Guide to the Dublin of* Ulysses

Next morning, as they all waited at the station, Florence saw the light in Little Audrey's eye (she refused to drop the Little, mostly to do with the fact that Audrey, very definitely, was not Little any more) and it did not please her at all. It was much the same as the light in Patrick's eye when he beheld some engineering marvel in one of his eternal books. But at least Florence could take comfort. Her son was not interested in *that* sort of thing even if Little Audrey was . . . Looking at the girl she saw how she had grown. Dark hair pulled back in a band, shiny freckled skin and big, clear brown eyes. Given to heaviness, though, Florence was pleased to see, so not all was perfect. And her son liked perfection. Patrick was a little heavy himself, but that was puppy fat, and his fair hair and blue eyes and flushed cheeks made him so beautiful that she could weep. Sandy, sitting behind them both on the station bench, playing with his cycle pedal, was like a little weasel in comparison. Most boys were. But she was very glad, weasel or not, that he was there.

She went over to him. 'Sandy,' she said cajolingly, 'those two think they are very grown up but *you* know they are not—and so do I. Will you keep a good look-out for them?' She reached over and tentatively patted his head. Sandy nodded, pleased with the importance of it all. 'Don't let them out of your sight for a minute,' she said. 'And in the Youth Hostel you stick close to Patrick at night. All right, lovey?' He nodded. She had only confirmed what Sandy knew. That so-called older boys and girls were too full of themselves by half. Florence slipped him a halfcrown.

Of course Audrey knew what she wanted from this trip. She had packed a lipstick, surreptitiously purchased from Woolworth's, for the purpose of . . . whatever, exactly, the purpose was (she was a little vague about it)—but she was also bright and interested in the world around her (as her school report said, nicely) and a bridge was as good as any other place to visit. If it pleased Patrick, it would please her. She had dreamed about being with him like this, without parents to bother them, without Florence to crack the whip. Patrick was clever, he was funny sometimes, and he was handsome. When she spoke to him on the phone her heart went a little faster. She was fairly sure she was In Love, and she had every intention of finding out. Pity about Sandy but you couldn't have everything.

In the train Audrey said what she had been

67

thinking on the matter of Patrick's interests. 'We've got a lot of bridges in London. You've got no bridges in Coventry to speak of,' she said. 'So it stands to reason you're interested in them. Everyone wants what they can't have—don't they?' She smiled, hoping it was invitingly. Sandy asked her if she had stomach ache. She kicked him—not very hard—and said, 'Hmm, Patrick?'

But he shook his head. 'Oh, those are mostly boring ones,' he said. 'I like bridges that amaze you, excite you . . . Most of those London ones just get you from A to B.'

'Nothing wrong with that is there?' said Audrey sharply. 'That's what bridges do, isn't it?' She regretted this immediately. She had planned to be nice to him.

Patrick sighed as if she had said that two and two make five. 'No, it is not all they do,' he said. 'Not Great Bridges. Great Bridges like the ones we are going to see are important for themselves. Grand Designs. Historical. Huge. They made their builders into—' He searched for the right words.

Audrey helped him: 'You mean household names?'

'That sort of thing,' he agreed, only it sounded a bit lame.

'Like Edmund Hillary?' offered Sandy.

'Exactly,' breathed Patrick with relief. 'Just like him.'

'Grand,' said Audrey, giving him her smile of confidence again. 'Tell me some more about bridges,' she added.

Sandy yawned.

As the train sped towards Birmingham (where, thanks to Audrey's direction, they managed to retrieve their bicycles and change platforms without mishap) and out of it towards Shifnal, he explained what they were doing and why.

First they would go to Coalbrookdale to see Darby's Ironbridge—seventeen-seventy-nine and the first true bridge of the industrial age— prefabricated. Audrey nodded wondering what prefabricated meant exactly. She immediately thought of all those little boxy temporary houses that went up after the war. Her aunt and uncle still lived in one in Wandsworth. She turned her fully absorbed gaze to Patrick's face. He was lovely when he got going. Sandy fell asleep.

After the Ironbridge they would go to Bristol and see Isambard Kingdom Brunel's amazing suspension bridge at Clifton. Audrey was confused and kept quiet—she thought of stockings and suspenders and did not dare ask what suspenders might have to do with bridges. If Sandy had been awake she would have done what teachers did when they didn't know the answer to something: turn to Sandy and say, 'Do you know what suspension is in bridges, Sandy?' And he would say no, and she could roll her eyes at Patrick and say wearily, 'You explain . . .' All she could do in the somewhat hazy circumstances was to nod encouragingly again.

He described it in great detail. The abutment that stands as a memorial to Telford's cowardice because he would not believe Brunel's original design with a longer span was possible (what contempt Patrick showed for such caution)—the glory of using Egyptian references (the golden age of building)—the catenaries, the links, the sheer bravery of it all. He paused for breath and noticed

69

the sleeping boy. He looked disgusting with his lolling head, his small wet mouth hanging open and his adenoidal rasp.

'Sandy,' said Patrick sternly. 'Wake up and pay attention.' He poked him in the chest. Sandy awoke and might have cried but Patrick was looking too fierce for that.

'I'm looking forward to seeing that bridge,' Audrey said quickly, noticing the rise of colour in her brother's cheeks. She gave Sandy a soothing pat on the arm. 'It's your favourite, isn't it, Patrick? The Bristol one. And he's your hero? The man who built it? Listen to this, Sandy,' she added. 'It's very interesting.'

Patrick nodded. 'I now know,' he said, in a voice that Audrey had great difficulty in taking seriously. 'That one day I will build bridges and be the new Isambard Kingdom Brunel.'

'Ooh,' said Audrey.

'Coo,' said Sandy. 'Well, so do I.'

'What?' asked Patrick, fearing for a moment he had a rival.

'Know what I want to be. I want to be like Stanley Matthews . . .'

Audrey gave him a clip round the ear and told Patrick, very sweetly, to go on.

'No, Sandy,' he said. 'I do not want to be *like* anybody. I want to be better, or the best. There was Abraham Darby and Ironbridge, and after him Isambard Kingdom Brunel—who is the greatest so far—and after him . . . there will be me. Patrick Parker.' He said it with such supreme confidence that Audrey nearly clapped.

'I'll build another great bridge. Here in England. The best bridge. The bridge of the century,' he said.

'I'll bet you will,' she said, fervently. The fervour was genuine.

To know what you wanted to do for the rest of your life, and to be capable of it, struck her as both exciting and a relief. So far all she'd got were dreams of being an air hostess, advice that she should concentrate on her sewing skills, and the comfort of her mother's words which were that she would get married one day and have children and that was more than enough for any girl to deal with. It didn't quite ring true to her after seeing the Queen being crowned because, after all, she was married, with a husband (obviously) and two children—yet she was Ruler of the World—Malaya and Africa and everywhere. When Audrey pointed this out to her mother, her mother told her not to be so silly, that the Queen of England had blue blood which made the difference. As Audrey knew very well that her blood was only red she accepted this explanation. Patrick's blood was red the same as hers. But it was different for boys.

'Do you remember when we went to see the Coronation decorations?' asked Audrey. 'And you looked up at those Coronation Arches and said they were too small?'

He nodded. 'And my dad explained about the stresses and the strains of them and how their proportions were perfect. Any bigger, he said, and they'd out-do Queen Elizabeth.'

'I thought they were lovely,' she said. 'But you didn't think they were big or grand enough?'

'Well, they weren't,' he said.

'Well, maybe they were for a queen but not for a king?' She was thinking that at home they had just

71

bought two new fireside chairs and the one for her father was bigger than the one for her mother (though her mother's bottom, if she thought about it, was considerably bigger than her dad's) so it seemed logical.

'When I build my bridge it won't just be for the Queen—or a king for that matter. It will be for posterity.'

'What's that?' asked Sandy drowsily.

'Eternal fame,' said Patrick.

'Like Greta Garbo,' said Audrey dreamily.

'*Not* like Greta Garbo,' he said, but he gave up. What did she or Sandy or any of them know?

Audrey gazed out of the window with longing as they sped past fields and cows and sweet little tucked-away cottages. She would like to live in one of them. With somebody clever like Patrick. They were what her mother called Little Palaces. Patrick stared out of the window too, half listening, also half dreaming. 'Trouble with that,' he said, 'is that she won't be crowned again. They only do it once.'

'Oh there'll be something else,' said Audrey to cheer him up. 'Something else to do with her wearing her crown and going in a coach and all that. She'll want a bridge for something one day.'

'There is always,' said Patrick, brightening, 'her funeral.'

Audrey laughed, but she was shocked. '*Patrick!*' she said. 'You could get your head chopped off for that.'

Patrick was so woebegone that she dared to take his hand in hers. She gazed into his eyes with adoring admiration. 'There'll be something else, you bet,' she said. 'Something big and historical. You can do it then.' And she snuggled up even further, liking it. Patrick quite liked it too, though he was also quite enjoying his troubled aura. Sandy suddenly threw himself between the two of them and looked up smiling. 'Oh no, you don't,' he said, and wedged himself firmly in.

*   *   *

When they arrived at the station nearest to Ironbridge, Audrey let the boys deal with the bicycles while she nipped into the waiting room, rolled up her shorts, put on a bit of lipstick in the mirror and emerged feeling suitably sophisticated. The map was consulted, water bottles filled and off they set. Despite her brother's best efforts Audrey made sure that she cycled right next to Patrick. Sandy was behind them and puffing to keep up.

'I'll tell on you,' he said, though whether it was the lipstick, the shorts or the way his sister ignored him, neither of the two front parties bothered to find out. Patrick hunched his shoulders, pressing on, longing to get there, and Audrey was cycling as languorously close to him as she could while keeping up. Patrick noticed that he was puffing and sweating considerably more than she was, which increased his determination to stay ahead. And she, also determined, kept up. In the end he could neither ignore her legs as they moved up and down, up and down so close to him and in such a mesmerising rhythm, nor her smile which appeared to be stuck on with glue. It was all very disturbing.

Eventually honour was served when he skidded to a halt and said that he thought they really ought to go a bit more slowly for Sandy's sake. She, still smiling that smile, agreed. Sitting on the grass

73

verge she undid the top two buttons of her blouse, threw back her head, and took a long drink of water. He was even more disturbed and vaguely irritated. He did not want to think about anything else but getting to Ironbridge. Once back on the road he cycled faster saying he thought single file was safer. She agreed. Sandy wailed behind them. She shouted to him to keep pedalling and shut up, gained and then slightly overtook Patrick. That was not what he had meant. It was even worse staring straight at her bottom and thighs which were now only a yard or two in front. He tried to suggest that he should overtake her but he needed all his breath. In the end he gave up and suffered the disturbing pleasure of it all.

When they were all very red in the face and sweating and when the sun was low and giving out an almost unbearably sultry heat, Audrey looked back at Patrick and, marking him and his confusion, was just about to deliver her *coup de grâce* and suggest they stop and sit on the grass and have a cheese sandwich from her rucksack (cheese being something of a luxury still) when Patrick suddenly took both hands off his handlebars, wobbled about dangerously, pointed with both hands and yelled ecstatically: 'There, look, isn't she *wonderful?*' Audrey nearly lost her balance but he did not seem to notice. He put his hands back on the handlebars and began to cycle like a demon towards the brick and iron bridge, lit up like a stage setting by the rich, rosy sun and rising romantically out of the early evening mist.

'It looks just like a fairytale bridge,' said Audrey, for it did to her.

He tutted. 'Nothing fairytale about it,' he said

firmly. 'A thirty-metre span, not particularly wide, and its architectural style is not unusual. But it does mark one of the most significant bits of progress in the development of bridge engineering.'

Audrey rather wished she had managed to mark one of the most significant bits of progress in something altogether different, but she said no more, except to go into ecstasies herself about the beauties of Abraham Darby's vision and what not. She was about to add, and then thought better of it, that she also thought the ironwork definitely had the look of a spider's web—but she remembered his contempt from the incident in the tree that summer and decided ecstatic silence would be sensible. Behind her Sandy was crying that he wanted to go home. Oh, how she wished he would.

From Audrey's lipstick and shorts perspective, the trip was not a success. They cycled so far that they were too tired to do much more than eat and fall into bed, separated by gender of course, in the hostel dormitories. Even had they managed to stay awake, Sandy was horrible and vigilant and either playing tricks with pillows and the like, or moaning. He seemed determined never to let them out of his sight.

They revisited Ironbridge the following day, and Patrick made drawings, took photographs, made Audrey stand on the bridge, by the bridge and under the bridge, to get the scale, and generally ignored any aspect of anything that was not directly to do with Darby's wonder. She posed as provocatively as she could but it was quite hard to compete and she felt a rising sense of resentment. After all, she did like the place too, and she did think the bridge was in a lovely setting and rather a nice bit of fancy work, but she also felt that you could do both—that is, enjoy being together (she was still vague about exactly what she meant by that) and enjoy studying the thing. Patrick seemed unable to do more than one of these, and it was not the former. It did not help that Sandy, when he was not crying to go home, spent a lot of time winking at her—a trick newly learned and in her opinion, on him, particularly grotesque.

The youth hostel they settled on before they reached Clifton was more hopeful as they were its only inhabitants. When she tiptoed into Patrick's dormitory at dawn on the day they were due to reach Bristol, she sat down very gently on the bed so as not to disturb her brother in the next cot and leaned over Patrick wondering what exactly to do next. In Doris Day films it was the other way round. He was supposed to kiss her. A girl, she knew, was not allowed to kiss first. But she felt drawn to that sleeping face. He was so, so beautiful. And she admired him, he was clever and artistic: she loved him, as she confessed nightly in her diary at home. He was so—well—different. Interesting. Better than she was.

In the end, as the dawn sent more silvery light into the room and Sandy began to stir, she shook Patrick's shoulder, leaning closer, putting her face exactly above his and smiling that Ring of Confidence for the umpteenth time. It worked in the adverts. Patrick opened his eyes and in the half light saw dark eye sockets and a row of gleaming teeth above him, upon which, not surprisingly, he screamed, and jumped out of bed and ran down the corridor for the warden. For the first time, but not for the last, Audrey suffered humiliation in

Patrick's wake.

When they returned, the warden holding a torch and a cricket bat, Patrick holding the warden's arm and peering from behind, she just about managed to explain her presence in the boys' room by saying she wanted to get an early start because she was so keen. The warden said that four-fifteen was a bit too early, in his opinion, and that anyway they had their tasks to do before moving on and that she was a very silly girl indeed not to check her watch. Audrey burst into tears. Patrick rolled his eyes, looked heavenward and went back to his bed. Sandy followed him, snivelling. Audrey went back to her own empty dormitory and lay there stony-faced and sleepless. Love was harder than she thought.

In the morning, by way of further humiliation and reprisal, she did both Patrick's and Sandy's jobs, cooking their eggs, washing up, sweeping the floor, and generally keeping her head down. The lipstick was put away, the shorts rolled down to a more comfortable length, and off they went.

On the next part of the journey the only thing that helped Audrey over her misery, apart from saying *bugger, bugger, bugger* under her breath with each pedal push, was that she could go faster than him, and she did so, and to hell with Sandy who could either get lost or keep up. He just about kept up, as did Patrick who was even more galled by her speed and her sudden indifference to staying together which she had been so good about until now. If she had but known it, at that precise moment Audrey had lighted upon one of the golden rules of girlhood. That less is more and to withdraw is to tantalise.

The Clifton Suspension Bridge, when they reached it, drew from Patrick the smile of astonishment and delight that she rather hoped her kiss might have produced. But at least she seemed forgiven. Love me, love my bridges was the message of this trip and not a lot of room left over for anything else. She decided to approach Patrick that way.

'This is wonderful,' she said, when they gazed upon the bridge.

Patrick sighed a deep and happy sigh. 'Yes,' he said.

She moved a little closer. 'I don't think there can be a better bridge anywhere in the world.'

'Yet,' said Patrick.

'Yet,' she agreed, and took the liberty of putting her arm around his waist. A liberty which he did not deny her, though even she realised that it was debatable whether he had actually noticed . . . Sandy, however, did—and he smacked his sister's bottom hard. The resultant fight between them put her, she was well aware, in a very bad light. On the other hand, after all the frustrations and humiliations she had suffered it seemed a great release . . . 'Oh,' she said, slightly less than under her breath this time, 'Oh bloody well bugger it.'

Later, when they had paced across and back and observed the masterpiece from every angle— Audrey dared to venture that it was a sight grander than Ironbridge. Patrick took this well and she gained in confidence. The bridge was also almost entirely empty of people and traffic, Sandy had his back to them, staring at a couple of boats very far off, and it was the perfect moment and the perfect place to kiss. She was just wondering how to approach it for the second time when Patrick said,

'Well done for getting us here so early, Aud,' and gave her a slap on the back. Not a hard one but it brought tears to her eyes and very little comfort. She looked down. It was a very long way to the water below which looked sludgy and greasy.

'His name is up there,' said Patrick, pointing at one of the Egyptianesque piers. She dutifully returned her gaze upwards.

'Still going strong,' said Patrick, shaking his head manfully. 'After all these years. And still known as Brunel's bridge.'

'Great,' said Audrey.

'I knew you'd like it,' he said.

She cheered up at once. He meant that she alone was capable of understanding and appreciating his special place.

'See what I mean about those London bridges?' he asked.

She nodded.

'Very boring in comparison.'

She nodded more emphatically. 'Oh, they are. Very, very boring.'

'Old hat.'

'Oh yes. Very, very old hat indeed.'

'Gothic, my elbow.'

'And mine,' she said, hoping to God he would not ask her what Gothic actually was.

They cycled backwards and forwards across the bridge for the sheer pleasure of having it all to themselves, while Sandy dropped stones and spat into the water. Then they stopped to lean over the railings once more and Patrick pointed out the abutment on the far shore that Stephenson's cowardice had caused.

'I suppose you could call it cowardice,' she said,

her toes tingling again as she looked down. 'But maybe he was just being careful?'

'Careful!' said Patrick scornfully. 'Do you know what Brunel said to him in reply?'

Audrey longed to say what a daft question that was, how could she possibly, and she very nearly said sharply *No but I think you are going to tell me.* Instead she shook her head invitingly.

'Brunel said, "What a reflection such timidity will cast on the state of the Arts today . . ." Meaning, of course, that you get nowhere without taking risks. Heroism is the Design of Risks.'

It crossed Audrey's mind to ask whose risk but she kept quiet. She wasn't very bright, and that was that, but she was happy leaning on the rail there with him. It was enough for her.

'You're not disappointed then?' she asked, eventually.

His eyes were shining as he looked into hers. 'Oh, *no,*' he said.

'Oh, *no,*' she mimicked, but he did not notice. She was getting just a little fed up with all this standing about. She liked the bridge well enough but she also saw that it had countryside beyond it, that it could take them somewhere new—and she wanted to explore. She gave him a sharp poke in the ribs. Then she laughed, and set off towards the other side calling, 'Come on, race you, race you . . .'

Patrick was offended. They were in the presence of his hero and she was laughing about it. He sulked. He wheeled his bicycle to where she stood and shook his head at her disapprovingly. Sandy called from the far-off riverbank below, and waved.

'Watch out for my brother, please,' she said, with her best effort at being hoity-toity, and she rode off. Leaving Patrick feeling even sulkier. Largely because he really wanted to follow her. But he could not and he would not.

When she returned, they both sat down, not talking, chewing grass and spitting it out. Stalemate. Eventually when she knew someone had to break the silence, Audrey suggested that they leave Sandy for an hour and go for a bit of a walk, and pointed to the trees in front of them—'It's the Gloucestershire side,' she said. 'I've been up there and it's really pretty.'

He said nothing.

'Please?' she asked quietly. 'For me?'

Patrick said that he had weak ankles.

'Don't believe you,' she said. 'Patrick Parker, you're afraid to be on your own with me.'

'Of course I'm not,' he said. 'I've always suffered.' And, as if to prove it, he stood up, proceeded to march off, and one of his feet turned over there and then and began to swell. 'See?' he said, pleased.

Audrey gave up. When they returned to the hostel he noticed that she wore her shorts longer, her mouth looked ordinary, and she scarcely spoke. Which was both a shame, and not a shame. All in all, he thought, she was a confusing person, and disturbing, not least because the image of those legs of hers going up and down, up and down, like strong, pale pistons, stayed with him and bothered him for far too long.

*   *   *

When he came back from that trip Florence was standing at the front room window, behind the

81

nets, once more looking as if she had never moved from the spot. Audrey and Sandy were safely on the train to London, she had sent George on several errands, and she could have her boy all to herself. Up the path he came and closed the gate with a flourish. Florence saw the jauntiness of his step, the new confidence about him, and did not believe it could only be the bridges. Her heart began to pound. Patrick waved and mouthed through the glass of the window, 'The bridge was a cracker, Mother. Let me in.'

Florence made her slow way to the front door and opened it. Straight away Patrick saw that she was—well—something. Ill or upset—affected in some way.

'I missed you,' he said, and kissed her cheek. And he lifted his turned ankle to show the bruising. 'I told Aud it happened all the time so we couldn't go for a walk.' He laughed. 'She was not best pleased.'

'Good was it?' she asked.

'Yes,' he said. 'But I'm very glad to be home.'

If this delighted her, it was short-lived. She was just putting the kettle on when Patrick said, 'Youth hostelling is good fun, Mum . . . We'll do the Royal Albert Bridge over the Tamar next and we'll ride over it by train because that's the best way to see it. Aud's OK for a girl . . . And we won't take stupid Sandy with us next time, either.'

Whereupon Florence scalded her hand, suffered her first serious heart palpitations and started wheezing.

*   *   *

Back in London and considering aspects of

82

frustrated love, Audrey suddenly remembered the toffee and the note from the woman in the shop. She told her mother about it. 'Wasn't it odd?' she said.

Dolly said that it was. And then added in a casual voice, 'And did Patrick give the envelope to his dad?'

'Shouldn't think so,' said Audrey, already bored with the subject. 'He's got a head a like a sieve. Unless it's about bridges, of course. I wish I'd been born a bloody bridge.'

Dolly's mind seemed to be elsewhere. 'Just as well,' she said, instead of telling her daughter off.

*   *   *

Audrey had one last try. In preparation for the trip to Cornwall she bought a brassiere and struggled into it in the lavatory as the train pulled out of Paddington. She then returned to their compartment with determined confidence, only to find that they had been joined by a woman with grey hair in a bun, some brownish knitting, and a willingness to talk. Audrey hitched up her straps, stuck out her chest and refused the woman's offer of a boiled sweet. If thoughts could kill, decided Audrey, the woman would be splattered all over the carriage floor with a knitting needle up her nose.

All through Hanwell Patrick was exhilarated, leaping from one side of the carriage to the other to pull down the window and peer out, telling Audrey and the woman (who looked up and smiled vaguely when Patrick accosted her) that this—he gestured grandly out of the window—*this* was the stretch where Brunel finally invented a new kind of U-shaped track. He paused for effect. Two pairs of eyes waited. Good. 'Well—it was safer and smoother because it did not have the mass—so it cooled evenly, free of latent faults . . .'

'Goodness,' said the woman.

'*Golly*,' said Audrey vehemently.

To which Patrick added, 'But the silly arse never patented it . . .'

Which made the woman tut and blink and return to her knitting.

Audrey, who had no idea what patented meant but was feeling quite confident with the brassiere in place, smiled.

Patrick, apparently addressing some distant, passionate vision, continued, 'Because he was not after the money. He was after the glory . . . And in the end he got both.'

'Smashing,' said Audrey, taking a deep breath and holding it. But it was pointless—Patrick had his head out of the window.

At Maidenhead she and the grey-haired woman learned that this bridge with its long, low arches was considered one of the wonders of Isambard Kingdom Brunel's world. To Audrey it looked very ordinary.

Patrick was frowning. His face, deep in concentration, was as handsome as James Stewart's in *The Glenn Miller Story*. More, really.

'Audrey?'

'Yes?' She blinked herself back to reality.

'I was saying—he managed to get the whole of that first run of track, up to here, rushed through in time for the Queen's Coronation. They told him it couldn't be done and he said it could—and so they

84

did. He got it done earlier, in fact. It was sensational.' Then he fixed his eyes upon Audrey, causing her to go bright red, and said, 'I expect to you now it looks very ordinary?'

'Gracious no,' she said.

He stopped and peered at her as if she were one of Mr Murdoch's hopefuls. Audrey had a definite urge to stick out her tongue but managed to smile. Patrick might be beautiful and tall and all that but he couldn't half go on about things.

'This,' he said, 'was one of Isambard's greatest achievements.' Again he paced about the carriage tapping his finger on his chin as if he were a schoolteacher. 'How to span a river one hundred yards wide without making a hump in his beautiful bridge.'

'Why?' dared Audrey.

'Because he had to make headroom for the masts of sailing barges—which would soon be made obsolete by the railway anyway but he had to accommodate them for the moment . . .'

'Why without a hump?'

Patrick sighed. 'He did not want a hump because it would spoil the beautiful simplicity of his design . . .'

'Why not make the hump part of the design?' asked the woman with the knitting.

Phew! thought Audrey, who was glad *she* hadn't asked that.

By the time they came to the Royal Albert Bridge, Audrey's head was buzzing with facts, all of which she had to deal with alone now, as the woman with the knitting (rather thankfully, Audrey thought) left the carriage at Exeter. She was determined not to make any mistake with this one and pronounced the bridge 'a wonder' and 'just as lacy as the Ironbridge.'

'I don't think so,' he said pitying. 'Bridges like these are known as lattice-girders.' And that, he hoped, was that.

As far as Audrey was concerned it bloody well was.

When Audrey, accidentally on purpose (as seen in a Marilyn Monroe film) fell against him in the carriage and he pushed her away quite roughly for the very important reason that they were just about to follow a curve which meant he could look back and take more pictures of the bridge and the setting, she finally gave in to her feelings and had a good long sulk. He did not notice. So she told him. 'I am sulking,' she said, arms crossed despite their hiding her chest, 'because when we went over that bump just then, I fell, and you couldn't be bothered.'

Patrick put down his camera and stared at her in absolute puzzlement. 'We cannot have gone over a bump,' he said.

'Well, I should know because we did and I fell on you.' She more or less believed it now.

'Nonsense,' said Patrick. 'There are no bumps.'

Audrey turned up her nose and uttered a rather enjoyable 'Hah!'

'There are no bumps,' said Patrick patiently, 'because this line was always known as Mr Brunel's Billiard Table. It's as smooth as a baby's . . .'

'My arse,' said Audrey, really fed up now.

He was torn at that precise moment. The prospect of Audrey's arse was quite an exciting image arriving so suddenly and unexpectedly—as was, oddly he thought, her pouting, sullen face. But Brunel won. He had notes to take and more photographs as well as absorbing the sense of seeing things with his hero's eyes. Girls and their arses would just have to wait.

By the time they reached journey's end Audrey had already decided to abandon Patrick as a potential romance. There was not a hint that he found her attractive and simple pragmatism told her to waste no more energy. It was something of a relief. They spent their overnight stop in a youth hostel and had fish and chips for supper sitting on the sands at dusk. Patrick seemed nervous and a bit twitchy and she was fed up with the whole thing. When he sat very near to her and brushed some sand from her knee, she was so overcome with emotion and wishing, that she immediately got up and went to paddle at the water's edge. She would always love him, she said to the sky and the waves, but it was too difficult. She would never be clever like he was and he would never be gentle and amorous like her. 'A Man Has To Do What A Man Has To Do,' she murmured to the wavelets. It was a quote from a recent cowboy flick and as she spoke it she nodded sagely, feeling old beyond her years.

Patrick was dashed. He had built up to the moment on the sand with the fish and chips. It was the obvious place, the obvious moment, with nothing of Brunel to distract him. He would kiss her. And now there she was with her toes in the water not even noticing him. He got up and called that he was going back to the hostel, that they were getting the early train back, hoping as he said so that she would come running to him. But she only followed at a distance, along the waterline, across the sand, onto the prom, trailing further and further behind.

Standing in the corridor that separated the boys' from the girls' dormitories, Patrick did not know what to do. Audrey, also standing there, did. 'Goodnight,' she said, and slipped through the doorway to her room without glancing backwards. She was looking forward to shedding a few private tears into her pillow as all her heroines did, the moonlight picking out the traces on her cheeks . . . Patrick was left standing there wishing she would come out again. Rationally, he decided that she had to come out again to clean her teeth. And when she did . . . So he waited. And he waited. But she never appeared. Largely because, forgoing the tears, she immediately fell asleep.

In the morning they cycled to the station in single file and for the journey back to London Audrey bought a comic. Into which she buried her pink-tipped nose as she read it, cover to cover, with her pink-edged eyes. Patrick asked if she had caught a cold at which she simply sighed. The brassiere was tucked right at the bottom of her rucksack. To be saved for somebody else.

The next day, at the station, as the train for Coventry pulled in, Audrey, caring nothing for decorum any more—why should she?—dared to throw her arms around Patrick's neck and give him the film star kiss she longed to try out. He would have returned it—only her father was watching him with a smile that was less kindly and more like the smile people wore when they watched a playful pair of puppies. Dignity was all. Patrick stepped back from the embrace and said stiffly that he had enjoyed himself, that he hoped they could do it again, and that perhaps Audrey would like to come somewhere with him next Easter? Get stuffed if I will, thought Audrey.

Patrick climbed aboard, opened the window, waved, called out, 'See you at Easter, then. We might go up and see Brunel's road bridge up at Balmoral. Maybe we'll meet the Queen . . . I can tell her to save one for me.' He laughed and waved again as the train pulled away. He was disappointed to see that Audrey had already turned her back and was walking out of the station. Arse swaying like billy-o, he thought, with regret.

Shortly after this Audrey found herself a real boyfriend and the cakes she used to send to Patrick through the post, and the phone calls, ceased. Which pleased Florence. If not her son. Of course it took him a little while to notice but when he did Patrick was alarmed and rang Audrey, only to be told by Dolly that she was out with William, and surely he knew about that? Patrick put the phone down, said 'Oh, sod the lot of them,' to the empty hallway and ignoring his mother's shocked protestations, went out for a very long cycle ride. Brunel's bridge and Audrey's shorts, the curve of Saltash and the curve of her pink, pink lips, sand on a knee and the perfection of a river's span batted their images around in his mind. The more he pedalled, the crosser he became, and he hardly knew why. When he went home to bed that night he absolutely refused, to the walls, to the ceiling, to the universe, to think of her in that way ever again. It took too much energy. It made him feel weak. What Brunel called 'dilution'.

*   *   *

In London Audrey put her arm through her boyfriend's and stepped out for a stroll. William, the new beau, might not be Great and Grand. Nor (she sighed to remember Patrick's fair face) as beautiful—but he knew how to kiss, he wanted to kiss, he never stepped back from her when she kissed him and she was practising very hard. Getting, she was sure, very Doris Day and good with it. She could turn William's face scarlet with just the touch of her tongue. Trouble was that sometimes—quite often in fact—it was Patrick whose lips she imagined pressed to hers. Bugger, bloody, bugger it.

*   *   *

'Now Aud's got a boyfriend,' he said to his mother. 'It means she won't be interested in coming away with me any more.'

'You'll probably get a lot more done without her,' said Florence, who was in great danger of clapping her hands and bursting into song. 'And anyway, I wouldn't worry about all that . . .' She handed him the local newspaper, folded back at a particular page. The headline read: MONEY AT LAST POURS IN TO REBUILD COVENTRY. NEW TEAM APPOINTED.

'See,' she said. 'And it won't be long before you are old enough to be part of all that.'

'There are no bridges in Coventry, Mother.' He spoke irritably.

'Exactly,' said Florence. 'So it's time there was.'

She sounded, he thought, just as daft as Audrey. But he could not be bothered to point out that an Heroic Bridge needs an Heroic Setting. Or at the very least a sodding river. Coventry had neither.

Florence smiled with satisfaction. Just the two of them again, even if George was sitting in his chair by the range and as usual slurping his tea.

'Bike held out all right?' his father asked for want of something to say.

Patrick nodded.

'You ought to give it bit of a clean and a once-over now,' he said. 'I'll give you a hand if you like.'

But Patrick did not appear to hear this. He never had cleaned it and had no intention of doing so now. His mother noticed he was restless. She considered her options. The matter was left.

*   *   *

When Florence stopped the elegant Mrs Ruby Boxer on Quinton Road and told her that Little Audrey had a boyfriend in London nowadays, the elegant Mrs Ruby Boxer was more than a little surprised. Such personal conversation was not a feature of Florence's relationship with the people who lived around and about her, especially not the publican's wife. Usually if you got a nod and a 'good morning' from Florence Parker as she hurried towards the shops, or back from the library, you were lucky. Of course, over the last year her Peggy had spotted Patrick, along with half the girls in Coventry from the sound of it—he seemed to be a very desirable young man—though Mrs Ruby Boxer liked them with a little more muscle to them. Her Peggy had said that she wouldn't mind but that when she enquired of Patrick's health, Mrs Parker told her very firmly that he was very well and courting Audrey down in London. Well—not any more.

'Really?' said Mrs Boxer, adjusting her dainty little homemade hat—or at least, drawing attention to it. 'And how does your Patrick feel about that?'

'To tell the truth,' said Florence in a low, confiding way, 'I think Little Audrey was far too self-centred for him. What he wants is to have a nice local girl he can go for walks with, or to the pictures sometimes. You know the sort of thing. Local.'

Mrs Boxer nodded the bit of navy buckram.

'He's got to concentrate on his studies if he's going to end up a famous—' Florence hesitated— she was never sure what the right word for her son's ambition was—she settled for 'Architect' since 'Builder' sounded too much like Eddying and Sons who had mended their skylight.

'He still wants to do the same thing then?' said the elegant Ruby.

'Oh, yes,' said Florence. 'Never wavered.' She waited a fractional moment and then asked with hitherto unknown interest. 'And your Peggy? How's she?'

'Starting in Orchard's next spring. In the Modes. If she does well she's hoping to be a buyer.'

'Nice girl,' said Florence. 'I'll tell Patrick. He'll want to know. He always asks after her. Nice hat too, Ruby,' she added.

May God forgive you, she thought, as she hurried away. Leaving the elegant Mrs Ruby Boxer standing on the pavement with her mouth wide open.

*   *   *

Alerted, Peggy Boxer began to observe Patrick as

he cycled to and from school. She watched him going in and out of the Library and into Stonor's Bookshop where she wisely left him alone. Only when he went to sit in the Cathedral grounds, gazing up and around at the shell of the new building with its scaffolding, and the old walls and the spire (which he stared at as hungrily as if he could eat it) and the sky beyond, his book discarded on the bench beside him, his sketch book open on his knee, did she reckon it was safe to approach.

High above her the workmen whistled as she stepped towards her prey. Nose well up, she ignored them. Patrick seemed not to notice her, though what he could find quite so interesting in the scaffolding escaped her when she was, she knew, looking particularly nice. She had progressed from bunny ears and bobbles to a nipped-in waist and full skirts (of her own creation) and she wore shoes that made her much taller and which she tied with a fancy little bow around her ankles. She sat down daintily on the bench next to him and said, 'Hallo.' He dragged his gaze down from the spire and scaffolding and the clear, blue sky and looked at her. Puzzled. She reminded him that they had been at junior school together. He pretended to remember her then, but she knew he did not.

Peggy Boxer was undaunted. His mind was on much higher things. Different. Artistic, so her mother said. With a good future ahead. After another respectful silence, she began to tell him that she thought this place was very interesting. All that history it had—and the bombing. He agreed. He told her that he was born on the night it was destroyed and that it was a miracle he survived, which impressed her. He saw that she was impressed and decided not to explain that he was actually down in London at the time. He told her that he came to sit here quite a lot, something which she knew but with her own economical approach to the giving-out of information, decided not to say. He liked, he said, to watch the new walls rise, get inside the spirit of the thing.

'Mmm,' she said. Peggy was game and quite as able as Audrey to appear as if she understood. Then he added, much more understandably as far as Peggy Boxer was concerned, that the Cathedral site was somewhere to go, something to do. That there wasn't much for the likes of them in Coventry. She agreed.

They sat on in silence for a few minutes more and then she said, quite pointedly, that they had just opened a coffee bar down Trinity Street. Patrick nodded, looking up again to where a scaffolder hammered more fittings into place. The noise rang out sharp and metallic, making them both wince.

'He's brave,' said Peggy in a sweetly breathy voice. 'I couldn't do that.'

'I could,' said Patrick. 'But I wouldn't want to.'

They watched the man flitting around the poles, agile as a bird or a bat.

'It's taking ever such a long time,' said Peggy, her peevishness echoing her parents and the whole town. 'You'd have thought they'd have finished it by now.'

Patrick turned on her. 'Of course they haven't finished it yet,' he said. 'Because it's the work of a committee. Not one man.'

'Oh,' said Peggy. 'Really?'

'If we had a Brunel working on that Cathedral,'

94

Patrick said, 'it would be finished by now.'

'Of course it would,' she said, imagining a Brunel to be some gigantic machine sending the walls rising rapidly into the sky like a scene from a science fiction film. Which reminded her . . . And she thought, nothing ventured. So she remarked that there was a good show on at the Picture House, a musical.

He nodded, but he was gazing upwards again. 'It's the only thing in this goddam town I'd care to build and I'm too young,' he said, with something of the picture house himself. 'Everything else is peanuts.'

'Yes,' said Peggy.

Then he turned to her and blinked. 'So,' he said. 'What are you up to now?'

'I'm leaving school this summer and I want to be something artistic. A window dresser or a dress designer or a photographer—something like that. Nothing common, anyway. I'm starting off at Orchard's . . .' She gave him a smile, waited, and then said casually, 'Are you still seeing Audrey?'

He ignored this but said, 'I'd have given them flying buttresses like they never knew they could have.'

'I bet,' she said. And wondered whether to approach the subject of the cinema again. Too late. He stood up.

'London's the place,' he said.

'What?' she asked.

'London. The *place*.'

'Oh yes,' she said.

'I'm going there next year.'

'Oh,' she said.

'So I've got to concentrate. Exams.'

'Yes,' she said, disappointed.

'Got a place in college.'

'Lovely.'

'Well, I might see you around.'

He nodded. Stood there awkwardly for a moment more and then said, 'Oh well—bye.'

'Bye,' she said, giving him a beautiful, lipsticky smile.

He moved away and then returned. She felt triumphant. But it was only to say, 'Don't tell anyone about the college thing yet, will you? I haven't told my mother.'

He set off, wheeling his bike, turned back once and waved, and she waved back. She looked a picture sitting there on the bench with her ankles crossed and the bows of her shoes dangling. The workmen whistled her again. He wasn't surprised. Damn, he said to himself as he pushed his bicycle across the road and headed home. Damn, Damn, Damn. She had a lovely pair of tits from what he could see.

As he pedalled the dull streets homewards he felt dull himself. Why was it all so difficult? Why was he so afraid to give in to what his Headmaster called *urges*? Everything about his ambition felt so vulnerable. Like his hero, he had what he secretly called his sacred, creative flame and he must protect it. Isambard once wrote to some woman or other, and how Patrick understood it now, 'I want you to know that if I appear to be taking things coolly it is because I feel them so acutely that I am obliged to harden myself a little in order to bear them . . .'

One day, he promised himself, pedalling like fury, one day he would be free of all these little-town constraints. One day he would take his place at the helm of the new world and be sure enough of himself not to worry about dilution, *urges*, or anything else. He could concentrate on designing great works, take his place in the Pantheon. And then he could kiss the girls. Once he was out of Coventry with its piddling canals, and its municipal geraniums, away from these flat Midland sounds and their flat Midland ideas, and off to London, he would become reborn. Blessed as Dick Whittington. To London, to London. But minus the cat. Which was all to the good. For as anyone who knows their pantomimes will tell you, The Cat is not only a companion to Dick, but His Conscience. His Heart.

6

In the Temple

I do not know much about gods; but I think
   that the river
Is a strong brown god—sullen, untamed,
   intractable,
Patient to some degree, at first recognised as a
   frontier;
Useful, untrustworthy, as a conveyor of commerce;
Then only a problem confronting the builder of
   bridges.
The problem once solved, the brown god is almost
   forgotten
By the dwellers in cities—ever, however,
   implacable,
Keeping his seasons and rages, destroyer, reminder
Of what men choose to forge . . .
   T. S. Eliot, *Four Quartets*: 'The Dry Salvages'

Patrick was one of the youngest students ever to be accepted for the London Academy's design course. He began remarkably well, something which did not surprise him and something which he was irritated to find surprised his tutors, by producing a critical essay in praise of Wren, Vanbrugh and Adam and damning what he called That Dreadful Reactionary Stuff which followed them and ended in the horror of Barry and Pugin's Westminster. He wrote it, as he proudly announced in the opening paragraph, for blind men who clung to the past instead of honouring it and moving on. He

98

declared himself a champion of the future. Both as architect, as engineer, and as artist. It was a gauntlet that many had flung down before, as his course tutor remarked to his colleagues, but there was definitely something about the boy . . .

'Concrete and steel perhaps?' said the Head of the Department somewhat acidly. 'Concrete and steel . . .'

The Course Tutor smiled. 'He thinks he's the natural successor to Brunel,' he said.

'They often do,' said the Head of Department, wearily.

'Oh but this one, sir—this one—I think this one may be different . . .'

The Head of Department settled back in his chair. 'I do not know much about gods,' he quoted. 'We'll see,' he said.' We'll see . . .'

*　　　*　　　*

At the end of his first year's assessment the Course Tutor called Patrick into his study and told him that, given his age, they had taken a chance on him and—they were delighted to affirm—he had not let them down.

'Of course I haven't,' he said waspishly. 'Age has nothing to do with genius.'

That had the Course Tutor reeling. He's the son of Brunel, all right, he thought. Now what do we do with him . . . ?

Patrick turned to leave. He cared little for authority and intended to show it. At this stage he believed that a Grand Talent would be enough to conquer the world—and if it wasn't—then Grand Ambition would complete the climb. If Faraday once stood on Giants' Shoulders—Patrick Parker must do the same. Newton to Science—Brunel to Engineering Design. If you showed that you knew you were superior to the rest of the world, then the world would believe that you were. Therefore, with his head held high and leaving the reeling Course Tutor with his head drooped low, Patrick marched out of the room. The Course Tutor (otherwise affectionately known as Old Socrates) was a wise old man and he knew that a touch of humility never went amiss.

'Reality and Humility,' he called after Patrick's retreating back, 'are good watchwords—in the world of design as in everything else . . .'

Patrick did not look back, just called out, 'Tell that to Brunel!' And went on walking.

'But he's dead,' said the Course Tutor to himself, and he sighed.

How many young men had said those words? How many young men thought they could recapture that peculiar age, the time of the Great Victorians? And failed? How many did not understand that the particular ingredients of any age produced the designs for it? Empire, heroism, arrogance, the satisfying pinkness of the map and the comparative cheapness of life helped form the great structures. As Patrick Parker told him—as if he were the first to do so instead of the umpteenth—he abhorred the way Samuel Smiles had left the Brunels, father and son, out of his *Lives of the Great Engineers*.

When the Course Tutor asked, mildly, if Patrick knew why, Patrick said that there could be no 'why' therefore the question could not exist. 'Very philosophical,' said the Course Tutor.

Patrick saw no irony.

'Perhaps I should set you an essay?'

Out came Patrick's lower lip.

'Perhaps I should set you an essay entitled "Although Samuel Smiles was very complimentary towards Brunel as an engineer, he regarded him as devoted to a suspect form of gargantuanism. Smiles suggests that his ruling idea was magnitude; he had an ambition to make everything bigger than he had found it . . . Being the very Napoleon of Engineers and thinking more of glory than of profit was good neither for investors nor for the public who would come to use his designs. What is needed now, as power and honour ebb away and money begins to be the only god, is a change of scale. Discuss." '

'Smiles was a damn fool,' said Patrick. 'It would be a waste of my time.'

'No, Patrick,' said the sighing Tutor softly. 'It would be a waste of mine.'

Most of the students were throwing off the old and embracing the new, but Patrick did it with more contempt than anyone else—just threw the balance of old wisdoms away as one might throw out a rotting vegetable. Appropriate, then, that he came from Coventry. So said the Course Tutor. But when it was put to Patrick that he might one day wish to transform his home town into a new age of design, he was scornful. 'Shopping malls, Walkways, Municipal Offices for Petty Bureaucrats, little houses for little people—'

'Then what would you build, Patrick? Another Reichstag?'

'If I had to choose between provincial design and that—then yes. But I won't. Because I am not interested in building anything domestic—anything that needs plumbing, electricity, waterpipes, doors, windows—all the stuff that has to be housed in a skin and dictates, no matter how hard you try to avoid it—the form. Oh no. I shall build bridges, which are the purest structures of all. And if there is one thing they have absolutely no use for in Coventry—it's a bridge. Little-town minds.'

'It's the people who pay,' said the Course Tutor. 'It's the people who use whatever you make.'

'Maybe—' said Patrick, 'but they must not dictate the form. Most people are idiots . . . I do not bow to making what people love. They must learn to love what I do.'

Ah yes—Mies van der Rohe. It often was. Usually—though not in this case—without the skills to carry it off. Patrick could—and he probably would. The Course Tutor had heard it all before, seen it all before. The trading of one lot of traditions and mores for a new lot that were simply the old lot's antithesis. New Wave—every few years. This season's young bucks were sharpening their teeth on Pinter, Barstow, Storey—rages against the banal, or paeans for it, depending on your point of view. Interpreting it—as every age does with every new thing under the sun—to suit themselves. They usually forgot real people. Too difficult to deal with, sweep it away—like Rembrandt hiding those difficult-to-paint hands. There was something touching about that.

He looked at Patrick Parker. He was not touched by what he saw: a tall, graceful—beautiful even—young man, with fire in his voice and contempt in his eyes. Those who forge ahead have no time for mortals and must forget that great building—truly Great building—even the biggest

Palladian masterpiece in Christendom—has a humble heart. It is, in the end, about people. Nothing the human hand and mind created was about anything else. How could it be? Men were not gods, but men . . . Mies creating a house that burned you in summer and froze you in winter was not Great Design. It was arrogance. And he thought he could see already that this young man . . .

The trouble with the lad from Coventry being so good was that nobody wanted to touch him. Nobody wanted to be responsible for reshaping such talent, or influencing it to the point of change. Even a little. They were all scared of it. This was the time of youth. His tutors were fazed by his ability, and, as he accused them quite rightly from time to time, they did not really understand Where He Was Coming From. And so they left him alone. Or guided him with a very loose rein and hoped for the best. One tutor, a religious sort who specialised in community housing, said that at seminars Patrick sometimes reminded him of twelve-year-old Jesus teaching in the Temple. Another thought he had about him the air of the young Giotto, as described by Vasari. A third cited Wren and John Evelyn's description: 'that miracle of a youth'. Patrick had a freshness of mind, a bounding invention and adventurous empiricism that matched Wren in his vigorous heyday. Whatever they thought of him as a man, as a builder of Great Bridges (bloody great bridges, said the Tutor into his whisky glass), they were sure he would go far. Which concurred, naturally enough, with the object of their estimation's view of things . . . Patrick Parker was already preparing himself for dining with the gods—he had evened out his vowel sounds and bought a suit from Savile Row (four-button cuff), and his aim was to walk away at the end of the course with the coveted gold medal and a public or private commission. Or two.

'He seems to take for granted that he will win the thing,' said another tutor. 'As if he expects his brilliance to be treated accordingly . . .'

The Head of Department agreed. But there was nothing to be done. If he continued with such startling originality and high technical standards in everything, his the gold medal would be. His transportable green Perspex-cladded hunting lodge was still the talk of The Academy and it was rumoured that he had already received a private commission out of it. Patrick's shrug of the shoulders and his public statement that 'You had to start somewhere' when the end-of-year commendations were given out was nowhere near humility and somewhere near the truth. It really was only a beginning. Somehow the Head of Department and the Course Tutor and the rest of them did not find this cheering.

'He will be our star pupil,' said one sadly.

'I know,' said the other mournfully. 'I know.'

The Course Tutor, wincing as he remembered this, reached for another very stiff whisky, a very stiff whisky indeed. The trouble with Patrick was that—if he *was* absolutely brilliant—he was also—somehow lacking in—he searched for the word—compassion. He was heartless, cold to anything that might threaten his ambition. That was it—not threaten his designs, but his *ambition*. So then—Patrick had chosen wisely for his hero. Brunel was a horse-whipper, too. And if the horse fell down,

104

there was always another one waiting behind. Patrick Parker wanted to be like him, did he? Well, thought the Course Tutor as he sipped his drink and slowly closed his door on Patrick's retreating, hubris-ridden back, it would end in tears. One day. If not Patrick's—then everybody else's . . .

7

Embracing the Modern, In Every Sense

A clapper bridge is a simple dry stone construction dating from the Middle Ages and is thought to be the oldest form of human made bridge. The name 'clapper' is believed to come from the Saxon world *cleaca*, an ancient word for stepping stones, and the clapper bridge was perhaps the most natural progression from fallen trees or stepping stones.

Lucy Blakstad, *Bridge: The Architecture of Connection*

Patrick wrote regularly to his mother, letters full of what he had done, what had been said, and urged her to keep the correspondence for posterity. Florence was delighted. She wrote that she was very proud, though she missed him badly and the house was empty without him. She had forgiven him for going. She believed he would be back. She spared nothing in the telling about his father's many irritations. He was getting worse, driving her mad—sitting with him and the clock and nothing else for the evening was giving her palpitations. Patrick wrote back that he was sorry she felt like that and that she should encourage his father to get out of the house, give him a job to do, stir him up. It was easy to dictate from afar and have it translate as being caring.

'Patrick says you should get going on something,'

Florence said, looking up from her letter. 'Let not slip the hour—' she paused to check the writing— 'is what he says.' She put the letter down and stared at him over her spectacles. 'I suggest you let not slip the hour and clear the shed out.'

It was the one place George dreaded visiting. 'Maybe,' he said. 'Better ask him about that bike before I start.' He added, pleased to have some respite, 'Can't move stuff past it, now can I?'

Florence wrote. What did Patrick think? Should they get rid of his old bicycle? She was mortified by his reply.

'No,' he wrote, 'keep it. I have met up with Little Audrey again and she might come up for a day or two in the Christmas vac. If the weather is any good we could go for a cycle ride.'

It is a wise parent who can keep his or her mouth shut. George did it of necessity. Florence had never learned. 'Be careful,' she wrote back. 'You need all your energy for your studies. Leave Audrey well alone for the time being, I would.'

Patrick laughed as he read it. More about dilution. Well—dilution be damned. He was a year and a half down the line, he was doing brilliantly, it was time for a little dilution in that department. Which is why, of course, he had sent that postcard to Audrey in the first place.

If he had hoped to meet a girl on the Design Course, he was disappointed. Of the twenty-seven students in his year, two were girls, and one of those was only approximate. She wore brogues, fisherman's sweaters, cropped hair and smoked small cigars. The most intimate moments spent with her were when she punched him in the chest by way of greeting. The other girl, called Sylvia, was very pretty, very clever, and engaged, by the end of the first term, to Lord Galton's son, also on the course (though he did not turn up very often). And that was that. He was disappointed but not surprised. A career designing buildings and bridges and railways and roads was not woman's work. Besides, mixed classes could do exactly what Florence warned and lay waste to young men's brains. Patrick had found his concentration wandering towards Sylvia's blouse once or twice during lectures and he was very aware of the Pitfall that was Girl.

What he was not aware of was the effect he had on the few girls he did make contact with, from other parts of the college—the fabric designers, the garden and interior designers—girls who hung around the entrance to the main building and eyed him as he strode past. If he desired a love life he had no way of communicating it—and no instinct for discovering who might reciprocate. So unversed was Patrick in the methods of the screen romance and its like, that when Millicent Carter—driven to distraction—plucked up courage and virtually fell at his feet in a welter of petticoats and laddered stockings, he stepped over her—apologising as he went on his way. Not quite daring to look. And when, in his second term, he received two Valentine's cards at his digs, he thought they must have been sent as a joke. So for Patrick there was no easy way to meet girls, which became—in the moments when his head was free of his college work, when he had set aside the lines and planes and conurbations and cantilevers—quite an urgent desire. He wanted a diversion. He was ready for a diversion. And he would have one.

His field trip that term was to Balmoral. He was amazed at the audacity of it when he saw Brunel's design for the young Queen Victoria. 'It's a splendid little bridge,' he wrote to his mother. 'Very modern. Genius in embryo. But it is only a very little one. No wonder Brunel thought he had better design something revolutionary to compensate for the scale of the thing. Otherwise, why bother? As for Queen Vic saying she hated the thing—well— what do you expect from someone who chose *Landseer*?'

To Audrey he wrote, 'I am staying at the YMCA up here, checking up on Isambard at Balmoral. More anon. And it made me think of you and our trips to Bristol and the Tamar. Will you come for a walk when I get back? This is my address. You can drop me a card.' He signed it 'Yours with best wishes, Patrick.' And added two Xs. Might as well get right stuck in, he thought. And put in a third.

On his return, and finding her card, he downed two glasses of cider in about as many minutes, asked his landlady if he could use her telephone, and then he rang Audrey. He told her that he would like to meet up and she told him that she had missed him. There was a pause. He wanted to say that he had missed her, but it was not the truth. So instead he told her that he was really looking forward to seeing her again, which he was. All of her.

'You sound just the same,' he said.

'You don't,' she giggled; he had forgotten that she could giggle so irritatingly. 'You sound like you've swallowed a silver teaspoon.'

'It's London,' he said. 'It just happened.'

That was not the truth either. But he'd be

damned if he was going to tell Audrey how hard he had worked at it. How closely he had observed Henry Galton, listened to his intonations, the terminology.

'I like it,' she said. 'I'll be at the college gates on Friday.' And then she was gone.

He sat down afterwards and took some deep breaths. He was pleased, and he was nervous. He reverted to calling her Little Audrey in his mind by way of keeping her in her place. Big College, Little Audrey, he thought. But when she finally arrived, long dark hair blowing about her face, little fur collar pulled up against the sharp autumn air, and that bright, happy smile, he saw that she was hardly that. If anything she was taller than him, though he was more than medium height, and she was as rounded and buxom and dark as he was slender, elegant and fair. He stared at her. Big College went out of the window. He could think of nothing else but the rosy prospect ahead. They stood facing each other on the college steps, and Patrick held out his hand. Audrey shook it. Two girls looked on enviously. Audrey, aware of them as one who is in love will be aware of rivals, decided to act. She leaned forward and brushed her lips against Patrick's cheek. The skin so cared for by his mother rewarded her efforts—it glowed in its freshness and was soft to the touch. He barely shaved. Audrey, as her cheek brushed his, said 'Oh.'

'Oh, what?' he asked, stepping back.

'Oh nothing—' she laughed. 'It's just that my last boyfriend had a beard.' She made that up but what the hell. It didn't do to tell him that the kiss made her stomach turn over with desire. Or to let him think he was the only fish in the sea. Which, in reality—because as soon as she saw him again, she knew—he was.

Patrick felt a little spike somewhere around his ribs. As usual his face was open to be read. Audrey was quietly contented. He was jealous. 'But I don't see him any more,' she added firmly.

'Good,' said Patrick. What he was thinking, with anxiety, was that she had probably *done it*—with this bearded loon—and he hadn't *done it* with anyone. Supposing he wasn't any good? He had been reading Lawrence lately (everyone at college was)—the first full text of *Lady Chatterley*—and he drew no comfort from it, none at all; somehow every time he imagined himself with a compliant Constance, his mother barged in. He looked at Audrey. You just could not tell. Lawrence also said that if a woman did not have a touch of the harlot in her she was a dry old stick—and you couldn't tell by looking at Audrey if *that* was true, either.

'Shall we go then?' she asked, happily.

And off they set, walking close together but not yet daring to link arms or hold hands.

In his pocket was a bag of honey and oat biscuits—his favourites—baked by his mother. The bag crackled. There was a little horseplay as Audrey tried to investigate what made the noise. It was exciting and silly and intimate to have a girl putting her hand in your pocket. In the end she brought out the bag and peered into it.

'Mum's biscuits,' he said, feeling slightly ashamed. The last thing he wanted to mention at this point was his mother.

'Like your oats, then?' said Audrey mischievously (truth was she had no idea exactly why oats were rude, only that they were). Patrick felt himself

111

going hot. This was more like it.

'Are you still seeing that lad who worked on the trains? William?' he asked. He was dying to ask straight out—if they had Done It.

'Oh no,' she said. 'He gave up being a steward and went into the Army. I think he liked uniforms.'

She wasn't going to say that she got bored with the kissing and that they never got past the hand-in-the-side-placket stage.

'Miss him?'

She shrugged. 'Plenty more fish in the sea.' She smiled at him, quite invitingly. Beneath her coat she wore something bright yellow and full-skirted and her legs made shushing noises from their nylons.

'And you?' she said.

'No time for girls.'

'Oh.'

'Much.'

He offered her the greaseproof bag. 'Have one?'

She took one and nibbled it and said, 'I expect they'd be nice with a cup of tea.'

'Well—let's do that next time,' he said, taking a deep breath and thinking Now or Never. 'Next time we'll have tea at my digs. I'll square it with the landlady and let you know when.'

It was then that Audrey decided the rekindling of their friendship was serious. Thank you, God, she said to herself, *thank you.* Patrick was perfect—and Audrey, though she had told no one, was extremely bored with being stuck at the virginal stage. She wanted to *know.* Not at first, of course. She did not want to appear easy. But eventually she would, as they said in films, Give Herself To Him. She loved him. She knew it. None of her boyfriends had made her happy. She knew more than they did. Only Patrick walked like a god and could tell her things. In the week between his telephoning her and their meeting up, whenever she heard Doris Day singing 'Secret Love' she always burst into tears. Proof.

Patrick was also considering being stuck at the virginal stage. As they tramped the damp London streets he didn't think he would ever get out of it either. Not at this rate. And it was such a liability—men were not supposed to be inexperienced; of course girls were—which did not quite add up and was best not thought about. He hoped Audrey would be a pushover. From the way his mother hinted at the twin evils, sex and girls lurked on every corner, in every situation, and both were just dying to grab their chance with him. Audrey in particular, according to Florence. According to Florence, all he had to do was whistle. Maybe. He still wasn't sure. As they walked, Audrey dared to take his hand. It was his turn to say 'Oh.'

A week or so later, with the landlady's permission, he took Audrey up to his digs. While he went along the landing to fill the kettle and wash the cups, she took a good look at the scattered letters from Florence, wondering if they mentioned her. But all she found were scathing references to George and motherly affection for Patrick. One particular letter caught her eye. Florence asked, Was he really sure he wanted to keep that old bike of his in the shed? The saddlebag was rotten and half falling off and needed a good clear-out—it was full of junk and probably ought to be thrown away . . . At which Audrey suddenly remembered their illicit sweets and the sad-faced shop owner.

'Did you ever give your dad that note and toffee from that woman down Chapel Street?' she asked later.

'What woman down Chapel Street?' he replied, his mouth full of biscuit.

*   *   *

Whenever they went out, Audrey encouraged Patrick to talk about himself. It caused him no difficulty. He talked and talked and she listened and listened, for she had little to say of her own that was worthy. Audrey herself worked at the telephone exchange up at Whitehall and, though it was considered a very good job, it was obviously not as fascinating as creating things like roads and tunnels and bridges and roofs and having posters on your wall with incomprehensible-sounding names such as Moholy-Nagy and images of ancient aqueducts and viaducts and siege machines. She reminded herself that she needed to know about such things if she was to keep Patrick happy.

He took her to the British Museum and showed her some drawings of a flying machine by Leonardo da Vinci and said it was over five hundred years old. For once she did not have to invent reverential rapture. 'But that's amazing,' she said. 'All those years ago. Weren't they still chopping off queens' heads then?'

'What on earth has that got to do with anything?' he asked irritably. She sometimes did this, came at something from a whole new perspective. He always felt ruffled when it happened. For her part, Audrey could not quite say what she meant by it but she felt that there was something relevant in

114

there somewhere. Just that Patrick was in one world and she was in another.

He took her to Hungerford Bridge (which she thought was remarkably ugly) and they stood staring at the cars below while trains whizzed past to the left of them, shrouding them in grit and the cloying smell of burning oil.

'Opened to the public in eighteen-forty-five,' he said. 'Crossing the Thames in the very middle of London.'

'Lovely,' she said.

'Yes—but only a footbridge. Brunel only condescended to create it. He knew he was worthy of something finer, bigger, more impressive . . .'

'I should think the people who used it couldn't have cared less whether it was bigger and grander,' she said, without thinking. 'They just wanted to get to the other side.'

'Oh, Audrey,' he said, shaking his head. He wagged his finger at her and she had a terrible urge to bite it. 'If building was merely a question of basic form kneeling to function, we'd still be living in the dark ages and making bridges with reeds.'

She nodded meekly. She would have liked to know about bridges made of reeds, which sounded very curious and quite impossible—but she knew better. The warrior's blood was up.

'Listen, Audrey.'

She gave him a Bambi blink to signify that she was all his.

'Brunel was a great engineer and an even greater designer—and probably the most resourceful builder of bridges the world has seen. Therefore, to say the people "just wanted to get to the other side" is—well—rubbish really.'

115

'Sorry,' she said.

He remembered that he was supposed to be softening her up. 'That's all right,' he said, kindly.

They visited the outside of the Great Man's London office at number eighteen Duke Street. She chose her words carefully and said how fitting it was that Brunel should show off a bit and work somewhere so grand.

'Imperative,' said Patrick. 'He had to win respect, and keep it, and give everyone a sense of confidence so that he could raise all the money for his projects . . . I'll have to do the same one day.'

'You will, I know,' she said, and she did.

'And to do what he did, and what I need to do, you have to fit in to society. Which is why I've left Coventry.'

'And lost your accent,' she said.

'How can you impress anyone when they know you come from a place as narrow-minded as that?' He shrugged. 'About the only exciting thing that ever happened up there was that daft woman Godiva and her striptease.'

Now, there were not many bits of historical information that Audrey remembered. School had been a bit sparing on the more lively aspects of English history. But, when Patrick said the name, she did remember Godiva. Largely because the story was not told to her class by the usual history mistress, but by a young supply teacher, a man with a beard and sandals who—so they whispered—was a vegetarian with left-wing views. He, for some reason, decided to teach the class about six extraordinary British women through the ages— starting with Boadicea. Until then she had not exactly been aware that there were that many. And

116

Godiva, eleventh—was it?—century, was the one that Audrey remembered best.

'She didn't do a striptease, Patrick,' she said, forgetting to be amenable. 'She rode on a horse through the city naked. And she did it to show up her husband who was imposing things on the people of Coventry. Cruel taxes—and other things . . .' Audrey was a little shaky on what the other things were. 'Anyway, when she went to her husband on behalf of the people and begged him to stop he said that he would only stop if she rode naked through the market at midday. So she did. She covered herself with her long, golden hair and asked the people of the town not to look and they didn't. Except one and they called him Peeping Tom. She's probably the lady on the horse with rings on her fingers and bells on her toes at Banbury Cross and—'

'Very interesting,' said Patrick impatiently. 'Anyway—it was a stupid thing to do. Fancy taking your clothes off just to make a point.'

Audrey stared at him. His lip had come out again. She was fed up with seeing it actually, a thought which very much surprised her. 'Well,' she said, her hands on her hips, 'it bloody well worked, though, didn't it?'

They stared at each other, stunned into silence.

'I mean,' said Audrey, a little less defiantly, 'it shamed him. And he stopped doing—whatever it was he was doing.'

Patrick was not pleased by her sudden uppishness. It conjured up the kind of images (naked, golden hair, warm horse between thighs) that warmed the parts of him that got in the way of clear thinking. The combination of irritation and desire—yet again—had happened. Audrey would question him and at the same she would sit near him or touch his arm—it confused him, it confused the issue and it confused the issue particularly now. They were on the trail of Isambard Kingdom Brunel, not fighting the ruddy battle of the sexes. He walked off briskly to show his disdain and then stopped and all but stamped his foot. Damn. He was supposed to be winning her over . . . But it was all right. Audrey followed. Over his shoulder he said, 'Anyway—Isambard had to mix with the great and the good in order to get what he wanted. And I'll have to do the same. Coventry gives the wrong image, completely the wrong image.'

'Of course,' said Audrey. 'Of course.'

She looked up at the blue plaque. 'It says he lived here.'

'Oh yes,' said Patrick. 'He got married and they moved into the house next door. He needed a wife by then.'

'Well, quite,' she said happily.

Everything was mended.

But later they argued about Battersea Power Station. She wished it didn't look quite so stark, though the chimneys were nice . . . And why not paint it a colour? Patrick was very short with her over that.

'You would hardly want it painted pale blue, now would you?' he asked, quite sharply.

To which she thoughtlessly snapped, 'Well—why not, it might be rather nice, cheer things up a bit . . .'

'You'll be wanting them to wallpaper it and put antimacassars everywhere next,' he said acidly.

118

She found herself apologising. All these outings together meant that they were moving towards the moment when Patrick would Make A Woman Of Her (as Belmondo did of Bardot), and nothing must get in the way of that. 'Sorry' had already become something of a mantra between them. She said it again now. 'Sorry,' she said, 'but sometimes I get a little confused about what to think . . .'

He nodded. 'My course and my beliefs *are* a bit of a mixture,' he told her as they wandered around the flattened site of the Festival of Britain. 'But they are all part of the systematic application of scientific knowledge to the design, creation and use of structures.'

'Gracious,' she said. 'I should think *so* . . .'

'Colour really isn't a part of all that.'

'Well no,' she said. 'It wouldn't be.'

They stared down at the murky water of the river. 'What are they building here?'

'Theatres, more concert halls—a whole arts complex,' he said gloomily, gesturing with his hands to indicate something grand and imposing. 'Born too late, again. If they'd needed a bridge I'd have designed them one.' He stared at the simple arch that took people and traffic over towards Covent Garden. 'And it would be a great deal more impressive than that.'

'I bet it would,' she said rapturously. 'My dad says we could do with another bridge across the Thames. He says the traffic is getting to be a nightmare.' She paused, thinking. 'Of course, I suppose they could just stop having so much traffic instead.'

'Silly,' he said, quite affectionately. 'But your dad's right. Another bridge is needed.' And he stood gazing across the water, eyes screwed against the afternoon sunlight, face bearing an expression of one who sees his own heroic place in its Pantheon. Audrey's heart skipped a beat, he looked so handsome and distinguished. 'Give me time,' he said. 'Give me time.'

'Oh, Patrick,' she said reverently. 'You'll be even better than your Brunel one day. I'm sure of it.'

What an intelligent girl she can be, he thought. And he put his arm right around her waist, smiling to hear her say 'Oh' in that special way of hers.

That evening he took her to a pub and bought her a gin and lime, and then another. Gin and lime, it seemed, was quite important if you were out to seduce a girl. Audrey did not appear to be the slightest bit unwilling (much as his mother had predicted) but you never knew and it seemed wise to get the thing right. He was extremely nervous. Audrey, on the other hand, was growing more and more animated and smiley. Desire, by the end of her second gin and lime, had reduced itself in him to an alarming feeling of tiredness. He sipped his pint of bitter and began to feel very ill. The dreadful spectre of failure gripped him. He had not felt it for a long time, not to this degree, and he was afraid.

'Would you like to . . .?' he began, but his voice trailed off.

Audrey gave him a dazzling smile. 'I thought you'd never ask,' she said.

He downed his pint in one. Now or never, he thought. The point of no return. She had acquitted herself fairly well that day, apart from the Godiva business. For most of the time she listened to him attentively and made sensible comments and she was, he could not deny it, enjoyable company. And attractive.

'Let's go then,' he said, standing up. Audrey tucked her hand under his arm and they walked out of the pub into the late November darkness. The stars shone in the heavens (which Audrey found very appropriate) and the air was cold and fresh. This was it. This was the future. They would be a couple at last. And she could almost, almost smell the bridal bouquet.

On the bus Patrick talked and she listened. They were taking their place in the modern world. They were Moderns. They must honour the past but build in the future. Modernity was everything. And Modernity did not—er—go with—er—virginity. She blushed at the word. Well, not for her either. 'You bet,' she said again, surprising them both, and she began to sing. 'Che sera sera . . .', not caring that the people on the bus turned to stare. We are Moderns, thought Patrick, trying desperately not to feel embarrassed.

'What does it mean?' he asked.

And she sang again, 'Che sera sera—whatever will be will be—the future's not ours to see, che sera sera . . .'

Exactly the opposite of the way he felt, which was that he knew every step he must take, and he would take it, he *was* the future.

And this would be an important step into it. With Audrey. Known and trusted. She was still singing, smiling away at him, eyes bright, shoulders swaying slightly in the seat. Uninhibited. It must have been the gin and lime, he thought, which was a very good sign.

Tiptoeing up the stairs, past his landlady's door,

she got a fit of silent giggles. Then he did too. Clinging to each other, shaking and almost bursting with it, they fell into his room. It felt as if neither of them would ever be able to stop laughing ever again . . . But when he closed the door behind them and they faced each other they were instantly silent and serious once more. The hour was nigh. No going back.

In preparation, with hope in his heart, Patrick had pinned up a new poster at the end of his bed. She could hardly look at it for blushing, yet she could hardly not. The name above the poster's black and white photograph was Eikoh Hosoe. The picture was of a male (very) torso and a female (obviously) torso, standing pressed frontally into each other—so close no leaf could pass between them—and photographed from the side. It was like a landscape of skin, joined at every place that—well—they should—or should not be . . . It was a confusing image to Audrey because there was nothing very rude in it—you could not see a nipple or any of their private parts or the—er—other bits—yet it was the most naked and exciting picture of two bodies she had ever seen.

When she did manage to look at it properly she sighed and said, 'It's beautiful. You can feel what they can feel of each other physically, and what they are feeling emotionally. It's a picture of feeling.'

Patrick was somewhat taken aback. 'Really?' he said. He thought it was a good, sexy picture. He peered again. 'Well,' he said, nodding with sudden gravitas, 'I see it as plastic forms taking on a sexual overtone. But at the same time appearing as detached as sculpture.'

'Oh no,' she said. 'Well, yes,' she said, going up to it as if she would drink it in. 'But it is also not like sculpture at all. It's living. Human.'

'I mean sculptural in its form. Not marble or bloody bronzes,' he said irritably.

She was still staring at the poster. He hadn't mean it to stir her brain up, only her body. Just when you want them to see the erotic, he thought peevishly, they go and find the artistic.

'Is it a new exhibition?' she asked.

'Yes,' he said impatiently, moving closer. 'But it's in Tokyo. He's Japanese.'

She read the words beneath the image. 'The full potential power of every medium is dependent upon the purity of its use.'

'Modernism,' he said, 'is purity. No taint, no homage, no leaning for support on the past. The New.'

'Why,' she said, still staring hard. 'It is not rude at all—it's pure. It's the heart speaking.' She read the quotation underneath the photograph. 'Quotation by the photographer: "I would like to express Love in my nude photography. This Love must flow like a stream beneath all photographs of the nude."'

'The Japanese,' said Patrick, 'are streets ahead of us culturally. Well—in everything really.'

'Even love?' she asked with daring. One of them had to get down to it.

'Particularly in building design,' he said. 'Way out front.'

They stood staring at each other. Love? he thought. She moved closer. Words came to him smooth on the tongue, and he heard himself saying, 'Well then—let's see if we can get ahead of them for once—'

They smiled into each other's eyes. It was going to be all right. They moved as close together as the picture above their heads.

Poor Audrey, yielding herself up to the romance of it, did not know what had hit her. In a moment of supreme clumsiness Patrick stepped towards her, overbalanced as she stepped back with a little squeak, and, with her beneath him, they both fell backwards onto the bed. Which might, thought Audrey, have been filmstar romantic if she hadn't caught her chin a right crack on the headboard. She saw stars and had tears in her eyes. Which was approximately how she knew it was supposed to be, even if it was for the wrong reason. They lay there, hearts beating, waiting for the landlady's step on the stair. It did not come.

More to the point, thought Patrick, neither did his mother.

Beneath him everything seemed to be taking place exactly as it should. Including Audrey's responses.

'Oh Patrick,' she said, very, very happily. 'You are wonderful.'

Perfect.

Afterwards she felt, as she looked up at the poster, that she was Modern at last. Although part of her, the secret part, was not Modern at all because that part of her was imagining walking down the aisle, holding white carnations and freesias, or perhaps little pink roses—or maybe something else—and finally changing her name from Wapshott to the infinitely more desirable name of Parker.

Patrick, on the other hand, enjoyed the entire experience intensely, until it was over, and then he was unsure what to do. He put his arm around Audrey's shoulders and lay looking up at the ceiling and wished that he smoked. They fell asleep and the Eikoh Hosoe poster was the last thing they saw until morning.

*   *   *

Audrey went about with a spring in her step that did not go unnoticed among the girls at the Exchange. Where it was still considered not quite the thing to do and where the claim 'I am a Modernist' fell on largely unimpressed ears. 'Just watch you don't get caught,' was the favourite phrase, muttered darkly. Audrey said that was not likely to happen because they only ever went to his digs together when the landlady was out. The speaker raised her eyebrows in mocking merriment. That was the trouble with the girls of today. Modern meant Half-baked.

Patrick waited for his brain to atrophy, his pencil-holding hand to become palsied, his eyes to cease to have their visionary clarity—and none of it happened. Instead, he felt miles better. Energised. As part of the course curriculum he was required to design a small factory and he had been fiddling around with various possibilities for ages. Now, for the sheer, shocking pleasure of it he threw out the more conventional ideas and created a series of very simple squinch arches, applying them to the roof of the building where they looked—well—astonishing. Good, but astonishing. A cathedral to industry. Brick, wood and glass was not what was expected. Steel and asbestos and plastic were more usual for factories now. But brick, wood and glass it was. 'Just To Prove I Can,' he wrote underneath

125

the finished elevation. The tutors saw this audacious use of materials and form and found it hard not to praise him—rather incautiously—to his face. The Course Tutor, eyeing the drawing, sighed. It was, without doubt, brilliant. More whisky was required. He gave his star pupil a large one, too. Patrick asked the Course Tutor, the only one to keep silent, what he thought. The Course Tutor deliberated for a moment and then he looked up, smiled, patted Patrick on the shoulder and said, 'I think you should take more water with it . . .'

So what? Patrick already knew his worth. He walked out of the college with his hands in his pockets, his head up, whistling.

'You seem to be seeing quite a lot of Audrey Wapshott,' wrote Florence to her son. (The use of her surname indicating strong disapproval.) 'I hope you are not letting her divert you from what you went down there to do . . .' Patrick wrote back that he was not, that they were just friends. Audrey, when she sneaked a look at Florence's letter, pursed her lips and said nothing. After all, there were some things a boy wanted that a boy couldn't get from his mother, and Audrey wasn't talking oat and honey biscuits.

Dolly and her father asked her flat-out if Patrick was behaving himself. She said that he was and that he was a perfect gentleman. He was teaching her things.

'Like what?' asked her dad.

'A Design for Living,' she said, off the top of her head. It was currently Patrick's favoured phrase.

'Well, if he's got designs on you,' said her mother, 'he can forget them unless he puts a ring on

126

your finger.'

'He's changing the world,' said Audrey. Dolly's expression made her rather wish she hadn't.

'All I ask is that he changes your surname,' said Dolly. 'The world will do its own changing when it wants to.'

*   *   *

Dolly asked Florence what she thought. Florence said that Patrick was following his destiny and didn't have time for all that malarkey. Florence asked Dolly a week or two later what she thought. Dolly said that Audrey was a sensible girl and they were just friends. Both mothers didn't believe a word of it. Dolly was worried that Audrey would miss out on marriage if she hung around with Patrick, and Florence, who felt the miles between mother and son, worried that Audrey might take her place.

Let battle commence, she found herself saying, as the days drew nearer for Patrick to come home for the holidays. She baked and sewed and knitted and even bought a copy of *Architecture Monthly* for his room. 'Let battle commence if that little madam thinks she can come up here and take him away from me.' He was, and always would be, her little builder boy.

8

Between Juno and Venus sits Apollo

To 'Make a bridge of gold for him' is to enable a man to retreat from a false position without loss of dignity.
  Old Proverb

Patrick arrived home. He did his bit by the turkey and plum pudding, he did his bit by the mince pies, and he ate a gratifyingly large chunk of Christmas cake. But Florence was not happy.

'Built anything yet?' asked George.

'They hold you back,' said Patrick. But he got out his drawing pens and soon sketched the rough plan of the factory—and the hunting lodge. For the latter, George suggested he might have added a roll-up walkway—in case the land was waterlogged. Patrick thought it an interesting idea and the two bent their heads over the breakfast room table, pens and pencils in hand.

Florence picked up the book Patrick had given her. 'Time to chuck out the cobwebs, Mum,' was what he said as he gave it to her. A particular insult for a woman who was known for her shining home. She had pursed her lips, couldn't help it. But then he put his arm round her. 'Take a look at it,' he said. 'It's about the art of food.' He emphasised the words *art of food* as if she was the village idiot. If she hadn't been so anxious to make this visit a happy time for him, she would have told him so. And queried why, apart from speaking down his nose to her, he was speaking down his nose in general. She was still coming to terms with his new accent—last Christmas he spoke his native Coventry—this Christmas he spoke like the Queen. Where would it all end? Patrick and George still had their heads bent over the table and the drawings and she thought that once there was a time when he would have only wanted her. She said nothing and turned the pages of his gift. A cookery book, by a woman called Elizabeth David. The wound went deep. She got up immediately and went to make turkey sandwiches. Patrick noticed the way she tossed the book down on the chair behind her.

'I thought you'd like it,' said Patrick stiffly. 'After all, it's hardly avant garde any more.' He said *avant garde* as if she was a dimwit. We'll see about that, she thought, and got on with the turkey sandwiches. He tucked into those all right. No Art about it.

Neither parent actually remarked on the change in their son's accent, nor did they appear to notice that he was wearing an orange silk handkerchief loosely knotted around his neck. It made a change from black roll-necks anyway.

'So how are you finding the capital city?' asked George.

Through a turkey sandwich Patrick said that London was amazing—inspirational. 'There's something in the air down there that feeds the mind . . . It's different. Exciting.'

We'll see about that too, thought Florence.

For his father Patrick bought a record. Jazz. While it played Florence looked at the wall with an expression of blank incomprehension. Not helped by George jouncing around in his chair and apparently liking it. It sounded like bellyache music to her. Where was the boy who liked John McCormack and Kathleen Ferrier?

'Who's it by?' asked George enthusiastically.

'Miles Davis,' said Patrick.

'Put the other side on,' his father said, sucking on his empty pipe.

Florence looked down at her horrible book. Even the illustrations were an insult. Pictures that were all black lines and harsh—no shading, no details—nothing like the pictures she admired of Constable and Gainsborough.

'He's good,' said Patrick, coming up behind her and making her jump. 'Johnnie Minton. Superseded now but at least he was trying to do something different.'

'Yes,' said Florence. 'He certainly was.'

When the Miles Davis ended Patrick produced a large, grey-lumpy machine. It was a tape recorder. 'Borrowed this from college,' he said. It was called a Grundig. German, thought Florence sourly, but she said nothing.

'And this was Audrey's present.' Patrick put on a reel of tape.

'Under Milk Wood,' announced the rolling Welsh tones of Richard Burton.

'By Dylan Thomas.'

They listened and when the grimly spotless Mrs Ogmore-Pritchard suggested that 'the sun could only come in if it wiped its feet' and Patrick slapped his knee and said, 'Isn't that just the way it *is* for the bourgeoisie?' Florence felt that she was being got at. She wondered, but again she kept it to herself—just what Patrick would do if she didn't

130

clean his room, wash his clothes, iron his shirts and send him back to college with everything clean as a pin. He never complained of it at any rate. He might wear his navvy's trousers of corduroy and his black jumpers—but he liked them to be washed and pressed all the same. She sat there and she listened without a word of complaint, because this was her son, her only son.

When it came to the courting couple, or *lovers* as they so brazenly chose to call them—and how Burton's voice rolled over the words—it was as if he was actually there in the room with them. Florence had had quite enough. Silly names and dirty people. Mog Edwards and Myfanwy Price were just plain rude.

'Well—' she said, beyond speech.

'Oh Mum,' said Patrick, enjoying himself (for he could take his place among them, the non-virginal, now). 'It's just the way of it today.' And he winked at his dad.

It was then that Florence knew her son and Audrey were more than just friends. She felt sick. It did not help that George took the pipe out of his mouth and laughed a little laugh—like he knew too. Well, he would, she thought, with Lilly-Her-That-One.

We'll also see about that, she thought, and tears came into her eyes as she looked upon her handsome, happy son. Peggy Boxer may have failed once, but she would make another plan. She took some comfort from hatching it.

When Patrick said that Dylan Thomas had died at the age of thirty-nine, from drink, Florence could not stop herself. 'I'm not surprised,' she said.

'Tragic,' said George.

131

'Oh I don't know,' said Patrick. 'Those whom the gods love die young . . .'

'Don't tempt Fate,' said Florence.

Patrick said airily, 'Oh—I'm not sure it isn't best for the creative spirit to die early. After all—what is there left once you get old? Nothing. All dried up.'

George put his pipe back in his mouth. 'You'll move the goal posts soon as you get there,' he said.

'The new cathedral opens next year,' said Florence. 'At last. I expect the Germans have been laughing at us.'

'Too busy rebuilding Dresden I should think,' said Patrick. 'What they've done there is amazing. We, on the other hand . . .' he sniffed his Florence sniff—'Well, I took a look on the way in. What a dog's breakfast.'

'They've kept the old cathedral walls I'm pleased to say,' said his father.

Patrick curled his lip. 'Basil Spence the architect? More like A Right Basil I'd say.'

'Oh?' said George.

'It's all whimsy,' said Patrick. 'Like the Festival of Britain.'

'Oh I thought that a grand show.'

'Your generation would . . .'

'You forget that I've got an eye for that sort of thing,' said George firmly.

'Oh?' said Florence.

'I used to build structures in Meccano, if you remember.'

She burst out laughing, ridding herself of some of her hidden spleen. 'Meccano!' she said. 'Pie in the sky more like.'

That shut him up.

Patrick remembered, fleetingly, taking one apart and putting it back together again in the shed. He might have mentioned it but the memory was not a happy one. He smiled to himself—Something Nasty In The Woodshed.

George saw the smile and misread it. It didn't do to venture anything in this house.

Florence said coaxingly, 'Well then—there'll still be plenty for you to do in Coventry when you've finished at college. You could start by building something that doesn't look like an army barracks and I'm sure we'd all be obliged.'

Patrick went and sat at the table. 'Any piccalilli, Mum?' he asked, picking up another sandwich.

'In the cupboard,' she said. 'I'm just popping out.'

They looked at her in astonishment. Four o'clock on Christmas Day?

'For a breath of fresh air.'

If George was amazed, it was as nothing to the amazement that the Boxer family felt when they received a personal invitation to the Parkers' for Boxing Day tea. It was the busiest time of the holiday for the pub and Mr Boxer declined. But Ruby and Peggy were delighted to accept. They decked themselves out in their very best attire and walked up. Florence, discreetly placed behind the front-room curtains, saw them coming and put a match to the parlour fire. She switched on the standard lamp, pulled the curtains tight shut, and went out to open the front door.

Ruby Boxer handed her a Christmas-wrapped gift—'No prizes for guessing,' she said cheerfully. It was sherry. If George's amazement was high already, the sight of his pledge-signing wife dusting off the little glasses and putting them on a tray on

133

the kitchen table with the bottle winking beside them, took it to new dimensions.

'We won't,' said Florence, smiling what she thought was a friendly smile and which, in actual fact, had Peggy and George's blood running cold. 'We're teetotal.' The smile, more horrible, widened. Ruby was smiling too. She said that she *would*, if it was all the same, as she'd been run off her feet. Florence nodded. 'And I'm sure Patrick will join you.'

Patrick was called down from the bottom of the stairs. And George, taking the opportunity while his wife was out of the room, poured sherry into each of the glasses. And took one. Florence returned. 'He'll be down in a minute,' she said confidingly, looking straight at Peggy. 'He's been drawing. He could do with a bit of livening up.'

George, top lip poised over glass, nearly choked himself.

It says a great deal for the agitation taking place in Florence's breast that she ignored George's throwing-off of teetotalism, if she even noticed. 'And you two young things can take your drinks and go into the parlour. I've lit the fire.'

Ruby smiled at her daughter encouragingly. Florence smiled at her son encouragingly. George smiled into the fire and sipped and said nothing. The two young things picked up their glasses and carried them, very gingerly, along the hall and into the shadowy room where the fire was just taking hold.

Peggy placed herself just-so on the rug by the fire and sipped her sherry and smiled at Patrick and waited for him to speak. He sat on the unyielding edge of the squeaky couch and drank half the glass straight off.

'Well,' he said. 'We don't usually have visitors at Christmas. You are honoured.'

'Am I?' she said.

He drained his glass. And got up. 'Would you like another?'

She shook her head. Sipping was the ladylike way and she wasn't going to let herself down. Patrick got as far as the door before Florence gave a little rattle of the handle and popped her head round. Her smile, if anything, was even more hideous.

'I brought you the bottle,' she said, handing it to him. 'Your father's got no control.'

And she was gone.

'My dad's just the same,' said Peggy. 'I'd like to get out—leave the pub and go to London too. What's it like?'

'Busy,' said Patrick.

The firelight was playing a halo around her hair and her skirt revealed a pair of very dainty knees. She sipped her drink again and looked at him over the rim. It was an inviting look. But Patrick, in the first full flush of new-discovered manhood, disdained it. 'I see a lot of Audrey,' he said.

Somehow Peggy Boxer managed to get the sip of sherry down her windpipe.

'Really?' she said. 'What's she doing nowadays?' The voice was even and Patrick was lulled.

'Telephones,' he said. 'Bit dead-end. But she's very bright actually. When she isn't being daft.' He said this last so affectionately that he surprised himself.

'Are you engaged?' Peggy also surprised herself. The daring of it came from disappointment. She had been led to believe . . .

135

'Oh no,' said Patrick. 'Just lovers. You know.'

There—he had told someone. Straight out. Lovers. It was a great word.

Peggy got up. 'I'm getting scorched,' she said. 'Where's the—?'

Patrick waited. Peggy pulled a face. 'Where—er—?'

Patrick picked up the bottle.

'Not that,' said Peggy, so upset she nearly hit him over the head with it. 'Where's the bloody toilet?'

*　　　*　　　*

When Audrey came up to visit, just for a night, which was as much as Florence would allow, and almost more than Audrey could stand, given the way she paced the floor of her bedroom, went up and down the stairs countless times throughout the night, and generally made it clear that there would be no hanky-panky in her house. The weather was so bad that they never set foot out of doors and the general frustration level on everyone's part (except George's) was electric. All notions of taking a cycle ride were abandoned, and the bike and the contents of the shed mouldered on.

It was the second time that the serpent placed before Audrey Wapshott's nose the irrefutable fact that, if you withdraw the pleasures of the bedchamber from your man, he will undoubtedly be all the keener for them—and—even if only incidentally—you. Love clouded Audrey Wapshott's vision. Or was it love? Might it not be something far more dangerous? Blind adulation?

A Consideration of Duty versus Genius

Steg uber der Mur: This combined footbridge and
cycle way plays an important role at Graz, as
indicated by a local commentator, who describes
it as a 'place for humanity, a symbol and a
cultural axis for the city, where a tension field
between tradition and receptiveness to the new
has been set up'.
  Matthew Wells, *30 Bridges*

The foodstuffs Patrick took back to London with
him doubled in volume, and Florence had made
him a pullover of the softest, finest wool which
would have taken an ordinary mortal months to
knit. It was in the colour she thought favoured him
best: royal blue. He looked at it for a moment, then
at her, and she was worried he might hand it back.
But he did not. He bent to kiss her, thanked her,
and boarded. There, she thought, as she waved him
away on the train, *there*—his father—old misery he
was—couldn't do anything like that for him, now
could he? As soon as the train was out of sight of
the waving hands, Patrick pulled down the window
of his carriage and threw the jumper to the winds.
  'Begone, Dull Bourgeois,' he cried. Then he
leaned back in his seat, letting the icy breeze sting
his face until a red-faced man in a scarf and hat
leaned forward and asked him, very nervously, to
close it.
  Audrey met him at the station. They tiptoed past

his landlady's door and spent the rest of the day in bed. In the evening, sitting either side of the popping gas fire, sipping beer, Patrick told her about Peggy Boxer's visit. He laughed and laughed about the mix-up over the bathroom (as he had learned to call it)—but Audrey did not laugh. She looked at him. If she was not careful she would lose him—not just because he was handsome—but because he really *was* somebody. You could feel it when you were with him. Of course Peggy Boxer wouldn't manage it—she was just a silly thing from what Audrey remembered—but someone would someday . . . unless Audrey developed into somebody, too. 'Teach me everything you know,' she said, leaning forward. He took her straight back to bed. After which he made her tiptoe out into the night. He returned to college in the morning and needed—as he said to her playfully— to rest.

*   *   *

If Audrey had not been wedged between a large man with several carrier bags and a lolling child, she would have danced down the length of the bus home. Instead she sat there and had a think. How to get on? How to be somebody? She would find a way. It seemed to her that if you loved, you could do anything—just like the best songs and films always said. If Patrick was going to build his bridges, what were her bridges going to be?

*   *   *

Patrick sent his father a copy of Dylan Thomas's

Adventures in the Skin Trade together with a copy of the tape of *Under Milk Wood*. Florence eyed both these items beadily. 'And just where does he think you're going to find a machine to listen to *that* muck again?' she asked the kitchen sink, rattling the dishes until she broke one. George said nothing. But he read the book and wrote back that he found it a bit strange but enjoyable. For the first time in his life George received a full letter from his son, addressed to him only, and in his own right. It had news of theatre trips, foreign films, a design prize for the college Gold Medal, part of which was a visit to Tokyo. It gave Florence breathing difficulties while George, delighted, wrote back and suggested that he might consider making a ticket collector's booth for the prize. In his opinion the signalmen were always looked after, it was the poor ticket collector who got stuck in a matchbox and took cold . . . Patrick wrote back and said he had his eye on something a bit more startling than that. George sighed. The letter ended with 'Love to Mum'—and that was all.

Florence waited for her own letter. Waited, and waited. No letter came and Florence became ill.

George nursed her. She became iller when, having written to Patrick that his father made a terrible presence in the sickroom, Patrick wrote back and said that he was in the middle of exams, as well as working on his competition entry, and couldn't return. He sent her a flowery card in pastels and wrote under the sentimental verse 'All My Love Your Loving Son'. Florence put it on her bedside table, continued to grow pale and not to eat and to have what she decided were fits. She wrote to Patrick that she was afraid she might die.

Patrick wrote back—hurriedly—and said it was nonsense. That she would be fine. What she needed was a bit of a holiday. Why didn't she and Dad spend a little of their savings and go away somewhere warm? He suggested Morocco and Florence nearly had another fit.

'I'll come up when I can,' he said.

Florence, beside herself, turned on George. 'And you can get out there to that shed now, George Parker, cold or not. For you're no use to me in here.'

But since she was lying down, George dared to stand up for himself. 'I'll go out when the weather warms up a bit,' he said. He waited for the heavens to open or the earth to swallow him up. But already Florence's mind had wandered off the subject. Tokyo. The very word on her son's lips made her shiver. It was Audrey who had done this. London was bad enough but it was a means to an end. But Tokyo? She lay in bed and fumed. All she got was another postcard. In the end, since she could not die and see the results in the pain her loss would cause Patrick, she got up again, but her recovery was slow. She was, if she thought about it, grieving for what might have been. She began knitting for him—like a Fury. This time in even finer wool, the thin, beautiful wool she used for him when he was a baby. Maroon. He suited maroon.

Patrick gave it to the first beggar he found. Audrey was shocked. 'What she doesn't know can't hurt her,' he said, triumphant to be so right. He was right about everything at the moment. His idea for the Gold Medal was brilliant—while everyone else strove to climb Olympus, he would design a children's playground. With the ghost of his

140

father's idea about the ticket collector's booth—he would include a shelter for the mothers—he knew it would win. It would be plastic, and indestructible and cheap. He'd got the idea wandering around Coventry, watching children kicking tin cans along gutters, turning somersaults around bicycle parking bays, hanging upside-down from trees . . . Quick, easy, temporary—there were still so many bomb sites unused. If they wanted humanity—they could have it. He was no fool. He knew that designing something for children would touch the hearts of the judges. You had to build up to the heroic slowly. Take them by surprise. If he used Corbusier's primary colours for the structures it would give the project just the right touch.

He told no one. Not his mother, not Audrey, not his father. Audrey had no idea that on the rare occasions they met (apart from when he sneaked her into his room for a couple of hours) and they went and sat looking at groups of children playing, he was less thinking about starting a family with her, than the basic requirements of the mini-human being in design terms. She sat looking fondly, imagining having his baby—he sat looking fondly imagining how his acceptance speech would go down . . .

'I'm on my way,' he said to her, patting her cold knee. 'What was the worst thing you ever remember about playing?'

'You wouldn't climb the tree with me.'

He laughed. 'No—seriously—what?'

She was being serious actually. 'Falling down,' she said.

He nodded and thought for a while. Then— 'That's *it*,' he said ecstatically, 'the final touch.

If they like to go head-first then what a playground needs is some form of mock grass, rubber based . . .'

Audrey agreed.

*   *   *

In Coventry, his moment of rebellion over and feeling quite glad to escape Florence's returned good health and accompanying misery, George set about doing his duty by the shed. He began with Patrick's old bicycle. The surprise he found in the old saddlebag once he had excavated it down to the Roman level (not a spanner or an oil dropper in sight—just old maps, used train tickets, sweet wrappers and assorted rubbish) had him sitting on one of the sacking-covered boxes for a whole evening, wondering what to do, how it had come to be in there, whether his son knew all about everything, what to make of it. It also had him rediscovering that distant land called Hope. After all, he had nothing to lose now—nothing.

He smoked several pipes, turned the note over in his hands, as if by doing so it would reveal more of itself, and wondered how long it had been in there. Indelible pencil. Smudged but still quite readable. Even on the envelope. He knew the writing and he wondered, his heart making little flipping motions, whether to take up what Lilly said in the note: 'If you are ever passing the door on a Wednesday afternoon you'd be welcome to drop in. We close at one and Alf gets picked up to go to his physio. It would be very nice to see you again.' And then, underlined, she had added, 'I have missed you. Lilly.' He had no idea when the note was written

142

but it had been over fifteen years since he had seen her. Perhaps it was best left. On the other hand, Patrick only got the bicycle six or seven years ago. So the note might not have been written that long ago at all.

'Cleaned out the bike,' he wrote to Patrick. 'Found a few surprises. Your mother still isn't eating properly. Couldn't you come up?' He waited for Patrick's response but there wasn't one.

*   *   *

In London Audrey decided that a good project to start off with was to get on the right side of her potential mother-in-law. She knew that if she was going to succeed with Patrick she needed Florence. Dolly said she was wasting her time. That no one who came between mother and son would be tolerated. But Audrey thought a little bit of bridge-building of her own might do the trick.

'You must go to her,' she said to Patrick. 'It will make all the difference and one day away won't kill you.' Truth was she was shocked at his selfishness but she managed to put the thought out of her head. Patrick was a genius and geniuses were different. She preferred to think of it like that. 'I really think you should.'

Patrick ran his hands through his hair and sulked and frowned and said 'Would bloody Michelangelo have left the Sistine to visit his mum? Would Pericles have allowed Mnesicles to leave the sodding Parthenon?'

Audrey said they very probably would.

'Aud, I'm in the middle of the Gold Medal. It's impossible. I damn well won't.'

Then she cajoled, enjoying the role which she more or less copied from a Katharine Hepburn and Spencer Tracy film. She liked watching those busy, bossy American women in frilly pinnies telling their husbands how to behave, despite being only housewives. She would be like that. In the end Patrick nodded. 'Oh well,' he said, 'If you think I should.'

Well obviously I do, she thought. But she just smiled. 'Tell her about your private commission. That'll perk her up.'

Patrick nodded enthusiastically. 'That'll please her.'

'I should think it will,' she said. 'A commission from royalty.'

'Not quite,' he said. 'The Galtons are only aristocratic.'

And up he went. Just For Twenty-Four Hours, as he told himself over and over again on the train.

*   *   *

It annoyed him to see how pale and thin Florence looked but after half an hour or so she perked up. 'Audrey was right,' he said, tucking the shawl more neatly around his mother's shoulders. 'She said it would do you good if I came.'

'Audrey did?'

He nodded. 'She can be quite firm with me sometimes.'

He said this with a smile. But his mother was not smiling. How dare the girl dictate to her son what he should do about his own mother? Indeed, she grew quite pink at the very thought, and Patrick misreading the signs, patted her arm and added several bushels of salt to the wound by saying, 'Audrey's pretty well always right about little things like that.' He laughed. 'Leaves me time to get on with the important things.'

'Where's your new maroon jumper? And the blue one?' asked Florence quickly.

'In the wash,' he said.

'I hope she hasn't shrunk them,' was all she could think of to say.

Patrick told her about the loggia he had been asked to design by Henry Galton. 'I'll take you to see it when it's done,' he said. 'We can have a day out at Coulter Hall. They're opening the place up to the public a couple of days a week. Death duties or something . . .'

Florence forgot all about umbrage. She saw herself in a nice navy two-piece with her arm linked through her son's and—though she knew it could not be—everyone was bowing as they passed.

'Mixing with the great and the good,' said Florence. For once she was satisfied.

Leaning back, she closed her eyes and smiled. 'I knew you'd have time for your old mother.'

'Not so much of the old,' he said.

But as she lay back he saw for the first time that she was. Old. And a shiver went up his spine. A shiver that said Responsibility. His father wasn't getting any younger either. One day he might have to do more than make fleeting visits like this. It was then, and almost idly, that possible salvation occurred to him. He needed a wife.

He rang Audrey that night. 'I wish you were here,' he said. And he meant it. She could tell. 'Good old Audrey,' said Patrick.

When Florence, feeling much better, was tucked

up in bed, father and son sat at the kitchen table and sipped tea and talked. Jazz Club was on the radio, turned down low, and they were set for an easy, harmonious evening of it. Or rather, Patrick observed, they might have been, if his father would just stop clearing his throat. Obviously in preparation for saying something.

'This is Charlie Parker,' Patrick said pointedly, hoping it would stop the intermittent rasping.

George nodded but he looked wound up, as if he had something pressing on his mind. 'I was just wondering if you really meant us to get rid of that bike?'

'Oh yes,' said Patrick. 'Don't keep asking—just do it.'

'There's nothing in it that you want to keep?' His father looked at him sharply, almost angrily. 'Nothing?'

'Oh no,' said Patrick airily. 'I'll be getting a car soon. The Gold Medal's worth a couple of hundred, and when I get the loggia money I can more than afford it . . .'

His father remained stern. 'You can think of no reason why that bicycle can't be thrown away?'

He shook his head as if in puzzled good humour. 'Dad—in a while I'll be travelling in style. Get rid of the bike . . .'

George relaxed. 'Fine,' he said, and poured more beer. He fingered the note in his pocket. Safe. 'You're on your way then? Big time?'

Patrick nodded. 'Once you get taken up by people of influence like the Galtons it's word of mouth. Not that I intend to spend my life doing domestic stuff but a bit of money and a few connections will be good. Then I'll go into partnership with someone and after a few years I'll specialise in big stuff. And then—bridges. Only bridges. No doors and windows and fancy frills. Just amazing, astonishing bridges. The world needs more of them.'

'No ticket collector's booths then?'

Patrick laughed and shook his head. 'Grand and monumental for me.'

'Good for you,' said George. He smiled wryly. 'Got it all mapped out. I envy you that.'

'You have to look ahead. Right now a man called Othmar Ammann has designed the longest spanning bridge in the world, over the Verrazano Narrows in New York. It'll be finished in a couple of years. One day I'll match it. That's the focus. And that is what I'll do. You make your mind up— you do it. Simple. Don't envy me, Dad. Do it.'

His father leaned forward. 'That—saddlebag. You're sure you don't want it?'

Patrick shook his head in disbelief. Little minds.

*　　　*　　　*

Florence, happy to dream about accompanying her son among the aristocracy, let him go easily. She did not accompany them to the station, which was a relief. Patrick kissed her goodbye and watched her pale figure waving from the front room window as the car rattled its way down the street. Freedom, he was thinking at each bump and squeak. Freedom. Even the car, a Ford Popular, was a lesson in what the terrible deathly hand of uninspired living could do to you. His father. His mother. This town. Grey to his Gold. It all needed blowing up.

'I'm reading some stuff by a French writer at the

147

moment. Jean Genet. I'll send you a copy.'

'Good?' asked George.

'Shocking,' said Patrick, with great satisfaction. 'It's about repression and hypocrisy. The illusory nature of reality. The ambiguous definitions of good and evil. He's a bit—well—lurid at times.' He laughed. 'I don't think you'd get it.'

George said nothing.

After seeing Patrick onto the train George drove across to the other side of town, running the car slowly down Chapel Street. Like a kerb crawler, he thought, avoiding the eyes of the girls who were already out. He had never been tempted. If it was bad enough leaving Lilly after those Wednesday afternoons, how much worse to pay and leave a stranger.

He drove slowly past the shop. It was in darkness, naturally, but the light from the little sitting room at the back glowed dimly through the big window. It looked inviting. In all his years of living with Florence nothing had seemed so inviting. He wondered what was going on in there at that very moment. Was Alf there still? Maybe he was dead. Maybe Lilly was dead. These were the years for it. But above the outside window it still said, 'Willis's Stores' in the same faded red paint. He could only hope.

He stopped the car and peered at the doorway. The list of opening and closing times was the same, Wednesday was still half-day. It was now Sunday. He had a sudden moment of déjà-vu. Around this part of the week, in the past, he always began to hanker for Lilly. He turned the car back and headed for home. Nothing changed.

148

As usual, Audrey met Patrick at the station. This is what couples did. They had absences, they met, they held hands on the tube.

'I could never go back to Coventry,' he said.

'Then don't,' she whispered, and snuggled nearer. 'Except for visits. You can stay here and I'll look after you and it will be just the two of us.'

Later, in his bed, whispering in case the landlady heard, he said, 'I've been asked down to Coulter Hall next Saturday. For the weekend. Dinner suit, the lot. I'd better buy one. I'll need one for the future anyway.'

'That's wonderful. I wonder what I should wear?'

'Oh no,' he said. 'I'm going on my own.'

'But—' she said.

'I could hardly ask someone I don't know if I could bring my girlfriend.'

Audrey lay next to him, staring at the poster of Eikoh Hosoe's nudes, the dream of which seemed as far away as ever. She wasn't good enough for him. That was what it was. And she reminded herself to do something about it.

'Patrick,' she said to the darkness. 'I really am going to improve myself.'

But he said nothing and seemed to be asleep.

*   *   *

Wednesday morning. George awoke and said, under his breath, 'D-Day, George, D-Day.' It was a strange and wonderful thing to wake up wanting the day to begin. In the morning he went to the chemist to get Florence's prescription. When he brought it back Florence was curt with him. 'You'll need to take the washing to the launderette,' she said. The doctor had forbidden her to do the heavy laundering.

'I'll go this afternoon,' he said, with irritating cheerfulness. He would leave it with the woman who ran the place and have a service wash. Wednesday afternoon—and he was free.

Of course the shop was closed when he tried the door, it being half past one. He stood there wondering what to do and then knocked on the glass. It rattled. Too much knocking and it would fall out. Needed puttying, he noticed. He stood back. There was no sign that anyone was in. He knocked again. Though which was the door and which was his heart at this stage he could hardly tell. And then, miracle of miracle, the door at the back of the shop opened, and out came—well— someone who looked familiar yet not at all. Wearing an old raincoat, a washed-out green headscarf, and carrying a brown, plastic shopping bag over her arm. The hair that puffed from the front of the scarf was grey with streaks of fairness in it, the face was pale, flat somehow, old and weary.

He backed away. But too late. The person, Lilly it was, looked across the shop to the door and saw someone standing there.

'Who is it?' she called. Her voice was nearly the same. She sounded nervous.

'George,' he called back. No help for it now.

As if she had been waiting for his arrival she walked quickly around the counter, reached the door, shot the bolt, and let him in.

Lilly never was one to be fazed by anything, he

remembered, as she stood to one side and let him pass. Not so much as a sound escaped her lips as she closed the door, which clicked very softly, behind him.

'Well, Lilly?' he said eventually.

'Well, George?'

They stood in that dingy shop light, facing each other. He twirling his cap in his hand, she slowly pulling off her headscarf and pushing at her streaked grey curls in a gesture he remembered. No nail varnish now. He took her note from his pocket and pushed it into her hand. She peered down at it and shook her head.

'Bit late,' he said, attempting a laugh. 'Only just found it. In the boy's saddlebag. We're throwing out the bike now. Well—he doesn't want it and he's more or less grown up and—' he stopped. There was a lump in his throat about the size of Iceland.

And she was looking at him. Washed out, but still with a bit of fire about her eyes. Smiling slightly. Familiar.

'My God, George,' she said. 'If I look half as bad as you do . . .'

He felt like crying. She was crying, or almost. He put his cap under one arm and putting a hand around her elbow, he steered her into the small back room and pulled the door to behind them. With the ease of sudden memory, he reached up and turned out the shop light. They stood staring at each other in the warm gloom. A low fire burned behind the fireguard, a Chianti bottle lamp, its shade at an angle, gave a dim light. The chairs were the same, one either side of the fire, same covers only more worn, on the table was a newspaper, a pair of reading glasses, a pot plant. Exactly as it used to be. Except for themselves.

Lilly moved away from him. She put her bag down on the floor, straightened up and looked at him with cold eyes.

'And is your Florence well?' she asked, indicating a chair at the table.

'She's been a bit poorly.' He sat down. 'But she's getting better slowly.'

'Pity,' she said.

She sat opposite him. The damped-down fire echoed his feelings. One good rake around in the embers and he could flare up. 'I am so sorry,' he said. A universal apology for his and her suffering.

'For what?'

'For staying away. For marrying the wrong woman.'

She reached for his hand. They gripped each other's fingers tightly. It was more than enough. Overwhelming. George wondered when it had last happened, that he had held somebody's hand.

'And Alf?' He raised his eyes to the ceiling.

She shook her head. 'Out,' she said shortly.

They went on holding hands. Neither of them spoke and both of them knew that they were not going to do anything else.

'At least you've got a fine son,' Lilly said eventually.

'Fine son?' he said. 'I haven't got a son. Haven't been allowed. I'll tell you what it's been like, Lilly, all these years. With her. And him. Shall I?'

She nodded.

And he did. The unburdening of it was joyful.

*   *   *

152

Later they walked along by the canal which had been cleaned and spruced up and now bore the occasional painted barge looking like a Disney Dream, unreal to the two of them who remembered the place when it worked for the town. She asked him if he still built his models of places. Dream places. But he told her that he had to stop all that nonsense. Nonsense be blowed, was what she said to that. She called Florence a tyrant, said that Hitler and Uncle Joe weren't in it. George said not to do so, nevertheless his heart sang with the justice of it.

'It was my fault,' he said. 'I've been weak.'

'You're kind,' she said.

They walked and they talked and had tea in a workmen's café well out of the way. Lilly would not let him buy her an ice-cream. She pleaded the coldness of the air but the real reason was that if he bought her one it would make her cry and they were both being strong. There was no other way to be. Florence was at home, Alf would soon be brought back. Time to go back to their dull old lives.

'We should have gone to Paris, Lilly,' he said. Safe to say it now.

'We should have done a lot of things.'

'It's hell on earth, Lilly.'

She stopped him. 'You have to live with it. You make the wrong choice and you have to live with it. You have to live with the mistakes you make.'

Simple the way she said it. Nothing else in life was simple, but that was.

'Patrick won't do that,' said George. 'Clever lad. A planner. Got his future all mapped out.'

'Clever is as clever does,' said Lilly. 'I didn't take

to him.'

'No,' said George.

On the little bridge over the canal, now painted white and looking bright and jaunty in the cold sunlight, they stopped. 'I wonder,' he said, looking down at the water.

'No,' she sighed. 'That was then.'

'We could run away together,' he said, laughing at the absurdity of the thought.

'Not with my legs,' she said.

They walked on, a dejected-looking couple, people might think, if they spared the time to consider it. At the shop, quite suddenly, they kissed like lovers and pressed their bodies into each other against the cold. Perhaps, he thought, that was their first real kiss. They spent a long time standing there, still as a statues, before the sound of the ambulance at the top of the street sent George scurrying back to the car and Lilly fumbling at the lock. Driving back, George thought that the only Dream Place he wished he could build now was a time machine.

*　　　*　　　*

Spring was late. By now they should have moved into the gentle rain of April, but over the next few weeks the frost set in and the ground was hard with it. Florence was mad with everything which meant she was more or less better. In London Patrick was working hard—or according to his postcards he was. Never a mention of anything, including Audrey. Dolly was cagey. She was not going to give Florence the satisfaction of knowing that her daughter did not seem to be seeing quite so much

154

of her precious son. 'It's his final year,' said Audrey defensively, when her mother asked. But Audrey was scared. Nothing had been the same between them since he came back from that posh weekend. He scarcely spoke about it, except to say that the place was fantastic, that the setting was perfect for him to create something spectacular and that he Bloody Well Would. He said this last so aggressively that Audrey was quite sure something had happened down there. Bad or good? She needed to know but he ignored her when she asked.

Something did occur at Coulter Hall. Something Patrick would never tell anyone but which had shaken him badly. At dinner he was seated between an elderly woman, the aged aunt of the family, who was quite deaf and hard going, but sweetly condescending to him, and Henry's elegant younger sister, Penelope, who was not. She looked him up and down challengingly. 'Henry said you were attractive,' she said. 'And you are.'

Immediately he imagined himself married to someone as elegant and beautiful as her. He did not pursue the idea of Penelope in later years and in his mother's house, looking after her in her dotage.

'And . . . ?' he asked, pleased.

'And I get very bored at these dos.'

'Let me entertain you, then,' he said, charmingly. 'You are too beautiful to be bored.' He was pleased with that. It was gallant.

And he, apparently, was attractive. This was living all right. She wore a black dress with no shoulders or sleeves and the top bit (of which there was not much) seemed to stay in place while the

155

rest of her moved around in it. She wore a huge diamond at the centre of her throat that almost hurt his eyes with its fire, and she had long, tapering white hands scattered with rings. He imagined her on his arm as they attended the various important functions that would accompany his creative progress through the world. From now on this was the kind of woman he would meet and mix with—this was the kind of woman a man of substance needed. Very definitely this was the kind of woman he would one day marry. It was exactly what he had shed Coventry for.

'You?' she said. 'Entertain me?' She raised an eyebrow. 'You can try.' She gave him a smile that made him feel completely inadequate. He took up the challenge. He began to talk to her about college and what he was doing for the Gold Medal and what he intended to build for her brother—for posterity—here at Coulter Hall. Eventually she said, 'Posterity, hmm?' and added, 'You have a very strange accent. I forget where you are from?'

He was shocked into silence. Afraid to say.

She laughed. She spoke just a touch too loudly. People were staring down the table. 'A very strange accent,' she repeated. 'You're not from where those Beatles come from, are you? Up North somewhere.'

He lied, then. 'No,' he said. 'I'm from London.'

Her smile hardened. 'London?' She laughed. 'Hardly London. No. You're a little Northern Johnny—Henry said so.'

His face was on fire. He said quietly, 'But I live in London.'

'I remember,' she shrieked. Even the aged aunt heard and turned to stare. 'I remember exactly.

You're from Coventry. Henry calls it the place that woman got her tits out . . . Godiva, wasn't it?'

Patrick laughed uncomfortably. 'A very silly woman. Taking all her clothes off in public like that.'

'Sounds heaven,' said Penelope. 'And you are a scholarship boy or something.'

'No,' he said, 'I am not.'

He turned his attention back to the Old Aunt and spoke no more to the beautiful Penelope. The beautiful Penelope, he was aware, neither noticed nor cared.

*   *   *

That night he sat on the edge of the damask-covered bed, sipped the whisky that had kindly been brought for him by the butler, and made some rough sketches. The humiliation of the encounter with the beautiful Penelope gave him an edge. My God he would show them. He would create something outrageous for the Galton pile. It would take them by surprise, it would be talked about, and the elegant, superior Penelope would know just whom she had snubbed. She would want him and it would be too late. Such were his twin dreams that night. He loosened his black tie, so perfectly learned, and lay back on the bed. The softness of the eighteenth-century façade with its dignified windows needed to be challenged. Oh yes. And by the time he had finished, those refined classical delicacies would have their eyes opened all right. And so they did.

*   *   *

Within two months the entire structure was drawn up. And Patrick had learned, from his first private commission, the benefit of shock tactics. When it was finished the press had several field days and the Heritage lobby was up in arms. He had designed the new extension from raw, unrefined materials and harsh, direct detailing. The elegant classical eyeballs of the eighteenth-century façade were not just opened wide—they were out on stalks.

'It's the new Brutalism,' he said to the assembled, when it was finished.

'Well, yes—it certainly is that . . .' Penelope stared at him with a new light of interest. 'Very—brutal.'

'One does not require good manners in design,' he said. He looked the beautiful Penelope straight in the eye. 'Where one needs good manners is at the dinner table and in bed.'

Everyone, including the press, laughed.

'Well you *are* a boy, aren't you?' she said.

'I should hope so.'

Then, with great dignity, and very deliberately, he turned his back and walked away.

＊   ＊   ＊

As one doyen of design put it in the conservative *Design Review*—it was Damn Well Plug Ugly. The radical *New Design Monthly* immediately rallied to Patrick's defence, and Henry Galton—who admitted to not really giving a stuff so long as he had somewhere out of the rain for the gin slings—was delighted at the way the publicity brought the visitors in. In building terms, even before his graduation, Patrick had arrived . . . At college his Course Tutor sighed and invited him into his study.

'Patrick,' he said. 'It is considered quite unacceptable for a student, even a final-year student, to undertake commercial enterprises.'

'Do you wish me to leave?'

The Course Tutor shook his head and sighed again. He handed Patrick a whisky. 'If it was down to me,' he said, 'I'd have kicked you out in the first term. You'd have survived very well.'

They both laughed.

*   *   *

The other result from the dinner-table encounter with the dazzling Penelope was that he now knew the sort of wife he needed, and it was not the Penelope sort. He wanted no sparring partner, no game playing, no one who was higher in any way, shape or form than he was. He needed to be top. It was important for what he would become. Yes. What he wanted was quiet support. Audrey might well be the one. He was still not sure. You did not need, if you were to be a hero in your field, a woman who tried to match you. Already she was talking about improving herself. Dangerous talk for a woman. He took his line from Isambard and Isambard married carefully. He knew how important that was. Patrick must do the same.

In this final year Patrick worked frenziedly to get his college work finished—to clean up with the Gold Medal and then to depart. He wrote an article, commissioned by *New Design Monthly*. The Course Tutor, on being shown the draft, suggested that he re-read Burckhardt on the subject of the

Renaissance and its Humanity. Patrick sniffed. It was one of the little mannerisms he had learned at his mother's breast. When in doubt, sniff superciliously. 'Burckhardt is as Burckhardt does,' he said. 'Give me concrete and steel.' He did not add, 'and plastic', for the kiddies, in Corbusier colours. Let them, when he revealed it, see it and weep.

* * *

George idled and daydreamed and began to dare to think that perhaps he and Lilly could make a go of it after all. He became so idle and so daydreamy that none of Florence's vitriol penetrated. He remembered his young days with Lilly, the Wednesday afternoons, the feel of her body pressed up against his and how empty he felt as he drove away from her.

'I don't know what's come over you these last few weeks,' said Florence. She was beside herself with the unseasonal cold and wanted the range lit though it was the middle of May. 'This country,' she said, 'always cold.'

George went on sitting at the table, pretending to read the paper, thinking of Lilly. Somewhere in the background Florence was going on and on at him, saying he'd put her back in bed and this time in hospital and was that what he wanted . . . ? George said that perhaps she'd got a chill. He nearly said he hoped she had, but managed to stop himself. Lilly would like that, he thought, Lilly would laugh at that. Wicked Lilly.

'Chill be blowed. I'm going to bed. And I'm not getting out of it until the range is up and running again.' And off she went.

'But it's May,' he called up the stairs. 'Nearly flaming June.'

'Flaming June yourself.'

He waited. When he heard the upstairs door slam and was sure that she was in bed, he tiptoed into the hall. The only room the telephone wire reached was the front parlour. Pushing the door as closed as he could, he dialled Lilly's number. It was a Sunday night. Always by Sunday . . .

She answered. He said, 'Lilly—dear Lilly—if you can't run away with me . . . then you can hobble, can't you?'

She laughed. 'Yes,' she said.

'I'll see you Wednesday. We'll make our plans.'

'Yes, yes, yes.'

He was happier than he could ever remember. He whistled down the path to get the coal and the kindling. If it was what Florence wanted, then it was what Florence should have. He was in his shirtsleeves but what did that matter? He was warm from within. There was a nip in the air and it had come on to rain but it only served to make him feel alive again. At the end of the path George gave a little twirl of pleasure and slipped. He hit his head on the path and lay there, quite still, pushed up awkwardly at the side of the shed. Something was not right about the angle of his leg. Florence, warm in her bed, heard nothing, thought nothing. The neighbours, warm in their houses, the windows sealed against the wet, the curtains pulled against the unseasonal night, heard nothing. It was many hours before a passing policeman (who should have passed a lot earlier but who found the station and his cup of tea more to his liking) heard him—

161

making weak little gurgling sounds. Cold and damp as death.

*   *   *

In the hospital the pain in his leg was so bad he decided that it was the best time in the world to die. Quite suddenly and quite silently he stopped breathing. Florence, sitting at the back of the room while the doctors fussed about her husband, could not believe it. Just could not believe it. Her first thought was that she had not given him permission to die. She came over to the bed and looked down at her husband. It could not be anything but illusion, she knew, but he seemed to be smiling. And young again.

10

Audrey and the Little Seed of Rebellion

Rodomont, the Saracen king of Algiers, loved the Christian Isabella. Rather than submit to him she tricked him into killing her. He built a great tomb for her that was approached by a narrow bridge across a river, and defended it against all comers.

The Christian Orlando, furioso with grief, naked and unarmed, came and wrestled with Rodomont on the bridge. They both fell into the water, unluckily for Rodomont who was in full armour . . .

James A. Hall, *Dictionary of Subjects and Symbols in Art*

Patrick received the phone call on his landlady's telephone first thing in the morning (no point in the boy losing a night's sleep, decided Florence). He went immediately, of course. Fortunately he had finished his article and the drawings could be done anywhere. He forgot to inform Audrey who stood for two hours in the rain the following evening outside the L'Illuminata cinema in Soho (getting quite a few offers, which did not help the situation) before going round to his digs to find out what had happened.

'He's gone, luv,' said the landlady. 'Got the train home first thing this morning for his poor old dad.'

*   *   *

She was shivering when she reached home. There was something about being left uncared for on a cold pavement, being eyed up and down by dirty men in disgusting mackintoshes, that went deeper even than the freezing rain.

'All right?' asked Dolly after telling her. 'Bit of a shock, I know.'

'Just a bit on the cold side,' said Audrey.

'Sit here then,' said her mother, 'and you can help me out. I'll be going up to stay with Florence tomorrow. See her through the next few days.'

'I'll go up with you,' Audrey said. 'He'll want me there.'

Dolly did her best to be tactful. 'It's a bit of a houseful,' she said. 'Why not wait and come up with your dad?'

'He will want me there,' she said even more firmly though she was really shivering now. 'To ease his pain.'

Dolly gave a little snort which she quickly turned into a cough. 'Well, well,' she said. 'You're dressed for the part at any rate.'

She was wearing black jeans and a black sloppy joe. Patrick's favourite style for her.

'If you want my opinion,' said Dolly. 'He's best off out of it. Poor George. She never gave him any credit. Well, neither of them did.'

They considered this in silence.

Her father came in and muttered something and then left them to it. Grieving being women's work.

'You sure you want to come up with me? Your dad could do with looking after.'

'I'll come,' said Audrey. 'Patrick will want me there.' She stared into the fire and her mother decided to leave it. *Che sera sera . . .*

164

After a while Audrey said. 'I'm thinking of applying to the International Service. I want to make something of myself.'

'You don't speak anything foreign,' said her mother, without looking up from the heel she was turning. 'So that's that.'

'Nothing to say I can't learn,' said Audrey. 'There's evening classes. And the school said I was bright, remember.'

If there was a hint of complaint in her voice, Dolly did not rise. Audrey had been just as keen as they were for her to get out in the world and start earning her own money. She put two pounds and a bunch of flowers on the table every Friday night and the rest was all hers. Now, having started all this carrying on with Patrick, Dolly wondered if he was turning her daughter's head . . .

'And who would be expected to keep you if you did that?' asked her mother in a voice that said the question was absolutely rhetorical.

'Evening classes are better than college because you go on earning. Best of both worlds,' said Audrey. But already she was yawning in the heat and the comforting dullness of the scene.

'And what does Patrick say about it?' Dolly asked, pursing her lips. She had a feeling that her daughter was being strung along.

'Oh I haven't—really—mentioned it to him yet,' she said. 'But I think he'll be pleased. He's so clever himself. He needs clever people around him.'

Her mother tutted once and the matter was dropped. Personally she thought that if there were any evening classes to be attended, they were better spent on pastry making and good plain

165

cookery. Her daughter had not inherited Dolly's light hand either with sponges or with pie crust and if a man had to choose between having a wife who talked foreign at him, and one who put a decent steak and kidney on the table, Dolly knew which he'd prefer.

Audrey decided, dreaming into the red hot caverns of the fire, that she would talk to Patrick about it and have a go if he thought it was a good idea. She fancied French. French was safest. Though Patrick would go on about how dynamic Berlin was nowadays, and Dresden and what a brilliant rebuilding programme they had despite being razed to the ground. He was also talking about his coming trip to Japan, which was also brilliant, apparently, despite its wartime sufferings. Anywhere where they had dropped a bomb appeared to be brilliant, she thought. Except, apparently, Patrick's poor old Coventry. She thought about trying to learn Japanese but one look at it convinced her she could be clever, but not that clever. Anyway, she was hardly likely to be able to go with him—not all the way to Tokyo—not on a telephonist's wages.

As for German—her father would never countenance her learning that particular language. Not with his feet. He always said that if he'd had George's feet, he'd have stayed at home all comfy. As it was he went out to Tobruk with a perfect pair, lovely to behold, toes all straight and everything, and he came back with bunions, corns and missing a toe. Every time the damp weather came and his twinges began, he cursed the German nation. And that bugger Rommel. As for Japanese—apart from the certain knowledge she would find it impossible

166

to learn—she would also be in danger of being thrown out on the street for that, too. Patrick was right—they should forget history and the war and get on with life. It had better be French, then, definitely.

Audrey sighed and poked at the coals and took up one of the socks by her mother's chair. He went through his socks did her father. Dolly looked over her spectacles at her. Despite the pastry, she was a good girl when she wanted to be. Audrey shrugged and smiled back. Might as well get on with something. Later she would try to read the book Patrick had lent her but it looked very difficult. Jean Genet—*Querelles of Brest*. She couldn't even pronounce it properly, she was sure. All her father said when he saw the name of it was 'Trust the Frenchies to call a book something with *them* in the title.' So even French would be tricky. But she had to do something. Otherwise Patrick would outgrow her.

*   *   *

The next morning, off the two women went. Audrey's face was pale with make-up and she wore the customary black. She was excited at the thought of Patrick needing her. This would be her moment. Dolly said not to get her hopes up, funerals took people in different ways. Not all of them good ones. And when they arrived at the house it was perfectly clear that Mother Knew Best. Florence, opening the front door and seeing Audrey on the doorstep with her mother, was firm. 'I'm very sorry,' she said, in a tone that implied she was actually highly delighted (by now Dolly had gone upstairs with her bag), 'but you can't stay here. We've no room. All the beds are taken as you well know.'

'I could sleep on the settee in the parlour,' said Audrey, determinedly walking past Florence and into the kitchen, looking for Patrick who was nowhere in sight.

Florence followed. 'Well, good luck to you if you want to do that—but the body's already in there.'

'I told you,' said Dolly, while Florence put the kettle on. 'You have to make room for people's ways with a bereavement.'

Eventually Patrick came down the stairs. He stood on the other side of the room and never even kissed her cheek. She felt humiliated.

'It was kind of you to come,' he said. 'But I think you'd probably better do what Mum says. Unless you can stay in a b. & b. ?'

Dolly said it was a good idea but Florence shook her head. 'Too much distraction,' she said. 'We've got a lot to organise.'

'But I can help,' said Audrey.

'Too many cooks,' said Florence, which Dolly thought was highly inappropriate. All the same, Audrey had been wilful in coming, she had been warned, and it was Florence and Patrick's wishes that counted.

'Better go,' she said quietly.

'Yes,' said Patrick, 'I think so.'

And since it was his father who had just died, Audrey did not think she could do what she wanted to do which was scream at him and hit him very hard right where—she had learned from sunnier days—it hurt.

'All right,' she agreed, and she stared at him with

168

such a look that he went back upstairs again. He did not care to be made to feel in the wrong. She still made him feel like that and it was one of the reasons he held back. Sometimes what he read in her face was disturbing. Love—if that's what it was—seemed a demanding commodity to him—what with mothers and lovers—and he was glad his affections were more realistic.

'She'll have a cup of tea and a sandwich first,' said Dolly.

'But of course,' said Florence, more warmly now she had won. 'Can't send you back on an empty tummy.'

But for the whole hour of her stay, Audrey had never felt so unwanted. To Hell With Everyone, was the way she felt about it. And she very grandly rang for a taxi to take her to the station. Patrick offered her the money for it, with Florence looking on, lips pursed, as she pressed out her pastry for the big day.

'No thanks,' she said. 'I've got my own money.'

'Hoity-toity,' said Florence quietly to the short crust. But she was pleased. The girl would not keep him if she behaved like that.

Patrick might be a Genius and Geniuses might need to be handled differently from ordinary men, but all the same . . . A girl has her pride and her limits, thought Audrey. He went to kiss her on the cheek and she stepped back. Too late, far too late, she began to get an inkling that she, also, had power.

The taxi driver set off towards the station. Anger won over forlorn. You could excuse Patrick when he was being dedicated—and she did—but not for something so emotional, not for your father's funeral, which was so very much the right occasion for having the woman you loved by your side to see it through with you. That was not the way the Tracys and the Hepburns, the Hudsons and the Days did it in films, and neither was it the way people did it in real life. In real life there was always kindness and romance and the seeing-through of things together. Up to the surface came the memory of Coulter Hall and how he had gone without her; up to the surface came the standing in the rain for two hours because he couldn't be bothered to remember her—and bubbling alongside them came a little burst of rebellion. How dare he? And for some reason, alongside that thought, came the memory of the woman and the note and the bicycle. How careless Patrick had been. All those sweets and she'd bet he never passed the message on. She'd bet a hundred pounds on it.

And then it occurred to her that George was dead. Really dead. And who was there to care about that, really? She had seen no tears in that house. None at all. She leaned forward—suddenly determined—and told the taxi driver to take a detour. He did so cheerfully enough, after all, it was a quiet afternoon. And when she stepped out of the cab saying grandly, 'Just wait,' as she had also seen in films, he smiled and saluted her. If this was the wrong thing to do, she thought, it was the wrong thing to do, but it felt right. Best not to think, she decided, as she pushed open the door and marched into Willis's Stores.

The woman was there on her own. Just about recognisable. Audrey thought that the horrors time wreaked on people must never happen to her.

Patrick would not be able to bear it. The woman's scarlet mouth was still there too, bright as ever, and so was the nail varnish. Odd the way women who were beyond all help still went on doing such things. The woman was humming softly as she swept behind the counter, so it couldn't be all bad. She looked up and said, very nicely, 'We're just about to close. Be quick now.' And she resumed the humming and the sweeping.

Audrey nearly failed and was on the point of asking for a quarter of mints instead. But she had come this far and surely the worst that could happen, when she gave her news, would be the woman staring at her blankly. Besides, right at that moment she hated Florence and if her suspicions were correct, this was a little bit of getting even that no one need ever know about. 'I don't know if I'm doing right,' she said to the woman. 'But George Parker died yesterday. Would I be correct in thinking that you would want to know that?'

The woman stopped her sweeping and her humming immediately and stood very still. She stared, half puzzled. The silence was chilling. Then she said, hesitantly, 'You might be . . .' Which was really a question.

Audrey said, 'I came in here with his son a few years ago, and you gave him a note to pass on to George. Patrick—his son—never did. And I am very sorry.' She could not bear the way the woman's face changed, how miserable she suddenly looked—and suspicious.

'How do I know it's true?' she asked.

For a moment Audrey thought she was going to hit her with the broom and she made to leave. The woman called her back.

171

'I'm sorry,' she said. 'My name is Lilly.' She crossed the floor of the shop to snag the door. 'Come through to the back.'

'I've got a taxi waiting,' said Audrey, afraid suddenly.

'Ten minutes,' said Lilly.

She put her finger to her lips as they went into the sitting room and pointed at the dingy ceiling. 'My husband's in bed up there,' she said. 'Don't want to wake him.' Somehow the whispering added to the bond between the two women. 'Please,' she said in a shaky voice, 'tell me . . .'

*   *   *

In the House of Death, Palace of Mourning, Patrick sat in his old bedroom—still with the narrow bed and its orange candlewick spread, still with the desk and chair and the blue tatting rug—and he was drawing. He had to finish the plan and he might as well finish it here as anywhere. In fact here, in the House of Death, Palace of Mourning (not strictly true this latter but he liked the sound of it) the silence and the peace were perfect for the completion of the project. And he had to get on with *his* life, that was all there was to it, death or no death. Time waiteth for no man, he told himself, nor for the Gold Medal. It was going to be a big year for him, a big life, and in the grand, rolling course of things, the death of a parent was both inevitable and small.

Florence, trying not to look as happy as she felt, came in every so often to give him cups of tea and cocoa and titbits, or to summon him downstairs for a meal. For these few days there was the most

172

perfect harmony between them and the harmony was conducive to genius . . . It reminded Patrick that what he needed was a wife—or, rather, (and this amused him) what he needed was a mother with sex.

'You'll stay on a bit after the funeral?' Florence asked, bringing him a tray of tea and scones.

'Perhaps,' he said, not looking up.

'You know there'll be a bit of money for you now your dad's gone. Just a little lump sum. Might be enough to buy a small house.' Not in London, he thought, but said nothing.

Florence closed the door softly, reverently, and he heard her padding her way—a little more carefully than she used to perhaps—down the stairs. He felt that freezing in his spine again. His mother was really on her own now. So was he. And he did not like the way she looked at him. Responsibility—that had to change. He would need a wife to sort that side of things out—but first the funeral.

11

After the Funeral

There is nothing romantic about the Ponte dei
Sospiri (Bridge of Sighs) which merely unites the
Courts of Justice in the Palace with the Criminal
Prison.
  Grant Allen, *Historical Guide to Venice*, 1898

The funeral took place, Patrick thought, like a series
of scenes in a theatre. Scarcely a sentence about the
qualities of the dead man was uttered by the Chapel
Minister without a nod or a pursing of the lips and a
strange and restless rustling through the crowd, all
of whom, including his own mother, had a shifty
look about them. And most of those shifty looks
were directed towards a woman who hung back at
the edge of the small group gathered around the
open grave. She looked vaguely familiar but when he
asked his mother about her—was she a distant
relative?—his mother looked as if she might have a
fit.

Florence was not far off having a fit anyway. Her
wishes having been flagrantly, *flagrantly* flouted.
For in death, if not in life, George Parker, RIP, had
got his own way. He could keep more than one
secret, could George. Among other things, some
years ago he had talked to the Chapel Minister
about the form of his last resting place and the
manner of his arrival there. It was one of several
conversations of a spiritual nature he and the
minister had together. George having found some

174

comfort in the piousness of the man's humility was able to lay his burden down—in part anyway. 'I married the wrong woman,' he said. 'And I have stuck by her . . .' (God would forgive the slight abbreviation of the whole picture.) 'I have had precious little chance to do what I want on this earth as a result of that, minister,' was how he put it. 'But I'd like to think that I've got some say in the going out of it.'

When it came to Florence and the minister there was quite a showdown. Florence insisted that she knew what her husband wanted, she hoped, and what he wanted was to be cremated. The minister, recognising his own wife in that stout bosom and determined chin, said he must demur and say, in the eyes of God, that he made a promise which he would keep. Florence railed. The minister stood firm. God was invoked and you couldn't go higher. God and the minister (and George) won. Which was why they all now stood around a gaping hole in the ground—'the most solemn reminder of man's return to worms and the earth from which he sprang . . .'

Patrick watched with particular keenness the drama of the mystery woman. She stood with her head bowed, her thin headscarf fluttering, the puffs of yellowish-white hair that escaped from underneath it looking oddly jaunty. She sobbed and gasped her way through the ceremonials. She had a lot more tears to shed than his mother—which was not hard since, as yet, his mother had shed none. The nods and curiosity and whisperings were directed towards this deeply affected woman, who seemed not to notice, or if she did, not to care. The few left over were for Florence. Patrick, observing

175

it closely, felt confused, with a mixture of curiosity at the event, as if he were standing outside it watching, and a sense of something else which he took to be grief. He thought about Dylan Thomas and jazz and how his father once made Meccano constructions, and he willed himself to cry, to shed even one tear, one drop of salt water—none came. He bowed his head and remembered what he could. That was all. But the memories were dim and inconsequential, like his relationship with his father—of no real substance—evaporating even as the coffin lay in the ground. He would talk to the woman afterwards—find out why she was able to mourn with tears and he was not.

The minister finished his few words. The woman stopped her sobbing. Nobody spoke. Nobody moved except Patrick who, feeling everybody's eyes upon him, bent and picked up a handful of soil. He threw the dirt onto the coffin, a gesture that was immediately followed by a strange choking noise. He looked up. The woman's head was bobbing up and down now, her shoulders were shaking, yet she stood alone. No one went to her, which was even more curious. People comforted his mother, who was dry-eyed; people comforted him—a pat on the back, and squeeze of his shoulder—but he too was dry-eyed. No one comforted her, who was soaked with her tears. Why?

He had a sudden thought—was she perhaps a professional mourner? Did they still have those nowadays? If anyone needed such a thing it was his poor old dad. He looked across at her and smiled. She smiled back, waterily. His mother moved towards him and tucked her hand in his arm. He could hear her breath, firm and heavy, as if she disapproved of what was taking place before them.

'Who is that?' asked Patrick.

'Nobody,' said Florence.

It might have been left there, set down by the graveside, just another mystery, had not Dickie (Cheffy's son) and Archie Bowles, old schoolfriends of Patrick's and subsequently workmates of his father's, smuggled a bottle of whisky into the teetotal post-funeral eats. At which the uninvited woman removed her headscarf and sat on the edge of the settee, knees together, cheeks very pink, eyes defiant and chewing very positively on a ham and cress sandwich. Not a pretty sight, thought Patrick. Tears had added to the effect of a pantomime dame, but at least she had managed to cry . . .

Dolly pointed out that it was just not done to refuse a guest after a funeral. Besides, Lilly Willis looked as if one sharp word and she'd tip over the edge and then what would the minister say? Florence did not care particularly about what the minister said as she had her own words to say to him later—but Dolly was probably right. It was easier all round. So Florence sniffed once and made the best of it. In a way she had a lot to thank Lilly for. Discretion, if nothing else, and taking away an unpleasant marital burden. As long as Patrick never found out then all would be well. He was still such a boy. Steering him away from Lilly's gaze, she handed him a plate with an assortment of sandwiches.

'Don't forget to eat,' she said.

'What's her name?' he asked, pointing at Lilly.

'Lilly Willis,' she said. 'And she's nobody.'

'Then why is she here? How does she know

my father?'

'Because they were sweethearts at school,' said Florence, smooth as butter.

Patrick looked more kindly at Lilly. He had the vaguest idea that he knew that bit of information already. She smiled back, a little cress caught in her teeth. Patrick looked away. Such things disgusted him. When he looked again she beckoned. He stood up and Florence suddenly executed a swift turn, blocking his way. 'You haven't eaten anything,' she said with extraordinary desperation in her voice. But he moved past her. She caught up with him, shrill now. 'You ought to speak to the Boxers . . . Just over there. Doesn't Peggy look a treat?'

He nodded and moved on towards Lilly Willis. Smiling at everyone as he went, feeling that he must show dignity on his father's behalf, enjoying the status of Son to the Star of the Show even if he was starring in Death rather than Life.

He spotted Peggy Boxer across the room and bestowed his sad, grateful smile upon her but she smiled at him in a different way from the others. For a moment dignity fled in the unmistakable sensation of desire. She had a very wide smile, and very red lips and her little teeth were white and perfect. Her mother, who sat straight-backed beside her, also smiled, but a little too eagerly, and she even gave a little wave. As if this was a social event. Ruby, who had high hopes, had dressed Peggy— rather appropriately if she said so herself—to kill. Ruby Boxer might have ended up as wife to the publican but her daughter deserved—and would get—better. Let the lower set of Coventry laugh at mother and daughter's stylishness—let them say they were fools and show-offs with their fashions and their elocution lessons—let them wink, let them nudge each other in the ribs and call her A Cut Above—the main thing was to better yourself. And one very good way of bettering yourself was to avoid, at all costs, marrying a publican. Ruby was still reeling from Florence's apparent interest in her daughter as companion for Patrick—and though Peggy had cried all the way home from the Parker household at Christmas, coming here today her mother had urged her to Put It All Behind Her. They were much encouraged at the absence of Audrey. Audrey being in London, feeling very sorry for herself, sulking, and having delusions that she was being severely missed. Truth was, Patrick was relieved. Withdrawing sexual favours only works when the circumstances are right. Since arriving in Coventry and up until this moment, Patrick had not had much in the way of carnal desire—too many other things going on—but now, as he looked across at Peggy, he was reminded, very pleasantly, that he could still have them.

Today Peggy was particularly chic, particularly dashing (perhaps a little too chic and dashing, thought most of the gathering) in a little black two-piece trimmed with black swansdown and with a shiny cock's feather stuck in her hat. Mrs Boxer noted, with smiling satisfaction, that even the grieving Patrick could not take his eyes off her. Nor the feather. What with the swansdown riffling and the feather flouncing, it was difficult to look away.

Peggy lowered her eyes at Patrick's smile and then looked up again quickly, so that the feather curved and trembled. It was, he thought with satisfaction, practically obscene. Peggy had perfected the art of peering from under the brim of a hat and Patrick liked the effect of it. He did not like himself for liking it, such foolishness being an old-fashioned foible of the median herd, but nevertheless he found himself wondering what she would look like naked except for the hat. The inappropriateness was good. He remembered his Nietzsche (always useful in his lack of convention) that man's sexuality reaches up into the ultimate pinnacle of his spirit . . . It was this very lust that produced his lusty designs. He realised that now. It underpinned him. The two were inextricably interwoven. To be bound by convention was to be lost to the Bourgeois. It was something he told Audrey over and over again whenever she showed signs of narrow-mindedness. Fling Off the Bounds of Bourgeois Principle, he quite often told her, which usually transposed into her flinging off her clothes.

Peggy and her mother were settled on the same settee as was Lilly. All three waited for Patrick to arrive—but Dick and Archie stepped out and blocked him.

'Mind out lads,' he said, and went to pass them.

They slapped him on the back, removed the plate of sandwiches from his hand, and offered him a glass of ginger ale to 'spice himself up a bit'. He took the proffered glass at face value, despite Dick and Archie winking at him. And he took a very large mouthful.

Of course he would have spat it out but just at that very moment his Aunt Bertha came up to him to be kissed and the very large mouthful felt as if he had hot needles going down the back of his throat. His eyes watered and every instinct, including the Flinging Off of Bourgeois Principle, told him not to swallow. But if he spat it out, then, in Aunt and Fairground terms, he would gain a bullseye. So he stood, tears streaming down his face while Aunt Bertha removed her little bit of black veil and leaned towards him so that he might kiss her cheek and said, 'Ah—so you are grieving after all. Well, I'm very glad somebody is . . .'

They stood confronting each other in amazed stalemate—until he, knowing there was nothing else for it, finally swallowed. She watched the tears rolling down his cheeks.

'There, there,' she said. 'You loved your dad after all.' And she smiled and patted him on his way and couldn't wait to get back to Florence to tell her. But Florence was gazing at Patrick as if she was about to witness some terrible calamity. Lilly.

'He's a good boy,' goaded Bertha. 'Poor lad. He's taking the loss of his dad very hard.'

Florence said nothing

'Crying he was,' said Bertha, triumphantly. 'Real tears.'

Florence removed her gaze from her son to stare at her sister in outrage. 'He was probably coughing,' she said, 'He has a weak chest as you know. Out there in the open with a hole in the ground instead of all neat and over with indoors.'

'No, dear,' said Bertha. 'He cared. He cared very deeply.' Florence saw that her son's cheeks were wet with tears, and she felt—added to the burden of Lilly, and George's betrayal from beyond the grave—enraged. With palpitations. If the worst came to the worst with Lilly, Florence could always turn blue.

Patrick, recovered enough to be pleasantly

warmed by the alcoholic experience, took another drink of what was supposed to be ginger ale and more hell broke loose over his tonsils. In London he drank either brown ale, Guinness, the occasional cider or rough, red wine. He stared at Dick and Archie in astonishment. 'You need it,' they said. 'Can't bury your father without a man's drink inside you.' And his glass was topped up again.

It brought him to life, made him confident. It also continued to make him weep. He approached Lilly with tears still rolling down his cheeks and she looked at him with approval. She beckoned him closer. He wanted to giggle but managed to contain it. And just as he was nearly there and about to speak he trod rather heavily on Peggy Boxer's foot which seemed to have arrived out of nowhere. He sat down so heavily between them on the settee that they both bounced.

'Sorry,' he said, feeling it would do for both of them. His voice sounded very loud.

'S'all right,' said Peggy. And lifted her foot up for inspection. 'No harm done.'

She removed her shoe and wiggled the little toes. They were encased in pale nylons, and looked like pink little prisoners. Patrick swallowed and turned to Lilly. What he saw in her face calmed his base thoughts. She really did look dreadful—ancient, ravaged—and still oddly familiar.

'Sorry,' he repeated, and he wiped his damp cheeks with the backs of his hands. 'I'm Lilly,' she said. 'Pleased to meet you.'

He remembered what his mother had told him. Childhood sweethearts. He leaned towards her and patted her hand and said, a little more roguishly, a little more loudly, than might be thought fitting at a funeral, 'I know all about it. I know all about you and my dad.'

'Do you now?' said Lilly, astonished.

'Oh yes. Love that bears the test of time . . .' he misquoted. 'You must have had some fun with him.' Patrick was feeling quite lyrical about the whole idea. He could imagine the two of them in the playground together. 'Dark horse my father, was he?'

Lilly blinked. 'Ye-s,' she said cautiously. 'Bit of a lad on the QT.'

'Like father like son,' said Patrick, and he slapped his knee.

Lilly looked faintly worried. 'Ye-s,' she said again. 'I never knew you knew.'

'Oh I do,' he said. 'It's hard to imagine, though.' He winked and gave her a little nudge. 'My father as somebody's sweetheart!' Now he fondly pictured them sitting in class, or walking in the fields, socks wrinkled, grubby hands holding on to each other tightly.

'How did you . . . find out?'

'My mother told me. Just now.'

Lilly put her hand to her mouth. 'Never?' she said.

Patrick nodded. He was still delighted. Conversation flowed. 'Did you do things like conkers together?' he asked.

'I beg your pardon?' she said, and then shut her mouth up tight. Whatever it meant she was not going to divulge anything of a scandalous nature. She straightened her back and said defiantly, 'Well, we had your mother's permission, you know, though nothing was ever said . . .' Her eyes filled

183

with tears again. 'And I do miss him.'

Patrick, who found the mention of his mother and the apparent duration of such feelings extraordinary, said, 'Really? You miss him after all that time? That's quite something.'

'It is.' She nodded, perking up.

'And how old were you when it first began?' he asked, just a little roguishly.

'Forty-one,' said Lilly happily.

Patrick sat quite still. He did not feel that he was altogether there. Then he shook his head and repeated the question. 'No. I mean, how old were you when you were—er—larking around with my dad?'

'Forty-one,' said Lilly. 'And he was the kindest, nicest man you could hope to meet.'

'Was he?' said Patrick faintly. He was confused suddenly and his head felt ready to split like a ripe tomato. Across the room he could see his mother staring at him as if her eyes could bore through to the very core of him.

Lilly's voice, perhaps to compensate for Patrick's faintness, was louder than necessary and she almost smacked her lips. 'He liked what he couldn't get at home all right. But he was discreet . . . And you never gave him my note. Never mind. He found me again.' He stared at her, trying to make head or tail. At last she lowered her voice. Patrick, head spinning, leaned over to listen. 'But red-blooded,' she said, giving his hand a little pat. 'Without any doubt of it. He certainly was that. I forgive you for the toffee.'

'Thank you,' said Patrick, braving it out.

'And I hope you'll follow in your father's footsteps.'

184

Patrick thought of the hole in the ground and began to laugh. It seemed ineffably funny.

Lilly, dabbing at her own eyes, gave him the benefit. 'I'm glad you, at least, can cry for him.' She shot Florence a look of pure venom.

'Oh no,' he said. 'I just swallowed some whisky the wrong way . . . Those buggers over there slipped me a Mickey Finn.' He could not stop laughing if he tried. 'I'm just not used to it. I'm not really crying at all!' He slapped her on the knee. 'Silly,' he added playfully.

Lilly stood up. 'May both of you burn in hell,' she said, almost conversationally, rearranging the knot beneath her chin. 'I'm off.'

Somewhere from within Patrick remembered manners. He stood up too and gave a little bow and said, 'So soon? Thank you for coming.' And watched in some confusion as the woman marched over to his mother. Forty-one? he was thinking. Forty-one?

Florence stood her ground. Lilly came right up close to her, beside herself, as Florence could see.

'I'll dance on your grave, Florence Parker,' she said. 'I'll dance on your grave.'

And then she went.

'Well,' said Bertha to Dolly.

But Dolly was looking at something quite different. She was looking at Peggy Boxer and Patrick Parker.

Patrick put Lilly and his father out of his mind. Peggy Boxer was there and she was smiling at him. He searched for something to open with. Something impressive. And—lately enamoured of Ionesco—he said, 'Have you seen *The Chairs*?' At which she looked about her, studied a few of them,

185

and gazing up at him brightly, 'Very nice,' she said. Patrick thought she was adorable.

* * *

Later that evening, with the beginnings of a headache, he found himself at the end of the garden, beneath the pale, full moon, with Peggy Boxer wriggling up against him and her feather tickling his ear and his nose as he inhaled her scent of Goya gardenia and busied himself about her body. She removed her skirt and her jacket, she removed her chemise and brassiere, and she even removed her hat for the final stages of it all, for which he was extremely grateful given the way the feather would catch him out just at the wrong moment. Her lower body, bathed in moonlight, looked like Roman marble, smooth and white and perfect where Audrey's had a few ripples and lumps. But it was warm flesh he was dealing with all right, and not the wishful contouring of some ancient artisan. Besides, Peggy Boxer appeared to be perfectly constructed. Each gesture could be read; beneath her taut skin each muscle, sinew, limb showed its connection. He watched it all and marvelled: Audrey never moved around like that, nor bent one knee while stretching out the other leg, which was so inviting.

'Canova made flesh,' he said.

'Really?' said Peggy Boxer happily.

'Really.'

The artist made free of his bonds, he remembered thinking, as the final great moment came.

186

Afterwards, while Peggy busied herself with the snaps and fastenings of her clothing, he was not so sure that it had been a good idea. He felt nauseous and the headache had intensified. He decided that this was less the effect of Bourgeois guilt, than the unaccustomed onslaught of neat whisky. He thought about Audrey, and in that startling moonlight, staring up at the stars in an attempt to control the waves of sickness, he knew that she would never understand. He had talked with her about Free Love but she muddled him by asking if it applied to her, too, which somehow did not appeal. That was always Audrey's problem—questions, questions, questions. So he would not tell her about this moment. She was not Modern enough. In any case it was just a moment of pleasure, an experience, and he would not repeat it.

*   *   *

In London Audrey put down her old school French grammars, turned off the radio and yawned as she went out into the hallway. She wondered about the funeral, what Patrick was doing now (Audrey, do not ask) and if her withdrawal had been noticed by him. She hoped it had because it had cost her dear (dearer than she knew). Surely he had noticed her silence, her absence, and at such a critical time, too—he would know from that how much he had hurt her. Surely? She traced her fingertips longingly over the top of the telephone but somehow managed to stop herself—as she did every night—from ringing the Coventry number.

Her mother would telephone tomorrow and Patrick would probably want to talk to her then. She would leave it to him. He must be missing her—he must. In fact, given how much she missed him, she had no doubt of it.

But when Dolly rang the next evening, Patrick was not in the house. 'He's a bit distracted,' said her mother cautiously. 'As is only to be expected.'

Audrey took comfort from that. 'When is he coming back?' she asked. But she had meant to ask when her mother and father were returning.

'Tomorrow—' said Dolly. 'We are. I couldn't say about him.'

'He's all right though?'

'I told you—just a little distracted.'

*   *   *

Patrick was most certainly distracted the following morning. What with the glaring summer sunshine and a sudden understanding of the current phrase regarding mouths and gorilla's armpits, he stared into the speckly old bathroom mirror and reaffirmed his decision not to see Peggy again. Besides, Audrey was waiting for him in London. It did not do to tangle with someone like Peggy. Her body and her movements might be perfect but her feathered hat was ridiculous on someone her age. And the way she folded her clothes. Those shoes of hers, too—he shuddered—it was all so—Magazine World. So oddly respectable. Audrey, when the time came for her to remove everything, just flung it on the floor, which was much more modern. He thought of her with affection. He would do no more than pass the time of day with Peggy when he

188

saw her next. And that was all. And he would talk to Audrey on the telephone that night. Dolly would be ringing her anyway.

But by five o'clock teatime that day, when Peggy came cycling by, he was ready—as he told his mother—to 'take the air with Peggy' again. And Florence smiled. When he came whistling home there was a look about him that Florence decided to accept. In a good cause. It reminded her of Wednesdays long past. But if the girl caught her son's fancy then she must accept the method of catching it, she supposed. Peggy Boxer had no ambitions to leave Coventry—Patrick would return to be with her—and she would make an easy daughter-in-law. Ruby, no better than she ought to be, would be glad of the connection. Patrick closed the front door and she went out to greet him. At least she had something to thank George's funeral for. It had cost enough. Which reminded her—she had not finished with that minister yet, not by a long chalk.

Patrick and Peggy spent the next few days 'taking the air' together. So much so that Aunt Bertha commented to Florence that if he took in any more air, Patrick would end up floating. Patrick found his old bicycle—minus the saddlebag—in the half-emptied shed and the two set off bright-eyed and eager for the woods. Dolly returned to London and for Florence it was like the old days having her beloved son home. She lived for it really. But inevitably, Peggy or no Peggy, the time arrived, a few days later, for Patrick to return. He did not ask Peggy to come to the station.

'I will write to you,' she vowed.

'No need,' said Patrick. 'Audrey will be waiting.'

But this time Peggy took it on her pretty little chin. She acknowledged that it had been fun. Everything comes to her who waits.

Florence, smiling a little, asked him what he thought of the Little Boxer Madam. Patrick said that he thought she was very Coventry. Florence agreed. 'Nothing wrong with that, though,' she said crisply. 'So are you.' Patrick swallowed hard and said nothing. He could not wait to get on the train. His mother, as usual, had everything washed and ironed for him and she packed it away as neat as a pin, including several new pairs of pants and some socks which she did not tell him about. The ones he had brought with him were too brief by half. And Aertex was better for you. Aertex was very Coventry. Everything up here was.

*   *   *

During the week of his visit he had taken a good long look at the city. He had walked around the parts that were already rebuilt and checked the drawings and plans for its further renewal—and he thought Ling the architect was a prissy person pleaser: a man who had trained with Fry and Gropius and yet saw the place as a series of chequerboard arrangements. Two tower blocks to pay lip service to the potential excitement of a waiting skyline, a pedestrian precinct that would be dead by six in the evening, and small places for people to sit and contemplate their navels. Such small-time concepts do not a New Age city make— thought Patrick—and turned his face back to thoughts of Tokyo.

At the station he carried his precious portfolio of

190

drawings as carefully and as proudly as if they were made of gold. Which, in a way, they were, for they contained the finished work for the Gold Medal (even better than he had hoped) and represented the golden future that lay ahead for him. Nothing was more important than that. Not Death, not Love, not the ties of Blood. Absolutely nothing came close. As the train for London drew in, he breathed in the excitement of it all. 'See you in the summer,' said his mother, 'if not before.' He kissed her on the cheek, said, 'You bet,' winked at her and jumped into the carriage. Thank God, he thought, thank God, I'm leaving.

In truth he would not go back to Coventry for a long time. He hadn't told his mother but he had already arranged to stay down in the summer vacation and get a job in an engineer's office. He was on his way. Now back to College, back to Audrey, and modern civilisation.

12

Endures the eternal clown/The eternal clown/
A naked woman . . .

Westminster Bridge, one of the widest and most
graceful bridges in Europe, consists of seven low
segmental iron arches, supported on granite
piers. It is 1160 feet long and 85 feet wide and
was opened in 1862. Wordsworth wrote of the
view from the bridge of his day, 'Earth has not
anything to show more fair . . .'
  The Charing Cross Railway Bridge had not then
been built.
  Guide to London

Well, Audrey forgave him everything, of course,
and Patrick, overjoyed to be back in London, the
very next day took her to the British Museum. He
stroked his hand lovingly over the curves of Danae,
admired the bits of frieze with their naked urgent
warriors, he stared up at Winged Victory and the
way her breasts pushed out against her drapery.

'Pheidias,' he said.

'My goodness,' said Audrey, picking her words
carefully, 'Pheidias, eh?'

Despite being Modern she was still slightly
embarrassed at the very obvious nakedness of it all.

'Mmm,' said Patrick. And then added, just to
clear things up for her, which it didn't but which
she was too polite to say, 'Controller of Pericles'
buildings.'

Audrey then rested her chin on her hand and

looked up at them pensively. 'Ah yes,' she said.

'And Mnesicles. Mmm,' she said. 'Well, well.'

He nodded, a little thrown by her easy reference. 'Metopes from the Parthenon. Those ancient Greeks knew a thing or two.'

'Well, I can see that,' she said.

They were both peering closely at them now. The delineation really was very clear. Given that the room was fairly crowded and the masculine gender of the marble riders was very obvious she did not, exactly, know where to look. In the end she settled for a horse's tail.

'Big frieze,' said Patrick, nodding sagely.

'Yes,' she said. 'But hardly surprising if they wore so little.'

Patrick burst out laughing, making everyone stare. 'You can be quite witty sometimes, Aud,' he said, and put his arm round her. She laughed too, wondering what was funny.

They sauntered on, arm in arm, and she felt close to heaven.

'The body,' he said, 'is probably the most perfect piece of engineering in the Universe.'

Audrey looked into his eyes.

He took a deep breath. Might as well, he thought, and added, 'And yours is pretty near the top of the pile . . .'

Fortunately it did not occur to her to ask if she was 'pretty near' the top, who then was actually 'top of the pile' or Patrick, coming over all Modern and bohemian again, might have told her.

'Now,' he said, suddenly whirling her around a plinth so that attendants wagged their fingers and visitors stared. 'Now— back for tea and crumpets and I'll show you what I've been doing for the Gold

Medal.'

Breathlessly she ran out into the Bloomsbury streets, following him on to a bus, running up the stairs, racing to the seat at the front. The conductor disapproved and tutted as he clipped their tickets making her feel happy and young and alive. They held hands and looked about them. 'I know what we'll do,' said Patrick. And they hopped off that bus and on to another so that they could ride over Westminster Bridge. Because, as Patrick said, it was one of the best bridges in London. 'And doesn't Mr Brunel's baby add to the view?' He pointed as the bus juddered over the river.

'I'll say,' she said, nodding vigorously, and thinking that it looked rather ugly really and blocked her view of St Paul's. But of course she wouldn't say. She felt so happy that she could have died at that moment. To be entrusted with his hopes and aspirations, to share in everything, including his body and hers, was total fulfilment. She forgot about Lilly, she forgot about being rejected, and her heart soared, once again, with hope and happiness.

Patrick extolled the virtues of being back in the Great City, saying how wonderful London was and denouncing Coventry. She asked him about the funeral. He had little to say. Neither had her parents—her mother being unusually reticent about the experience. When asked how Patrick managed, Dolly just said, 'Well enough,' and clamped her mouth shut.

Dolly was praying it would pass. All of it.

'He's sensitive,' said Audrey.

'My elbow,' said her mother. 'I don't think either of them shed a tear.' Then she turned to her

194

daughter and asked her if she was truly serious about Patrick. 'More to the point,' she added, 'is he serious about you?'

'Of course he is,' Audrey said. 'But we are not going to do anything Bourgeois.'

'I'm very glad to hear it,' said her mother dubiously. 'All the same, I think you should hurry up and get that ring on your finger and marry him. Before someone else steps in.'

*   *   *

'The funeral,' said Patrick, almost joyously, 'is over. And that is all you need to know. All right?'

Of course it was. She was in love with Patrick, in love with London, in love with Westminster Bridge. And it seemed, for the first time ever, that Patrick might also be in love with her.

With this in mind, and borne aloft on a cloud of feminine expectancy, Audrey started removing her clothes as soon as she walked into his room—a piece of boldness that she had never dared before. Patrick went ahead of her into his dear, beloved workplace that he had missed so much, and opened his portfolio. He spread out the copies of the Gold Medal drawings in order on the floor, kneeling above them, beckoning her, without looking up. 'See,' he said, pointing. 'It's fantastically revolutionary. *Fantastically* . . . And full of bloody humanity . . .' He touched the drawings lovingly, delicately, as if they might bruise. 'Notice,' he said, 'that I have used the colours Corbusier used—red and blue and green—and this is a cross section of the rubber mat . . .'

Now normally Audrey had a good instinct for

195

what to do and what not to do and when. But on this particular occasion, buoyed up by their separation and with Patrick's enthusiasm and the idea of his glorying of her body—she misread the position. While he leaned admiringly over his work she removed the last of her clothing and knelt on the floor and leaned over him, actually putting her knee on one of the drawings. And then she said, rather seductively she thought, 'Can't we put those things aside for a little while?' She picked one up and tossed it gently away. 'Just for now? I've missed you so much.'

He looked at her amazed. Then coldly. Then he looked back at his beautiful drawings. Then back at her again. She began to display goosebumps. 'They are not—as you put it—*those things*. They are my future.'

The silence was long and terrible. She broke it. 'Sorry,' she said. She willed herself not to look at the poster or she knew she would cry.

'I suggest,' he said, 'that you put your clothes back on.'

*   *   *

They did not meet for several weeks. Patrick remained silent, too busy to think or care beyond his work. The Galton Loggia—much photographed —was opened to the public. He did not take Florence to the ceremony—in his heart he knew she was not the kind of mother to impress—and the thought of her meeting Penelope in public was too awful to consider. But he did take her there afterwards. Already aware of the usefulness of publicity, he suggested to Henry (who was about to

196

leave for his summer in Antibes) that he might—
with his permission—invite the press along. The
Daily Graphic and *The Times* were the only ones
who showed up. But he was pleased. It was a start.
And whatever else his mother could not do—she
could certainly look quite smart. She brought a
message of congratulations from Peggy, and he,
feeling jubilant with everything, sent a friendly
message back. His meticulous maquette of the
children's playground was complete, all the
drawings had already been submitted in sealed
envelopes. All he had to do now was to sit back and
wait.

He put Florence on the train, kissed her cheek,
and watched her smile and wave from the train all
the way out of the station.

'And hallo, Tokyo,' he said to himself as he ran
down the steps and back into the street. 'Not long
now.'

*   *   *

Audrey, meanwhile, had two options—either to
take to her bed or to do something positive; she
chose the latter. Whatever had happened between
her and Patrick could only be temporary—but
while she had the time she would use it. She began
looking at her French books in earnest. And she
went back to the British Museum, and walked over
Westminster Bridge—and past number eighteen
Duke Street. Later she bought a postcard of
Isambard Kingdom Brunel from the National
Portrait Gallery. Looking at it, studying it each
night, propping it on her dressing table, she grew to
hate him—hate the cocky stance, the cigar, the

place he held in her lover's heart.

The press cuttings were sent on from Coventry and Audrey swallowed hard when she saw Florence standing there instead of her. But it was no more than she deserved. She had not been thoughtful enough. This was her period of self-awareness (a new concept) and she took it very seriously. She would put aside girlhood and become an adult, thinking woman. She ploughed on with the French.

When Dolly was told by Florence (of course) that Patrick had won his medal (of course), she sent him the Brunel postcard. She wrote: 'I congratulate you with all my heart. Please forgive me. Your loving Audrey.' And she waited. One thing she knew for certain. Patrick would never throw the postcard away. Not with bloody Brunel on the front of it.

*   *   *

Patrick, meanwhile, was introduced to the Grandees of Design as the College's most promising undergraduate. He noted that they wore suits and ties and spoke the Queen's English. Yet he knew for a fact that one of them (bathetically named Ronald Wilkins), with a practice in London, Toronto and Sydney now, and the title 'Sir', had been born in Bradford. Another had been a Barnardo's Boy. They were international men now—no trace remained in either of them of their humble origins. His instinct to remove the stigma of Coventry was right.

When the Gold Medal was announced and Patrick was presented with it, there was a dinner. And at the dinner Patrick sat next to the guest of honour, who happened to be the Great Man from

Bradford. The Great Man from Bradford, who spoke so impeccably, congratulated Patrick on the Galton Loggia—he had seen it in the press. Clever stuff. Brave. Go far. Emboldened by a glass of wine and his own substantial achievement, Patrick asked the Great Man to tell him what else (after talent) was needed in the professional life he led that had enabled him to achieve and maintain his Greatness. The Great Man, having enjoyed his bumper, smiled broadly, picked up his glass and raised it to a straight-backed, sweet-faced woman, with blue-grey hair in a tight perm (just the sort of neat little woman Patrick thought he despised) and said, 'Get yourself a good wife.'

The Great Man appeared to be serious.

'I only employ married men,' said the Great Man, still apparently serious. 'The unmarried ones are bound to be wild and go off at a tangent.'

Patrick studied the women sitting at the table. The staff and the Academic Hierarchs' wives were distinguishable by their short, grey hair and serviceable outfits and the way they got their heads down, saying little, eating much. The wives of the Grand Outsiders were distinguishable by their air of relaxed ease, their blue rinses or coiffures unflecked by grey, and their discreet but sparkly frocks. Nothing cool about them. Just nice ordinary women with one thing in mind. The success of their husbands. It made perfect sense. He envied them all—the Great Men and The Great Men's Women. He thought of Audrey with irritation. If she were only more conventional—less restless. None of these wives would have dismissed his work as 'those things' and suggested putting them aside for sex (clearly!). Food for thought. Definitely. He thanked the Great Man for his advice. 'Get a wife,' he said, now very much further on with the port. 'And I might just employ you.'

He telephoned Audrey quite soon after. Out of the blue.

'OK?' he said.

'OK,' she just about managed to reply. But it was not from anger, it was from relief. As she danced out of the house she called to her mother that she always knew it would be all right really . . . Dolly went on with her knitting. Maybe, was all she thought, maybe.

*   *   *

Just as Audrey arrived back in his life—and to be fair he was very happy about it . . . yes—he could say it—he had missed her. Just as that happened Peggy Boxer began writing to him. He sent her one polite note back saying that he was very well and he hoped she was and thank you for the congratulations—and then—just as out-of-the-blue as his phone call to Audrey, Peggy Boxer appeared on the college steps one day. Off her own bat, and telling no one, she just appeared and waited for him. She had lightened her hair, pencilled in her eyebrows, which seemed to go on to infinity, and wore a very fetching little suede box jacket. She looked—as the other students (male) showed from their stares—pretty bloody sexy. The female students did not stare—not at all—which showed that they thought so too.

'Hi,' she said, with a little wave.

He was flattered, distinctly flattered. They spent the night in his room before he put her on the

200

train, and he had forgotten how good it was to enjoy yourself without responsibilities. Audrey could be quite serious nowadays. Not one question but twenty. She knew all there was to know about beam bridges, arch bridges, suspension bridges— and when he tested her she really did know the difference. 'Talk to me about them, Patrick,' she would say. 'Tell me more.' Peggy required no such input. She wore amazing lace underwear, too. Amazing. Nevertheless—back on the train she must go. And that must be that . . .

*　　*　　*

Peggy wrote again, this time with endearments. He did not reply. He was busy working on his Tokyo itinerary. Audrey was busy doing something or other about her French—and Peggy wrote again, with more endearments; he sent a card. Perhaps, he suggested, he would see her when he returned from Japan—if he came up to visit his mother. That should do it, he thought. But it didn't. One evening Peggy Boxer telephoned. Saying that she just had to hear his voice because he was going away for so long (two weeks!) and that Florence had given her the landlady's number—and how was he? He, as it happened, was having palpitations and difficulty with his bowels on account of Audrey being in his room at that very moment, with her kit off. He only managed to grunt. Peggy Boxer said that *she* was quite well *thank you*, in a funny sort of voice. And rang off.

Back down to London Peggy came. 'I want to see some of the sights,' she said. But unless you called his room, its posters, the two Heal's mugs and the

201

inside of some rumpled bed linen memorable scenes of interest, she did not achieve her ambition. Or—retrospectively—maybe she did? She certainly went away quite happy. She was—no doubt about it—very attractive and lively, and Patrick was always—after the initial shock—glad to see her. She glowed where Audrey was all vampire pallor (Max Factor panstick being the new thing), she laughed where Audrey questioned . . . She was, he dared to think, something of a relief. The last thing Peggy said to him at the station, was, 'I do understand. You are busy. That was fun. Have a wonderful time in Tokyo. Bye.'

Audrey was not so considerate.

If he stayed away for any length of time, or forgot to telephone or cancelled arrangements . . . it was oppressive compared with the way he could stand there on that platform and wave Peggy Boxer away. Comparisons are odious, as he knew, but he could not help making them.

With profound relief, a week later he flew to Tokyo. Audrey cried, his mother cried and the note his mother brought him from Peggy Boxer was covered in tears, too (apparently). If he could shake the dust from his heels over that little lot, he would be happy. What he really wanted, what he dreamed might happen, what he thought was very possible, given his Gold Medal status, was that someone in Tokyo would offer him a job. Then he could stay for as long as he liked and all three women would be quite irrelevant. He'd get himself a geisha. He'd joked about it with Audrey often enough. Though she didn't seem to see the funny side.

13

Darkest Before the Dawn

We're getting married under Brooklyn Bridge.
Until you're a bride, you just don't understand. It
transforms you, it makes you feel lovely.
  Marnie

The first place the welcome party took Patrick to
visit was old. The Imperial Palace. More than three
hundred and fifty years old, they told him. There it
stood, half-ruined, a traditional Japanese royal
building, surrounded by a great moat and massive,
sloping volcanic stone ramparts. Patrick was
unimpressed. Such ancient monuments bored him.
They laughed. 'Come closer,' they said. 'Look.
See . . .'
  The building was not traditional at all. It was not
even half-ruined. It was being rebuilt and it was
being rebuilt from non-flammable ferroconcrete.
Clever, brilliant in fact.
  'Firebombs, nineteen-forty-five,' they said. And
bowed.
  'And I am from Coventry,' he told them. 'Also
firebombed.'
  They all shook hands.
  Sometimes one's history could come in useful.

*   *   *

Then they took him to the business area, west of
the Shinjuku station. Behold, he thought amazed,

203

Mammon. Here they were making buildings that reached for the clouds—his eyes ached trying to focus on their tops. 'Most expensive real estate in entire world,' said his guide. 'Per metre. Soon.'

Patrick licked his lips.

He asked to be taken to the site of the new Olympic Stadium, to pay homage to Kenzo Tange. 'Brunel is my hero,' he said. 'But Tange comes close.'

They approved.

The rudiments of the building were taking shape, the magical sleight of hand that would one day support—without appearing to—the already famous sea-shell roof was beginning to happen. It would one day shelter thousands and make the architects of the world fall to their knees with envy. Patrick would have given his soul to have thought of that.

'Can I have a job here?' he asked, only half playfully.

The escort bowed before him one by one. They were smiling. 'You are not old enough,' he was told. 'Here we value experience.'

A man approached and plucked a grey hair from his head. He placed it on his upturned palm. 'When you can do the same,' he said, 'return to us.'

Patrick bowed. 'One day I will. And I will build you such a bridge that Tokugawa himself would approve.'

They all clapped.

Personally, Patrick did not think they would need to wait for his hair to grow grey for that little prophecy to come true. But he also realised that now he was out in the big wide world it was better not to say such things. If it wasn't the dash of humility his Course Tutor had asked for, it was a good pretence at it.

He also learned, as many busy high-flying men before him, the usefulness of airport shopping. He bought his mother a duty-free fan and he sent Audrey a postcard of a geisha—full costume, smiling and serpentine, painted as a piece of china. 'My new girlfriend,' he wrote. The card was three-dimensional, very clever, and if you moved it around the geisha would wink and take off her clothes.

*   *   *

He returned to London and prepared to take up his rather inferior position (given that he had hoped to remain in Japan, sitting on the right hand of Tange, it was something of a comedown) with a City-based architect. Humble stuff, all bingo halls and Mecca ballrooms. And the most they allowed was some clever use of glass wall dividers and the occasional bit of drama with an exterior finish. Rough plaster, smooth plaster, plaster to look like a hacienda. But at least it was an income, it was in London, and he could look around for something else. He had a week before he started there. Just enough time to find a proper flat—or at least somewhere with its own front door and no questions asked. Somewhere big for his work table. And somewhere near the river. Definitely near the river. London's artery. He wanted to feel the pulse of it.

Audrey was delighted.

'You should do the same, Aud,' he said, get a bit of independence. Which was not exactly what she had in mind. '*D'accord*,' she said, but she didn't.

Upon one thing he was resolved. He did not have time for two lovers. He asked his landlady to say he was out if Miss Boxer telephoned, and his landlady obliged. She fielded two calls before the letter arrived. He recognised the tiny handwriting and nearly didn't open it but something about the way she had written URGENT all over the envelope made him open it. It would be undying love, he knew, so he was doubly winded when he read it.

He sat down. He got up. He read it again and then he went out into the night and he walked. He felt as if he was floating through a very bad dream—down Ladbroke Grove, along Holland Park, through the decay of Shepherd's Bush—right the way into Richmond. Dark and empty the water below him on Twickenham Bridge—which was how, approximately, he felt about his life at that moment. He had no doubt the baby was his. That, he told himself, nodding at the water, was what happened—a man and a woman made love—they made a baby. He was the fool for having let it happen. At least Audrey—dear Audrey (he winced at the thought of telling her) wore one of those rubber things. She wore it whenever they met, just in case, she had told him. It never occurred to him that Peggy Boxer wouldn't do the same . . . Now what should he do?

And then there was his mother to think of.

There must be a way out.

There was not.

He walked all the way back again, and by the time he let himself back into the house it was another beautiful dawn in early summer. Birds singing, sky blue, air freshened by the night. He should have

206

been stepping out in hope and promise. He had it all to play for. Instead he had this lot to deal with.

*   *   *

He sat in his room with a bottle of Delmonico's roughest red wine. From Soho. Where the real cats hung out. On one level he quite liked the drama of it—drinking at five in the morning, the creator cast down by despair—but every time he thought of his mother he was Coventry all over again. He winced. Every time he thought of Audrey he winced, too. He tried not to think of Peggy at all—because if she floated into his mind he felt very close to tears. He was all buggered up. He ran his hands through his hair over and over again. All buggered up. Bloody well bugger it, as Audrey would say. For what? And for whom? And then—two glasses down—oh Miracle of Miracles—he had a thought . . .

He wrote a letter of his own, in his finest hand, and he posted it that morning. The following day, he received a letter back. An appointment for an interview was given at the end of the week. It was successful. Which did not surprise him. The following morning, a Saturday, he took the train to Coventry. Nettles and Horns, he told himself as the nine-forty-two gathered speed. Nettles and Horns. He had grasped them both and come up smelling of roses. He was not surprised at that, either.

*   *   *

Audrey was not surprised when Patrick's note arrived from Coventry. He had only just got back from Tokyo and he would want to see his mother. Besides, she was busy herself, preparing for Night School in September. Her mother and father were still lukewarm about the whole thing, but at least she had given up the vampire pallor and the black and they were grateful for that bit of good sense. If you were going to impress your employer, especially the Post Office, then being a little conventional was wise. She still kept an old black sweater at Patrick's and a pair of leggings—but that was more by mistake than anything else. Well, that was what she told Patrick—but it was not a mistake at all. She admitted, but only to herself, that she left them there because it made her feel part of the place, as if she had a role there, like leaving your toothbrush at a schoolfriend's house because it meant you were part of the family.

Now she wore skirts with nipped-in waists, blouses or thin sweaters, and a little boxy suede jacket in brown. Dolly thought she looked a bit heavy in it all though her height just about saved her—and the milkman whistled when she passed his float in the mornings so she must be doing something right. If she could get her hair cut and then to stay in flick-ups it would be better but you couldn't tell Audrey anything—she wanted long hair and she was going to keep it. She did not tell her mother that it was for Patrick's sake. He thought all girls should have long hair. The longer the better. Even if you were up half the night washing and drying it.

It was in just such a conventional outfit that Audrey arrived at Patrick's the following Friday night. She came straight from work, he straight from Coventry. And she was so happy to see him that she misread his mood. Which, when she looked back on it, was quite obviously pretty bloody bleak. But love is blind. Or hers was. Having learned not to remove her clothes until he said she should (which avoided any further misdemeanours), she sat on the bed and waited, twirling a lock of hair around her finger, sipping the red wine she had brought, and letting a little bit of stocking-top show. It worked. It always did.

'I forgive you,' she said, falling back on the pillows and smiling up at him, 'for not bringing me anything back from Japan. But I don't see how you can love me if you can forget me so easily . . .' She did the Kitten Pout. And she waited. Above her, Patrick's facial expression was one of someone with very bad toothache. 'Are you all right?' she said, alarmed.

They made love in silence.

Afterwards, just as Audrey was drifting off to sleep, and bloody well bugger it yourself, her world turned upside-down.

'Audrey,' Patrick whispered in her happy, hopeful ear.

'Yes, Patrick?'

'Sit up. I want to talk.'

She sat up. This was it. This was the big one. She could almost feel the ring on her finger.

He said nothing for a while, just moved around a bit, plumped up his pillow, sipped from a glass of water. And then he asked her how the French was going. Which was odd.

'Very well,' she said. 'I shall be able to translate for you by this time next year.'

He was right. She would eventually find something of her own to do, and it would take the place of—all this.

'That's terrific,' he said. 'Really terrific.'

She was even more surprised. He had never shown much interest before. It did cross her mind that even though he went on and on about Simone de Beauvoir and Jean-Paul Sartre being such an egalitarian (*liberté, égalité, fraternité*!), when it came down to it he was rather weak in his active support on the subject.

'You really think it's a good idea?' She hugged him. He did not hug her back. 'You're sure?' she said, faltering a little by now. Something was not quite right . . .

You can say that again, was another thought she had later.

'Absolutely sure,' he said. 'It'll take your mind off things.'

'Things, Patrick? What sort of things?'

When he ran his hands through his hair she began to feel really worried.

'Well,' she said nervously. 'What?'

'Things like—the fact that—I'm getting married to Peggy Boxer next month.'

He paused. Somehow that sentence, though true and complete in itself, did not seem quite enough. Something else was required. So he said, 'I'm afraid.'

Neither did that.

'Sorry,' he added.

*   *   *

Outside the window the stars were winking at him. He was not sentimental about omens, not at all, but he felt he was now on his way up there to join them. Once this terrible night was over there would be a new and beautiful dawn. Sir Ronald was as good as his word. And even though it was only a very junior post, a very, very junior post, it was in one of the best practices in London. A wife *and* a baby on the way were compelling statements of settled, committed intent. As far as Patrick was concerned, Peggy Boxer would do as well as anybody else. Of course, he did not exactly put it like that, to himself or to anybody, and he did feel sad about Audrey, but he had his life, and she had hers, and he had never, ever told her it would be for ever. And he had too much to do, too much to think about, to hang around sorting out complications. He summed it up for himself in the useful phrase, For The Best.

14

Success and a Martyred Mother and a Wobbly Wife

As soon as the Brooklyn Bridge opened in 1883, people began trying to hurl themselves from its steel cables and majestic limestone arches into the water below . . . From the top of the tower to the water is about 270 feet . . . Any safety net extended becomes useless because a falling body will go through it like a sieve. The net will hold but the body won't.
   Gary Gorman, NYPD

The exchanges between Mrs Florence Parker, mother of the groom, and Mrs Ruby Boxer, mother of the bride-to-be, were made in private. Just as well. Mrs Parker was of the opinion that Peggy Boxer was no better than she ought to be. Mrs Parker was also of the opinion that she had been let down and let down badly. Neither a baby nor a removal to London was on the cards when she took a back seat and let the pair of them get on with it, and now here she was having to deal with both. She also pointed out that she was no fool even if her Patrick was and that Peggy's little problem might have been caused by any one of half a dozen boys. Mrs Boxer pointed out that not only had Patrick agreed that he was responsible, but they had been seen by Archie Bowles's mother at least twice in the woods after George's funeral if you please, when she was walking her dog. This did not, apparently and according to Mrs Parker, clinch the argument. No. Not in any way whatsoever. Rita Bowles. Rita Bowles—hah! Dogs or not, she was hardly one to talk given the kind of war *she'd* had. Why, she'd say anything to anyone . . . As for Peggy! She was a chip off the old block all right and Patrick was doing the right thing because he felt obliged. There was no love lost *there*, she said. How could there be with a silly chit of a girl like that? She would hold him back, she would, because she was brainless. And then wouldn't everyone be served?

'Well, you thought it was a good idea at the time,' said Ruby. She didn't care and she spoke as she found. Her hat would be the star of the show in any case.

*   *   *

Florence wrote to her son and told him, very firmly, that he did not have to marry the girl and that she would stand by him. 'You do not have to stay down in London. You can hold your head high up here.' She hoped that would clinch the argument. Patrick wrote back that he had found them a house on the Northern Line, that it was small, needed a bit of work, but it was a start. They would move in directly after the wedding. Argument *not* clinched. And with no more ado, Patrick, wedding suit and all, duly arrived. Just as well.

Mr Brian Boxer, father of the *enceinte* Peggy, an aficionado of John Wayne and a follower of the Great American Western, arrived on the Parker doorstep and took a quite different view about the clinching of arguments. He arrived at the house to make sure of it. With the view that if Patrick wanted his face to remain in roughly the same place as it had always been, he had better get cracking and marry Mr Boxer's Peggy. Patrick, who was very calm, felt that Mr Boxer meant it. Peggy said that he had been acting very peculiar ever since 'The Alamo' came to Coventry so he probably did. Over the huff and the puff of it all, Patrick made himself heard. He had every intention of doing his duty.

Only in need of a gun to complete his Wayne-like stance—Mr Boxer's parting shot, fired at the quivering Florence—was guaranteed to seal parental antagonisms for life. 'At least her Patrick knew he was going to get a bit of what a marriage was all about now and then—unlike his dad . . .' They knew where the bodies were buried in Coventry.

Patrick could not wait for it to all be over and leave. Finally. Peggy, despite Florence's hopes and expectations, wholeheartedly agreed. There was, in her opinion, only one drawback to living in London. 'What about Audrey?' she asked.

'She will get over it,' said Patrick. 'I'm still very fond of her.'

Which did not, altogether, make Peggy Boxer feel secure.

*   *   *

It would be chapel of course. When Florence went to see the minister she was deeply, deeply offended when, after her outpourings about the vicious brutality of the Boxer tribe, the minister smiled at her and patted her hand and said that he

214

thought—and he thought that God thought—Patrick was doing the right thing. And that Peggy Boxer would make him a good and handsome wife. As if that were not humiliation enough he gave her a choice of several dates for the wedding which had already, he said, been given to the Boxer family first.

Florence hit out at God. About the only one left she could blame. It was all right for Him—He'd got His boy up there sitting on His right hand. What would she do for the rest of her life now? She tottered out of the chapel and did not look back. When this was all over, she would never, ever, walk through its doors again.

*   *   *

The wedding was more like a battleground. Florence stood to one side of Patrick, granite-jawed, wearing black and clutching a damp handkerchief. She cried for her son as she had not cried for her husband—an irony that was lost on her. Afterwards she glared at the lens of Cyril Horner's camera, photographer for the *Weekly News*, with a malevolence that would not have disgraced the Erinyes. Mr and Mrs Boxer standing on the other side, looked as if they were about to be transfigured on some wonderful white cloud, so much material was there billowing around their daughter's ankles. It was to be thanked that Empire-line dresses were all the go.

Mrs Boxer wore a maroon and peach suit, with matching hat (which was, indeed, the star of the show as it kept blowing away) and her husband's tie co-ordinated. As, it might be said, did his face. Mr

Boxer had begun a little earlier than the other toast-givers, a fact conjectured upon when, on being asked 'Who giveth this woman . . .' in church, he replied, 'Me. Thank God.' Peggy went very pink but kept on smiling. The wedding, the frock, the husband and the forthcoming baby were quite enough pleasure for her. She could forgive her father such a slip when she had so much.

Patrick did not smile. He was longing to get back to London and real life. His mother had not spoken a kind word to him since the whole thing began, her only comment on the wedding being that Dolly would not be attending *obviously*—and that she doubted very much whether Dolly would ever speak to her again. Privately, she thought he looked so young and beautiful in his grey suit and navy tie. Distinguished. She looked at the jacket label as she hung it up and she saw that it was made in Savile Row. Wasted, she thought, all wasted on this crowd of simpletons. And now they had taken him away from her.

*   *   *

Patrick sent his new address to Audrey. He hoped she was getting on with her life and would she send on any things of his that she had. He added again that he was sorry and signed it with very best wishes. It was as much as he could do.

*   *   *

For the honeymoon they spent four days in Disneyland, just coming up for its eighth birthday, courtesy of his new firm. While there he could

216

check up on this phenomenon—a new way of building for the consumption of leisure. As he suspected, Peggy adored it. She loved the whole idea of a dimity, fantasy town in which your every dream could come true. Patrick studied it with interest. This was the ultimate madness of giving people what they wanted. Building for plebs. You had to dictate the higher possibility—not offer the lowest common one. He had in his wife the perfect example of what he was put on earth to enlighten. And he would. One day he would build bridges for heroes.

'Wasn't that lovely?' said Peggy coming back on the plane.

'Lovely,' he said. 'Why not?'

He gave Sir Ronald a full report on the place as his first act as employee. Sir Ronald was impressed. He put in a tender for something similar that might or might not be built in Japan. They were a busy practice and they could afford to wait.

*　　　*　　　*

Over the next few weeks Peggy was busy painting the rooms of their little house white. She had rather fancied some daring wallpaper—to jazz it all up a bit—but Patrick said that white was the only acceptable colour for walls, though she said she wanted lilac for the nursery. Lilac, she argued seriously, would go with either blue or pink when the time came. 'So would white,' said Patrick, but he let her have her way. A nursery, a home, was woman's domain. The world was his.

Then Peggy fell all the way down their newly sanded staircase. Patrick had worked on them, pulling up the old carpet and throwing out the old stair rods with a savage joy. But he had not quite thought through the practicalities. Twelve uncarpeted steps, and the entire reason for the wedding was lost that night in the local hospital. Peggy Boxer's first thought on coming round was that Patrick would want to go back to Audrey now. When he arrived with a bunch of white lilies (an unfortunate choice in the matron's opinion) she said so. She turned her head away and stared at the window and said, 'I expect you'll want to go back to Audrey now.'

To which Patrick looked amazed. Of all the things . . .

'Audrey?' he said. 'Why?'

She only hoped he meant it.

Of course he meant it. He was busy. He was focused. Just about the last thing he needed was to keep chopping and changing all the time. He had married her and that was that . . . Not the most ideally romantic way of putting it but better than nothing. She lay back and decided to live.

*   *   *

Out of darkness came forth light . . . He designed some anti-slip studs for the edges of the stairs, neat little things that became all the rage with the emergent lifestyle stores. Terence Conran shook his hand.

*   *   *

Florence was icily polite when he rang to tell her about the baby. Her 'so sorry to hear it' would have

218

broken several sets of crystal glasses. It wouldn't last, she told herself. She left him, meanwhile, to get on with it.

But it did last. And Patrick had a little thing he liked to say about them. It was that he and Peggy constituted the three Ps—Patrick, Peggy, Perfection. Of course they would have children one day but it did not matter if they waited. Patrick was quite happy to be alone with Peggy while his career blossomed. And Peggy made sure that he remained happy. She did not want him to ever, ever think she was inadequate—which is how she felt sometimes when she thought about the day she slipped down the stairs and what she had lost. So she put Patrick at the centre of her life—why not, he was the star— and she made sure he was well served in everything he required. It was a continuation of his mother's approach. He was used to it, barely remarked it as a matter of fact. It was—if he thought about it— exactly what he had once wished for. A Mother With Sex.

Poor Peggy. Despite being the three Ps, she did not feel absolutely secure. Audrey maintained quite a strong presence in their lives for the first year or two. Patrick might make the odd remark about 'Remember when you first saw the Elgin Marbles?' or he might read from the paper that they were going to attempt to make a film of 'that Genet book I lent you' and each time it happened Peggy felt, in the words of a centuries-old superstition, as if someone had just walked over her grave . . .

Once she dared to enquire about Audrey's whereabouts. 'I think she's working in Paris now,' he said. And then with an affectionate little shake of his head. 'Who'd have thought it? Little Audrey.'

*   *   *

Patrick enjoyed an excellent sixties. London was the place to be, and he was very much a part of the scene. He was beautiful and witty enough to be part of the beautiful set and he even had the opportunity of dancing at a nightclub with the Galtons' Penelope—which he was very happy to decline. She, it must be said, rather regretted her earlier behaviour as she watched him walk away. Times were more democratic and he was both attractive and something of a star. And he had been photographed for *Vogue* by Snowdon.

These few years were a great time to be young, successful and creative. There was big money around for building projects, and youth was premium. At the age of twenty-eight he became the youngest partner in Sir Ronald's practice—and he was given his first serious project: to design an entire housing complex. It would be smaller than Leslie Martin's Roehampton Estate, about a third of the size (only a dozen point blocks, several high slabs, twenty blocks of flats of seven storeys and around fifty clutches of small two- and three-bedroom houses) and far less important in its siting—which is why Sir Ronald risked giving it to Patrick Parker. But it was a time for youth and if you wanted to compete in both the home and international markets, you must use dashing, dramatic young designers. Patrick took the opportunity and he laid out his own particular, peculiar, prodigious (another three Ps) design stall. If the children's playground was never produced

220

except in prototype (too advanced for mortal eyes still used to detail and definition) the housing estate was.

He interlinked (bridged, he insisted) all the community buildings and shops—and the places for people to wait for buses, the places where they might sit in the sun, shelter from the rain—with a series of elegant walkways—plain, undecorated and efficient. He threw out the idea of geometric patterning and staggered balconies and followed a ruthlessly, simple path, letting the lines and planes and layout of the buildings themselves dictate the cohesion—not invented patterning on façades. The whole was laid out by referring back to the eighteenth century's love of the picturesque. But not with parks and gardens and the building's relation to them—Patrick threw that aside and applied the principles of irregularity, intricacy, surprise, informality to the relationship of the buildings to each other. It was a huge success for the practice, and an even greater success— triumph—for Patrick personally. He went on to design an office building for Beggar Records, a pavilion for the Venice Biennale (a shadow of Tange about it) which won him a medal, another small housing complex but this time in the north of Sweden. Each major design by Patrick Parker carried his hallmark trait—somewhere, somehow, he would include some kind of bridge. Not too difficult for the annexe pavilion in Venice, ingenious staircasing for Beggar Records. Photographers loved him. The golden age of the colour supplement loved him. Anything creative was worshipped in those late-sixties days, and anyone young and creative was swallowed whole.

Patrick Parker, aware of the game, played the part. He was the 007 of the design world. The Hockney of architecture. The Ginsberg of design. He dressed in style, drove an E-type and appeared in all the right places. Peggy, if she accompanied him, smiled and looked just like a pop star's bird. Sir Ronald was quite right. He would never starve—not with caviar and champagne and Langan and photographs at the Bunny Club endorsing the way the Bunnies were dressed. 'As a piece of engineering,' Patrick said, for the benefit of *The Times*, 'their costume is without doubt perfectly designed to maximise their strengths and minimise their weaknesses.' The reporter blinked. 'It is all a matter,' he said kindly, 'of stresses and strains . . .'

He became one of the five or six most used architects, working less and less in England, more and more in Europe. But London was still the only place to be, the centre of excellence. Coventry tried to claim him but he ignored it. Small-town ways. He could never go back. Money began to roll. Their small house south of the river was replaced by a larger one on the fringes of Chelsea. After a few more years, with the commissions beginning to form a queue, an even larger house was bought, just off the King's Road and very much in the heart of Chelsea—while across the water Patrick bought the lease of a building and set up his own partnership, which he called a workshop because it meant that the egalitarian principle was not supreme. He was in charge and he was playing the long game. His eyes were set on glory, not trendiness, on heroism not style. He had displayed his capacity to be fashionable and quirky—now was the time—just on his thirtieth birthday—when he must eschew a bridge as a trademark and make it the centre of his design universe. When the Norwegians—who had already grown excited at the prospect of North Sea oil, decided to prepare for the transport revolution and bridge some of their fjords and mountains—Patrick took the commission. His very first major bridge. The footbridge in Italy, which had won him his first prize and about which he was once so excited, became no more than a footnote—the medal gathering dust in one of his desk drawers. Now he was getting somewhere. Now his real designer's profile began. Brunel. He would stand on his shoulders.

A classic suspension bridge—simple—with direct, unselfconscious detail. It was as if Patrick was saying to himself and the world that the flowers were over—that the power now lay in going back to basics, to beautiful structure again, the bones of design. It had barely a span of 420 metres (not much more than a thousand feet) but it was greeted with wonder and delight, and all antagonism that he was English forgotten in the pride of it. He was on his personal Brunel trail in earnest. He declared to the listening world that the foolishness of Romance and eccentricity were in the past. A good plain, wholesome diet, was his message—kept the body healthy, and the soul. Years on from this first Big Baby, there was another Norwegian bridge, at Ollsten, even more beautiful and sublime—a real bridge builder's bridge—with a wonderfully structurally unnecessary arch of steel, abutment to abutment, that he had painted blue to match the sky. When the rays of the sun hit it, it looked like a rainbow. It was entirely romantic.

223

Not long after the Ollsten bridge was opened, Peggy obliged him with a son. 'The New Brunel', said the headlines in the *Daily Mail* as Patrick was photographed crouched over the wrinkled, sleepy newborn thing. Little Isambard had arrived. You could barely see the baby for Patrick's teeth.

The following year their second child, a girl, was born. Eventually they named her Polly. It took Patrick four weeks to register the birth because he was so busy working . . .

Success after success followed. Money flowed. Grand schemes sprouted and soared throughout a buoyant Europe—and London was at the heart of the boom. Patrick was commissioned to work with a Japanese architect to design a series of high-rise buildings for discerning workers and residents in docklands. He gambled and nearly won. He said he would work on the project for a smaller fee if they would also raise half the finance for a bridge across the Thames—his grand ambition—a Parker bridge for his Nation's capital. If they put up one half of the money he was sure he could raise the rest from the government. They agreed. Foolish not to. What a wonderful addition to the Thames. But somewhere in the deserts of the Middle East a decision was made that changed everything that year. Patrick's bridge was shelved. Almost everything was shelved. People got up in darkness and went to bed in darkness. Everything and everyone was a victim of the oil crisis. It was the first real disappointment of his creative life and he never forgot it. How many opportunities does a man get in one lifetime to build a bridge over the Capital's River, to place his monument within the very heart of the Nation?

Peggy could only rock her baby and tell Patrick that it would all be all right one day. Florence, who grudgingly arrived in London to see the baby, pronounced her quite unlike her side of things again (a statement which privately made Peggy feel very relieved) and departed again. Florence felt ousted, cheated, humiliated—and though she dutifully, even proudly (for of course inside she was still proud) sent all press cuttings to Dolly and occasionally rang her to point out her son's success—she had taken such a large of dose of umbrage that she was in danger of choking on it. In all their years of marriage, Patrick and Peggy had only visited Coventry twice. It wasn't her fault that there wasn't a double bed for them and that they had to sleep in separate rooms. Did they think that Florence should give up her own comfort just to recognise theirs? Once Patrick had called in on his way to Edinburgh—but he had only stayed for a bite to eat and a cup of tea. It was on the tip of her tongue to say that in half a jiff she could have a bag packed and go with him, but those days of ease were gone. The proud joy of being escorted around Coulter Hall, on her son's arm, with the press in attendance, was gone for ever—Peggy Boxer had seen to that. If Florence could not forgive her, she also found it hard to forgive her son. All in all, Florence Parker had lived for her son, and now it looked as if he was slowly killing her.

*   *   *

Gradually Europe licked its economic wounds and wealth began to mount again. The London river project was shelved largely because the days of big investment and city money had gone for good—quiet, long-term planning were the watchwords and in Asia, Japan was having a crisis of its own. Boom and Bust. Patrick had returned to Tokyo only once—and in triumph—bringing his few grey hairs as testimony—to accept their commission for the longest-spanning bridge in the world. Now he must turn his face to Europe again and Europe was very pleased to have him. He was invited by the wise French to submit designs for creating the link between the old building and the new building of one of the proudest and most sensitive architectural sites in France—the Louvre. The original grandeur of the east front must connect with its brand-new modern extension. A BridgeMan was needed, and Patrick Parker was to be the BridgeMan. It was an honour and it mended his heavy heart; the international accolades that followed even swelled it again. He was awarded the Prix des Arts et des Lettres (French letters as he liked to joke in his speeches) after his name. 'They brought Bernini from Rome,' he said to his wife, who wondered if it was some kind of pasta but who had wisely learned over the years to wait for the clue—it came—'And now they are bringing Parker from London. Not bad, eh?'

Clever, wonderful, brilliant, top of the tree—these and other words and phrases came from her lips. And she meant them. But she also dreaded the whole thing. *Audrey Wapshott is in Paris, Audrey Wapshott is in Paris.* It echoed and echoed around her brain even after all those years.

'Your mother said she'd heard that Audrey was still living in Paris,' pursued Peggy miserably. (Florence liked to turn the screw on her daughter-
226

in-law whenever she had the chance.)

Patrick sighed. 'She also heard that she had been skiing with Princess Margaret,' he said scathingly. 'And Jackie Kennedy. Now I ask you. Is that likely?'

Frankly Peggy thought anything was possible.

'Do you want Isambard and Polly to come?' she asked, hoping they would so that she had some moral support.

Patrick actually winced. 'Why? he asked. 'Will his probation officer let him leave the country?'

'Oh now, Patrick,' said Peggy. 'You know he's not as bad as all that.'

'Yet,' said Patrick.

Polly was not even part of the equation.

*   *   *

The Grand Opening was to be Grand in that peculiarly overstated way that the French do so well. Not so overstated to be vulgar like the Italians, not so understated to be taken for a British diplomatic funeral. Opulence was its hallmark, and being the best and being seen to be the best. On the chosen night anyone seeking to hire a car of any quality to take them there in style would be disappointed. The guests knew they would find cameras awaiting them—and an April night is not always the most balmy of occasions. Coiffures can be damaged, chill air can hide the cut of a décolletage. Those men who chose to wear a little enhancement in the matter of mascara or foundation or a touch of black about the hair line, would not wish it to streak in a sudden squall. The French, in advance of everyone else on the Continent (though not, it must be said, America),

227

had got Celebrity about ten years before anyone else. Celebrity was dressing itself up like a starlet going on camera for the very first time. And Celebrity had hired all the cars. Including the car designated for Patrick. A wadge of francs—and pouf! It was gone! Peggy, nervous enough at the vague possibility of Audrey turning up with Jackie Kennedy and Princess Margaret, was also put to another, more physical disadvantage—she and Patrick had to walk from their hotel.

Now—Patrick did not mind because the exercise helped his nerves. And like Brunel, whom the evening would honour along with the New Extension's architects, he liked to walk to places. Peggy—aware that she had to pull out all the stops in her *toilette*—and not aware that they would, once pulled out, be subjected to some very severe meteorological conditions—wore very high heels (one needed height at such gatherings she had learned), very big hair (precariously perched), and flounced shoulders padded to a degree not unlike her father's beloved John Wayne (it being the time for it).

Thus it was that Peggy arrived, having hit the unpredictable squall that was quite predictable following the argument of Sod's Law and she arrived looking and feeling less than radiant; in fact—not to put too fine a point on it—she was wet through, flattened, and with two odd-looking growths, one on each of her shoulders, that gave her a look of the Munsters. Not an auspicious start. A little madness followed. Had Patrick done this deliberately? she wondered. So that if Audrey was there—she, Peggy, would look sad and disadvantaged by comparison? It played on her mind as the rain dripped on to her neck. Unusually, she snapped at Patrick. 'Do I have to check *everything* myself?' she said. 'Couldn't you have just for once pulled your finger out?'

And Patrick—less unusual—took umbrage. 'If my wife can't support me tonight of all nights,' he said through gritted teeth, 'then what hope is there?' The mess she looked did not lean him towards sympathy. She was usually so radiant and stylish and able to talk so much small talk that you'd swear she had a mincer in her throat. But tonight, of all nights . . .

Madness was in the air about her, too. A hunted air, a searching look instead of her usual quiet, dignified aplomb. As soon as they entered the place Peggy began seeking out the crowds for that familiar face, the haunting one from her dreams. Audrey.

But Audrey never appeared. Patrick disappeared at the opening party—disappeared for quite a long time—and that made her jumpy. But he turned up again. Of Audrey there was no sign. No sudden, shocking, reappearance.

'Why on earth should she?' Patrick had asked her, irritably, on the way back to London.

*   *   *

After their return he remained irritable. At first Peggy thought it was like post-Birthday Party Syndrome. But it was much more as if he was out of love with her . . . The Three Ps were never talked of now and the photographs of the event were not placed in an album and shown to visitors—they were kept in Patrick's study. And he seemed to study them, for some odd reason. The few that were taken of Peggy had been burnt by her. Ten minutes in the Little *Dames* Room that evening had not improved her much and it was best forgotten. Could it, she worried, be as simple as that? Her looks had gone? She always kept herself so trim and attractive. Suddenly, and for the first time, she found herself looking at her life. Without Patrick it was—well, despite her two children—empty. Emptied out. She had given everything to her husband. What could she do if he no longer wanted her? She stayed quiet, kept her head down, waited for the ill-feeling to pass. It would all be made better, she was sure, if the commission for a new bridge, a bridge for The Millennium, in London, came to him.

Peggy had not lived and worked for Patrick for all those years without knowing him. She was right. They were preparing to commission a bridge for the Millennium and Patrick knew that he—and the world—would expect it to be his. Yet as they moved towards the nineties there was a sense of egalitarianism abroad—the word 'caring' had crept into the social vocabulary. An architect, even world-class, could not be certain of anything. Even one who had designed and built a bridge with the longest span in the world. After that, how the Japanese would look askance—would laugh—if he were passed over by his own people.

She came into Patrick's workroom one evening and found him re-running the video of his interview with French television made during the Grand Opening of the Louvre. The last time, she thought, that they were ever happy. She sat down with him and watched too. 'Just look at how your tie is all skew-whiff,' she said. 'And your jacket collar. And whatever *had* you been doing to get your hair in a state like that?' It brought it all back to her. The long absence. When he did reappear he looked as if he had been in a fight. There was very definitely something of the little-boy-caught-out about him.

Patrick immediately switched off the video and stood up. Interview over, was the message. 'I'm going to bed,' he said. And left the room. Peggy got up too. Perhaps, she decided, it was because *he* was getting older. Perhaps Paris really was his last great moment? She puffed up the cushions, tweaked the drawn curtains tidy and switched out the light. To be truthful, she'd be rather glad if it was. It would be nice to have a holiday.

*   *   *

Florence continued to sit in her kitchen in Coventry and fume. She fumed over the press cuttings that never mentioned her. She fumed over the place at his side that Peggy Boxer had stolen. There was never, ever, anywhere, mention of her, the fount of everything. She thought of Liberace and his mother—she thought of Noël Coward and his mother, and when she thought of Patrick Parker and his mother—it made her feel ill. The world thought very highly of him, as indeed the world was right to do. But the world knew nothing of her. And that was very wrong.

It was then that Florence, who had given up on a kindly, approachable, chapel Heavenly Father, took to the Higher Church. She tried a few before she settled on St Michael's. Largely because most of the priests, vicars, ministers she approached in the town told her the same thing—that we must let our children go, that they do not belong to us, if we want to be happy we must have no expectations, remember God's gift of free will, etc. etc.—which she found quite opposed to her taste in spiritual counselling. Father Bryan, on the other hand, had taken a kinder view. He, too, thought mothers were good things and to be treasured, never having had one of his own, nor a father (which is why he took to the church since God the Father and Jesus Christ His Only Son gave Father Bryan an instant family and standing in the community). It seemed to Father Bryan that if he'd had half the help Patrick Parker was given by his mother, he would have been a bishop by now. At least. 'You are welcome here,' he told Florence. 'You and your bruised heart.'

That was more like it. She got on very well with this God and wished to encourage Him. Her first act in this direction, since she was mother to one of the leading architects in the world, in the ruddy Universe actually, was to kneel before a bank of candles in that ancient, silent, scented air, and apologise for the appalling monstrosity they had stuck on the outside of the new Cathedral (also St Michael's, which made her all the more proprietorial). Jacob Epstein, so they said, was the nation's greatest sculptor and this statue of St Michael, his very last work before he died, was supposed to be his Triumph. Florence had had enough of Triumphs. The operative words regarding Epstein for her, as she said with head bowed, was 'his very last work before he died'. 'Well, good,' said Florence to God. 'You did the right thing there.'

232

The church was her salvation. A place to go and communicate all that she felt as the years went by and Patrick succeeded without even so much as a mention of all that she had been to him. There was sour rage in every glitter of her eye as it beheld the Host. There was quivering righteousness during the Creed. And there most certainly was a woman scorned each time she knelt to take Communion. She told the piously sympathetic Father Bryan, as she pressed money into his hand for some good cause or other, that it was enough to kill a woman. Father Bryan absolved her from the sin of taking the name of death in vain and said that she was an angel in the sight of the Lord.

She was still convinced that one day her son would come back to her—and she would forgive him. She would. She told Father Bryan this and he nodded gravely. 'You have the power of earthly forgiveness,' he said. The knowledge of which kept her going for years. Her favourite Bible text was from Luke chapter 15, verses 11–32.

The Prodigal Son. With relish did she say aloud the words '. . . and took his journey into a far country and there wasted his substance with riotous living.'

Never a truer word, she thought.

15

Moving On: Life and Death

Mary Cassatt's *In the Omnibus* includes a bridge
across a wide river in the background. This
picture shows three people—a mother, a baby
and the nurse, who is the bridge between them.
They are isolated as if no other people exist.
They are indifferent to their surroundings, which
are passive. And indeed, the mother seems to be
in a world of her own. Only the nurse, attentive to
the child, shows any sign of activity.
  Brantacan Bridges,
  brantacan.co.uk/bridgeupdates.htm

Florence received the news about her son like any
member of Joe Public. She turned on the
television and there he was with his family (the
boy looking like an idiot, the girl sulky) grouped
on the steps of their grand London house,
confirming the news that he was to meet the
Queen. He was to become Sir Patrick. She
noticed, in the midst of her rage, that Peggy
Boxer looked nervy and that her bust had
dropped. That's what came of being nursemaid to
a Genius, my girl, and didn't she know . . . But she
waited that night, just to see. Perhaps it had all
happened so suddenly he had not found the time
to let her know . . . Or perhaps . . . Her heart beat
faster at the thought . . . She had waking dreams
that Patrick was already driving up to tell her,
pressing her hands, saying it was all thanks to her,

she must come and be a part of it all . . . But of course it did not happen. Eventually she telephoned. She tried not to sound upset as she congratulated him. He merely sounded relieved.

'At last a KBE, Mother. And no more sharing the list with footballers, cricketers, people with no hands and B-grade comedians. Now I'll get the Millennium Bridge commission—you'll see. Won't that be something?'

'I'm very proud of you, my son,' said Florence, keeping her breathing as even as she could.

'Birthday Honours—means I should be getting in sometime in October. I'll send you a photograph.'

Florence swallowed, said goodbye, and put down the telephone.

* * *

As the time for Buckingham Palace drew nearer, she asked Father Bryan what to do. He—born into orphanage and bringing his sanctified view of mothers and sons to bear—suggested that she telephone Patrick and say how much she would like to share the special day with him. Surely his wife (Father Bryan did not have a wife, nor intend to) would not grudge a mother this? Sitting there in that still little room with the waxy candles (never lit) and the plaster Virgin in her sweet sky-blue robes, it all seemed possible. Why should Peggy Boxer As Was accompany her son? When she had given him everything? 'Thank you,' she whispered to the priest, who was gazing through the door and up at the stained-glass window in which Bishop Heatherington had himself immortalised, in full regalia, in 1892. She leaned forward and said that she had a small offering for Father Bryan; Father Bryan—in an enjoyable state of ecstasy—merely nodded and suggested she put it in the box by the door. Florence had had quite enough of people dismissing her one way and another. She stood up, and without another word, she departed, pausing only at the door to do as the heedless priest had said. She shoved the entire bag of oat and honey biscuits through the slit in the top, one by one.

She took Father Bryan's advice. When she reached home she telephoned her only son. 'I am very well,' she said to his enquiry. 'Never felt better. And I have a favour to ask . . .'

*   *   *

Peggy Boxer As Was wore a very unpleasant shade of custard yellow and an odd-looking hat that looked like a cake decoration. She still seemed nervy but she obviously had on better foundation garments for this occasion. Peggy Boxer As Was looked a fool. A custard fool, Florence laughed grimly. Nevertheless he had chosen her, not his mother, to accompany him to the Palace. The television news showed them for perhaps a second—outside the railings now—smiling and hugging and slightly tearful while the BBC man said it might be thought a little overdue given Patrick's other honours from all round the world . . . And Patrick looked so young and so handsome and modest, smiling to the camera. It was as if he was goading her with it. Shoving it in her face. She remembered him at his father's funeral. He had tears in his eyes then, too. For his father! He had never shed a tear for her, never. This is what

236

Florence thought. It was a great comfort to her to think it. She who had given so much and so willingly was never to get her reward here on this earth. And so, Florence Parker, wronged Madonna, took the last possible superior action she could manage and decided to leave it. She slumped forward in her Garwood TV chair—present from her son—delivered by liveried van . . . and died. She was there, in *rigor mortis* and out of it again, for four days before anyone took any notice of her absence. Patrick rang and rang but thought she was probably just put out and ignoring his call. She'd come round. But of course, she wouldn't. She couldn't. She could only be found, eventually. And that was only because the flickering of the television very late, night after night, was noticed by a passer-by. 'She seemed to be smiling,' he said to Patrick. 'I'd say she died happy.' And so it might be, for the one thought that crossed Florence's mind as the last breath left her body was that *this* would put a spanner in the works of the new Sir Patrick Parker. And if she was going where she hoped she was going, she'd be able to observe it, too.

*   *   *

It did. Put a spanner in the works. For Patrick was not totally bound up in his life's ambitions. No— not by any means. He had arranged a surprise for his mother. It might be a surprise that could do no harm to him either, but it was around and for her that he arranged it. He suggested to the *Daily Mail* that if he brought his mother to London (he would not take them up to Coventry, obviously) to share their family joy, they might like to interview the two of them together. After all, he owed her so much. His mother had been everything to him in his formative years. The *Daily Mail* journalist, warming to the idea, asked if his father could be interviewed too—Patrick probably gained a lot from his dad? Patrick shook his head. 'It was my mother,' he said. 'My mother alone.' If he felt a little unfair about this he justified it by saying that George was dead and that anyway, small Meccano models were hardly the sort of thing with which he wished to be associated. The *Daily Mail* were quite happy with just his mother. They imagined a sweet old lady with faded blue eyes and a brooch at her throat and thought it was a great idea. Human Interest.

The *Daily Mail,* though expressing disappointment when Patrick rang with sorrow in his heart and informed them of Florence Parker's untimely death, thought it was an even greater idea to suggest that they would like to cover that aspect of things instead—if he was willing? He considered saying that grief was private, but only for a minute at most. It could do him no harm, it could certainly do his mother no harm, and though the whistle would be blown on his Coventry antecedents, the spectacle of Great Britain's Most Honoured Architect (their caption) brought low by his grief— and so soon after the award that would have brought joy to his mother's heart—was too serendipitous to miss.

Besides, he had just learned of the Millennium Commission's decision to put the bestowal of the Bridge Design out to competition. By the end of the beginning of the nineties, the notions of egalitarianism and No More Sleaze were making everything democratic again. Which would, Patrick averred (perhaps with just cause) in due course create a land of bridges and buildings fit for Lilliputians. But for the time being—in his bereavement—a little solid, sober, goodhearted publicity could do his cause no harm at all.

*　　*　　*

Thus Patrick, fresh from the glories of his Honouring, though still a bit downhearted that only *The Times* and the *Telegraph* had reported it with a picture—and still collecting news cuttings and photographs and letters and telegrams of congratulation from around the world—drove back to Coventry.

He wandered around the house. It depressed him. His mother had even refused to exchange the old range for something more modern and the walls in the kitchen were still that aged cream. How could he have ever brought anyone here? He shuddered remembering his brief hope of marrying Galton's sister—it would have been mortifying. No. He had chosen well, or Fate had chosen for him. He stood by the Garwood, where she was found apparently, and he was both sad and amused. At least she had died comfortable.

Out in the neglected garden he remembered childhood and playing with Audrey. He wondered where she was. Couldn't ask Dolly—she'd long gone to her Maker. It probably *was* a bus conductor she married.

He peered through the shed window, which was caked in dust and grime. He could just make out the shape of his old bike—so they hadn't got rid of

239

it in the end. He tried the door. It was locked. And a distant childhood memory came to him. He felt beneath the lintel. There was the key. It was an odd sensation—no one to stop him from coming into this forbidden place any more. It opened without much effort and there, wrapped in newspapers, were some of his father's models. He unwrapped the Eiffel Tower, put it on the bench and studied it. How small it was. He wondered why his father had made it so small. He hunted through the other wrapped shapes for the forbidden signal box, curious to see it again after all these years, but it was missing. He felt a small flutter of something like sadness as he dropped the model of the Eiffel Tower back into the crate and closed it. Have to get all this lot cleared before the house could be sold.

Outside he returned the key to its hiding place and stood in the overgrown garden for a while, thinking. The old-fashioned Meccano of that model gave him an idea. His bridge over the Thames could reflect that simplicity of form and function. There would be shadows of memory of the Festival of Britain, of the last vestiges of Empire and the New Elizabethan Age—a time when the metal building kit was at its most popular. How simple, how clever. He sat at the old kitchen table and began sketching some ideas. The house was very peaceful.

The following morning he went to see Father Bryan (of whom Florence wrote often as sainted and nearly a second son) to discuss how he wanted his mother's funeral service arranged—the music, the readings, the shape of the event. More than just the *Daily Mail* were interested. Human interest was in all their hearts for it sold newspapers. 'Such a poignant time,' said the journalist from *The Times*.

'So Pitiful—so Tragic,' said the *Telegraph*.

Only the *Guardian* forbore to get involved. Largely because Patrick was fifty.

When he arrived and sat with Father Bryan, in that same pale room with the unlit candles and the plaster cast of Mother Mary (pushed to the forefront of the desk on this occasion) he was shocked to be told, very firmly, that Florence had made her wishes known to the church, that she had written them in her own hand, and that things would, therefore, be arranged accordingly. (If nothing else, Florence had learned from George how such behaviour could pull the rug from under the feet of those left behind.) If Patrick could be firm about things, so could Father Bryan. He called Patrick 'my son', which got Patrick's goat. And when he tried to remonstrate, the priest actually patted his head. 'A sad loss, my son,' he said. 'A sad loss.' He fixed his eyes on Patrick and there was fire behind them. 'She was sorely sorrowing by your neglect,' said the priest.

*   *   *

All that Patrick had come away with of his original plan for the funeral was his address to the congregation on the subject of his mother's great beneficence. This Father Bryan had slotted in between the finale of *Paradise Regained* . . .

From the opening lines . . .

> But thou, Infernal Serpent! shalt not long
> Rule in the clouds. Like an autumnal star,

Or lightning, thou shalt fall from Heaven,
   trod down
Under his feet . . .

To the closing . . .

Thus they the Son of God, our Saviour meet,
Sung victor, and, from heavenly feast
   refreshed,
Brought on his way with joy. He, unobserved,
Home to his mother's house private returned.

Which Patrick found a very unpleasant and
disturbing reading, really. He wondered quite how
it was that his mother, not a scholar as far as he
knew, had any knowledge of Milton. But if he was
disturbed by that—having expected something
along the lines of 'All Things Bright and Beautiful'
or 'Golden Lads and Lasses Must . . .' it was as
nothing to the discomfort he felt when he found his
own words were to be followed by a stout rendition
of the Parable of the Prodigal Son, to be read by
none other than Father Bryan. Who was not
without voice.

'Are you sure?' asked Patrick, who was not
without peevishness.

'Of that,' said Father Bryan very fixedly, 'your
mother was most adamantine.'

Had Patrick been a keener scholar he might have
deduced from the use of the word 'adamantine'
that his mother's preference for seventeenth-
century devout verse was somewhat echoed by
Father Bryan's own interest and knowledge of
Milton (as in Satan's adamantine chains). But he
was not. He was far more interested in how to work

in some Dylan Thomas. He knew Florence had hated him, but—well—Patrick had been practising 'Do Not Go Gentle Into That Good Night . . .' in the car on the way up (which could bring tears to his own eyes, never mind anyone else's, he was so good) but Father Bryan refused. 'This is her order of service,' he said, 'and the order of service it remains. Besides it would hardly fit with the Pope that follows.'

'*Pope?*' said Patrick, horrified.

> Happy the man, whose wish and care . . .
> A few paternal acres bound
> Content to breathe his native air
> In his own ground . . .

'But why?' asked a puzzled Patrick. 'What's that got to do with my mother?' He could not see it at all. Father Bryan smiled knowingly.

'The funeral can't be for some time,' said Patrick. 'They'll have to do a post mortem.'

'Ah yes,' said the priest. 'Because she died all alone.' And he gestured that Patrick might leave. The good man was feeling just a little ragged that afternoon as it appeared that some time ago an ill-disposed and very nasty piece of work had obviously thought it amusing to stuff biscuits into the Poor Box. This, being opened every two months or so (seldom was it worthwhile sooner), had not been discovered until a family—a considerable family—of mice were discovered having taken up residence. Mrs Moggs's scream would echo in his mind for many a year and if Father Bryan ever got his hands on the perpetrator . . .

Patrick left.

The date of the funeral was fixed at last. The invitations had been sent. At least no one argued with that. In London Patrick felt quite mortified. He had wanted to pay a particularly warm and meaningful public tribute to her. Full of meaning and drama and catching the hearts of his public. He felt cheated.

He felt even more cheated when Father Bryan refused, absolutely refused point-blank, to let journalists into a funeral. If he was ever going to get a bishopric you could not afford to have things like that on your CV.

And then once the body—his mother—what to call it—was released, as if the cheated feeling could not get any worse, just before the funeral, when they were due to set off for Coventry, Peggy went down with a temperature of one hundred and two. Influenza.

'But I can't organise the thing,' he said, pacing the floor of her bedroom, running hands through his hair. 'I expect I will go down with it too, now.'

But though he tried and tried—he did not. Just for once, despite his mother's upbringing, saying the deed did not induce the illness. It was a fine time for him to find that out.

He was forced to set off for Coventry alone. Polly was dragged out of her nest on the other side of London to nurse her mother. Isambard could not be found. Not that he ever could. And if he was found he'd probably have nits and that rash of his again. Peggy used to wail that he never had nits *once* when he was at school . . .

There was nobody else left to help. Dolly was dead. He thought—oddly enough—of Audrey. 'Pity I lost contact,' he said. Peggy's temperature shot up. 'Anyway, she's probably fat and married somewhere with a couple of kids and a bus conductor for a husband.' Her temperature went down, but only a little.

So much to do, so little time, but at least Patrick had remembered to place the announcement in *The Times*. And *The Times* thought they would come up anyway, funeral or not, and take a few pictures of him. Perhaps at the grave or something. That kind of thing. Patrick certainly did not want them going anywhere near his old home.

When he arrived at the house it felt cold and strange and unpleasant and chills ran up and down his spine. Here he was, at the forefront of his world and he had no one to help him. No good asking any of his London or international friends or their wives—think what they would do when they saw his humble home. No—it was his wife or it was nobody. Pity about Aud—she'd have been good. He rang Peggy again. 'Are you absolutely sure you can't make it?' he said plaintively. 'It's not long on the train.' She just gave a gasp and the phone was passed to Polly. Who hung up.

The flowers pleased him when they arrived. Florence might have stolen his thunder in the order and content of the service, but the floral tribute was entirely his. Daisies, lilies, irises and masses of curly greenery, which he had ordered to be shaped as the bridge to heaven. 'A touch,' he said, 'of which my mother would approve.'

The press arrived the day before to photograph the inside of the church, already arrayed with

245

flowers, the pictures of which would accompany a short piece by Patrick on how much his mother had influenced his early years of dedication. Accordingly, on the preceding day, the press were also taken from the church grounds (pensive shot of Patrick leaning on the marble arm of a slightly bird-spattered angel) to the chapel of rest to see the coffin and the Bridge to Heaven. 'For My Dearest Mother. My Help and My Inspiration. Without You I Was Nothing.' A statement of which the press, if not Father Bryan, heartily approved. Close-up of Patrick and the floral tribute. Also distant shot. The great man brought low.

Patrick made a touching figure bowed down with grief, without the help of his wife or his children (who had all, as he told the press, succumbed to the flu epidemic. He said this quite unblinkingly because—well—son Isambard *might* have got it. Wherever the ungrateful little bastard was. Come to think of it, if he hadn't already got it, he bloody well deserved to get it.)

'I feel,' he said to the world, 'alone in the world. And as if my right arm, my drawing arm, has been cut off.'

The *Daily Mail* waited to do their piece later, as they needed a charming picture of the entire family grouped around Florence's grave. Patrick could only keep his fingers crossed about Isambard.

*   *   *

'Bridge Man, honoured by Japan, France, Italy and Norway, finally recognised: Patrick Parker's Muse dies. "My mother was my prop and my rock. She died happy that I had been honoured properly by

246

my own country at last," ' was the caption, with photograph, in *The Times* the next morning. It made page two.

The funeral was set for 3 p.m.

'Another blow for the newly honoured Sir Patrick Parker. His wife and two children are all victims of the flu epidemic and will not be able to attend the service with him. Sir Patrick will attend alone.'

TWO

AUDREY

Excellent Opportunity for Single Woman

There were three men in suits in the first-class carriage. The three men in suits all had distinguished greying hair and held a copy of a daily broadsheet and they had spread their arms wide to read them. They had earned the right to this space. They had earned the right to travel at offpeak times and in maximum comfort by dint of working their way upwards in the various companies they now steered. They were fulfilled men, men of substance, players.

Were they to stop and speak to each other (a thing unheard of and most *infra dig*), they would find that their experiences of business life were very similar. A good school, a sound college, a little word from a member of the family here, a little directorship there, the slightest of nods from a chairman there, a part-time consultancy here, etc. etc. All understood. All on the nod. The men who steered but never got their hands dirty. The men for whom business meetings in those unprepossessing Midland or Northern towns away from their familiar City of London territory would be set for the hour just before lunch, rather than the hour just after breakfast. Power—these men had it, and they wore it very lightly—almost as if it was not there at all.

Each one looked over the top of his newspaper as covertly as possible to consider the woman in the carriage. If she had power she, too, wore it discreetly. Not in the first flush, of course, but very well kept. Late forties perhaps or early fifties.

Quite youthful to them, really, given that they were ten years older. Good legs, and wearing a skirt (thank God)—money, of course, as the discreet gold jewellery and the smart black suit quietly declared. Not too much make-up; that streaky blonde hair about which they knew because of their wives. A slight touch of brazenness in the stare that met theirs. Their eyes went back to the legs again, encased in very sheer black, crossed at the ankles, feet in plain but delicate high heels. Also black. Altogether a striking woman. One who looked as if she knew what was what. She terrified all three of them and they retreated behind their newspapers as soon as their eyes met hers.

The woman smiled a little smile. She was used to such men. Had built her life around one of them. She knew them inside-out and sideways and she smiled again at the thought. Travelling on trains was quite a sexy business really. It was usually somewhere around this ratio of men to women—in first class anyway—three to one. All that trapped, anonymous testosterone. All that understated money and power. She smiled as she sipped her coffee and then wrinkled her nose at the taste of it. She must, she supposed, get used to British coffee again. Foul stuff—thin as dishwater. Some institutions still had not learned that the indigenous palate had changed and now demanded the standards of Starbucks and Coffee Republics and Caffe Neros. Or perhaps it was less a question of not learning, and more a question of choosing to ignore. No doubt the people who ran the restaurant car thought only of profit and never of pride and were probably on the fiddle. Always had been, always would be, in her opinion. One of her boyfriends in the old days had been a train steward. Used to give her catering-size Maxwell House to take home to Mother.

She replaced her cup. Ah well. There were compensations . . . At least the British abided by their rules. This was a mobile-telephone-free carriage and the steward (bless him) had already seen a pink-faced young man off earlier who had the temerity to get out his spreadsheets and start making calls while they were still in the station. None of these would do anything like that. They were Grandees and Grandees did not stoop to being available all the time. She knew all about Grandees. She had lived among them for long enough. They held no fear for her.

She looked at each newspaper front in turn—two *Daily Telegraphs* and one *Times*. Very nice, very predictable. England—she was definitely back. She saw one of the men flick another quick look above his paperline again before retreating. I might be in my fifties, she thought, as she leaned back and recrossed her ankles, but I've looked after myself. From the look in their eyes, she decided cheerfully, the men in the carriage thought the same.

She, too, opened her newspaper, which was also *The Times*—though not for the first time that morning. A copy had been delivered to her Bloomsbury hotel room at seven-thirty a.m and she sat up in bed with her early morning tea to read it. By eight-thirty a.m she had breakfasted and was on the telephone first to her travel agent and then to an Old Folks' home (or 'Ferndown Retirement Community', as the voice answering the telephone said) and then to a manse. By nine-forty-five she was leaving the hotel in a black cab. At ten on the dot she was the first customer in a small boutique she knew behind Tavistock Square, and by ten-forty-five she had made her various purchases. She left the shop exquisitely dressed in black, tucked herself back into the cab and headed off for the station. Her ticket was waiting for her and she even had time to have a cup of coffee at Starbucks and to buy another *Times* for the journey. It was amazing what you could do if you were efficient, determined, and had enough money.

By eleven-forty-two she was in her seat. Her hat—small, black and with a tiny veil—was safely stowed in the rack above her head, and she was comfortably settled when the train pulled out of the station—on time—for Coventry. It was then that she requested her second cup of coffee of the morning and looked about her at her travelling companions. If she had not had her mind on much more amusing matters, she might have had some fun with a little flirtation—but not today. Today she had enough to keep her occupied. She leaned back and refolded her newspaper with the photograph face-up and re-read the short report 'Patrick Parker's Muse dies . . . Sir Patrick will attend alone.'

'Not necessarily,' she muttered, under her breath. 'Not necessarily, Patrick dear . . .'

*　　　　*　　　　*

Lilly was wheeled into the church in a chair that squeaked and squealed. A general tutting rose up towards the lovely beamed roof and the carved round bosses—surely the people who looked after the woman in the wheelchair could use an oil-can?

But Lilly, who had made little commotion for most of her life, quite liked disturbing the Universe now.

Patrick turned round and stared out from the front pew. What he saw approaching seemed a vision of hell. 'It's Baby Jane,' he thought, and he gripped the pewback to save himself from passing out. The chair screeched its advance and stopped a few pews back. He found himself looking at a twisted, smiling smudgery of a red mouth and bright scarlet splodges on the cheeks beneath the sunglasses. It looked as if someone had pressed red-hot pennies into the flesh. The figure lifted a small, bent hand with great difficulty and waved it at him very slightly before being settled at the end of a pew. He was just congratulating himself that at least the apparition wore sunglasses, when these were removed and he distinctly saw Lilly—for there was no mistaking who it was—wink. He shuddered and turned back towards the altar. He wondered how on earth she had found out about the funeral. Small town, he supposed. But with her there lolling and winking it made standing alone (he did not count his deceased Aunt Bertha's husband's brother's son, Roger) in the front pew all the more stressful. He ran his hands through his hair . . .

Suddenly, sliding past him in a black softness of fabric and a sweet smell of perfume, came a woman. She managed, seemingly without effort, to insinuate herself between Roger and himself. Perhaps it was Roger's wife? But Roger did not have a wife. He had never married, lived in Bromsgrove where he sold wet fish and wore plastic gloves to do it and—it was clear—never touched anything alive and warm if he could help

255

it. It was all he could do to shake Patrick's hand at the door to the church, and say 'as your godfather, er, as your godfather . . .' Which was about all he ever *had* said to him over the years. Patrick looked at the woman's veiled profile as she stood facing the altar and then he had the added shock of feeling her warm hand take his and hold it and squeeze it. He peered harder, the profile turned towards him and beneath the little black hat, behind the enticing little bit of veil, the smile was warm and sympathetic and vaguely familiar. Also, he thought, attractive. Well, for an older woman. A very well-kept older woman . . .

'Poor you—' she said, in a soft, sweet voice. With just a trace of a south London accent. 'Alone at such a time.'

Patrick did not know what to say. The hand holding his squeezed gently again.

'My wife—' he muttered helplessly. 'My son and daughter—'

'So I heard,' she said. 'Shame. But I'm here now.'

'Thank you,' he said, confused. It was familiar yet unfamiliar, that voice, the phrasing.

Behind them came the faint sound of squeaking wheels and a faint voice, but one which was quite distinct in that hushed gathering, saying, 'He should have married her. She'd have given Flo a run for her money. Not that silly bitch he ended up with . . .' before someone said, 'Hush, hush . . .' just as the organ and choir began with 'Lead us, Heav'nly Father, Lead us . . .'

Patrick was literally and metaphorically lost for words. What with wondering if he had heard right, and the proximity of the woman who now took her hand from his and picked up a hymn book from the

256

shelf in front of him. She removed one black glove and flipped through the book's pages with confident fingers, manicured and painted with dark, blood-coloured polish, the sight of which gave him a frisson, despite the solemnity of the occasion. When she had found the right page she handed it to him and nodded encouragement. He opened his mouth and sang. He sang, 'Who are you and do I know you . . . ?' To which she merely replied, 'O'er the world's tempestuous sea . . .'

Father Bryan spoke warmly about the good qualities, the bounty, Florence bestowed on her family and community. The various readings were given with tremendous feeling by the various members of the congregation designated to do so. None of them had been on anything more than hassock-bumping acquaintance but they gave it all they'd got anyway. Patrick found the floor riveting.

A short stocky man with a toothbrush moustache began with an extract from *Pilgrim's Progress* subtitled, as he boomingly announced, 'From this world to that which is to come.' The selected passage—made by his mother, *his mother*—Patrick found peculiarly disturbing: 'Then I saw in my dream, that when they were got out of the wilderness, they presently saw a town before them and the name of that town is Vanity; and at the town there is a fair kept, called Vanity Fair . . . It is kept all the year long. It beareth the name of Vanity Fair because all that there is is there sold, or that cometh thither is vanity, as is the saying of the wise . . .' He could only think his mother was going through some terrible mental crisis about herself in her final months . . . He was rather glad, after all, that the patronising priest had banned the press.

Throughout the proceedings Patrick either stood in a daze, with the woman in black standing next to him, her hand tucked in the crook of his arm, or sat in a daze with the woman in black's hand tucked in his. If he stole a look at her face, the profile seemed a little familiar and he liked the way just the ends of her mouth curled in a hint of a smile. But who was she? If this intimacy was meant to comfort, it merely disturbed. So much so that when it came to his moment to stand up and speak he nearly missed the summons.

'It's you now,' said the woman sitting next to him, breathing in his ear. 'You will be fine.'

And up he went.

It was only when he was a few sentences into his maternal eulogy that, facing the woman in black front-on so to speak, he realised who it was. There was just something very familiar in the way she tilted her chin as she looked up at him. Good God, it was Little Audrey. *Little Audrey* blonde. Transformed. The last time he had seen her, he remembered, she was naked and weeping on his bed. He was astonished—and very relieved. Well, she'd done all right for herself after all. He had said so at the time—he also remembered saying that she'd get over it—and she obviously had. Well, well—she was a very sophisticated-looking Little Audrey nowadays. Elegant and *expensive*. Also a lot younger-looking than he might have expected . . . Mind you, he managed to think, despite speaking aloud about something completely different, mind you, he wasn't too badly kept for his age either . . . He breathed in and continued 'My mother was always there for me, quick to praise . . .'

From somewhere in the congregation a voice

258

muttered, 'Shame,' and he guessed it was the intruding Lilly. Her and Audrey—both uninvited. Odd, very odd.

He wondered how these women managed it. Did they have second sight or something? Or perhaps that's what funerals did? Brought out the past? He searched the congregation to see if his ancient, pickled, Stetson-toting father-in-law had managed to forsake the Ram and get there, but no sign of him. Peggy's mother had gone to the Great Fashion Show in the Sky a couple of years ago. His Dearly Beloved Mother was up there in the front resting in her coffin. There was no one to take offence, or indeed remember that there might be any offence to take by the presence of Audrey. It was quite— interesting—exciting—that she had turned up, out of the blue. He had a sudden thought—his whole family was down in London with the flu—and— well—he was free . . . It was a thought so cheering that he found himself giving quite a noticeable chuckle—just as he reached the more solemn part of his eulogy. The bit about his mother sacrificing so much to get him where he was today. Ha-ha was not really the right way to punctuate such a statement so he quickly interjected the bit about his mother saying that since his birth had apparently single-handedly brought about the razing of Coventry—it seemed the very least and most appropriate thing he could do to turn himself into a builder-upper . . . The congregation tittered (though Lilly seemed to give a very faint boo) and he put his mind back to the task. Father Bryan's glittering eye was upon him. He must do well.

Back in his pew he gave Audrey a look that asked if she approved. Her expression behind the veil was difficult to read but she gave him a little nod which he took to be approval. Suddenly he wanted her approval very much. Damn it—he wanted *somebody's*. There was no one else here who appeared very keen to give it. Father Bryan rose to the pulpit and read the Prodigal Son. 'As requested by our dear, departed friend and mother Florence Mary'—he seemed to relish the announcement, staring into Patrick's very soul. He was going to go off the deep end with it, Patrick could tell, and to feel Audrey's hand in his was balm indeed. As the opening words rang out, Patrick could not stop himself from making a low moan. He remembered the story from school, more or less; he knew what was coming. The penny dropped. He realised, suddenly, what all this was about. His mother, God damn her, had taken offence . . . Sorry, sorry, he found himself muttering in prayer, sorry, sorry, I did not mean to say that, My Lord.

'What man of you, having an hundred sheep, if he lose one of them, doth not leave the ninety and nine in the wilderness, and go after that which is lost, until he find it . . .' Father Bryan looked him right in the eye. Audrey's squeezing hand helped. Oh, how it helped. Patrick looked right back. With a woman like her holding his hand, he felt he could conquer such prejudice.

'I don't know why she always liked this so much,' he whispered as Father Bryan rang the beautiful rafters and shook the round, old bosses with 'Father, I have sinned against Heaven, and in thy sight, and am no more worthy to be called thy son . . .'

Squeeze, squeeze, squeeze went Audrey.

Patrick squeezed back. He had a sudden flash of

memory of her cycling in very short shorts. Wildly inappropriate.

Somehow the happy ending of the parable—'. . . It was meet that we should make merry, and be glad; for this thy brother was dead and is alive again; and was lost, and is found'—made very little impact compared to the sinful nature of the rest of the story . . . 'But as soon as this thy son was come who hath devoured thy living with harlots, thou hast killed for him the fatted calf . . .' Patrick could barely get the idea of *harlots* out of his mind after that. The Bible was an unfortunate choice of book for spiritual matters sometimes. Audrey went on squeezing his hand, wafting her perfume; or was he squeezing hers?

He raised his eyes to the Madonna, who gazed down at him soft-eyed. Even she was beginning to adopt a faintly lascivious leer as he shifted uncomfortably on the pew. Audrey's scent had something of the musky feral about it—or it had now—though when he smelled it before it seemed wholesome and flowery and pure. It wasn't even as if Peggy would be waiting to warm the bed after all these rituals . . . He had expected, really, some kind of acknowledgement by the priest of his own achievements—the dead woman's son is a very great man—something like that. He felt slighted. After all, half the people here in the congregation had only come to goggle at him. He was no fool. His mother had never been as popular as all that.

Audrey turned and smiled at him gravely. He watched her damp lips part, and looked away. Bang, smack into the Madonna's eyes. She, he was appalled to see, was alive with erotic desire. Practically throwing the baby out of her arms to get at him. If not the entire congregation. This was all absolutely wrong—he was even beginning to find her *wimple* seductive—*Stop, stop, stop,* he cried inside. *Stop.* He was so busy getting his brain back into a semblance of sanity that he did not notice the order of service had changed. What should have been a roistering finale as printed in the order of service—and most incongruous for the soaring arches and incense laden air—was chosen by Florence to be one in the eye for Chapel. It was one of her favourite hymns from girlhood—when the world looked as if it might be a wonderful place.

> Give me the old time religion,
> it was good for the prophet Daniel,
> it was good for the Hebrew children,
> it was good for sinking Peter,
> it was good for Paul and Silas,
> it was good for sister Mary,
> it was good for brother Noah,
> it was good for our old Mothers,
> it was good for our old Fathers,
> it is good when we're in trouble,
> it is good when we are dying.
> It will land us in safe glory . . .

But it was no finale. The loud and joyful rhythm gave way to the sound of a wheelchair moving slowly, with celebratory screeching, down the aisle. Father Bryan was beckoning. Any shred of erotic desire left Patrick as he looked round. Lilly was on the move and advancing. Pushed by a dim, self-important-looking youth with a baseball cap placed widdershins over a horrible, thin ponytail. Audrey, neck straight, shoulders back, turned towards the noise and nodded encouragingly at the occupant. Lilly, lolling and smiling, gave a thumbs-up sign as she passed. Patrick gave another little moan. Now what?

Father Bryan was ready and skipped lightly down the altar steps towards her for all the world as if he were a television compere with a roving mike. Patrick hoped he would stop her—some kind, quiet word, firm but courteous—but instead the fierce-eyed priest leaned down, suddenly dove-like, to hear what she was saying. There was, Patrick thought, something of a Titian Pope about it—the very ear of God being corrupted. Father Bryan nodded to what was said and took the handles of the chair from the hands of the helper—Patrick assumed he was about to march her back to her place—but no. He watched in horrified amazement. Instead of sending her back down the aisle, the good Father guided the wheelchair around—it shrieking like a banshee—so that its occupant faced outwards at the base of the altar steps. Lilly would speak. He would be ill.

'Old friends such as Lilly here,' said Father Bryan with warm gesture of congregational embrace, 'have come to speak and have the right to do so. For they *chose* whom to love . . . A son is *born* to do so, it is of no consequence to him. But a friend makes the *choice*. So, speak, Lilly—and have your say. Let out your praises and let the rafters ring with them.'

Lilly smiled, horribly, and bent to kiss his ring finger, which he seemed to enjoy.

'Oh my God,' said Patrick quite audibly. Given what was about to follow he could only call upon his Maker. But his Maker seemed not to be at home . . . Given the expression in the eyes of his father's one-time mistress, what the rafters were about to ring with was unlikely to be much to do with praises at all.

Lilly settled her wobbly little hands in her lap. There were those in the congregation who thought the trembling came from her stroke, there were those who thought it came from her nervousness. It occurred to no one—except Patrick—that its source might be anger.

'Florence Parker was an extraordinary woman,' Lilly said. She slurred, swallowed, and added, 'How I wish I could dance.'

Father Bryan, settling himself down in a fine, carved chair, nodded appreciatively. His raised his eyes to the coffered ceiling, and was pleased that even the broken were welcome in his church. No squints for him. He looked very holy and let his mind drift in the pleasure of it all.

Lilly gathered herself. 'Very extraordinary,' she said. 'And such a piece of work as one could hope never to see again.'

The congregation shuffled—as if perplexed. Surely that was wrong . . . ?

Patrick felt Audrey's hand seek his again and he took hers gratefully. He squeezed, hers stayed still. He dared to raise his eyes to the Madonna. She was back to being a Queenly Maiden again with the child tucked safely in her arms. That was something to be thankful for. But he did not have long to be thankful before Lilly's voice quavered out, stronger than it ought to be.

'She had a good husband,' said Lilly. Father Bryan drifted off. 'And she ruined him.' She flung out her knobbly old hand and pointed a twisted, shaking finger at the coffin. 'Her. That one.' Her laugh, for one so frail, was rich. It echoed around the shocked silence and even the candles seemed stilled by it. There was a shuffling, someone dropped a hymn book and bent to pick it up, but otherwise nothing stirred. This, they seemed to be saying, was more like it. Father Bryan sat on, smiling up at the smoke-dimmed panels of the Angelic Host and clouds with saints soaring upwards. Their eyes, too, were fixed on the above.

Patrick closed his and waited for the uproar but none came. Only the silence of the assembled who could not—no, not one of them—quite believe that they had heard such a thing.

'Florence-bloody-Parker,' went on Lilly a little indistinctly, but not indistinctly enough, 'rotted his teeth with her baking—where she got the sugar from in rationing we'd all like to know—and rotted his heart too. Pretended it was the immaculate conception. George didn't feature, Oh no, nothing to do with him, Patrick wasn't—not even allowed to hold him—called it love—mother love . . .'

Father Bryan nodded benignly.

'Mother love. Cracked love more like it,' Lilly said contemptuously. 'And you, Patrick Parker, should be ashamed of yourself for letting her take you away from your dear, dead father.' She raised a bony, mottled finger. 'He gave you everything you know . . . . Everything you've got now was down to him and his dear, clever hands.'

Father Bryan, mishearing, nodded at the idea that Florence had given her son everything with dear, clever hands. It was certainly what she told him in their little private talks. Father Bryan could have been a bishop if he'd had a mother like that.

265

Lilly's voice continued, 'Nothing clever about Florence. She had no special gifts. No—it was George with the talent—who passed everything on. Little models he used to make, lovely things . . .' Lilly drifted off for a moment, remembering. 'That's where you got the knowledge from, my lad—so don't think you did it all on your own. And little thanks he got for it. None, actually. This man—this selfish stuck-up builder bugger couldn't even cry at his own dad's funeral until he took a bit of drink down the wrong way . . .' Lilly stopped. She was worn out by the effort and the rush of vengeful adrenalin.

This time they knew they had heard right and the congregation responded accordingly with a communal intake of breath, and an almost-hiss as it was let out.

Father Bryan went on appearing to listen devoutly but was in truth now caught up in the mental picture of how well he might wear his mitre and hold his crook. He was running an interesting conundrum through his mind. Outside it was drizzling with rain. Now—if he were a bishop he could expect someone to hold an umbrella for him during the external ceremony. But for him to request it, a mere priest, would be considered too proud. But surely once a bishop you were supposed to be even *more* humble? If you were a bishop and it was raining you should be glad to go out and get soaked to the skin and never count the cost. The higher you rose, the wetter you should get. But no. He sighed and adjusted his surplice, which was as ornate as he dared to wear for Coventry. The real reason bishops stayed dry was not to do with holiness, actually. The real reason was the embroidery on the cope and whatnot. It would be ruined and that would be hundreds of pounds down the pan. If not thousands. All those widows' mites. Which brought him back to Florence. He'd have to go out there soon, rain or no rain. Maybe it would stop and be a little miracle for him. He prayed for that and began staring downwards, preparing himself for feeling unpleasantly damp.

Patrick turned his head with difficulty and found himself staring into Audrey's veiled eyes. She, it must be said, had lost some of her cool in the heat of the experience. 'Lumme,' she said. And then even more softly, '*Lumme.* I never thought she'd go *that* far . . .'

Patrick was too far gone himself to consider this statement odd.

Lilly continued, tiring now, her voice getting more and more indistinct, until she came to saying, 'So I've come to say it for George. He was a wonderful man and he didn't deserve any of it. She was a very bad woman and good riddance to her. I'm nearly done.'

The congregation began shuffling their feet, moving in their seats, rumbling with dismay. Patrick wondered what the *fuck* he should do? What was the protocol when someone decided to give an anti-eulogy? He looked at the priest who appeared to be transfixed now by the ancient tiles of the floor, as if enraptured with what he heard. He looked up momentarily and nodded once, and smiled encouragingly, in Lilly's direction, aware that she had gone quiet. He gestured with his palms upward that she should speak up, up, *up*.

So Lilly did. With amazing strength given how weak she really was. Nothing like getting the bit between your teeth, as she told her minder afterwards, for the Finale. She dabbed at the wet corners of her mouth and eyes and went on, 'And she was so pleased about it, Florence was. Not having to do what a wife should and letting me do it instead. Thought she controlled both of us. Well—she *didn't*. And I want you all to know that George was wonderful, wonderful and—' She broke off. Very tired now, tears trickling down her cheeks. 'And I am very happy to say that Florence Parker did not die a happy woman. And I will.'

Patrick went into a numb little corner of hell. It occurred to him that he might die, too, which would be handy for the undertakers and the crazy priest—two for the price of one—two for the— then a voice broke through the pain barrier and called him back to life.

A voice. Her voice. His saviour. Audrey.

*   *   *

'That's quite enough now, Lilly dear . . .'

'Oh no, it's not.'

'Oh yes, I think it is.'

Audrey took both handles and spun the chair around—Lilly appeared to genuflect in her chair towards the Host—in fact, she was so shaken by the whirl that she bounced. As she was wheeled past Patrick's pew she pointed her finger and said, 'He was a wonderful man, your father, Patrick Parker, and you should always remember it.' Then, thank God, the wheelchair screeched past and was silent.

Father Bryan, coming to, stood up and smiled benignly. He walked towards the altar steps rubbing his hands. Outside he could see that the

268

drizzle had stopped. A thin sun was glimmering through. He was blessed after all, and now he could look forward to the next bit—there just was something *impressive* about a burial, and he was extremely good at them. He put himself at the foot of the altar, in the place where the pale shaft of sunlight was at its brightest and he beamed at everybody.

'Thank you Lilly,' he said. *'De mortuis nil nisi bonum.'* Latin, how he loved the sound of it.

Audrey, half pleased, half scared, put Lilly very firmly back at her pew. She had summoned her so that she could make Florence do a turn or two in her grave. Not the full Dervish.

Father Bryan held out his arms as if he would embrace them all. 'Hymn number three hundred and sixty,' he said, and while they were riffling he lifted up his voice and his chin and spoke to the rafters ringingly, 'All is feeble shadow—a dream that will not stay; Death comes in a moment, and taketh all away . . .'

At which point he was shocked to hear a reedy voice pipe up, 'Bloody Good Job Too.'

Father Bryan lowered his eyes from the rafters in time to see the elegant woman from the front pew put one hand over poor Lilly's mouth, and another over her own, and both appeared to be laughing. Hysterical women. He thought of the Magdalene at the sepulchre.

*   *   *

'Oh,' said the triumphant Lilly later, as they pushed her out behind the long trail of coffin followers. 'But it was worth it. I tell you it was worth it

269

in *cartloads . . .*'

'Get her away from here,' said Patrick through clenched teeth. It was all he needed to have a scandal at his own mother's funeral.

'Don't catch your death,' was Lilly's parting shot, as her minder, much excited at the interest, wheeled her once round the gaping hole in the ground before taking her, shaking but exhilarated, away.

How refreshing, some thought. For how many so assembled in churches and chapels throughout this good Christian land, gathered together to see off the last of a fellow human, have not wished—just once—that someone would tell the truth? Certainly the minder thought so. He had been up for it all along. You don't get very good wages, after all, so there has to be something in it for a grade three council helper class two. After all said and done.

'Were you laughing?' asked Patrick.

'Patrick,' said Audrey, 'how could you suggest such a thing?'

Patrick chose to believe her. He needed her too much to do otherwise.

*   *   *

When the earth had been thrown and the hands shaken—those who wished to do so—and they were many, given Patrick's fame—they made their animated way to the house and ate and drank well. Thank God the press were banned from the service, thought Patrick, and he practically hugged the guzzling priest.

Peggy rang to see how Patrick was managing. Patrick said he was not managing at all well. He was still feeling very roughed up by the service. 'I suppose you hated my mother, too,' he said.

There was a silence, and then an 'Oh' and then a non-committal 'Hmmm', which he took, irritably, to be assent.

The difficulty with true influenza is that it leaves one feeling weak and low and Peggy had hoped for something along the lines of 'How are *you* feeling?' Instead of how *she* might be feeling about his mother. Instead of denying her true feelings for Florence (unspeakable) and doing the Peggy-usual ('She was Wonderful'), Peggy just said that fateful 'Hmmm.'

It was a 'Hmmm' that spoke volumes. Patrick felt offended by it. Peggy's role was maximum support —not 'Hmmm'.

'Anything in the post yet?' Patrick asked stiffly.

'I haven't looked,' said Peggy wearily.

'I'm expecting a letter from the Millennium people.'

'If it comes,' she said, 'I'll send it on.'

'Thank you,' he said. And he put down the receiver. Without Peggy—and without his mother —he suddenly felt very alone. Orphaned. And grass-widowered. He went back into the gathering feeling very sorry for himself.

The front room looked no different from the way it looked at his father's funeral. The settee was in the same place, the grate held faded paper fans, the curtains were half drawn to save the furniture from the invasive sun. The only real difference was that the catering was more sophisticated, there were proper flower arrangements and one end of the table held glasses and drinks. Nothing too fancy, of course, no champagne or cocktails—just wine, beer, sherry and whisky. He thought he might have one of those now, and remembered his very first taste of the stuff. He was used to the best of it now.

Across the room Audrey was talking to his godfather and Father Bryan. Father Bryan was saying how wonderful the addresses were . . . and how brave of the woman in the wheelchair—who had been so determined, so determined. He was, Patrick decided, either a consummate bloody actor—or insane. He made his way to the table and poured himself a tot of the malt. Of course, there was *one* big difference with this funeral—one very big difference: this time Audrey was there, and Peggy wasn't.

THREE

AUDREY ALONE

1

Be Strong, Audrey

In the year of the humiliating of Audrey Wapshott, when her world fell apart and Patrick announced that he had made Peggy Boxer pregnant and was going to marry her, in another part of London altogether, on the poor side of the river, in a seamier, undeveloped, ugly part of London, where houses were cheap and groups of immigrants hung around together, afraid to break away from their familiars, a girl was born. Inconsequential event. Many girls were born there—some survived—some died—some dreamed—few achieved. This one—named Apsu by her hopeful parents—will be a dreamer and an achiever. She will grow up surrounded by people, and she will take it as a matter of pride and conscience to observe their needs. As they will observe hers. It is a poor community that has seen much, been through much, and is tempered with compassion accordingly. As she grows and takes her place in the New Land of the West, Apsu will dream this knowledge into an achievement. One day she will become wedded to the two confusions of Architect and Engineer, Art and Science, but for the moment she sleeps in her parents' bed, and knows no more of the world and its designs than the happy arrangement of having a reachable thumb at the end of her hand to suck. Perfect design.

*　　　*　　　*

When Audrey awoke she was still naked, still lying in Patrick's bed, but the light was now crepuscular. He had a little etching by Hans Bellmer called *Crépuscule*. It was one of his favourite words. Audrey had looked it up—it meant twilight. It also meant 'dim, not quite enlightened'. She felt sick, now, when she thought of it. It was the perfect word for her. On the table at the side of the bed was a note, in Patrick's stylish hand. It refreshed her memory about why she lay there feeling ill.

I am sorry. I thought it would be best if I let you sleep. I am not feeling very well either and will stay at college tonight. Be strong, Audrey. As I must. Patrick. PS. Would you leave your key?

*　　　*　　　*

Had he said more? She vaguely remembered a long discourse—Patrick rambling on about something or other—it was hurting both of them—it was not what he wanted but what could he do? But perhaps she made that up? Over quickly, for the best. She seemed to remember that, too.

Best if I let you sleep . . .

Sleep? She could not believe it. *She* had been asleep following *him* having told her he was going to marry *Peggy Boxer*? How could she have slept? How could she? And then she realised. She had not been asleep at all. She had been *unconscious*: knocked flat. Out cold. Down for the count. Sleep, indeed!

She got up from the bed and staggered. And she was still punch drunk. She felt as if she had been

276

kicked, drowned in too many gin and limes, and beaten all over again. She picked up the stylishly written note, screwed it into a ball and hurled it at Patrick's stylish three white tulips in a stylish pale blue Japanese bottle balanced on the window sill. Good girl. Bullseye. It toppled, nearly righted itself, and then fell. Breaking very satisfactorily. Mental note, thought Audrey—when the world throws stuff at you, you may topple, but you must not roll over. Or you will break.

The water from the vase dripped down the poster of Brunel's bridge at Clifton. A present from her to him. His present to her was to explain how it was constructed. While she was romantically remembering their visit there, he was telling her how the bloody abutments worked. The water, she thought, looked like tears. She held on to the thought for a painful moment—and then let it go. It looked like water running down a poster, that was all. From now on she would keep both her feet on the ground. Roll over and you will break.

She opened the window and breathed in the warm night air. A passer-by, masculine, giving his dog its evening walk on this fine night, nearly strangled the unfortunate animal. It was the stuff that dreams were made on—you looked up at the just occurring stars while your dog crouched and strained in the gutter having his walk, and you expected to see nothing more than faint pinpoints of light in the sky, the fading trees, colourless brickwork, the beginning of a moonsheen on a roof—and instead—staring quite mindlessly up at an extremely scruffy house, you see an angel leaning out of the upstairs right-hand window—stark naked—white-shouldered, with breasts quite open to the elements, arms straight

277

beside her on the windowsill, dark hair tumbling around her neck—and no shame—absolutely no shame at all. When she saw that he was looking at her, she waved and threw white tulips down to him. He pulled hard on the leash and ran. With the astonished dog trailing its nightly turd all along the pavement.

Patrick's landlady was pottering around downstairs preparatory to going to bed. Audrey, still naked, walked out of Patrick's room, across the landing and into the bathroom and slammed the door. She then bathed noisily, using the ancient, hissing geyser at full volume. When she had finished and came out of the bathroom the landlady, standing at the bottom of the stairs, just about managed the terse opening bars of her hymn to her tenant's selfishness when her jaw dropped. Naked Audrey stood at the top of the stairs and told her what she could do with her shitty old bathroom. If this surprised Audrey—and it certainly did—it was as nothing to the landlady's surprise. Her shocked old voice rose to a crescendo, addressing her husband: 'Henry—don't come out . . .' Which, of course, he did. 'Best moment of me life,' he said in The Lamb and Flag the next day.

Then the bravado left her. She was a reject. That was what she was. And some old husband of some old landlady giving her the eye scarcely changed *that*. She dressed and went home to Mother. Dropping her key down the drain on the way. The little act of vengeance did nothing to make her feel better. Neither did her mother's first words to her, which were, 'You look a bit ragged round the edges, my girl.' Dolly was standing by the dying embers of the range in her dressing gown and plaiting her long greying hair. 'You shouldn't stay out all hours when you've got to get up for work.'

Audrey slumped into the chair recently vacated by her father. He always went up early to warm the bed. She told her mother what had happened. 'Apparently she's pregnant,' said Audrey. 'So that's that.'

And did Dolly the Mother throw her arms around her only daughter's misery-ridden shoulders? Did she stroke her still damp hair and coo tidings of great comfort? No she did not. 'Be glad it's not you,' she said. 'Never did like that Patrick. Spoiled he was. Flo.' She flung the finished plait over her shoulder. 'You want someone a bit more settled. You'll be wanting to settle down yourself soon enough.'

And make sponge cakes, Audrey mouthed to the blank beige wall.

'I'll ring that Florence and give her a piece of my mind in the morning,' said Dolly. 'In the meantime, I'll make you a nice, hot milky drink and you'd better get into bed.'

Bed. Even the word hurt. Audrey thought of Peggy Boxer, pregnant, a baby growing inside her, married, Patrick's for ever. All the things she had dreamed of. She poked a bit at the dying embers and saw them spark up. 'Leave the fire,' said her mother exasperated, 'we're off to bed soon, aren't we?'

Audrey nodded. 'You know,' she said, 'I think I will carry on with French. Then I'll see what happens at the Exchange.'

*   *   *

279

In her first interview, with her immediate superior, the supervisor, whom she was certain wouldn't know French from double-dutch—she merely peppered her speeches with the titles of some of Patrick's books that had been translated, but kept their original titles. Books by avant garde writers like Jean Genet (never finished on account of its being unfathomable and, if the jacket was anything to go by, very probably disgusting), Jean-Paul Sartre (never finished—what was an existentialist?) and Honoré de Balzac (finished but not with pleasure because the neglect of Balthazar for his loved ones in pursuit of the absolute stone made her feel frightened).

'So,' said Mrs Pugsley. 'French?'

'*Querelles of Brest*,' said Audrey, with the kind of shrug Jean-Paul Belmondo gave in *And God Created Woman*.

Mrs Pugsley looked uncomfortable. 'The International Exchange demands a very high standard, you know.'

'*Les Chemins de la Liberté*.' Audrey smiled. And added, with another, smaller and wholly convincing shrug, '*Le Sursis . . .*'

Mrs Pugsley made a few notes on the sheet of paper before her.

'Well,' she said, now slightly pink. 'Of course, if you have a smattering already it might be easier to recommend you.'

Audrey leaned back and looked Mrs Pugsley straight in the eye. '*La Recherche de l'absolu*,' she said.

'Yes, well, that's all, I think, for now.'

'Balzac,' said Audrey, and left.

2

Balm for the *Reject*

The child Apsu, daughter of immigrants, still living in impoverished circumstances, can walk now and express tactile and visual interest in the world about her. She likes the contrasts of hard and soft, scuffed and shiny, sharp and blunt, and she watches the way the people about her are with things—careful with knives, laughing with balloons, respectful of fire, pleasured by light. Her grandmother holds her and sings to her when she can, but little Apsu does not stay still for long. 'Ah, she is a bright one, that one,' says her grandmother, who knows about these things. 'Even if she is a girl.'

Somewhere around the time that Patrick's career began to take off, when he started to show just how full of bright ideas and innovative he was, and the Practice put his salary up so that other practices would not steal him away, Audrey travelled to Brighton to take her French examination. She was, if not the star of the course, certainly among its most dedicated. It was, she knew, the value of an otherwise empty life. And an angry one. Her engine was driven by both. When her mother told her that Peggy Boxer had lost the baby, Audrey just said, 'Good.' And that was all. She returned to her books and her verbs, the only sign of any inner activity being the tapping of her foot as she wrote. The word *reject* would come into her mind, no matter what she was doing, and she was determined, *determined* to erase it. A shocked Dolly had learned to keep her mouth shut.

Madame Minette, her evening class teacher, recognised the jilted woman in her pupil, and she felt, with a Frenchwoman's love of romance, that she should participate in the drama. She invited her pupil to her flat in Bayswater for extra lessons, free. Even the address made Audrey sigh. It was a far cry from the grubby bit of south London where she and her parents lived. Bayswater!

'You be careful,' said her mother, as if she was venturing to a foreign land.

At first they spoke only in French. Her teacher offered her a cup of coffee which she poured from a small metal jug into tiny white cups. No milk was offered, nor sugar. It was bitter as medicine but it smelled wonderful. Just for a moment, sitting there by the enormous floor-to-ceiling window, perched on a scuffed, gilded stool, Audrey felt she was taking part in a film, that this was a setting full of props, everything beautiful but somehow wrong. Later she was to learn that this was all that was left of Madame's family's château after it was looted and burnt in the war. She liked Madame more for it. She felt she had been consumed by fire, too.

On that first visit she was very nervous. She who had thought she was so Modern and sophisticated realised that she was not sophisticated at all. She and Patrick drank frothy coffee that tasted of nothing. This was the real thing, so real it burnt the back of your throat.

'Next time,' said Madame Minette, speaking in English again as her pupil was so jittery, 'next time we will have an Armagnac, too.' Audrey assumed she meant cake.

On her next visit Madame Minette held up, as if for applause rather than inspection, her Chanel suit. Audrey did not know what to say. It looked quite dull on its hanger. Black and white and bobbly instead of her favoured prints or pastels. Her teacher also dangled before her its matching bag. Too small to bother with, Audrey thought, but she smiled agreeably enough. It was all a bit of a mystery to her. But as Continental women knew—and as Madame Minette instructed her—one good stylish purchase made up for fifteen inferior and transient fashion items. There was simply nothing better for one's confidence—under the sun—than knowing you looked elegant. Audrey wanted to say that her French lessons had given her confidence but she was too polite. She was perfectly prepared to concede that this was small beer compared with looking good. Audrey wriggled into the tight checked skirt and buttoned the big, shiny buttons on the waist-cinching jacket.

Madame nodded and looked pleased. 'But, Audrey,' she said critically. 'You must lose no more weight. Or it will hang.'

Audrey nodded. The entire French lesson was given over to the dressing of Audrey.

'And you must have a hat. No chic woman can impress without a hat. It makes you hold your neck just so . . .'

Audrey said that it would have to be the headscarf. Madame Minette went rigid. 'You wish to look like your *Queen*?'

Personally Audrey could think of a lot worse and said so. The Queen, in her opinion, wore some lovely frocks. And be blowed to modernity.

There was a fairly hot debate between the two women—certainly very hot on Minette's side. 'You cannot, I will not allow it, she dresses either like a cake or a horse . . .'

'Oh, now—' began Audrey.

'And the only elegant members of your Royal Family you send to the devil. You throw away. The Windsors . . .'

Judging by the passion in the Frenchwoman's eyes, Audrey decided not to pursue it. So she shrugged. 'Well, I haven't got anything else and I can't go hatless.'

Minette's own hat had gone to be refashioned in Paris but she would not be gainsayed. She eyed the standing Audrey up and down, touched her lightly here and there to make her more straight of shoulder, more serpentine at the hip, and then said, 'My God—I see it—you are like your namesake.'

'Who?' said Audrey.

'The Hepburn . . .' said Minette, in a voice of wonder. 'In which case—it is easy—you will wear a little black beret.'

'A beret?' said Audrey horrified. 'But I'll look like a schoolgirl. Or a French onion seller.' She remembered something else, something painfully connected with Patrick. 'Or Picasso.'

But the woman had already hurried away to the rear of her flat, returning with a black beret which she placed on Audrey's head.

'It is a shame about the hair which is not *elfine*—but—oh, my dear—' Minette held her at arm's length and smiled at her—'the only schoolgirl you could possibly resemble would be a sly one—and you certainly could never look like an onion seller in a million years. And as for Picasso?' She led her to the full-length mirror in the hall. 'The only connection with him—if he met you now—is that he would want to eat you . . .'

It was a very great shock to Audrey—weaned as she had been on sensible cardigans and pleated skirts and nice fresh shirtwaisters for the summer, and then turned by Patrick into some kind of waking vampire—to behold herself transformed into a long, thin, elegant, *dangerous*-looking Frenchwoman. How had this happened? Where were the heavy thighs, the solid calves, the heavy, rounded shoulders that she used to press against Patrick to arouse him? Even her breasts had nearly disappeared. 'Oh *blimey* . . .' she said, in a that's-torn-it voice. For this was what the pain of lost love had produced. She had been whittled away by it and never noticed, whittled away to a *gamine* young woman with eyes too big for the smallness of her face and elbows sharp as gimlets as she rested her hands on her bony hips. She would never be Little Audrey with the statuesque curves ever again. So this is me, she thought. Let's see what this new me can do.

She thanked Madame Minette for the loan of the clothes and promised to bring her back a stick of Brighton rock. Madame Minette pulled a face. 'Non,' she said, just like de Gaulle. 'Non, non, non . . .' The English were really absurd if you thought about it. Seaside rock was, actually, quite horrible. Audrey laughed. Then, with Madame's '*Bonne chance*' in her ears and butterflies in every other part of her, she left the apartment. On the way home she realised that they had not gone over any

285

of the vocabulary she had prepared. And now she was just too elated, too tired.

In her bedroom she pushed the cardboard box and its expensive contents safely under the bed, where she lay, wide awake all night, worrying that the bed would collapse upon it. She was in a twin state of excitement—first for the effect her new self might have on the world, second for the examination. But it was the first which, as the French would say, called up her *passion* . . .

Somewhere, perhaps, the Goddess of Bluestockings, bored out of her skull with it all, went to sleep. Because Audrey never did sit the examination. Having not slept a wink all night she finally fell asleep about an hour before she was due to get up. Which meant that she was late for everything. Late for the Northern line to take her to Embankment, late for the District line to take her to Victoria. Which put her in a rebellious frame of mind. Why did they make you go to Brighton? What was all the fuss about? Why not just give her the job and try her out? And did she want the stinking old job anyway—all those old biddies in cardigans still talking about the war while they made foreign connections for other people and never wanted to travel themselves.

As she tip-tapped her kitten-heeled way along the platform unable to take anything but the smallest of steps due to the tightness of the skirt—the train whistle blew. So far she had not passed one carriage with a spare seat, except the first-class carriages of course. When the whistle blew again she hopped on and began the slow, pushing, prodding journey back along corridor after corridor of the crowded second class to arrive, eventually, breathless and pink of cheek, at yet more first class. Just as she was about to turn away a guard sprang to attention and slid open a carriage door for her.

'Madam,' he said, and saluted.

In she went.

So that was what happened? She might not be dressed like an over-iced cake or a horse but she knew how to borrow a gesture. She gave a little queenly movement of her hand, and settled herself elegantly into the corner by the window. The guard saluted again, and slid the door shut very smartly. She crossed her legs and gazed, from beneath her jaunty little beret, across to the carriage's only other occupant—a man already busy at his papers, his brown leather briefcase flapped open on the seat next to him and his fountain pen in his hand. He was much absorbed.

He wore a dark suit, and white shirt, a slate-blue silk tie and his thinning hair was dark grey. His shoes were black and very well polished and on one finger he wore a black and gold signet ring with an E. She took all this in and as she stared, he suddenly looked up. He raised an eyebrow. Then he smiled. And there was no doubt about it, it was an appreciative smile.

'Good morning,' he said.

And Audrey, completely taken up with her new role in life, said, 'Bonjour.'

To which he smiled broadly and said, '*Je suis ravi de recontrer une charmante bilingue . . .*'

She then looked down at her hands and went a very delicate shade of pink as she answered. '*Merci, je suis flattée, mais je ne pense pas parlez assez bien français pour mériter ce compliment.*'

After which there was no stopping them. The fountain pen was laid aside, the briefcase flap was closed, and the *charmante bilingue* and the one who was charmed by her, leaned back in their seats and talked. In French. 'If only Patrick could see me now . . .' she thought.

*   *   *

The man's name was Edwin Bonnard and he was In Business. *Les investissements.* He worked in Paris where he had his own offices but he had many British connections. His mother was English and lived as a semi-invalid in a home near Brighton, his father was French, thought he was Maurice Chevalier, and lived dangerously in Nice, Biarritz, Paris and—occasionally—since it was the home of the family château—in Perpignan. Obviously Edwin Bonnard was travelling down to see his mother who liked to lunch at the Metropole but he was also interested in buying an apartment on the seafront to save himself the tedium of staying in an hotel on these visits. He was married with two children, both at the Sorbonne.

And the elegant linguist?

The elegant linguist—working on an instinct that told her not to speak about Patrick nor about her mother and father and, still reeling mentally from his easy use of the word *château*, not about her humble home either—brought herself back to the realms of reality and explained that she was sitting an examination in French—and why. She felt that to mention the telephone exchange was acceptable. It was, after all, her job—and a very decent one.

He put up his hands in horror at the very idea of

the elegant linguist having to do such a thing as sit an examination. He said that her grammar and her pronunciation were impeccable. She explained that unless she passed such an examination she could not further her career on the—she hesitated, aware suddenly that perhaps after all a telephone exchange did not go well with a Chanel suit— business side of things. She managed a little shrug which she felt was quite French and which she hoped embraced the world at large.

The man listened intently, raising an eyebrow here, giving a little sympathetic cluck there, smiling all the time. As they came nearer to their destination he gave a little start as if he had just remembered something, slapped the flat of his palm on his knee, and said, as if he had made up his mind, that he himself was looking for an assistant in his Paris office. Might she consider the position?

The elegant linguist became, frankly, neither. Her mouth was open in quite a large O—and words— English or foreign—would not come. Breathe—she reminded herself—and just about managed it. She distinctly heard her mother's voice saying 'White Slave Trade' but decided that if it *was* such a thing, at least it was exciting. Better than sitting at home and moping and forever thinking of Patrick. She put her chin on her gloved hand, her head on one side, and listened hard.

It seemed, according to Mr Edwin Bonnard, that there was nothing much to being a personal assistant. She would have to make sure his diary was kept up to date, know how to answer the telephone (they both laughed at the absurdity of this and Audrey said, with spirit, that she jolly well

289

ought to) and get him to the places he was required to attend, on time. She would have to buy gifts on the right dates, and send greeting and thanks and all that kind of social thing that women were so good at. Audrey looked at him doubtfully. Then she thought of Patrick. Always when she thought of him the word *reject* floated into her head and made her tap her toes nervously. *Reject, reject.* But she need not be. She could do this job. After all, she had done all those things for Patrick—once. Remembered when it was his mother's birthday, when the film started, when he should return his library books. Not hard at all. She enjoyed being useful. So she said she would think about it, which—they both understood—meant Yes. Then, buoyed up, Audrey asked Mr Edwin Bonnard (Edwin, please) if he was related to the painter, Pierre Bonnard. She did not say that she had heard of him because she had once had a boyfriend who took her to see some of his work. She just let it trip off her tongue as if the question were entirely her own.

Mr Edwin Bonnard raised an impressed eyebrow this time and smiled. He was very distantly related to the painter but, alas, he had only one small pastel by him, a smaller version of the famous *Woman and Dog*. Audrey nodded. She remembered it from Patrick's books and she liked it. But when Edwin started to talk about Bonnard's intimate depictions of the Bourgeois, Audrey nervously changed the subject. Patrick used the word Bourgeois a lot too, and she did not want to think about that side of things. Being Bourgeois was not a good thing. And she had a nasty feeling she still was. Whatever the opposite of it, it

290

seemed to Audrey it was largely to do with taking off your clothes and laughing at people who kept theirs on. The Bonnard pictures Patrick showed her seemed like pictures of her parents and their friends and their ordinary homes. Not the proper kind of subjects for art—not like the Elgin Marbles or Leonardo. Patrick used to say these paintings were like bridges—their strength being as much to do with what was hidden as what was shown. Patrick.

To change the subject she asked Edwin about the apartment he was considering buying and she was thinking how lovely it would be to have somewhere of her own to live. A little bedroom, a little separate room, maybe, to eat and read in, a kitchen, didn't matter how small, and—impossible dream—a bathroom of her own. The sort of place she once dreamed of sharing with Patrick. She imagined the bed, large and lacy, like Lucille Ball's, but it turned into something small and familiar, Patrick's, and she remembered the last time she saw him. It still hurt and she was still his *reject*.

Edwin suggested that better than describing the apartment, and since he had about three quarters of an hour before he was due to meet his mother's car, perhaps she would accompany him to see it? And they could talk on the way about Paris? He was entirely serious in his offer. It was clear from the way he looked at her that he knew the truth. If she went with him now she would miss her examination. Her heart thudded. She experienced a very peculiar mixture of feelings—fear, excitement, joy—and something else that felt like surrender. She was weary, suddenly, of her old ways. Weary of living a life that looked like a

Bonnard painting. Her mother would sit in her kitchen chair by the fire most evenings, and knit. Then, after tea, Dad and she watched a bit of television. Quite contentedly. But just occasionally Dolly would look up at nothing in particular and smack her lips and say to no one in particular, 'I fancy a little bit of something and I don't know what . . .' And that was exactly how Audrey felt. She wanted a bit of something and she didn't know what. Maybe what she wanted was a bit of the White Slave Trade? She nodded, and agreed, she would like to see the apartment very much.

There was nothing unseemly about the visit. Not the slightest hint of The Sheikh. She felt slightly disappointed. A little bit of her thought that it would be quite exciting to be made to lie in silken sheets and eat oranges (if that is what they did)—to have her clothes ripped off and be given spangled see-through bloomers and a sequinned bolero in their place. Fairy stories. Fantasy Land. She knew all about living in those. So she said yes in her heart. What did she have to lose?

'It will be better,' he said, 'when we get rid of all these mouldings and cornices and ornamental claptrap . . .' Audrey felt warmed by the way he said 'we'.

'What do you think I should do with these windows?' he asked. She walked over to them. They reminded her of Madame Minette's floor-to-ceiling windows, only there were many more of them. At the moment they were swathed in heavy, shiny, patterned curtains, as complex as a dowager's dance frock. She thought that she could never live where there were little square windows ever again. She studied them critically and remembered Patrick. Patrick had always wanted shutters and blinds at his windows. 'Shutters,' she said, 'and plain white blinds.'

'Bravo!' said Edwin, clapping.

The estate agent looked horrified. 'The apartment is sold with the curtaining,' he reminded his client.

Edwin dismissed this with a wave of his hand.

He told the estate agent he would take the place and he told Audrey, as they strolled back towards the Metropole, with Edwin holding her hand through the crook of his arm, which felt very pleasant because she trusted him now, that she was *just* the sort of thing he needed to bounce his ideas off. Audrey said, Oh Yes, because, of course, she had been used to that with Patrick. And then she could not help adding, 'But what a shame to waste all that curtaining.'

Then Edwin laughed a delighted laugh and stopped and looked at the sea, still holding her hand in the warmth of his arm. 'What would you do with them if I gave them to you?' he asked.

She said, 'I could make a dress. Well—I could make two dresses really.'

'Then they shall be yours.'

He put his briefcase down on the steps of the hotel and held on to both her hands. 'I will see you back here at five,' he said. He looked anxious. 'And if you get lost you must take a taxi and I will pay.' It was almost worth getting lost for but she had no intention of going very far. Supposing he wasn't there, supposing something had happened and he had gone back to London early, she would have to pay the fare herself and that would be the last of her wages for the week.

'I think I shall go and look round the Pavilion. That'll do me.'

'I am so sorry,' he said, 'that I cannot buy you lunch.' He shrugged. The shrug said, 'Mothers'.

'That's all right,' she said. 'And I hope your mother enjoys herself.'

*   *   *

She was still in a state of shock when she walked back later to meet him. She took it very slowly because she was so early, the last hour of the afternoon having dragged almost unbearably. She wanted to be in France, *now*. She walked back in the lowering light, with the waves gently breaking, the seagulls making their last screeches of the day and the streets bustling with people going home from their work. She felt very happy and not at all guilty at having missed the exam. Indeed, she felt happier than she had felt for years, despite the ache in her heart that was Patrick. How he would have hated the Pavilion. More than anything, she realised, as she walked slowly back, she wanted to stop seeing the world through Patrick's eyes.

They re-met at five. Edwin took her hand and put it in the crook of his arm again and led her up the steps and into the big hotel. It looked very peaceful as well as grand, she thought, after the glaring excesses of the Pavilion. Edwin asked her what she thought of it and she said that, on the whole, she preferred somewhere like this to that.

'I looked at each and every thing that was on show,' she said thoughtfully, 'and I wouldn't have wanted any of it.'

That pleased him. He told her that everything

294

glorious and visionary stopped with the reign of Charles II. Yet another bell rang in her head. 'He liked Rubens, didn't he?' she said (Patrick liked Rubens)—she had tried to like all those fat women but they looked ill to her—very flushed . . . 'No,' said Edwin. 'That was his father.'

'Oh yes,' she said. 'Now I remember. Charles II was *Wren* . . .'

He looked at her in some surprise.

'I'd like to go to Paris,' she said. 'They were Heroic builders, the French. They invited Bernini to build for them, you know.' If she said this slightly parrot fashion he did not seem to notice. 'But though he came and designed a new bit for the Louvre they never used it. But Wren was there in about sixteen-sixty-nine and he saw the plans and he said that the Parisian School of Architecture was probably the best of his day . . .'

'You have a knowledge of such things?' said Edwin.

She liked the fact that he was surprised. 'I helped someone through their history of architecture exam once,' she said in such a way that no further comment was required.

Edwin just said, 'Oh.'

They drank a cocktail in the hotel bar before he deposited her back on a train, with his card firmly pushed into her little Chanel bag, and her own telephone number and address pushed firmly into his wallet. And home she went to tell mother.

Mother, who up until now had thought this French thing was just a bit of a way to get over the miseries, was distraught. 'You can't go to *Paris*,' she said, horrified and very firm about it.

'Why not?' asked Audrey, serpentining her hips

295

like crazy and pointing out one toe.

'He's a stranger. You'll never be heard of again.'

'He's a very respectable man. He's married with two children at university and he needs a bilingual personal assistant.'

'It will do you no good in the end,' said her mother.

'Why?'

'Because you've got to think about the future.'

Audrey looked puzzled. 'But that's exactly what I am doing,' she said. She changed hips and pointed her other toe. She was beginning to feel a new sensation as if she had actually grown a few inches. 'What's the point of speaking French in London?' she asked. 'Mother—it is a good job.'

'What will people think?' asked Dolly, lost for anything else to say.

Audrey re-angled the beret a little more jauntily, staring into the mirror over the hearth.

'Let them eat cake,' she said.

Her mother stared at her blankly. 'And what on earth has cake got to do with anything? You can't even bake a decent sponge.'

Audrey did not look at her, happily posing and posturing in front of the mirror, like a girl who was not to be pitied.

'And get that suit back to your teacher before you singe it,' added her mother, feeling that somehow, in some indefinable way, it was the suit's fault.

When all else failed Mrs Wapshott invoked her husband. 'We'll see what your father has to say about this,' she said grimly. But Audrey was unconcerned. 'I'm over twenty-one,' she said, and, she thought, I am Audrey Hepburn.

She handed her mother his card. 'You or Dad can

ring him up and talk to him if you like.'

But neither had the courage.

When the parcel arrived Audrey and her mother put it on the kitchen table and circled around it for at least five minutes—prodding and poking and lifting flaps of brown paper, until Mr Wapshott came in and told them not to be so daft and to get on with it. Audrey found the sewing scissors and her mother cut the string. The parcel was addressed to Audrey but that made no difference, Mrs Wapshott pulled the packing apart. By the time she reached the tissue level, Audrey realised what it was. She began to laugh, a forgotten sound. And a frisson of something called courage, confidence, certainty entered her. He had kept his promise—even in this small, humorous action, he had remembered what he said and stood by it. He had sent her the curtains from the Brighton apartment. He could be trusted.

'I think Mr Bonnard will make a very good boss,' said Audrey. 'And I'm going to Paris whether you like it or not.' She gave a little swivel on her perfectly turned heel, and added, *'Tout de suite.'*

3

A Lesson in Poetry

Now Apsu is no longer in her parents' bed. She has a brother who has taken her place. Now she lies in her own cot and has time to investigate the many variations of texture and shape that surround her. Also the way light plays on the bars of the cot and how it is held together. Sometimes she stands with her hands gripping the rail and she bounces up and down on the plastic-covered mattress, watching the bolts jump and rattle. Her grandmother peels her an apple and keeps the peel whole. She says that little Apsu will see her future husband's initial letter in the shape it is when it falls to the floor. Apsu takes the fallen peel and builds with it, enclosing space, making walls, making bridges. Her grandmother smiles, not knowing what the child thinks about but pleased to see her so happy and absorbed.

At approximately the same time, Audrey, much amused, much excited, took the curtaining from the dreary Wapshott kitchen into the exotic space of Minette's apartment. The sewing machine came out, scissors flashed, fingers flew, fabric took shape. It was like starring in a *Let's Do It Here* film and she had seen enough of those, and dreamed enough, to be happily absorbed.

*   *   *

Edwin Bonnard telephoned, spoke to her parents, told her the arrangements. He would meet her at the airport. Later he sent her a letter confirming her employment and enclosing her ticket. 'One way,' said Dolly sadly.

Audrey cried a little too, but whether with sadness or excitement she wasn't exactly sure. Here was something of her own at last. She was going to make her own place in the world. And bloody well bugger Patrick.

*   *   *

The dresses were finished. It was a joke, of course, but it was a seductive one. For the cocktail dress, Minette's use of the plum-coloured braid, scooped to follow the lines of Audrey's bosom, was shocking and chic. Audrey laughed when she tried it on. It was a far cry from Patrick's black on black. It was also a far cry from Wapshott parental approval. They did not laugh at all. When Audrey modelled the off-the-shoulder, tight-bodiced, straight-skirted dress of a dress, Mr Wapshott asked where the rest of it was. Her mother shook her head. But when she slipped on the little suit, with its neat jacket and short—well above the knee—skirt, neither parent had even the breath for a quip.

'You can't go out with your legs showing like that,' said Mrs Wapshott. But Audrey did. All the way to the airport, and all the way on the aeroplane to Paris. She felt liberated. And she began to like the way men looked at her. From behind newspapers, from corner seats, they stared. She crossed her legs. Let them, she thought. What harm does it do?

The only drawback was that Patrick was not here to see her Triumph. He, apparently, and according to Florence (who could scarcely be trusted) was having many a Triumph of his own at some wonderful job in the City of London. The news was passed on to Dolly (who nearly broke off speaking terms again when she heard it) and thus passed on to Audrey, who had a little cry. So . . . Now she was flying off, leaving London behind, glad to be far away. And it was real. She could see it was real by the dwindling fields and the retreating cliffs of the English seaside. It was a real fairy tale. Certainly that was what the girls at the Exchange said about it. You meet a man on a train and you end up in Paris? That's called dreams come true. Even if what caused it to happen in the first place was not very nice.

Man Trouble—she heard her mother using the term to a neighbour as if it was a disease she, Audrey, had contracted wilfully—well she supposed that was the reason—Man Trouble—it sounded right for the times. The sort of thing the New Young Woman had—Man Trouble. It was a good deal more promising than a Broken Heart. 'Sex and the Single Girl' was a phrase being whispered among the more forward of the girls at the Exchange. Man Trouble sounded as if it went with that. If Edwin ever asked her why she was so happy to leave England, that is what she would tell him. Man Trouble. It sounded cool and it went with the kind of clothes she wore now.

With only the grey English Channel churning away beneath her she breathed a sigh of contentment. Fussy and stuffy old England, she thought. Never again. Begone, Bourgeois

Sentiment. Oh, Patrick. Somehow she had to learn to live with the fact that he was still in her head.

*   *   *

Years later, when Edwin and Audrey were in Brussels looking for a new apartment for his business trips, and they viewed a place with similar windows and curtains to the Brighton apartment, she reminded him of that first meeting, on the Brighton Line, and how naive she had been. And he reminded her how he thought, as he looked across at her in that airless little carriage, that she had tumbled out of the sky with her Parisian chic and her English blushes and the very definite air of virginity that hung about her.

'Hmm,' she said, addressing the Brussels curtains. 'The air of virginity didn't last very long . . . How right Minette was to put me in those clothes.' And she wondered, as she said it, *Was she?*

Audrey never told Edwin that her seduction was, in the event, rather a relief. It followed on very swiftly from the airport meeting and confirmed what Minette had already told her. 'This man is half French,' she said with a shrug. 'He may wish you to work for him, but he will also wish you to sleep with him.' Audrey thought about this. It was probably true. She hoped it was true. In fact, if she thought about it, it would be something of a blow if it were not true . . . A view of Man Trouble in the new magazine world was that as one Man went out of the door, another Man came in through the window. She had waited far too long to replace Patrick. No one had come close. Insurance salesmen, electricians, bank clerks—how could she

301

be interested in the likes of them? How to admire them after Patrick? No: Edwin—if he wanted her—would be perfect. Mr Perfect, her Prince, if a little older than in the fairy tales, had come along.

*   *   *

She daydreamed on the plane. First of all he would sleep with her and later he would divorce his wife and marry her. That is what she thought would happen. As they made their way to the hotel restaurant (it was too late to go to her apartment and she would see it in the morning) that first evening, he told her with grave sorrow that his wife did not understand him. To which she nodded consolingly, feeling immensely grown-up to be given such a confidence. Yes, she felt sure, he would divorce his wife eventually. Madame Bonnard she would eventually be. She would seek out Patrick somehow and show the elegant Monsieur Bonnard off. Then wouldn't he be sorry and too, too late . . .

On that first evening, at dinner, Edwin presented her with a ring set with a large turquoise. 'The joyous colour of sun and sea,' he said. 'And the way you make me feel every time I look at you.' She accepted it, put it on, admired it and was pleased. Which meant that when it was perfectly clear, about halfway through the next course, that Edwin wanted—indeed expected—to spend the night with her, she accepted his proposal. It was definitely a step in the right direction. And the Modern way. Whatever Patrick used to say about the Bourgeoisie and marriage, in the end he had gone and tied the knot with Peggy Boxer. As Was. So why shouldn't she? So much for *his* avant garde principles. He had changed from being a man with a room and a Bauhaus poster and plain white blinds, to a man with a wife (and no baby, she was pleased to recall) and a house with orange curtains and a neat garden held behind a privet hedge. She knew this because—not long before she left for Paris—she took the bus to the neighbourhood and crept past the house one night, and though it was small, from what she could see through the gaps at the window, it was a definite home. She could even hear music. He played the same for Peggy as he had once done for her. *The Reject*. She crept away.

Edwin told her many years later that if she had not let him seduce her that night, or at least, if she had not shown signs that she might soon agree, he would have packed her back off to London in a day or two. 'Just as well that I did then,' she said to him crisply. 'For both of us.' But back then it had all been romance. She could still picture the hotel room high up above the Champs-Élysées and the feeling that she was in a fairy tale. Patrick and all the pain of him—that disease called Man Trouble—felt as if it rolled off her shoulders once she lay down with Edwin. It was that simple.

With the early spring trees blowing in the breeze and the moonlight falling sharply across the bed, Edwin settled her back on the pillows, rested his head on one hand, played with her body with his free hand so that she could barely concentrate on what he was saying, and told her—very nicely, very softly, but very firmly—that if she expected him to divorce his wife, he would not. But that if she expected him to love and cherish her—he would do so. He was quite matter of fact and she found that she was without embarrassment. It was just as if he was setting out her terms of employment. Which, of course, he was. She saw nothing immoral about it all because she did not believe a word of it. Not really. Not when they were like this. She smiled amenably, obligingly had her first orgasm and thought she was having a fit. 'This,' he said, 'is our first priority. Then we learn the rest.'

* * *

Waking with Edwin in the morning, the memory of Patrick, the weight of him, was indeed rolled away, like an immense rock being lifted from her shoulders. She kept this to herself. An ancient wisdom ran through her veins, a sudden understanding that honesty, in matters of the bedroom if not the heart, was best left unpursued. When he said he must go and that he would be back soon, she waved him away lightly. Who would have guessed that she had ice in her stomach in case she had not passed the test and he never returned?

But he did return. And she was still asleep. He called it the sleep of youth. They left the hotel and walked. Edwin explained that she would have an apartment nearby, that she would be known as his personal assistant, and that she would have a salary . . . Not wages, then? Her mother had specifically asked her to find out what the francs were in pounds, and how the annual sum translated into wages. It would be very grand to say that she was paid monthly and into her own bank account. For this salary she would have to do very little—there would be occasional entertaining and she would

304

keep two diaries for him—the official diary and the other one—but her real job was to keep Edwin happy in her company, in all respects. She must consider the apartment her home and if she wished to change it in any way, she could. He then gestured. They had walked around the block in a large circle and ended up near the hotel. They were standing at the foot of some white steps. He pushed open the double doors, they ascended in a lift, and they arrived at her new home. If what went before seemed a fairy tale, this was the end of the rainbow. What more, what more could she possibly wish for?

Here was the room to sit in, the room to sleep in (though the bed was wide, very wide, knocked Patrick's skinny little thing into the shade), the little kitchen and—considerably bigger than the kitchen—a bathroom. All to herself. It really was like the films. With a shower thing and what he later showed her how to use and to call a bidet. Things like these her mother could only dream of (they still had a gas geyser and the bath enamel had long seen better days). If she had a fleeting sense of loss—a sense of disappointment—a sense that she had thought herself to be so clever to have landed a real job—she brushed it away in the magic of having all this. She said, daring herself, '*Prenez-vous de relations sexuelles?*' Just to remind herself how clever she had once been with languages. He laughed. But he also said, afterwards, that he would like it if they could speak English together. She would have plenty of opportunity to speak French with other people. Which subdued her a little.

Gradually, throughout the day, in bed and out of it, Edwin explained the pattern of her future. He would pay the rent, just as he would pay the bills, and he would expect loyalty and sole ownership of her, just as if they were man and wife. She would have some work to do—she would be expected to keep herself looking fashionable and she would be expected to learn about the things that interested him—just as he would (and here his hand became unbearable) just as he would be sure to find out what she liked and provide it for her. It was her duty, like any good wife, to enjoy herself to her fullest capacity. Could she do this? She found that she could.

There would be small parties for his friends and a few formal functions to attend with him. She would learn which occasions were for him and his wife, and which occasions were for him and his mistress. Her. The learning process would take about six months and she would have an old friend of his, Madame Hélène, to help her. Hélène knew everything. It was the way in France and no one thought any the worse of it. Her role would be well understood. She could ask him anything, anything at all, and he would help her. Then he gave her that reassuring smile of his. He did not expect any of this to begin overnight and there would, of course, be a settling-in period. Just like a job.

'Since we met,' he said, 'I have been very happy thinking about you—the way you are now—and as you will be in a few months' time. You will learn quickly and we will be very happy together.'

She then felt what she could only liken to an earthquake in her body—another kind of fit—which was clearly the Greater Things to Come. It seemed she was quite capable of doing her duty extremely well. Nothing like that had ever happened with Patrick. She also kept that thought to herself. A maturer sense was already weaving around her and she realised that it was not a good idea to mention a past lover to a present one. Patrick was not of interest to Edwin and she hoped that soon, sooner than soon, he would not be of interest to her either.

She did ask him about his wife. 'Doesn't she mind?' she asked.

'My wife will not interfere,' he said. 'It is always discreetly arranged.'

'Always?' she asked. 'I am not the first?

'You will find,' he said, shaking his head, 'that it is sensible not to ask too many questions. The answers will not always suit.' He touched her beneath her eyes, where an unexpected tear had formed. It was not jealousy, nor was it sadness, it was that she no longer felt quite so special. Not quite the fairytale princess any more.

'But as far as I am concerned, if you will stay, and be a good girl, then you will be the last. I make you that promise. I am forty-seven—and I think we will make good harmony and you will see me out.'

Years later, remembering that moment, she wondered how she could possibly have let him say such a thing without popping him one.

Arithmetic was never her strength. Patrick always told her how good and logical figures were, but she never thought so. It did not occur to her, now, to do the sums and wonder what would be left for her when she had Seen Him Out. For heaven's sake— she was in an apartment high up over the city of Paris—looking down on people for a change, and with a man (so what that he was old?) who loved her. Patrick was gone, banished. She silently sent

307

that message across the seas to him. Patrick. And turned her face and her fortune resolutely towards Edwin.

*   *   *

'Do you know Robert Browning's work?' he asked as he dressed.

She did not. She kept silent. He could be anything.

'A poet. Let me quote a favourite piece of his poetry. It's the Duke of Ferrara speaking to the agent of the father of his proposed new bride.' She stretched herself and smiled. A little confusing, but she was sure it would be lovely. He began,

> That's my last Duchess painted on the wall,
> Looking as if she was alive . . .

He quoted the whole thing without stumbling once, though he paused a long time at the lines.

> . . . She had
> A heart . . . how shall I say? . . . too soon
>   made glad,
> Too easily impressed; she liked whate'er
> She looked on, and her looks went
> everywhere.
> Sir, 'twas all one . . .

After Patrick's pleasure in something called Concrete Poetry—'where the form, Audrey, begins by being aware of the graphic space as structural agent'—which she found unfathomable stuff, written by people with peculiar names that sounded like illnesses—Arp, Schwitters, Klee, Malevich—and which you never knew if he was stumbling over or not because none of it made any sense . . . after that she found the lines quoted by Edwin pleasantly straightforward, even if he did read them in the kind of voice that made her shiver.

> . . . Oh, Sir, she smiled, no doubt,
> Whene'er I passed her; but who passed without
> Much the same smile? This grew; I gave commands;
> Then all smiles stopped together. There she stands
> As if alive . . .

'Lovely,' she said. 'Sad. And very romantic. He missed her very much, the Duke.'

Edwin gave her a look quite similar to the looks Patrick gave her from time to time—usually followed by the word 'Daft'.

Oh well, she thought, what is wrong with liking things to do with romance and love? *What?*

When he had gone she hung the now crumpled chintz suit in the wardrobe, where it swung self-consciously in all that empty space, and she unpacked her bags and hung up the rest of her clothes, which looked even more out of place—except for the cocktail frock. The bathroom with its extraordinary appliances did not welcome her little red plastic washbag, and the cream button-up-the-front nightie looked quite affronted as she put it over the end of the bed. Nevertheless she understood now that she was in Paris, that she was out of her depth, that she just looked wrong, and that this would change if she was—as Edwin had asked her to be—amenable—*raisonnable*. She had a strong, oh so strong, urge to ring her mother and tell her about it all—but of course she could not. She could tell no one about all—or any—of it. If she rang her mother she would want to know how her first day in her new job had been. Audrey looked down at the rumpled linen and smiled, wryly. She would also start suggesting things like a nice serviceable pleated skirt and a plain, navy jumper and asking her if the rooms were clean and if she was being a good girl.

*   *   *

Madame Hélène was at least as old as Edwin, tall and stick-thin, a bit like the Duchess of Windsor. 'She would be flattered,' said an amused Edwin. She arrived the following morning and said that they had a bargain—if Audrey would speak English with her—she would help Audrey become French. She seemed to know her way around the apartment very well and, after her inspection, suggested that if Audrey found anything inconvenient she should let the concierge know and the concierge would pass it on to the correct individual. Everything was quite calm until Madame Hélène opened the doors of Audrey's wardrobe. Whereupon she shrieked. She clawed at all the clothes, including the wonderful cocktail dress, and threw them in a heap on the floor. 'You are from London?' she said, frowning.

Audrey wondered what on earth she had done. 'Yes,' she said, cautiously.

Madame Hélène's English was extremely good.

310

'They are saying that London is the epicentre of style—it is reported so in *Paris Match*—yet I look at this and I am astonished, amazed—Mademoiselle Audrey I am—I am—'

Audrey looked down at the crumpled clothing. Some of her favourite items—her black toreador pants, her big, comforting, floppy jumpers, her chiffon-sleeved dress for special occasions. All lying there, defeated somehow. Ashamed of themselves. She was near to tears suddenly. It was as if she was seeing her very self discarded. But she swallowed hard. And she straightened her back. She had made this bed for herself and she must lie in it.

'Madame,' she said. 'Edwin has left me some money. He said I should trust you. I do trust you. And I am in your hands.'

Madame Hélène beamed at her and nodded. As much as a stick insect can beam. It seemed that with Madame Hélène it was money that talked.

4

Odalisque

While Audrey pirouetted in front of her mirror or sat out on her balcony reading her books on etiquette and learning to live the life of a *jolie mademoiselle*, the child Apsu began attending her first school. She showed an extraordinary gift for drawing. At five years old she could copy a picture from a story book and had an understanding of perspective that was quite beyond her years. Her parents nodded when they were told. Of course their little Apsu was a good girl. And clever. She had gifts, of course. And their son, they knew, would be just the same. But they were liberal in their outlook. Apsu would be educated just as her brother would be educated. She could go to the good state school nearby and receive a good education there. This could be done because the school was only for girls. The teacher emphasised that Apsu was special, gifted. The parents nodded again. Of course, of course, and beautiful too . . .

Audrey was quite used to her duties. Learning what the man in her life wanted her to learn. Same ethos, different man. Not hard to adapt if you were prepared to be amenable. And bright. She had her appearance organised again—but this time by Hélène. She had her cultural interests and her views on the world sorted out again—by Edwin.

312

She went to the right art exhibitions, shopped in the right shops, heard the right music and read the right books so that she could converse quite satisfactorily at dinner when required. Of course she was very good at it, very quick, for she had done it once already. Only this time, luckily, her mentor was kinder.

Sometimes at night Paris seemed a disturbed city. She would hear police cars, shouting, screams and if she looked down from her balcony she would see—usually—young men, dark, being beaten or kicked or bundled into police vans. No one seemed to do anything—except the odd passer-by who shook their fist or shouted. Once or twice when they were driving through the city she saw similar ugly scenes during the daytime.

'Why are they hitting those people?' she asked. 'Who are they?'

'Probably the rump of the Front de Libération Nationale—Algerians.'

'What have they done?'

'We have just given them their independence. Now they want revenge . . .'

'Why?'

'Because we were not—very—kind.'

She shivered. 'In what way—'

'Enough,' he said. 'Politics is a dirty, trying business. Best left.'

'My mother always said it was best left to my father.'

'Well,' said Edwin, 'there you are then.'

He gave her a little squeeze, as if to reassure her, and no more was said. Within a few months the incidents died away and her sleep was no longer disturbed.

313

The standard joke among Edwin and his friends (most of whom had mistresses or—shockingly— beautiful young men) was that whereas the Englishman required of his mistress all the subtlety of Barbara Windsor and Diana Dors, the Frenchman wanted something between de Beauvoir and Jeanne Moreau—with a sprinkling of Lesley Caron. Someone you could read Proust to afterwards, went the joke. There was a flaw in this argument, though Audrey did not yet see it. At least half of the mistresses she met were English— and not given to reading anything much. They were good at cards, and some enjoyed needlework and knitting (which they hid when their Masters were in town) and doing beauty things. If they thought about Proust at all, they tended to call him Prowst. Audrey only knew that was wrong because she listened carefully to Edwin and his friends. At least, thanks to Patrick, she knew that Genet was not pronounced Jeannette. But who cared? 'We give them cachet,' said one giggling girl from Broadstairs. 'And they give us cadeaux. Fair enough.' Nobody spoke of love and marriage and Audrey kept quiet.

A few years later, and a little less naive, when she and Edwin went to a Delacroix exhibition, there they were, *The Women of Algiers*, Odalisques, lying around looking beautiful, luscious and bored out of their skulls. It had the ring of authenticity. She kept that thought to herself, too. Edwin gazed at it for a full five minutes before moving on to *Liberty Leading the People*. 'Ah,' he said enraptured.

314

'One of my favourites—the greatest propaganda painting of all time.' Liberty, she was interested to see, was shown as a woman.

*   *   *

On one of her morning visits Madame Hélène brought with her a doctor, Dr Claude, who examined her and pronounced that she was healthy.

'Well I knew that!' said Audrey, feeling a little cross at not being consulted. 'Of course I'm healthy.'

Madame Hélène laughed. 'You really are quite, quite innocent, are you not?'

At the very beginning of their understanding, Edwin told her that there were to be no children. Since she had grown up with the knowledge that children, if you were not married, were a bad thing, the undertaking was not at all difficult.

Thus, along with the vitamin supplements and the light-dose sleeping pills that Doctor Claude gave her (at night she was sometimes restless—especially if she had seen no one all day), there were six small foil packets containing little pink pills in individual slots. She asked Madame what they were for.

Madame winked. 'You must take one of these every day at the same time,' she said, 'and you will not become *enceinte*.'

'Good,' said Audrey. 'What's in them?'

'Magic,' laughed Madame.

'No, I mean how do you stop a baby with a pill?'

Again she gave that French shrug. 'How should I know? Just be grateful that Monsieur Edwin is

315

a Protestant.'

*   *   *

Dolly buried the hatchet enough to go up and stay with Florence where they both sat on opposite sides of Florence's fire and talked about the great achievements of their respective children. Neither listened to the other very much. Afterwards Dolly passed on snippets of news to Audrey—Patrick now drove a Jaguar car, was tipped for a partnership and was the youngest architect to run a full team, Peggy still hadn't fallen again, Florence never seemed to see them nowadays . . . Audrey showed little enthusiasm for these nuggets. Florence passed on almost nothing at all to Patrick, largely because she had no opportunity. She was still waiting for a reply to her letter of two months ago and though the telephone was there she did not see why she should be the first to use it. It was all Peggy Boxer As Was's fault, of course. Her who couldn't even hold a baby.

Part of the reason that Audrey did not return to London for several years was fear of discovery— and guilt. As time went on and she was less and less sure of being made an honest woman of, she was more and more aware that it was one thing to live in the midst of semi-respectability in Paris—and quite another to go home and tell lies. Occasionally she looked in the mirror and willed herself to ring her mother and tell her everything and hope it would all blow over—but she always baulked. No. She had made a silken web for herself and she was all tangled up in it and though it was quite a nice life really, she began to see that she was trapped by

316

the very fact that it *was*.

'Everything all right your end, Aud?' Dolly often asked on one of her—slightly nervous because it was such a long way—telephone calls. Audrey said that it was. All perfectly fine. And invented a whole string of things that had happened to her. Then she rang off. Shed a tear or two. Wandered around the apartment a bit, thought about telephoning Edwin but he was with his wife and children that evening—and eventually rang Madame Hélène instead, saying that a little game of bezique was just what she fancied—and Madame Hélène obliged.

'How do you avoid boredom?' she asked her guest.

'So soon?' Madame Hélène replied.

'A little,' said Audrey.

Madame shrugged that familiar French shrug. 'You have many years ahead of you. You could always get yourself a little dog.'

Instead she put aside the sleeping pills and began to read. She was right. Jean Genet was absolutely disgusting.

*   *   *

Long after Madame Hélène declared there was nothing more to teach her, and when she had learned to sit down and dine without gagging on beef that ran blood (Mrs Wapshott liked to give her joint a damn good roasting before she released it on the world. At the slightest hint of pinkness it went straight back in the oven which she then guarded, arms crossed against all offenders, until she was sure all signs of life had ceased), it was decided that Audrey should learn to ski. Edwin was

317

very good at knowing when the moment came to find her a diversion and each time—about once a year—she reached a point of rebellion because of boredom, he provided a new interest. She had already learned to ride, for there was a stables in the middle of Paris, and she could now drive tolerably well though it was a skill only there for emergencies. (Edwin said that if he bought her a car she might run away in it. She was not entirely sure he was joking.) She now had an account at the best bookshop in Paris, opened for her by Edwin, and a monthly luncheon club (ladies only) at which she and the other *jolie mademoiselles* wore their latest finery. But skiing was much more exciting than all these—because for skiing they must travel. When Edwin told her they were going to Gstaad and she wrinkled her nose and said couldn't they go somewhere that sounded nicer, he laughed delightedly. Gstaad, it seemed, was about the best you could get, even if its name wasn't very promising. They would go in the middle of February. In previous years he went away with the family for most of that month—a bad time for Audrey who became more restless than ever—but Madame Bonnard was now a little stiff in the joints (good, thought Audrey)—and the children went away with friends of their own. If she felt a little frisson of anger at being second on the queue, she kept it to herself. Slowly, slowly catchee monkee, she thought—or was it softlee?

Edwin was pleased with how she looked in her ski outfit and he was even kind about her goggles (a mortifying moment when she put them on), which helped her through the more trying bits of learning to stay upright and eventually to move about on her skis. Part of the Parisian training was to look elegant and unruffled at all times, which was quite hard when your bum was covered in snow. Repeatedly. In the end she began to enjoy the exercise and the experience and to look about her at the beauties of the place. It was all like a fairy tale in its icing-powder sparkle. The whiteness and the silence were beautiful, and Edwin made her feel beautiful, and that was about as much as she could dream of asking. She forgot the occasional dullness of city life, the restraints, the two diaries, the sense of being second-class, and instead she became his fairy princess again. He liked to watch her and she liked to be watched. Once she could stay upright, of course.

Edwin scarcely skied. His excuse for not joining her on piste very often was that he preferred to watch. She knew that really it was that his joints were suffering, too. Whereas she—she—had so much energy and vitality fizzing out of her that she decided, very probably, she would live for ever. It was happiness—confidence—to be good at things was *good*. Edwin, on the other hand, was apparently saving himself for the nights. And for the first time she found the lessons of being a mistress tough going. One thing to be out on the slopes all day and exhilarated. Quite another to feel every ache in her bones and to just want to fall into a hot bath and bed—to find Edwin in her bed each night. She longed for him to remain in his own room next door, even for one night, but no—still she must smile him into her bed. For a moment the telephone exchange looked the better bargain.

The exercise became her, the boredom of the city had lifted and the air pinkened her cheeks. The young skiing instructor whispered things and held her arm or touched her leg a little too lingeringly. Nobody seemed to mind, so why should she? It was enjoyable being with someone of her own age. Edwin looked on. He might smile, but at night he warned her: 'Remember "My Last Duchess",' he said. And now she understood. It made her flesh creep—like something out of a Hitchcock movie. 'You mean he murdered her? Just for some imagined dishonour?'

'Oh no,' said Edwin, laughing. 'The Duke of Ferrara didn't murder her ...'

'Well, that's a relief,' said Audrey.

'He had someone else do the deed. It is the lot of a mistress to be at the master's mercy, you surely see that?'

Audrey had no idea if Edwin was joking or not. But it reminded her where the power lay. Youth might be hers but the power and the pleasure lay with him.

On one or two of the days, instead of skiing, they walked, shopped a little, dined at the Eagle Club, drove into Rougemont, took a hot-air balloon over the snowy range and tobogganed near the Schonreid. She pinched herself. Impossible to imagine the Audrey from London doing any of this. The dream was continuing and it was lovely, lovely, lovely. From a distance she saw Princess Margaret and her group, and she saw Jackie Kennedy and her party. 'Ah, the merry widow,' said Edwin, and bowed low. Audrey sent her mother a card the very next day, underlining the names of both Princess Margaret and Jackie Kennedy. It was fairyland all right.

One lazy morning, when she could scarcely stop

320

yawning and he called her his dormouse, which was just about right, they were due to take a sleigh ride and stay overnight at a little inn above Zweisimmen. He woke her. She rolled over and went back to sleep. In the end they left in a rush and she was still half awake as she snuggled up to Edwin during the ride. Through sleepy eyes she watched the beauties of the journey and felt very loved and very cherished, even if she was only a mistress. The next morning she discovered that she had not brought her little foil packet of pills and she also remembered that she had not taken one the day before either. Well. What was the harm? She decided to say nothing and take three the next day when they returned to the Palace Hotel. Such, she thought in later years, was the extent of her naivety, and the last of it.

*   *   *

Six weeks later she realised that something was not quite right and she called the doctor, who came and examined her. She had been very sick for a couple of days—what could it possibly be? The doctor telephoned Edwin and they both came to her apartment. She was pregnant. A wonderful warmth ran through her. With child. I am so happy, she thought. She waited for Edwin's rapture. For the first time she saw that he could be as ugly as a thwarted child himself. 'I said no children and I meant no children,' he said, stony-faced. 'Dr Claude will see to it.'

Then she wept. First real tears since Patrick. She was aware of that amid all the bucketings. It could not be happening. To be told to grow up? She had never felt smaller. The days before the appointment at the clinic were spent weeping. Surely, surely he could not mean it? She tried asking him again.

'If you have a child,' he said, 'you will not have me. I have a wife and I have a son and I have a daughter; that is as it should be. I want no more. I never said we would have children. I have been honest with you. You must be honest with me, now. Does our bargain stand?'

Impossible to say that she had never believed in it because she certainly did now.

He softened a little, almost became Edwin again. 'I should be more sorry to lose you than you might believe at this moment. You must decide.' He hesitated—then picked up his hat and left the apartment. Audrey continued to cry.

*   *   *

Afterwards, in the little private room, at the small discreet clinic by the Forest of Fontainebleau (Napoleon's favourite retreat, so she was told), she received a small bouquet of spring flowers and a note which said that Edwin would be away for a while, that he hoped she would soon be restored. It was sent with his love, he said. Audrey continued to cry. She cried in the clinic and she cried in the taxi, she cried in the apartment and she cried in the street, and when Edwin arrived back, three weeks later, she was still crying. 'Either the crying stops, or I go,' he said. 'Which?'

Audrey stopped crying. The prospect of being sent home at such a time was completely beyond her.

5

Scar Tissue

'You are cleverer than your brother,' whispered Apsu's mother to her, 'but you must not let him know it. You are a girl.'

Immediately Apsu rushed to the door of her brother's room and shouted at the top of her lungs: 'I am cleverer than you, I am cleverer than you. And I am a girl.'

Her brother threw his much chewed pencil at her. She caught it, and laughed.

She needed to heal both physically (there was an infection) and emotionally. It seemed a good time, therefore, to return to England and visit her parents. Edwin suggested it and Audrey welcomed it. He, also, would go to England and visit his mother. This simple statement caused Audrey a sharp pang, reminding her of how she was the first time they met. How excited she felt, how delighted with her he was. Now she had learned so much, and presumably still had so much more to learn.

London was different. Everyone, it seemed, who was anyone, was young. Even the Queen wore skirts above her knee. Audrey had already passed her quarter of a century and she suddenly felt very old. She watched the laughing long-haired youths and the wide-eyed mini-skirted girls and saw that the world belonged to them. She felt even more angry with Patrick for abandoning her. For abandoning this. It was exactly the way of living he believed in, talked to her about—it was what all those books and posters and plays were driving towards—a dream of the future—the future he would design and build for and which together they would be a part of. Brave New World. All that. And now here she was outside it. All cried out. Seeing the colours and the joyful silliness as if she was staring through a goldfish bowl. The Revolution was here and she had missed it. Free Love, it said in the headlines.

But she was charging for hers.

* * *

Mr Wapshott shifted from foot to foot as they waited for Dolly to come back from the florist's. Dolly had gone to get some flowers to put in a vase for her room. Audrey felt strange. She did not want to be treated like visiting royalty, she wanted to feel normal.

'I'll make a pot of tea,' she said, for what could be more normal than that?

'You will not,' said her father. 'Your mother would skin me alive. You sit there and I'll do it.'

If her father was prepared to make the tea, then what hope was there for normality? But it was better once Mrs Wapshott returned. Excited she might be, but there was little outward manifestation of this. She gave her daughter one, long look and said that she looked peaky. This was, apparently, all the fault of that foreign food—the oil, the garlic, the frogs' legs—she'd read about them. And she set about putting it right in the English way. She baked a ham and she mashed potatoes with plenty of butter and the top of the milk, and she laid out the pickles.

Audrey, who still seemed to see babies in everything, poked at the bright pink, fleshy ham and tried to go back to being the girl she had been, the girl who would have eaten it up without blinking. But she could not. 'I wonder,' she said, without considering the consequences, 'if I could just have a little cheese?' Mrs Wapshott's mouth puckered and Audrey knew that she was thinking along the lines of Hoity-Toity. A large piece of yellow cheddar was placed on the table, along with half a dozen Jacob's cream crackers and the glistening, even yellower, butter.

Years later, if ever she began the torture of self-doubt and was casting around for something, *anything* to remind herself that she was better than that, she remembered that particular meal and how—against all odds of gravity—the cheddar, the biscuits, the butter, they all stayed down, along with the milky tea and baked rice pudding. In one of those peculiar twists of reason, she thought that if she ate of the foods at the table of her mother, it might—somehow—compensate her mother for what she, without knowing it, had lost. A daughter who would one day get married, put into practice all the skills her mother had taught her (like baking a ham) and produce grandchildren to be spoilt.

Staring at the pink meat she had pushed aside on the plate, she suddenly understood that Edwin meant every word. There would be no marriage, and there would be no children—his loving and his cherishing were real, but they were finite. Now she could never come back here (she stared, as if through a stranger's eyes, at the cream-painted kitchen, the old polished Rayburn, the multi-coloured plastic strips hanging at the back door that supposedly kept out flies); she had moved on from this and into a never-ending twilight. She was a princess in a cage who would never be Queen.

'You look very down in the jib,' said her mother more softly.

'It'll be the travelling,' said her father.

'Yes,' she said.

And everyone was content.

If Audrey was worried about how to avoid talking about her job in the days that followed, and the telling of more lies, the difficulty never materialised. Of all the conversations she and her mother had at the kitchen table, or queuing at the Co-op, there never was one that asked her, outright, exactly what she did. Dolly was much more interested in whom she knew.

'And have you seen any more of Princess Margaret?' she asked her loudly one day, when they were taking the bus up to the Junction.

Audrey decided to indulge her. 'Oh no,' she said, 'we only meet skiing.'

Dolly looked around at the passengers in the bus in triumph.

She was no longer herself to anyone. Not even her mother.

*   *   *

Edwin did not care very much for the Beatles. He thought they were brash in their music, rude in their manners. In Paris, if she listened to them at all, it was on her own. Now, in London, they were everywhere, flooding the city, the shops, the radio, with wonderful, raw sound. By comparison her French chic was old-fashioned and alien in the

326

London streets. She bought herself a mini-skirt—Edwin did not like her to wear them too short (though she noticed how his eyes lingered on the Lulus who wore them)—and she bought herself a pair of wine-coloured patent knee-high boots.

She was stared at, whistled at by builders, asked out by the postman and Dolly raised her eyebrows—but it did not go beneath the skin. This was all disguise. Underneath she was, and always would be, an alien. *Avortement. Abortion.* They were the same in either language. *Article-déclasser. Reject.* Those, too. No matter what the clothing, the person stayed the same. When she returned to Paris she donated the skirt and the boots to Sandy's new girlfriend, a plain, friendly, dumpling of a girl who was sure the skirt could be made to fit. Dolly approved of her—she was very good at sewing.

In the kitchen one evening, not long after she arrived, and when her father was at the pub and her mother was relaxed, Audrey dared to bring up the subject of Women's Things.

'Did you mind,' she said, tracing the squares on the tablecloth as if she were not really there, 'that you only had two children, Mum?'

Her mother laughed but without much joy. 'Why should I? Two's more than enough.'

'Yes—but—well—there might have been—well—I thought—'

'Thinking doesn't do,' said Mrs Wapshott pointedly.

Audrey was still in slight pain from the infection. She put her hand over her lower stomach, feeling the comfort of the warmth of her palm. 'I've—um—' She squeezed the place. She was desperate to talk about it. Mrs Wapshott was not.

'You need an aspirin for that,' she said, and got up and fetched one, as relieved to do so as one who is drowning is suddenly relieved at her toes touching sand.

'Did you—' said Audrey as she took the tablet, 'um—ever have—' she whispered, 'an—infection?'

*   *   *

There, it was out. And along with it came the tears. What Audrey had heard as she dressed after the painful examination—that *sotto voce* conversation between Edwin and Doctor Claude—returned to her, and the tears increased. 'It might,' Doctor Claude whispered, 'mean that the matter is out of our hands.'

'In what way?' the anxious Edwin had asked.

'In the possibility of any future—er—such mistakes.'

'Explain?'

'Scar tissue, Monsieur Bonnard, and the damage to—er—'

Afterwards she had looked up the whispered French '*trompe de Fallope*' and then she had looked up the function of that part of the anatomy, and then she had understood. The good doctor was telling the good lover that her *fécondité* might be gone for good.

She stared at her mother, willing her to answer. Her mother shook her head, then she stood up again, took the kettle and shook it, a gesture so familiar that Audrey in her jittery state could barely stop the tears. She put it on the Rayburn and began making the tea things dance. Audrey was nearly beside herself.

328

'Infection?' her mother said uncomfortably. 'Not that I know of.' And then, with her back to her daughter, and as if addressing the cups and saucers, she added, more softly, 'It's natural to feel it a bit down there. It'll be better when—well—when you get married.'

For one moment of confused astonishment, Audrey had a vision of herself dressed in a frock made up entirely of white crocheted daisies As Worn By Mary Quant, walking down the aisle to meet her bridegroom, while carelessly chucking away bottles of aspirin and packets of Anadin over her shoulder into the smiling congregation.

'Er—how will it . . . How different?' she mumbled to her mother's back.

Mrs Wapshott continued to busy herself. 'You know.'

'I am asking.'

'When you are—well. *Married.*'

Back came the crocheted daisies. 'I don't understand.'

Mrs Wapshott sighed into the tea-caddy. 'You—and your husband—the honeymoon—it's what married people do.'

'What? Go on holiday?' said Audrey incredulously. She was practically hysterical. 'You mean going to Bournemouth for a week?'

'A bit more than that.'

'A bit more than what?'

Her mother tutted with embarrassed irritation. 'I'm talking about what they *do* on holiday—'

Audrey's hysteria grew. 'What? Make sandcastles? Ride donkeys? What mother, what, what, what?'

Mrs Wapshott was defeated. She picked up the

steaming kettle and poured its contents into the pot. 'You'll find out soon enough,' she said, with a wearily kind—but definitely dismissive—nod. 'Now have a cup of tea.'

As if to cheer her daughter up even further Mrs Wapshott produced a packet of chocolate digestives, hidden behind the flour bin and for very special occasions, and from a kitchen drawer she removed a newspaper. 'I was saving this for you,' she said, as if it were priced beyond rubies. Audrey took it and spread it out on the table. Mrs Wapshott turned a page and—lo—there—suddenly—was Patrick's smiling face.

'He's won a foreign medal for something. Florence is over the moon. And now he's off doing something else.' She went on talking, oblivious to Audrey's hungry reading of the piece. Not a mention of his wife, she noticed, not a mention of anything beyond the fact that Patrick Parker was the youngest engineer ever to win the *Globo de Milano*.

'Only a foot and bicycle bridge,' said Dolly. 'And it's only in Italy. Early days, Florence says Patrick says.'

The headline read 'Genius of the Juniors'. And Patrick himself was quoted as saying that he had a very long way to go to match his hero, Isambard Kingdom Brunel. He had designed *his* footbridge for the Thames at Erith when he was three years younger than Patrick. That it was little known about and never built was immaterial. It was and always would be a very fine design . . . Patrick was pictured on the steps of his workplace in the City. He looked every inch a part of Swinging London. Sharp shoulders to his suit, wide lapels, big cuffs—

hair curling over his ears. What Edwin called, in Paris, a brave young buck. Last time Audrey saw him he was wearing corduroy jackets, sweaters and jeans. To be more accurate, she corrected, the last time she saw him he was wearing nothing.

'It's good that he's got on,' she said, as calmly as she could.

'He'd have been hard put not to given all that effort his mother put into him,' said her mother waspishly.

'Then why,' said Audrey, 'didn't you do the same for me?'

The cry rang out in the kitchen. Her mother paused. Looked at the tablecloth, looked at her cup. And then she softened her voice and said, 'It wasn't your fault he went and got someone else in trouble. Or you'd be in clover with him now.'

'In clover? In clover? You show me one mention of Peggy Boxer in this.' She stabbed the article with her finger and her nail broke. That was appropriate.

Dolly blinked.

'Why didn't you do for me what Florence did for Patrick? Why didn't you say Yes to me? Instead of always saying No? I might have built something, too.'

Dolly looked at her incredulously, as if her daughter had gone raving mad. Audrey immediately backed down and apologised. Which just about summed everything up. And that was an end of it.

*   *   *

When Audrey came to pack, she put the newspaper

331

cutting at the bottom of her case. She also took from her room some of the books that Patrick had lent to her to help her expand her mind—books on Brunel's projects, books on planning and building and conquering and the heroism of design—all those things that Patrick set his star by. He had requested that she send them back and she never had. A little rebellion. A mini-revenge. Hers by right.

By the time she set off to meet Edwin in London she was better, or at least, resigned. Dolly told her to go carefully (the outburst in the kitchen she privately put down to nerves) and Audrey thought how apt the warning was. After so long apart, Edwin was bound to be ardent. Better than cold, anyway. So she shed London. Shed the zestiness—shed the feeling of being young again—shed the skirt and the boots which had been like dressing up and being someone different—and now it was back to work. She was certainly physically better, anyway, which as she told herself on the train was just as well. No good returning with dud currency. She was a different person, though. Scarred. It really did not do to venture in this life unless you were feeling strong. And she was feeling particularly weak. Weak and Scarred, then. But she smiled, composed herself before the train pulled into the station, and she remained smiling and composed as Edwin walked eagerly along the platform to greet her. Smile, smile. Though something burned inside her—flaring up in moments when she was alone—making her restless and downright angry, without her quite knowing why. Paris, she hoped, would make her feel calm—real—again.

Edwin had a car to take them to Gatwick and she

found that a comfort. He had bought her a gift—a dress—she found that a comfort, too. Now she knew where she was again. La Dame aux Cadeaux. When he asked her if she had had a good time, she said, very brightly, that she had. She really and truly had. She hung on his arm as she hung on his words. She smiled, she laughed. The thought of Edwin going out of her life now was more than she could bear.

* * *

In the plane he asked her, very pointedly, if everything was now 'all right'. She knew what he meant.

'Everything is absolutely settled,' she said, with complete conviction, and she damped down the familiar little fire that began flaring. 'One hundred per cent *fine*.'

The matter was not referred to again.

Patrick was just a press cutting, a mound of books in her case. He had escaped. She was forever locked in.

6

A Touch of Rebellion

Apsu began to notice her environment. The buildings. The streets. At the age of eleven, about to start senior school, a large comprehensive close to home, she began to walk around her neighbourhood of London, along by the river, the desolate areas, and slowly she saw that she was part of a whole, yet an individual, and the walking gave her a vision of both the journey and the beyond. Her grandmother talked about the past, how their lives might have been, the baking, the growing things, the days of heat and cold. Her parents cared only for the future and she felt that she was somewhere in between. A mixture of ancient and modern. She could not put this into words, but she could put it into drawings. Which she did. And in every drawing of every cityscape, real or imagined, she put people at the centre. 'This girl has a special talent,' said her new teachers. 'Of course she has,' said her parents and her grandmother, and they left her alone. She wrote in her notebook, alongside her drawings, 'Our present way of building and living is one that denies what we hold to be natural in so many ways . . . I would like to change such things.'

Back in her apartment, in familiar, delightful Paris, as the year passed and another and another, she began to wonder what had made her so unhappy. The lovely sitting room was always filled with flowers, the bedroom was sweetly orderly and inviting, the bathroom gleamed and glistened, and Edwin was loving. She worried about nothing material. And as she became more involved in the life she and Edwin led together, she became more important to him. He trusted her. She trusted him. They had a contract. If it was not marriage, then it was as good as. Peggy did not appear in Patrick's professional life, she did not appear in Edwin's. They were both little pendants.

Audrey became more and more—so Edwin said—indispensable to him. She spent time at his office. The others there, if they knew of her role in his life beyond the office walls, looked the other way. Indispensable was a good word—it made her feel safe. And it took away the days of boredom. She involved herself more, arranged his travel if he was to be away, reminded him of things left undone, sent gifts and thanks to whoever required it, dealt with his tailor, his shoemaker, his hatter— even his dentist and his barber. If, on occasion, he was late for a meeting at his offices, or a meeting overran, she engaged the waiting appointment in general conversation and called for coffee or cognac or tea to placate. I work for my living, she told herself, and felt better about herself for that. I am, in all senses—save one—his dutiful wife.

But she could not make friends. She must remain aloof. Her friends were the others—the giggling girl who talked of cachet, the men who liked men and could hide their preferences from their wives. There was no one in whom she could confide. Even her maid was paid for by Edwin. The memories of films in which the heroine talked into the mirror as her maid did her hair and dispensed wisdom were not real. And her weekly telephone conversation with her mother was almost held by rote. When she asked Edwin if Madame Minette could come to stay for a few days while he was away being something grand, he seemed unwilling. She began to wonder if he was as scared of losing her as she was of being abandoned by him. 'Please,' she said, resenting having to ask. He smiled. There were exhibitions to see—a new one on costume at the Musée des Arts Décoratifs, a new one on Goya at the Louvre for example; she was to have dinner with the Maguires—two of his friends from the English connections—when they came over; he wanted her to attend a couple of book auctions on his behalf . . . she would be very busy. And it was only a little less than a week—then he would be back.

The flame flared up again, surprising her. She stroked his arm, let a tear fall, and said, 'Edwin— you have no idea how it feels when I know that you are away on some grand business pleasure with your wife.' This was true—but not, perhaps, in the healthy way of simple jealousy—more in the darker way of feeling wronged and wanting revenge. Madame Bonnard did nothing except be Edwin's wife. This coming trip would be interesting, she knew, because she had helped arrange some of Edwin's part in it. There would be many meetings with cultural officials from the European Union regarding a new, Union-financed, business and arts complex. There would be a banquet given by the President of France, and—among other hospitalities —a lunch would be hosted by Madame Bonnard.

The woman walked in sunlight while Audrey was permanently in her shade. It would not do . . .

Madame Bonnard—only ever glimpsed by Audrey—was the same age as her husband. She was square in the way some French women end their days, short of stature, well-groomed, perfectly cropped hair, large-chinned—and probably hairy, though Audrey never could get close enough to see. Madame Bonnard would eat with the President of France, sit smiling and nodding next to her husband as the photographers' cameras popped, she would be gracious as she presided at the Ladies Only Anniversary fundraising lunch for the families of soldiers killed in Algeria. And she would have done—not a thing. Not even warmed her husband's bed. Audrey had done all three—the organising of the lunch, the dispatching of the invitations, and the surrendering in bed.

The flame grew more fiercely. If Minette had come to stay they might have shared a bottle of wine and laughed it away. But she did not. Chattering lunches in the latest smart bistro bored her to distraction; a game of bezique which she tried to play with the now withering and crotchety Madame Hélène irritated her. When it came to *Marriage* and *Royal Marriage* in the trumps she clucked at her cards acidly. When it came to pointing out to Madame Hélène (who was losing her memory, fair enough) that in *both* Royal and Common Marriages, widowed spouses may not remarry, she threw her cards across the room. Madame Hélène, who had seen it all before, said nothing and departed. Audrey then drank a bottle of wine, *toute seule*. Which, of course, made the fire grow hotter. It was, in any case, summer—Paris was steaming—and had Edwin not been away on this trip they would have been cooling themselves in Cannes by now. Unfair, she thought, and slept badly and woke in a temper. She would do something about it. If nothing else she would have a little revenge.

She arrived in Toulouse in baking hot sun, wearing a pure white silk dress, large dark glasses, a white bandeau covering her hair, and enough jewellery (nearly all of it) to sink Cleopatra's barge. The doorman at the venue for the luncheon was nonplussed. Yes she had her invitation. She helped him tick her off by running her finger down the guest list. And there she found what—or whom—she was looking for. A Madame Delphine Bolle—who was invited and had accepted and had then—late—sent a note (which Audrey had not yet passed on to Madame Bonnard's private office) to say that she could not attend after all. She must be in Biarritz to oversee the furbishment of her new Indian and African Artefact Galleries.

Delphine Bolle, whom Audrey had never met and of whom Edwin did not wholly approve (being in business in her own right when, as the wife of a distinguished politician, she should be thinking of charity work only), was apparently one of those rarities—quite young and very wealthy. A second wife. Edwin spoke of her with a mixture of contempt and admiration. To be in business in African artefacts was, apparently, rather vulgar—but presumably her money, when it came to Madame Bonnard's charities, was not.

The lunch was a buffet so there would be no place names, which was fortunate. More fortunate still, the event was one of the larger functions on the good Madame Bonnard's fundraising calendar. Eighty guests. If she so chose, Audrey could simply arrive and blend. But she did not so choose. She wanted to provoke. And she therefore arrived startlingly dressed. Since it was a charity lunch, and since when it came to matters of charity, the attendees were nearly always somebody's wife or widow, they were usually of a certain age and—though often glamorous—they were certainly not young and lovely. Audrey was glamorous, young and lovely with that added dangerous spark to her that denotes a hint of madness. As she made her way up the steps, across the foyer and into the luncheon room, she drew the questioning looks of each of the women that she passed. And she heard them asking each other who she was—and she heard them mutter and saw them shrug their shoulders. Her presence, and the questioning about it, went through the assembly like a wind through corn.

This, incautiously, she found pleasing. She stood by the heavy, swagged gold curtains at the end of the room so that the sunlight poured down on to the white of her dress, the gold of her jewellery, the flash of her eyes. She put her hand on her hip, held her Audrey Hepburn pose, and was transformed into a goddess. She took three dry martinis in very quick succession; Edwin had taught her to make them—two parts gin (kept in refrigerator), one scant part martini, no olives—and she knew they gave a quick hit. Or in this case a heavyweight punch. She immediately felt very powerful, very beautiful and very determined. Slightly shaky on the legs—but perfectly in control. Why, she could conquer the world. Well, certainly poor, ugly, hairy, square Madame Bonnard whose husband must loathe her so much. There she was, right in front of her, a few metres away, feet apart like a prize fighter, strong jaw jutting, talking with chin-shaking urgency to a woman who looked like a road map she was so lined. The Cannes Skin, it was called. From too much sun and too little to do. Edwin had pointed it out to her. 'Wear a hat in the sun all your life,' he said, 'and one day you will be grateful you did so . . .'

Audrey approached her prey. With one hand she took up the hem of her flimsy white frock and held it out so that the sunlight flowed through the fine fabric leaving little to the imagination regarding the shape of her thigh. Let them look, she thought, for all their Molyneux and Chanel. In the other hand she held her martini glass outwards, and just so, and proceeded in a southerly direction towards the unattractive duo. She followed the squares on the carpet for a straight line—it seemed the easiest thing to do—and came up close. Both women stopped talking and smiled at her. Audrey noticed that Madame Bonnard had a gold tooth. Age made your teeth drop out too, then. The hostess stood to one side as if to invite the newcomer into the group, and the newcomer obliged. Then Madame Bonnard made a gesture of apology and said that she would introduce Mad'moiselle—Madame?—if she knew—she must forgive—who Mad'moiselle was? It was politely done, kindly done, but an imperative all the same.

'Well,' said Audrey coyly. 'I could be Delphine Bolle . . .'

Both women looked at each other, then back at Audrey, then they laughed, both puzzled and polite.

Audrey laughed too. 'Or I could be Dolphine Belle . . .' She swayed slightly, like a child with a secret.

'But,' said Madame Bonnard, with slight embarrassment, 'you are not.'

'Might be,' said Audrey petulantly.

'I do not think so,' said the woman with Cannes skin, smiling indulgently despite her nutbrown lines. She looked her up and down. 'I do not see how you can be . . .'

Audrey turned on her with a haughty stare. 'And why not? Do you think I am not good enough? Do you think I am not rich enough? Do you think I am not *old* enough? Or perhaps, Madame, you think I am not suntanned enough?'

Both women laughed at this, both amused and bemused.

'Ah well—' said the wrinkled woman, stepping back to avoid being splashed by the martini remaining in Audrey's wayward glass. 'Not— suntanned—exactly—but—you cannot be her . . .'

Audrey wagged a finger and said confidently, 'But you are not absolutely sure—now are you?'

At which Madame Bonnard sighed and raised her eyes, beneath their heavy brows (need plucking, thought Audrey idly) and said through perceptibly gritted teeth, 'Oh yes, Mad'moiselle—I am absolutely sure.'

'How can you be? You have never even met her.' Audrey played this trump as if she were playing bezique.

'Even so—' And both women laughed. The crowd around them, listening now, tittered too.

The wrinkled woman nodded and said, 'In a

341

million years you could not be her. Unless you are wearing a great deal of powder.'

Audrey turned a contemptuous look upon her rival. 'Madame,' she said, '*I* do not need so much make-up . . . Whereas you—'

'Well, you would if you wished to be taken for Madame Bolle,' said the woman sharply. 'Madame Bolle, my little impersonator, is from Senegal.'

'Senegal?' said Audrey shrugging. 'So?'

Madame Bonnard stepped back, shook her head in mock sorrow and said, 'So—she is a Negress. And you—most obviously Mad'moiselle—are not.'

Audrey paused for a moment wondering whether to run for it or faint. But she did neither. Instead she straightened her neck, looked down what now seemed to be her twin noses as coolly as she could, and said, 'All right then, I'll tell you who I really am.'

And then she thought, sadly, mawkish with the martini, But Who Is That? 'And who I really am is—' Out splashed the last of the drink as she saluted them with her glass, the crowd pressed forward, amused—'I am Audrey Wapshott.'

Edwin would kill her, was her immediate thought—never mind His Last Duchess . . . Ah well. Too late now.

Did Madame Bonnard's eyes flicker before she said, 'So?' Did the group surrounding them intake their breath? Audrey could not be sure—but something stirred—perhaps it was the pumping of her own blood. She had waited for this magnificent moment—waited and waited for it.

'And do you know what I do for a living, Madame?' She stepped closer. The older woman stood her ground. The jaw jutted and the eyes snapped, but they did not waver from the pink and animated face that looked down at her.

'You must tell me, Mad'moiselle . . . What do you do for a living?'

'For a living, Madame, I sleep with your husband.'

This time there was no mistake. The crowd hissed a breath, Madame Bonnard looked—for a moment—as if she had been slapped. She stared around the room, perhaps seeking escape. But then she recovered. Looking Audrey straight in the eyes and with never a waver to her voice, she laughed a rich, ringing laugh—surprising, to Audrey, for one so squat and plain—and she said, 'Well Mad'moiselle—I thank God for it. Every day. For while you do—it means that I need not!'

At which the crowd murmured their laughter.

If it was wit that she was after, Audrey was upstaged.

Forgetting to follow the squares on the carpet, she wavered her way out of the room. Behind her she heard a united sigh of relief. The pretty, silly girl had gone. They could resume their grown-up ways.

'She has much to learn, that little one,' said Madame Bonnard.

'And she will. He has not begun on the others, yet.'

7

Little Sweethearts

At school they were allowed to choose their project. 'Name two buildings that have impressed you and say why.'

It was an exercise in formulating ideas, understanding research. Apsu cared little for the academic side of it—she took the brief at its broadest and chose two bridges—two bridges, she wrote, that made her tingle, but for very different reasons. Her teacher who was about to explain to Apsu that, for the project, they meant buildings, not bridges, thought again, and said, 'A very good idea. Well done.' And left it at that.

Her choices were the Sydney Harbour Bridge, at five hundred and three metres, the largest steel bridge in the world. And the Kingsgate Footbridge, Durham. Eight hundred houses were demolished, she noted, to build the former—without any compensation to their owners. In the latter the architect and engineer, Ove Arup, spanned one of the most sensitive sites in the United Kingdom: the gorge across the Wear connecting Durham Cathedral with Durham University buildings. Sydney Harbour Bridge, she noted, provides an heroic climb for the brave few kitted out like crack troops who dare to make the two-hour trek to and from its 304-metre summit. The Kingsgate Footbridge, she contrasted, joins a thousand years for the students who cross and return on its quivering structure. Like a spider's web, she wrote, it feels alive. It is alive. It is made for ordinary people. It is this bridge, for its living qualities, that has made the greatest impression on me. She received excellent marks.

Audrey never knew if Madame Bonnard told her husband about his mistress's little rebellion. At first, back in the apartment, she was fiery with hope that she *would* tell him, and that in some miraculous way it would change things. But nothing of the incident was mentioned. Edwin returned, talked of the trip, described the various schemes and plans they had put their names and signatures to—and things went on much as they always had. For a while. But then something between them did change. And at first it seemed like the end of the world. The mistress became no better than the wife. Edwin lied to her. It was to do with what was called, in the Wapshott household, Having Your Cake. Audrey, who had been thinking along the lines of making a campaign for herself, of even frightening Edwin a little so that he might reconsider his cast-iron marriage vows—was banjaxed. There was a rear flank that she hadn't even considered. Less Cake, more Little Apple Tarts.

It was not difficult to discover. Even for the unsuspecting Audrey. Edwin was not particularly clever, nor overly concerned, in the matter of keeping his dalliances a secret. He was prepared to be discreet and he was prepared to avoid humiliating her by flaunting them—but the truth was there to be discovered if she looked a little more closely.

Audrey saw some of it in those first years. If Edwin saw a pretty girl, or even just a fine pair of legs, or an inviting bosom, he would drink in the sight as if it were wine. He might even go after her—talk to her—tell her with a flirtatious smile how much he admired her—but Audrey assumed it was part of his way. 'I am an Epicure,' he once said to her when he was slightly in his cups. 'There is art, there is music, there is fine living—and there are always—pretty girls. An Epicure.' She was puzzled and looked it up. 'One given to sensual pleasures. A follower of Epicurus (341–270) who taught that pleasure was the chief good.' Nothing wrong with that, she thought innocently, that is what I am here for.

The first time she discovered the reality of Edwin's 'Epicurean' principle was on her birthday. Flowers were delivered—including two diamond tulips for her ears—and as he paid the pretty girl who delivered them she saw him hand her his card. Not in a businesslike way—but in the way he had once handed her his card on Brighton Station. She said nothing. She watched him, as he watched the girl. Audrey had seen her before—in the shop near the apartment building—and had seen how Edwin gazed at her through the window glass. Fool that she was, she thought he was gazing as he might gaze, had gazed, at a Renoir nymph or a languorous Goya. But now, suddenly, here she was, in this very apartment, darting about, quite legitimately, under the very nose of, and brought there to do a job for, the mistress of the man who now gazed at her so raptly. The girl, who knew she was being watched, became more and more provocative—bending, reaching, showing off her feminine attributes as she set the flowers to show themselves off around the room. Audrey, who saw it all, could do nothing. She felt slow and old by comparison—the birthday could have been her hundredth—and now she knew how Madame Bonnard must feel and she was sorry for what she had done. Too late, she thought, always too late. Bloody, bloody, bugger it. But at least Madame Bonnard had a life of her own. Audrey Wapshott, growing older, fluent in French and very little else—except in the Epicurean department—had not.

A day or two later Edwin excused himself from her bed for a few days, saying that he had to go to Perpignan very early the next morning to deal with urgent family matters. No, she could not accompany him—it was—he hesitated so that she felt a frisson of suspicion—purely family. She must stay here. There was plenty to do. When she said, quite sulkily, 'What?' he shrugged in that maddening French way and reminded her, too tersely, that she was in one of the most cultivated cities on earth. She reminded him that when she arranged to have painting lessons with a sweet, bearded old man in Montmartre, Edwin suggested he would rather she did *not*. Edwin then laughed, but not very nicely, and reminded *her* that the old man was known to be a great lecher. So she reminded *him* that he had also refused to allow her to engage one of the younger painters. 'Dangerous,' he said cheerfully. Then he kissed her on the cheek, and was gone. It was the closest they had ever come to rowing. She rather enjoyed it.

The following day, when she walked past the flower shop and peered in, the girl was not there. She went in, bought a little spray of something, asked where the pretty girl had gone. The owner pursed her lips. 'She is arranging the flowers for a man who has a château in Perpignan,' she said. There was that French shrug again. The woman did not believe it either.

Desolate, she returned to her apartment and telephoned the château. Edwin answered. She said that she knew he was there with the girl and that she was hurt and humiliated and leaving him to go back to England.

'But I love you,' he said. 'And I will be home in three days. I should not like to return and find you had gone away.'

Audrey sat on her large and beautiful bed, in her pretty room, with the sounds of the city drifting in through the balcony windows, and sobbed—at first with rage, then with pity for herself—and finally with resolution. She would leave. She began to pack, tearing the beautiful clothes from their hangers and throwing them on to the beautiful bed. Opening the drawers of her Louis—whatever number it-bloody-well-bugger-was—cabinet and hurling out the contents. From the back of the cupboard she hauled out her big suitcase and opened it. There was Patrick's face, smiling up at her from yet another news cutting sent to her by her mother. This time it was about a new housing estate he had designed, somewhere in England. The headline was 'Head in the clouds. Sir Leslie Martin gives approval. Patrick Parker continues to create a Brave New World.'

She stared at the photograph. Happy the man with talent, she thought despondently. In the photograph next to Patrick there was a more detailed picture of the design. A tall, plain block of flats, with a walkway (the famous bridge motif, as the caption commented) at its base leading to a long, low-rise, unadorned shopping complex. Outside the plain-looking shops were two prams and a couple of dumpy-looking women. Patrick was quoted as saying that he 'had expected some argument or dissent from some quarters, given the height he had chosen—but so far there was none. I have always enjoyed a good debate.'

Debate, she thought amused, was—debatable. She remembered him telling her not to be so passive—couldn't remember what about—might have been whether to have the top of the milk on your cornflakes, might have been the Value to Man of building rockets to the moon. She also remembered that what usually happened if she said her piece was that he told her she was being silly—or that she didn't know enough about it. Whatever it was. Oh, happy the man who has talent, she said again, But where am I? In Paris, actually, she reminded herself. Which was a great deal better than a woman of no talent (bar one, apparently) could expect. When her maid arrived in the morning she was still there, her clothes scattered.

When Edwin returned she was cold. Firmly unforgiving. He went away again. He telephoned her. 'I am alone,' he said. 'And I want to make love to my beautiful mistress—whom I love—and not some unkind iceberg. You will telephone me and I shall come to you.' Then he hung up.

Audrey paced the apartment. She had already thrown away the birthday flowers, tearing them apart in her hands. Now she prepared to break the vases—she had seen it done in films often enough. She selected the first, held it, looked at it, one of

Edwin's favourites, Venetian glass, light and delicate as air. She prepared to dash it to the ground. After all, she had the right. And then she stopped herself. What would she do once she had finished with the vases? Would she wreck the rest of the apartment? Would she then leave? And go where? Her heart was not broken by his behaviour, it was merely humiliated. She knew the feeling of a broken heart and it was not like this. She decided to take her mother's eternal advice and be a good girl. She replaced the vases carefully on the writing table and picked up the telephone. She apologised for her harsh words. He accepted the apology. While she waited for him to arrive she dressed herself in white linen. The right clothes for the right job. And when he arrived—she laughed at herself. He was right—it meant nothing.

*   *   *

So it happened from time to time. Edwin was not secretive about it but he was discreet. She did not pry. And it was usually over as quickly as it began. Just once, when the little sweetheart had a bit more mileage left, and Edwin went from Perpignan down to Cadaques still with her prancing ballet-girl delights in tow, Audrey felt a mixture of jealousy and envy. Jealousy because Cadaques was somewhere special on account of its picturesque red roofs and dazzling white houses—and the memory of the overwhelming moment when Salvador Dali *himself* had bent to kiss her hand at a luncheon. Envy because she had only the dimmest memory of what it was like to lie with a supple young body—Patrick—and know the

350

pleasure of smooth, unblemished skin. She fretted in between both emotions until they fused into anger.

Paris was hot again, and restive, with much activity going on in the streets below. She had seen headlines on news stands—about Vietnam and Cambodia—and once she and Edwin saw the French and American flags being burnt together. It reminded her of the street violence they witnessed over Algeria but Edwin said it was different.

'Why?' she asked.

'Because they already have their independence from us. It seems there is no such thing as gratitude nowadays—only rebellion.'

'I know so little,' she said.

'Oh, I don't think Vietnam is something you need bother yourself about.'

*   *   *

Out on the midday boulevard—dressed as provocatively as Edwin's little sweethearts, in a pink clinging sun top and a very short skirt—she picked up a pretty boy-man with dark, angry eyes, long curling tresses and no shoes. At the Café de Lilas. The streets were full of them—all young— somewhere between twenty and twenty-five, wearing red bandannas and pictures of heroes printed on their T-shirts. They were students, they were protesting, and they were—so Audrey's told her—going to change the world. 'How?' she asked. And laughed when he said Free Love might do it. He had bloody hands and filthy broken nails. From ripping up cobblestones to fling at the police, he said. She ordered red wine for them both and when

351

it came it tasted like vinegar. He laughed as she spat it out and asked for something better, for she had never drunk such poor wine before. He taunted her for her soft ways and urged her to come and join them that night. He told her that, just as in the days of the Revolution, the women were at the barricades. 'This,' he said, 'is the second revolution, this is the one that *counts*. This one is truly Power to the People.' He gripped her hands and told her that their votes counted for nothing, armed rebellion was the only way for governments to see sense.

Audrey nodded at every word he said. She was quite relieved that their votes counted for nothing, because she had never—actually—voted.

He was so beautiful, she thought, but he was still talking, talking, talking. 'Come and join us,' he said again. 'They are waiting.'

We will see about that, she thought. And she leaned towards him, taking a mouthful of the sour wine and putting her mouth to his so that it trickled through his lips and down his chin.

So much for the Second Barricades. She took him back to her apartment and, while the Revolution That Counted raged throughout the capital, they smoked dope and rolled around and drank Cointreau as if it were schnapps. She kept him there for a night and a day while the cobbles flew and the tear gas swirled in the streets below. When Edwin telephoned in something of a panic to see that she was all right and staying safely indoors, her boy-man, her *petit frisottis*, was still there, naked in her sheets, and she was still giggling. She tugged on his curls and indicated that he should make some kind of little noise—perhaps a cough—just so that Edwin would know. It was not to hurt him, it was to establish that she, too, was a separate entity with a life and entitlement to its pleasures of her own. An Epicurean.

The *petit frisottis* dutifully coughed and then laughed. He blew a raspberry right into the receiver, and laughed ever more loudly. She was mid-sentence, saying that she was desperately missing him, when Edwin put down the phone. She rolled over on to her naked back and laughed and laughed and laughed.

The beautiful boy left the next day, urging her to come with him. For a moment she considered it. Sitting on the rumpled bed, cross-legged, watching her lover dress, his hair wet from the shower, his body so different from Edwin's—fire in his eyes instead of sophisticated *ennui*—she almost went. But the past held her back. Where did following a man with fire in his eyes ever get you? She waved him goodbye from the balcony and watched him swing off down the busy street below, his hair streaming behind him as he started to run—free as air—already linking up with others—ready to die for the cause. She yawned and went back to bed.

It felt good. Right up until she knew that Edwin had returned to Paris and did not come to the apartment. She waited. And she waited. It was then that Audrey Wapshott discovered she did not have a separate identity—nor an entitlement to her own independent pleasures. She was not and never would be an Epicurean. She had not been a good girl and she would be punished for it.

*　　　*　　　*

Edwin refused to speak to her on the telephone, his

door was not open to her, his domestic staff were instructed to turn her away and he did not go near his office. All business was conducted through his male personal assistant, whose expression remained as still and cold as a Napoleonic marble in the face of all her importunings. Edwin remained incommunicado for a month. He wrote her one chilling letter saying that he was destroyed by her disloyalty. She had broken their agreement. If she wished, now, to return to England, he would not stop her.

How could she go home? Instead she went down on her knees at the door of his house until—as he said afterwards—he thought her wailing would awaken the dead (he lived near the small Cimetière Fatidique, which he said would be convenient one day)—and brought her into the house, if not immediately into his forgiveness. Eventually, when he did speak to her, he said most seriously, 'That is not your part of the bargain. If you do such a thing again—' She hung her head. He relented and put his arms around her, telling her that—providing she was truly sorry and would never do it again—they would be happy ever after. 'It is not something,' he said, 'that a woman needs to do.'

She learned to accept her own passivity. It was easier to look the other way when he became enchanted elsewhere. Easier to welcome him back, to not ask questions. Safer too. While she remained quiet, she remained. She learned to enjoy the pleasurable part of a mostly unpalatable soup, the pleasurable part being that—once he returned to her—he was more happy to be with her than ever. He was right about this, as he was right about always wearing a hat in the sun. Once

354

she learned these rules she could bear them. And as the years went by he seemed less inclined to make his little visits to Perpignan.

Audrey never did vote. When she asked her mother about it, Dolly said she had never voted either, apart from Anthony Eden. But then—he *was* lovely-looking. What was the point? thought Audrey. Wiser and sharper now, she knew that the *petits frisottis* of today would be the Grandees of the future when they were sixty. Already, from press cuttings, she saw how far Patrick had already travelled down the road of respectable living, to understand what became of so-called rebels. Anyway—neither Harold Wilson nor Edward Heath was the slightest bit attractive. So she just didn't bother. Instead Audrey tucked the memory of her passionate *petit frisottis* away—and she never drank Cointreau again.

Nor did she call herself an Epicurean. The new word she used was *Pragmatist*. From Pragma, she told herself (1941–?), British, meaning a woman who just shuts up, and gets on, and makes the best of it.

8

Florence and Lilly

It was time for Apsu to consider marriage.

She refused.

Her grandmother hid her face in her apron, her mother cajoled, her father threatened and her brother said she was no sister of his.

'Don't be so silly,' she told them all. And resumed her studies.

Audrey rarely went back to London but always, when she did, her mother had kept some new cuttings about Patrick for her. It was as if Dolly could not stop rubbing in the salt and Audrey could not help holding open the wound to oblige, though she always affected indifference. At these times she rediscovered a painful hollow inside herself. And if she thought about it at all, the word fulfilment came to mind. But she tried not to think. There was one press cutting that cut more sharply than most. The photograph of Patrick, proud father, with his newborn son.

'At last,' said Dolly. 'And now *we* won't hear the last of it.'

Not a sign of Peggy Boxer As Was anywhere. If Audrey did not exist in her world in Paris, Peggy Boxer scarcely seemed to exist in hers. Faceless and voiceless seemed to be the way of things when you served Genius. Faceless and voiceless for both of them then. Which seemed fair.

The years moved on, slipped by, rolled away—quite easily. In Paris there was a good rhythm to life. Sometimes she would try out the words to her mirror 'kept woman' but it caused her more surprise than shame. At least Edwin *had* kept her. Patrick just threw her away. How had she gone from being Little Audrey Wapshott, climbing trees and marvelling at spiders' webs, to this wicked sophisticate? She could hardly remember. But she knew she had done it quite easily. Very easily. Too easily, was the next stage in the consideration, but she never went there.

'We are not kept,' said Pauline, fourteen years with the head of Parisian Police (now retired). 'It is us who keeps *them*.'

*   *   *

Gradually on her visits to London her mother ceased to say the word 'grandchildren' and look at her meaningfully, and instead concentrated on her son Sandy's offspring—overpraising the poor little dribbling, snotty things in Audrey's opinion, though she smiled and nodded and looked interested at every informative morsel. It was highly unlikely that they could talk, write, draw, play any musical instrument, do sums, have several sets of the finest teeth and make you laugh till your eyes dropped out at the tender ages of two and four—but Audrey accepted it. She also accepted that Jeannie, Sandy's wife, was probably the best mother in the world (barring the Queen Mother) and that Dolly could not wish for a better daughter-in-law. If the

357

implication was that she *could* wish for a better daughter, Audrey did not rise. Her mother made the best of it and referred to her daughter as 'a successful businesswoman'. Audrey hoped that fate would not intervene and inform Mrs Wapshott just what business it was at which her daughter was so successful.

She went on keeping the cuttings her mother saved her about Patrick. Couldn't help it. She tucked them into her suitcase to take back to France to read. And in France she hid them away at the back of a cupboard under piles of yellowing linen.

'Interested are you?' said Dolly, watching her fold them into her packing so carefully.

'I'm always interested in old friends,' she replied sweetly.

Audrey knew all about discretion. It did not do to tell anyone that she thought of Patrick every time she crossed a bridge—that she thought of him when she looked at a painting in the Louvre or at the Prado—that when she heard a certain kind of jazz or saw the title of a familiar book—she still thought of Patrick. As to what she felt when she thought about Patrick, she could not say. It was not love, that was certain. It was just a something. Like her mother saying she could fancy a little bit of a something but she didn't know what.

And her life in general? Was she happy or not? Happiness, it seemed to her, was what other people required it to be on your behalf. 'Are you happy?' Edwin said occasionally. What he meant was, 'Reassure me things will continue as they are . . .' And her mother—not that she ever actually came out with the word, happiness being an extravagant

358

concept—sometimes asked, 'So—everything all right, then?' which came to the same thing, and as with Edwin, required a reply to reassure. She gave it. It was a nice life, easy. Edwin spent more time with her as the years went on. He talked to her about European Union Cultural Matters. She listened, politely, but she was never engaged by any of it. Art, music, poetry, buildings—they were painful things. Items upon which a door had been closed. When she looked at that smug little Maya with her neat naked body and her dainty, silly feet, she merely wanted to smack her. She didn't know the half of it, locked into paint like that. And neither, actually, did Goya.

In Paris she had an elderly maid, Evie, who commented if she hummed to herself, or did anything of a foolish, spontaneous nature, saying, 'You seem happy today, Madame . . .' in that doubtful way of the true Roman Catholic. All in all it seemed that the world was made anxious by happiness and its existence or not was best not speculated upon. Pragma, she reminded herself, I am Pragma.

When her father died she was relieved to go home and take with her real, deep feelings. In the chapel she put her hands together and bowed her head and thanked her father for being real. For being someone about whom she did not have to pretend. She was so used to impersonating the woman that everyone in Paris thought she should be that she was unsure where she ended and the real Audrey Wapshott began. At least these tears were her own. At least when she put her arms around her mother she meant it. Even Sandy touched her heart with his painful face. Well—those were her bridges, she supposed. Small compared to Patrick's, of course. Hardly worth considering.

'How's Florence?' she asked, to take her mother's mind off the day for a while.

'Flo is a very bitter woman,' said Dolly, nodding into her teacup with deep satisfaction. 'Too upset to come,' she said.

'I never thought she cared for Dad that much.'

'Nor does she. No—she's upset about Patrick and that wife of his and the children. Never go up. Never see her. If they remember her birthday it's a miracle, she says. And after all she's done, she says.'

'I know how she feels,' said Audrey wryly.

'Oh she's bitter,' said Dolly. 'Just sits up there in Coventry and gets bitter. *Very* bitter.'

All Audrey could think was, Good.

Perhaps it was something about funerals. Or mention of that town, but Audrey decided to take the train up to Coventry. Dolly was busy enough with Sandy and Jeannie and the children (all those grandchildren—and thank God for it, thought Audrey) and she could be spared for a day. She went to see Lilly. It was a cold, grey day and the journey depressed her. Not so much for the lowering clouds and the dull light over the fields, but because she remembered the way she used to feel when she travelled up to Coventry. No matter how bad the weather, how low the light, she was always excited, expectant, alive with possibilities. Even when she travelled up that last time to see Patrick, to be by his side at his father's funeral, even then—guiltily—she had felt excited at the thought of being with him. All that innocence. Hardly bore thinking about.

360

Ghosts were there to meet her as she left the train—she saw Florence and Patrick on the station—she saw George sucking on his pipe—Poor George—and she heard herself, suddenly, saying 'My arse' to Patrick when he launched into yet another lecture on the virtues of bloody old Brunel. Bloody Old Brunel. She wished she had said it to him more often. Just once, she thought, as she skittered down the station stairs and hailed a taxi, just once, she would like the chance to meet with Patrick again and tell him what she really thought about his bloody old bugger-it Monumental Odyssey. My arse just about summed it up.

As the cab pulled away she looked about her. She had not been back since George's death and it was strange to find that—despite Patrick's scathing dismissals—she still liked the town. The Cathedral had mellowed, the surrounding buildings did not look quite so stark and there was a sense of community in the streets as busy people hurried about. Such boring little lives, Patrick used to say. How arrogant he was. How arrogant she let him be. Looking at them now, they seemed nice, ordinary, kind. She could well imagine them turning their faces to the wall to preserve a lady's dignity. She had a warm regard for Godiva, despite the way Patrick used to dismiss her as That Silly Woman. Now she could think beyond the drama of her naked ride and wonder how she ever managed to return to her husband after he had humiliated her so. Probably like the rest of Womankind, Audrey decided, she kept her head down, said nothing, and just got on with it. Pragma, Godiva. We are all at it, she thought. And smiled. 'That Silly Woman', indeed.

To Audrey she seemed remarkably wise. After all—
she got what she wanted—it was her husband who
ended up with egg on his face. And then, just as the
taxi turned into Chapel Street, she had a little
thought . . . Just a very tiny one—a little daydream
. . . Which made her smile. Just a little thought about
egg on a face . . .

*   *   *

Lilly was pleased to see her. The shop was to close.
You could not compete with the clever, industrious
work-all-hours Asians. Nor did she want to. Lilly's
husband was dead now so she had time to spare.
She often thought about George and cursed
Florence. 'One day,' she said, smiling a wicked
smile, 'I will dance on that woman's grave. I told
her that. And I will.'

'I know how you feel,' said Audrey. 'She's a bitter
woman.'

'It's no way to be,' said Lilly. 'Don't ask for wages
in this life. You have to look forwards, not back. It's
what might be—not what was, that counts.'

Audrey nodded.

'How's that son of hers?' said Lilly. She said it
with such fierce contempt that Audrey was
shocked.

'He's doing very nicely.'

'Nicely is as nicely does,' said Lilly
contemptuously. 'Unfeeling little bugger. Needs
taking down a peg or two.'

Audrey nodded again. Wise old bird, Lilly.

She kissed her on the cheek as she left and waved
until the taxi turned the corner of Chapel Street.
Lilly looked sad, orphaned almost, as she stood at

the kerb, waving back. 'Keep in touch,' she said and Audrey thought that she would. Then, on a whim, she asked the driver to go slowly past Patrick's old house. A low light was on in the hallway, otherwise it was in darkness. Inside lives a bitter woman, thought Audrey. And I must not let that happen to me.

*   *   *

It was harder to leave London this time. Not so much in the leaving her mother because Sandy and his family were there—but because one of her roots had died and it made her remember, even to cherish, the rest. In her heart she was no different from Little Audrey Wapshott who would one day want to come home. And be forgiven? Only one person could do that, and that was herself.

In the meantime she and Edwin moved into a life of comfortable affection. Edwin was satisfied that her love for him was love and she did not say any different. Frankly, she thought, his own view of love was wonky enough; quite as strange as the Duke of Ferrara's, if less fatal. He had kept his bargain and she would keep hers. To him she was now—if not youth—and if not Simone de Beauvoir mixed with Lesley Caron—then at least an attractive, sometimes beautiful, woman. Audrey liked to call herself, with irony, a very *well-kept* woman. She had adapted over the years as a companion (less bed, more read nowadays) too, and could converse in an informed and amusing way. Edwin had a good bargain. She was something between a female Faustus and (Edwin loved her to read Oscar Wilde to him) a Dorian—Dora?—Gray

. . . Except that if she were the heroine of that novel she would be found at the end with a dagger through her heart, her face unlined, and the painting crumbled to dust. The wages of sin, it appeared, were smooth features.

Well—she deserved something for being a Duchess in a Cage and in a land dedicated to such pursuits she put it down, publicly, to the excellent face products she used. To herself she put it down to her ability, hard won, to detach herself from too much reality. And to remain untouched. True, if she stood on a bridge with Edwin, it was Patrick she always remembered; and a litany of phrases—'tensioned cables and struts', 'open lattice work without masonry skin', 'multiple span', 'heavy catenaries and slender timbers'—all sounding more poetic than they looked. And then maybe, while she stood there, the little flame would leap up again, fear or anger, sadness or regret, something intangible was ignited—but on the whole she kept the damper down. Lilly was right. Look to the future.

As part of the less bed and more read rhythm of life, she began, on a whim, subscribing to the English-language *Architecture Today*—which certainly surprised Edwin when he found her curled up with it. She lied to him. She said that she was losing her grip on the more difficult aspects of English and this was good exercise. It saved his questioning her. Whatever her motives, they were private.

She was equally surprised at how much she enjoyed reading it, and—even more surprising—how much of it she understood. If things had been different, she thought, if things had only been different . . . But she remembered her little *frisottis*'s face when she told him she had never voted. Despite his claim that the world was beyond needing such puny stuff, he was clearly astonished—horrified even. It took a while, quite a long while, for her to understand that things could only be different if she had made them different. And she had not. It was as simple as that. She had fallen into Edwin's arms without giving anything else a second thought. A random moment changing the whole course of her life. But a random moment caused by—Oh Bugger Lilly and her Good Forward Planning—caused by Patrick Parker, and it was him she blamed. Oh and Florence, mustn't forget Florence. But at least it seemed that Florence Parker had got her Come-Uppance, was paying the price. Patrick had not. Unjust. She saw the happy newspaper cuttings with all those smiling teeth of his. Oh, no. Patrick had paid for none of it. Nor ever would . . . All the same—she liked to daydream—that one day he might.

*   *   *

Gradually a few minor changes in Audrey's status took place as Madame Bonnard became less sprightly. Invitations occasionally arrived which would once have requested 'Monsieur et Madame Edwin Bonnard'; now, sometimes, they tactfully suggested that he bring either an unnamed guest, or—occasionally—they mentioned Audrey by name. She understood that she was a recognised—even accepted—fixture. Edwin's children were grown up with families of their own and quite unconcerned about their father's morality. Life had moved on since her youth. Many great men had been delivered of their haloes by the women they once kept and then abandoned thinking they could do so with impunity. The world had seen enough to find it salacious amusement rather than genuinely shocking. It was the way of things, now, thought Audrey. The world was confused about its women so it was the women's job not to be confused about themselves. At least she was clear on where she stood and she did not mind. A kept woman without an independent existence of her own, she thought, can be anything. Edwin was growing old now, and as he once predicted, she was still young. Or young enough. Caterpillar, Chrysalis and Butterfly: if she had lived in the days when heraldry designated status and belief, that is what she would have borne on her shield. In the meantime, she was content enough. Like a good bourgeoise. Indeed, sometimes Audrey laughed outright to see how much they appeared to be living in a painting by one of Edwin's ancestors.

And then, as if to spite their calm, affectionate, almost bourgeois life together, along came a fierce little zephyr to blow on that near-dormant flame of hers. It happened in Paris, and it was thus . . .

9

Madame Bonnard *Regnant*

Apsu wrote an answer to one of her A-level papers in which she suggested that if the world designed its new roads to be curved, then people would necessarily drive more slowly. A short answer, she wrote, to some of the gravest ecological problems, and a way of taking the masculine style out of fast driving. She was marked down for making design a gender issue in such a blatant, unprovable way. She objected. Her examiner, one Peter Greene, who was very keen on the stylistic qualities of garden decking, fought back. Apsu fought, too. Taking it to the very top. She stood before the panel and she made her apologia. 'Testosterone rules such things,' she said. 'It is drawn on the caveman's walls.' But she also produced statistics kindly provided by the Automobile Association.

She won. She was granted her A level. Peter Greene gave an interview in the *Daily Express* saying that the world had gone far too far in its political correctness—it was all the Americans' fault with their *vertically challenged* for short and their *sight impaired* for downright blind.

Apsu countered this with an interview in the *Daily Mail*. She said the issues had not been taken far enough. They asked her to pull her skirt a little higher over her knees for the photograph. She turned on her heels (flat), and left.

'That is some young woman,' said the journalist. With admiration. She wrote a scathing piece about Apsu and her arrogance.

The French had long recognised the gifts of J. M. W. Turner, smiling to themselves at the English who took such a long time to understand the bridge he formed between the old and the new, the living world and the sublime. How absurd, they shrugged, that he has no museum of his own. How idiotic that there is no monument. Well, they would show those Philistine English how they regarded genius. Like buccaneers rifling through a stolen jewel chest, they plucked him out. They would honour him if his fellow countrymen would not. The French cultural establishment licked its lips and clapped its hands as it began to arrange a grand exhibition of his work to be held in the newly built Centre l'Arlésienne. Along with works from the great collections by artists who were known to have been influenced by him. Girtin, Cotman and Gilchrist, of course, and all the 'landskip' greats—but also the French moderns, Monet, Van Gogh, Cézanne, hung there in homage. The English, but only in very rare exceptions, were once more fashionable.

Audrey became excited. She expected to be asked to accompany Edwin and there was something delightful about the appropriateness of her first major public appearance with him coinciding with this essentially English exhibition. A landmark in her life. A moment of acceptance. Head held high.

But no.

Not to be.

Madame Bonnard would accompany her husband to the opening of 'Turner and his World', and to the banquet afterwards. Audrey swallowed hard and accepted it. But a few days before the exhibition's official opening, and when the show was hung, Edwin took Audrey for a private evening viewing. Edwin and the Curator were old friends and the Curator also had his little secret sweetheart. It was, Edwin suggested to Audrey as they walked around the exhibition, a handsome show. And a fitting opening to a fine building, which, curiously enough, was also designed by a British partnership. 'Really?' said Audrey, wide-eyed, though she already knew: it was Patrick's. Dolly had sent her the cutting. With exclamation marks in biro all over it. Not that she needed that, either. It was all very well documented in her *Architecture Today.*

'Monsieur Parker and his colleagues will be taking on the Louvre next,' the Curator said, highly amused at his wit. 'I am told that his practice is one of the best in the world. So—naturally enough—they do most of their best work abroad. Oh, the British, the British . . .' He laughed even more uproariously.

At the private dinner, later, she congratulated the Curator on his remarkably outward-looking vision—'Not only painters, of course,' she said. 'As you say—we have produced some of the finest engineers, the finest architects, the finest design visionaries in the world . . .' She waited for his response. 'It would make a marvellous exhibition, don't you think? "Brunel and His World"?'

The Curator smiled at her politely, if a little uncomfortably, as he filled her glass. 'But yes,' he said smoothly. 'Take a little more of the *foie gras,* why not?'

Such men were nothing if not polite. Then he turned to Edwin and resumed his conversation.

Once Audrey would have said nothing more. Taken the hint. But this time she had something to say and she wished to speak. She interrupted them. 'Think of Telford,' she said. 'Think of Stephenson. And think of the great, great genius that was Isambard Kingdom Brunel. And then there's all the other great men—' She thought desperately. 'Darwin,' she said triumphantly. 'Even Prince Albert in his way.'

The Curator and Edwin both looked at her and blinked. Sometimes the notion of de Beauvoir and Moreau met the reality and that could be awkward. They both gave her a polite smile. The Curator's little friend looked from one to the other and smiled prettily, too. What *was* going on?

Audrey, suddenly annoyed, raised her glass in defiance. 'Perhaps, Monsieur, you should have an exhibition about Brunel next,' she said. 'After all— he was half French.' She sipped her drink before adding, 'Normandy, I believe. And he was educated in Paris. I've always been *very* fond of his Box Tunnel on the Great Western. Haven't you?'

It would have been a good victory had it not been spoilt by the sudden flash of vivid images from the past—the posters on the wall, the bed—lying there listening to him, believing in his genius and happy to be chosen by him. That Silly Woman, she thought, Daft. 'To Isambard Kingdom Brunel,' she said loudly, and then, much more quietly, 'My arse.' And she downed the rather fine Saint-Émilion in one.

Edwin patted her hand and suggested, in an aside, that she should perhaps calm down a little . . . The *foie gras* really was exceptionally good.

But she was still looking fixedly at the Curator.

The Curator smiled. As if to humour her. 'Indeed, indeed,' he said, 'Isambard Kingdom Brunel is—a—future possibility.' He made a note on a little pad he requested from his mistress's handbag, before moving the conversation on to the quality of the wine. Later the Curator said quietly to Edwin that women were always a surprise. Edwin agreed. But by now Audrey was properly and safely demure again.

*   *   *

And so Madame Bonnard took her husband's arm for the L'Arlésienne Grand Opening and the Grand Opening Dinner and Audrey waved Edwin off from her balcony with her usual good humour. Not the end of the world, she told herself, not the end of the world. But she would have liked to take a peek at Patrick in the flesh again after all these years. Somewhere in the apartment she had a pile of his books—never returned. She could have returned them to him tonight—and dropped them on his foot. She closed the windows of her balcony, thought for a moment, then went to her cupboard and lifted from under the yellowing linen the pile of books, still wrapped in Wapshott brown paper and string. She settled down with them by the fire. Memory Lane. Here was the Clifton Suspension Bridge, the Great Western Line with its revolutionary Box Tunnel, and the gigantic Great Eastern—the heroic construction which she had once referred to innocently enough as Brunel's Big Boat to Patrick's horror—'Ship, Audrey, it's a ruddy *ship*!' She reached the biographical section. What she wanted to find was the man.

371

10

Florence and Audrey

Apsu was offered several places at several universities and colleges and by chance she chose to become a student at Patrick Parker's *alma mater*. She took the Parker Bursary. Though personally, as she told her tutor afterwards, she did not trust the man as a designer of bridges at all. All thrust and bollocks, she said of him. Too big for his boots, she called him.

She had the English vernacular to a T.

But not in her designs which were, so all agreed, entirely her own. When Patrick visited the college, as he did from time to time, and gave a seminar or two, he found Apsu difficult. Sometimes, when he was halfway through a remark, she interrupted him and suggested that there were always multiple ways of looking at the shape of things and it was unlikely that theirs would agree. At the same time he was fascinated by her mixture of old and new, simple and complex—and he used (though he would never acknowledge it) her idea of stayed walkways as developed from the rigging and spars of sailing boats.

Apsu wrote to him afterwards, long afterwards, when the bridge was built in Georgia, and told him that she knew very well what he had done, she forgave him, and that one day she might take something of his in return . . .

Now, there was method in Audrey's submissiveness: if she was a woman of little existence, she was not a woman without property. The selling of feminine charms in return for barterable goods to be used when the feminine charms have gone is a feminine way forward at least as long as history. Like it or loathe it, Goods Is Safe. No doubt back in the Savannah, or in those caves of Apsu's, a woman would behave wisely in order to secure her old age—somewhere between twenty-eight and thirty-two presumably—and whoever brought back the biggest rhino horn to hang around her neck was quite within his rights to demand a bit of rumpo in the tall grasses. She undoubtedly buried the tribute at the back of the charnel house, along with a few others, to be brought out when some other, younger female sashayed up without visible signs of rheumatism. Wealth has a strange effect on aching joints—it soothes the savage knees.

So—Audrey now possessed her own income from investments Edwin selected for her. When she asked what the investments were he just waved his hand dismissively and said, 'Various, various . . .' in a way that she knew meant 'Don't bother me with trifles . . .' He had placed them in the careful hands of his own broker and that was all she needed to know. She made a note of the broker's name and put it somewhere safe for later.

He also gave her the apartment in Brighton, his mollifying gift after the Turner Exhibition. His mother was long dead, he no longer found himself so interested in *jolies filles*—and it was a handsome way of showing how much she meant to him. He had currently let it on her behalf, on a seven-year lease, which ensured she would stay with him. If he was indulgent, he was no fool. Since his seventieth birthday he had suffered two mild heart attacks, which prompted Audrey to suggest that they both move back to England. If the worst happened, which was inevitable anyway given the difference in their ages, she did not want to live alone in Paris. England would be a good thing for them both, she argued. For Edwin, because he now found Paris and Cannes full of rich, bored, uncultivated creatures (was it, he argued, any different in London? With that ignorant Queen of the Bourgeoisie, Madame Thatcher? She could only shrug.) For her it would be good because she would be home at last—funny how as you got older you dreamed of living back in the old country—her mother was getting on, and her brother and his family were there and—well—she had served her stint in exile. She wanted to go home. But Edwin would not be persuaded. He was quite philosophical about his selfishness. 'It will not be for long,' he said. 'And then you will be quite free to go wherever you will.' But it was Dolly who went first, not Edwin. And that was hard.

*   *   *

There was some debate about it but in the end Florence Parker came to London for the funeral. Audrey was curious to see this woman who had created such a son, who had wished her such harm, and who had then been dealt such a blow herself. And curiously, when Florence arrived on the doorstep, Audrey's immediate reaction was fear.

374

Her second was that she was quite glad, after all, not to have that for a mother-in-law . . . Certainly she looked frightening. The hard jaw and the jutting chin were now like steel and rock. A belligerent, angry, unforgiving woman, with lines at the side of her mouth and a pious regard for the one she referred to as Our Lady, Queen of Heaven, Mother of Jesus, who has pity on all mothers and just as well *somebody* has . . .

Audrey kept her distance. They nodded to each other from their respective pews, and she felt Florence eyeing her up and down, but they said no more until they were back at the house. After her second sherry she dared to approach this Mother of Mothers—and even dared mention Patrick's name. Florence was sitting alone on the edge of one of Dolly's old armchairs looking as if not to take comfort from it was a matter of pride.

'Can I get you another cup of tea?' she asked.

Florence shook her head. 'One is quite enough, thank you.' The taking of even one piece of refreshment was—it seemed—a clear sign of weakness. 'Poor Dolly.' She added, 'Us mothers. What we have to bear. You went away and never came back and I know what *that's* like.'

'Ah,' said Audrey, 'yes.' She waited for a moment and then dared to say, 'How is your Patrick?'

Florence looked up at her. Her eyes were hard and bright. 'Not mine,' said Florence. 'Not any more. And certainly not yours. Not anybody's, I doubt.'

'No,' said Audrey. 'But he thought the world of you.'

Florence sniffed. It was a familiar sniff, and Audrey was suddenly Little Audrey again, eager to please.

In a mixture of pride and betrayal, Florence said, 'I gave that boy everything, everything . . .'

'You did,' said Audrey. 'And George did, too.'

There was a dreadful silence as Florence cast her baleful eye upon the humble Audrey.

'George had nothing to do with it.'

They both stared at each other. Little Audrey departed and Big Audrey returned. It was a ludicrous statement. She wanted to laugh and say that he must have had *something* to do with it—but managed to contain the vulgarity. 'You were certainly,' she said, searching for the right words. 'You were certainly very close to him. And he's done very, very well.'

Florence eyed her. 'All thanks to me,' she said. 'And now he scarcely comes near. Born out of the fire and rubble,' she said. 'What I went through. And look where it's got me.' She sniffed once more, pulled her mouth back into a line of chilling disapproval and added, 'All I get is the children sometimes. If they can't think of what else to do with them.'

'Children?' said Audrey.

'Two,' said Florence, the first softness appearing in her face. 'Boy and a girl. Isambard and Polly.'

'Nice,' said Audrey, though her heart pounded. 'He always admired Brunel. He'll be very busy then? Erecting his bridges all over the world? He was always good at erections.' She stared at Florence. Would she or wouldn't she? But Florence had no sense of humour where her son was concerned. I suppose, thought Audrey, that I never had any where he was concerned, either. The difference was that she had learned to laugh at herself, so she could laugh at others. Florence had never, would never, learn that lesson.

Florence gave her another baleful look. 'Oh yes. All the time in the world for his bridges—building them here, building them there. And *she* does the running after him nowadays. Peggy Boxer!' She leaned forward and poked Audrey's knee-cap, giving her a terrible urge to giggle. 'You should have been a bit flyer, my girl . . . You could have kept him.'

'I'm not sure I would have wanted him,' she said, keeping her smile as bland as possible. What a huge and wonderful irony it was that this pious, prudish woman who had encouraged her own husband's sad little side-show should be telling her deceased friend's daughter that all would have been well if she had only opened her legs a bit wider. What was it that Mahatma Gandhi said? 'I would have become a Christian if I had ever met one . . .'

'I'm very happy as I am,' said Audrey. Good Lord, she thought. I really am.

'Not married though,' replied Florence.

'I believe that may be why I am happy,' she said. And walked away. Leaving Florence to contemplate the possibility that she might, just, be right.

*   *   *

Back in Coventry, and almost before taking off her hat, Florence telephoned her son's house in London. As usual the call was answered by her daughter-in-law. On the pretence of wishing to talk about the funeral and Dolly and the day, Florence managed to let Peggy Boxer As Was know that Audrey looked about half her age, had a nice little figure to her, wore very smart clothes, and was—all in all—a credit to her mother (no greater tribute could she give). Audrey Wapshott—for she was not married and never had been and was probably still holding a candle for Patrick, Florence wouldn't be at all surprised the way she talked—continued to live in Paris, and was obviously very, very wealthy. She enjoyed hearing the intake of breath and the nervous breathing, as Peggy received the news.

11

Patrick in Paris

It was the talk of the college. The fabulous exhibition due to open in Paris. Housed in a spectacular new addition to the Louvre designed by the donor of her bursary. Apsu underlined the word 'spectacular' and signed up for the student trip to see this wonder. Paris was—if nothing else—a city of bridges and she never tired of it. And she was interested to see what Patrick Parker and his cohorts (all men) would do with such an illustrious site. She had, she told her tutor, very grave doubts. Her tutor opened his eyes very wide. It was as if she had said that Michelangelo was possibly not all he was cracked up to be and that she was off to investigate the Sistine.

Apsu looked at the catalogue. Even the subject of the opening exhibition was a strange one to choose in this age of open-mindedness and simplicity.

Spectacular? Spectacular bothered her. She just did not like the word. It conjured up images of Disneyland. It went with the word Celebrity. And all three of them made her shudder.

She liked the Eurostar, though. Now who else was it who once struggled to create such a tunnel?

After the funeral when Audrey returned to Paris after being away for nearly a month, Edwin was ardent as he used to be after their separations long ago. She understood. Now the boot was on the other foot, the sauce for the goose was transformed into sauce for the gander—Edwin was afraid she might leave him. She saw how much frailer he looked. And she saw it in the way he clung to her. He had played the field, behaved cavalierly towards her, controlled her—and now he needed her and they were equals. Equals in a very pleasant way of life which she doubted would last for very much longer. In the meantime, 'It was very pleasant' struck her as perfectly acceptable. What the French call *le mot juste.*

There were virtues, as Edwin remarked wryly, to choosing to live and therefore grow old in France. Good medical practice for a start. He willed her to agree. Audrey did not argue. In Pleasant Land you did not need to. Once a month he took the train to Perpignan to visit his wife who was now in a nursing home. A very nice nursing home, so it seemed, with fine views and an interesting group of companions. Edwin played cards with her and read to her and then came home. One afternoon, when he returned, he took Audrey's hand in his and said sadly, 'I knew you would keep me young. My wife is . . . pitiful now. Perpignan will be her last resting place.' The humiliations of the past seemed as nothing. Here she was, alive and healthy while Madame Bonnard lay in her lonely bed and her husband visited her once a month only. She noted, but said nothing, that it never crossed Edwin's mind to nurse her. She, at least, had been with Dolly at the end.

He continued to visit Perpignan and he continued to say that Madame Bonnard would not last long. Her not lasting long, thought Audrey mildly, seemed to be lasting long enough. Indeed, it began to look quite likely that Edwin would leave the arena first. But at least Audrey no longer felt her inferior. Equals in the land of Égalité she was now, and she liked the feeling. It had been a long time coming and she had been patient enough.

And when an invitation and press release arrived inviting Edwin to his old friend the Curator's retiring exhibition, Audrey smiled to herself. And so the circle finally turns, she thought. For his old friend the Curator had moved on from L'Arlésienne and become, very grandly, Director of the Louvre's Modern Programme. In the press release he explained, with the pedantic wisdom of the Grandee (French or otherwise) that he had become, that when one reached three score years and ten, one could no longer be considered a Modern and should begin to make plans to slip quietly away, which he would do now that this, his last and greatest achievement, was realised. He had persuaded the Higher Grandees that the Louvre should have a new addition to its galleries. He had argued that it was not long until the Millennium and that—being Paris—the world should find them well prepared. 'We have only to look across the sea and observe the foolishness taking place among the British about extending their own National Gallery,' he wrote. And he proposed that his Fellow Keepers of the Arts should forsake Nationalism in the cause of Excellence.

This was his final wish as Director of the Modern Programme.

And it was granted.

*   *   *

381

The best Architectural Partnership was used. The Higher Grandees were persuaded to commission the same people who created the L'Arlésienne Centre. Alas—they were British—but then they were requested to forsake Nationalism—and they did. When the building began nobody rioted in the streets. Now it was finished and—it was agreed—was a spectacular success. Spectacular.

Audrey had read about the proposal in her *Architecture Today*. Of course the team, as before, was Patrick Parker's. When building began she drove past the site occasionally, sometimes she walked past, sometimes she lingered, but it was shrouded like a Christo sculpture and she never saw in. Of course she might have requested a visit around the site—it would not be difficult to achieve—but—well—she did not. Chance was interesting, Planning was not. Besides, if there was a possibility of glimpsing the designer, she thought of it as a very remote one, and in any case, you could not tell the men apart in their hard hats.

Also in the press release the subject of the inaugural exhibition was announced. Clever, brilliant, wonderful, were the epithets for the idea and its progenitor, The Retiring Director of the Modern Programme. For it would salute another Franco-Anglais union. The work, influences and times of Isambard Kingdom Brunel. Everyone thought this was a Splendid Idea. Another one in the eye for the Philistine British who, as with Turner, were unable to recognise their influential geniuses.

The French would share the honours with the Japanese, as well as half the cost of the exhibition, and it would travel to Tokyo and Yokohama. The Japanese were a nation of bridge builders themselves and admirers both of the Great Brunel and The Parker Partnership (indeed, very early on in his career they had honoured him). Everything was set, and everyone was happy and proud. It was all going to be absolutely glorious.

'Well bloody well bugger it,' said Audrey out loud when she had read to the end. 'He's pinched my idea.' It was too much, no, really it was. The sensation she felt somewhere in her solar plexus was rather like being punched and her heart raced again. She gave a little gasp. Edwin looked up startled from the invitation. She put her hand to her chest and saw his expression change to fear. She smiled. 'Indigestion,' she said, 'only.'

He relaxed and took the invitation from her and read it.

'Will you go?' she asked, trying not to sound too hopeful. 'Your friend the Director would be glad to see you. And I should enjoy it. Very much.' She felt safe to suggest it now that Madame Bonnard was so frail, and according to Edwin (who wandered off the subject himself occasionally and was inclined to be vague), also apparently more or less senile.

'You should go,' she said, with incautious urgency. 'If you don't, you'll be missed. Noticed. It will be the exhibition of the decade—like before. You should be seen to be there at the opening night.'

Edwin said, 'You knew Patrick Parker once, I think? You mentioned that once to me.'

Sometimes he was *quite* the opposite of vague. Usually when you didn't want perceptiveness.

Perhaps she had told him—once—when she was

383

still angry about being left at home while he played The Good Husband. 'Yes,' she said. 'He was a family friend. I grew up with him.'

'Ah,' said Edwin. 'I see.'

She waited. He nodded. Yes, yes, he would attend the evening. Audrey relaxed. She allowed herself the pleasure of considering what to wear, how to behave, should she have a new hairstyle, perhaps? All the foolish things that she knew to be foolish yet seemed important, exciting. So what if she was frivolous? So what if the prospect of a beautiful dress and change of hair appealed to her? She called it, without bitterness she hoped, dressing the puppet.

And then the most bizarre and enraging thing she could ever imagine happened. Madame Bonnard scuppered her. Again. In an amazing rally, Edwin's apparently not-so-senile wife decided that she would go to the Ball. Madame Bonnard would rise from her bed and accompany her husband to the Grand Opening.

Audrey palpitated. Edwin apologised. But he was intractable. It was the honour of it. 'You could have fooled me,' said the surprised Audrey. He flinched but remained firm. One did not dishonour one's wife in one's public duty. It would, perhaps— almost certainly—be the last such occasion they would attend as man and wife. Propriety should be extended to Madame Bonnard to the last. Audrey, dearest Audrey, must understand this as she had always understood. Dearest Audrey shouted. 'I thought it was The Last, The Last Time—' She turned her back on him and refused to answer any further questions. Edwin therefore returned to his other home. He seldom did so now, seldom needed to, but whenever anything difficult occurred, home he went. His going reminded Audrey, obliquely, that he still held all the cards. She was a dab hand at piquet, bezique, chemin-de-fer—but she could not compete with a Full House.

So—Dearest Audrey sat there—blinking back the tears, rage, frustration and self-pity commingled. But she knew better than to argue. She calmed herself. She welcomed Edwin back. And she waited for the right moment to suggest that Edwin could get her an invitation in her own right so that she might just slip through the evening anonymously. Isambard Kingdom Brunel fascinated her—always had. Edwin said that he would take her in due course but that he did not think it would be seemly for her to go to the Grand Opening. She could not be anonymous nowadays, she was too well known as his companion. That if his wife knew, and most likely she would find out, she would be offended. That the President himself would attend with his wife, rather than the woman he had lived with for all these years and who had borne his three children. If the President maintained a protocol, then Edwin must maintain it too. And he repeated that it was not seemly. Wives, it appeared, had a way of clinging on.

A little bit of the dam broke. 'Edwin,' she said. 'What we have just done in my bedroom is not seemly. Shall we also dispense with that in case it offends?'

'My dear,' he said with mocking gallantry, a touch of the old Edwin emerging (he could be intransigent, oh how he could be), 'if that is what you wish—and it is certainly not what I wish—I will go from your life immediately.'

And in the usual way of proceeding, she ran to him and tucked her arm though his and kissed him and said, 'That is not what I meant. Not what I meant at all.' She always submitted to the way of things. But this time—bloody well bugger it *and* my arse—she would not. More ways to skin a cat, as her dear old mother used to say. She closed her lips with a smile.

*　　　*　　　*

By way of consolation Audrey was presented with a handsome, clothbound, limited edition copy of the catalogue. She wondered, but without much hope, if she was acknowledged in the Foreword. She was not. She therefore wrote the Director a thank-you note and ended it with her congratulations on the exhibition and a desire to know wherever he had found such a clever idea. He did not reply.

So far as Gallic opinion was concerned, the success of the previous 'Turner and His World' exhibition laid to rest the ghost of Waterloo. The new exhibition, 'Tribute to Genius: Brunel and his World' would cause an even greater sensation. The British, if they thought about him at all, considered Brunel to be an English Victorian through and through. But this exhibition would show that he was Normandy Man to his backbone. The Anglo-French détente of the European Union was parchment thin, tightly drawn, prickable by the first tiny pin of rancour. And rancour there would be. For if the Curator's Turner exhibition was limited to the visual arts—and it was well known everywhere but in England that the English were visually illiterate and therefore might not feel quite so proprietorial—this time, in his capacity of Director, the exhibition would include *everything*. Even original lengths of the famous—or notorious —seven-foot-gauge rail. And of the huge, dramatic chains that held down the *Great Eastern*. Japanese money had seen to that. There would be artefacts, books, paintings, photographs . . . Let the Modernists squeal, said the Director. The Louvre was an ancient institution. 'Brunel and his World' fitted it supremely well.

Their cousins across the water trembled yet again. But there was no way out of it. La France had been very generous in the matter of lending works for both a Toulouse-Lautrec and a Renoir show in London and Birmingham (sell-outs, obviously, as the French shrugged to themselves, since even the Philistine English had heard of *them*) so it would look nothing but mealy-mouthed if British institutions refused to comply with French requests now. The Cultural Establishment of the British Isles was privately biting its knuckles. It wished it had never gone for the easy options of Toulouse-Lautrec and Renoir, and it wished— above all it wished that it had thought up and executed the Brunel idea first. But It Had Not. To the French was the victory. Again.

The exhibition took the halfway stage in the century as the closing point of the Great Victorian Enlightenment. The moment, the Director averred, when the British took too much Empire with their brandy, and lost out to the rest of the world, could be pinpointed to a quotation from Walter Bagehot's letter to his father, written in 1851, year of the Great Exhibition in London, year of Louis Napoleon's *coup d'état* in Paris, the discovery of which delighted the Director. For the young Walter was visiting Paris and observed the street fighting and wrote to his anxious parent that, 'If you go calmly, and look English, there is no particular danger . . .' This statement, maintained the catalogue, was the high point of the golden age, after which the great days of benign politically inspired social reform were at an end. After that the Victorians descended into absurdity—Doers became gentlemen and Did no longer. The exhibition would celebrate the days before men allowed themselves to become imprisoned in the petty notion that there was a superior purity to science and maths known only to initiates, and that visual art and literature were inferior, feckless, non-absolutes. Darwin was allowed in since, even though he published *The Origin of Species* in 1859—he was working on it throughout the preceding decade. The French could be very fair like that.

Audrey, who was feeling very sorry for herself, and angry, as she looked through the catalogue, smiled a little sourly to note the lack of the feminine in all this. Presumably some Victorian women were also not imprisoned by this inferior, feckless thinking? It seemed not. Apart from a little sensitive and ground-breaking botany and whatnot, women did not climb the trees, they planted them. Women did not build the bridges— they sketched or painted them once they were designed, built and functioning. And the only drawings of buildings women drew were of the sweet, domestic variety—with rose bushes in the garden and the sun glinting warmly on the bricks. Why didn't they do something about it? she

388

wondered. It was a wondering that made her feel quite uncomfortable.

The Director concluded that 'Looking back to a Golden Age of Paternalism and Intelligently Applied Generosity and the sacrifice of self for the common weal seemed entirely wise. Brunel was just such a man. Whence comes such another . . . ?'

Audrey thought she knew one such another who thought he might just be whencing it right now.

* * *

In bed alone one evening, shortly before the Grand Opening, Audrey sat up surrounded by books on Brunel, the Brunel exhibition catalogue, and her new *Architecture Today* with a picture of the Great Man on its cover. Together with a picture of the other, more recent, Great Man. And she was reading everything avidly, and sulkily. The latter, she felt, even though she was now a supposedly mature woman, was allowable under extreme provocation. Patrick Parker. Designer. Smiling his toothy smile, told the world of the ziggurat bridge links between the new tower and the old palace. Blah, blah, blah, she thought. Blah. Since her mother's death she no longer received any information or cuttings about him so she studied his photograph carefully. He looked, she thought, well cared for and not so old as his years, but certainly not as young as she looked by comparison. This pleased her. Even though, she thought, feeling sorry for herself again, even though it seemed to be all the ammunition she had.

Patrick was also quoted in the catalogue as saying 'At the very best, Modernism is free of its chains. I

389

look to the past for my inspiration in the future. Brunel, in particular, is a very great hero of mine and he would applaud this celebration of the first half of the nineteenth century in England. I am honoured to design the bridges that will link and lead you around the exhibition. Thus proving that the design of buildings and great structures is the most enduring and international of all the plastic and graphic arts. This building is neither Museum as Shrine, Museum as Temple, nor Museum as Spectacle, but a living, organic building in which the exhibits are as important as the spectators and the building is a beautiful, fulfilling space. I think the Babylonians would have liked it. And its international, cross-cultural relevance is clearly recognised by the fact that after Paris it will travel to Tokyo, and Yokohama, the new heartlands of futuristic design investment.' Blah.

Babylonians? He had never mentioned *them* before. She lay back on her several pillows and gazed at the ornate mouldings in the ceiling—cherubs, flowers, fruit and frolicking naked ladies—and she smiled to remember how Patrick would have hacked them all off, smoothed the surface, painted it all white or perhaps cream. And she would have agreed. Well—she liked the cherubs and the fruit and the frolickers (indeed, since Edwin was hardly Lochinvar in the saddle nowadays, she had quite a lot of time to study and grow fond of them all). She smiled to herself, and closed her eyes, and made a mental note to look up the Babylonians. Patrick's ego, she thought, might one day be Patrick's downfall. She also thought, remembering long ago, that sometimes, when he got too much on his high horse, what Patrick needed was sex. The only way to stop him—she yawned—was sex, sex, sex. The one thing she was very good at. Which set, in her sleepy, sulky mind, an idea. Cinderella shall not attend the ball, she thought, as she drifted into oblivion, but someone else might. The shadow of Delphine Bolle made her shudder for a moment with the memory of the humiliation, and then drifted away again. It need not be like that. She would think of something, she would. And with that comforting thought she was soon, very soundly, asleep.

*   *   *

Delphine Bolle's shadow might flee, but the idea of attending the opening did not. Indeed, the following morning the idea had grown considerably more solid. Patrick would be there. And it seemed that she would not. Faceless again. Voiceless again. Hidden away. The Director's lack of acknowledgement for her idea made the sting of it all the sharper. For all anyone knew half of his blessed Victorian males in his bloody old show had got their ideas from women in the first place.

'Oh, Charles—don't you think that amoeba has the look of our little Samuel about it?'

'Oh, Isambard—how my garters do keep breaking so—if only I could have iron suspenders . . .'

'Well,' she said to herself angrily, tearing at her breakfast croissant. 'Well. And who's to say the women had not?'

Le Monde that morning was full of tributes to *Le Temps Japonais*—theatres, art, music, dance— which had grown out of the nucleus of the Louvre show. Paris now embraced a cultural invasion by

391

the exotic east.

By the time she had eaten her croissant, Audrey knew what she was going to do. She would after all and in a manner of speaking Dress That Puppet.

*   *   *

She telephoned the Director's assistant and said that she was calling from the Japanese Embassy and that they wished to send one more dignitary. A Madame Koi. 'Is that C-o-y?' asked the assistant. 'No,' said Audrey, much amused, 'it is *not*.'

The assistant assumed that all Japanese women giggled, having seen *Sayonara* with subtitles, and Audrey spoke in what she imagined was the slight sing-song of a Japanese voice, as she had seen *Sayonara* too. The ruse worked. They all agreed that since there was only a week before the Grand Opening and the post was not good, it would be best if the Embassy sent a chauffeur to collect the invitation.

The deception went smoothly. Audrey had been doing deception for nearly thirty years and she was good at it. With pleasure she removed the deckle-edged card from its thick white envelope and placed it in the cupboard with the yellowing linen and the Brunel books. Another little secret. If it worked it would be very, very funny.

Naturally enough Edwin could not visit Audrey on the Big Day for he had to attend his wife. Which was just as well, really. If he had called on his mistress of nearly thirty years' standing (or lying) he would not have found her at home. Instead he would have discovered a Japanese Lady of strange and distinguished appearance, pouting and

392

pirouetting in his Dearest Audrey's place. The shock might have killed him.

Madame Koi surveyed herself in the mirror. Something between a geisha and a high-class, traditional Japanese wife looked back at her. Madame Koi giggled and remembered to put her fingers to her cherry red lips. The wig would be hot, but it was correct and from the best theatrical costumiers in Paris. It was neither stylised split-peach geisha, nor a flat, black bob, but something in between, and it looked the part. Madame Koi's scarlet gown, embroidered with cherry blossom, was an elegant adaptation of a kimono, with a bright ochre belt that was wide enough to give the impression of the traditional obi. The costumier explained that to wear the full regalia—which Madame Koi had hoped to do—would render her more or less unable to move. This outfit, he explained with pride, came from the original stage production of *The Teahouse of the August Moon*— costumed by Molyneux no less—at the Théâtre de Savoie—*before* the foolish American film version. Such a gown was designed—as perhaps only a French House could achieve—to keep the essence of Japanese style without the encumbrances. 'So that the wearer may move around the stage quite easily and freely.'

Since Madame Koi thought that she would probably have to move around her particular stage more easily and freely than most, given the number of people who would be at the gathering and from whom it was incumbent upon her to be able to move freely and easily away, she accepted the compromise. Indeed, as Madame Koi remarked to the startled costumier, it might be

393

less a case of moving around a lot quite easily and freely than running away a lot and rather fast.

'In which case, Madame,' he said, with the merest hint of a leer, 'you will not require the traditional *okobo* which are designed entirely so that the wearer may be caught . . .'

He removed from her reluctant hands the shiny lacquered wedges and replaced them with flat, beaded shoes in the design of a dragon. 'The sign of sin,' he said, 'in any language.' His hand had lingered on hers. Not bad, she thought, for a woman of fifty. It gave her courage.

*   *   *

Once back in her apartment she told her maid, still the God-fearing Evie, that she would not need her that night. That she would probably go to bed early. Evie was glad. She thought she would go and watch the crowds of distinguished *personnages* arriving at the Louvre.

'Good idea,' said Audrey. 'Say hallo to Gérard Depardieu from me . . .' she managed to sound wistful. 'And Catherine Deneuve.' Evie stroked her arm, said she was sorry, that it was such a sad life sometimes, and left. Audrey instantly began to dress.

When she finally slipped on the beaded dragon shoes she smiled—as much as the heavy make-up allowed her to smile. Like the wig, her face was painted to look something between the full geisha face and the stylised application of a good Japanese wife at a formal evening function. In other words, Madame Koi looked the business. She bowed into the mirror three times and smiled. She felt oddly liberated. Oddly at one with the part. Unfettered, in fact. Strange how being in disguise could set you free.

When Edwin rang at a few minutes to six, apparently to seek her reassurance before he left for the exhibition, she even found herself doing a little geisha knees-bend bob at the telephone. Never could she more honestly say 'Yes' to his 'Are you sure you are all right about this?' Indeed, it was all she could do to stop herself from saying 'Hai'.

They usually spoke English but—without thinking —she ended their conversation with '*à tout à l'heure*'.

'Dearest,' said Edwin, 'you know that I have to accompany my wife back to the house tonight.'

'Sorry,' she said lightly. 'I forgot.'

'Sleep well,' he said, and the telephone was replaced.

'*À bientôt*,' she said, before replacing hers. '*À*-bloody-well-bugger-it-*bientôt*!'

12

Enter Madame Koi

Bridges were interesting, thought Apsu. They were romantic, they were useful, they made connections and they divided. But, she asked herself, looking up at the mounting ziggurats, the harsh jaggedness, the soaring heroics, 'Why build a bridge? What effects, negative and positive, will it have on the people who use it? Who will use it and how much Heroic Requirement would *they* have? More to the point—why didn't Patrick Parker just install an entire bank of lifts?' Climbing from floor to floor would be so *hard*. Well, of course, there were other ways of getting to each of the floors on the new extension—by coming through the old building—just as they were planning for the Sainsbury Wing at the National—but that, at least, was gentle to the eye. To Apsu's mind, while this design was exciting, and she could not deny it, it was also—yes—no other word for it— Spectacular. God made Spectacular, she wrote in her notebook—Niagara Falls, Grand Canyon—Man made things for Humankind.

Madame Koi's car pulled up a little late, which seemed wise. If she arrived too early the number of guests at the reception would be sparse and she would be too approachable. And while she wanted to make an impression (no doubt about that) she did not want to be taken under anyone's wing. She especially did not want to have to talk to Edwin, obviously, and he and his Madame would arrive early. It was his way. She was perfectly aware of the risk that nearly thirty years of intimacy created. There might be something in the movement of her wrist, or the way she walked, that gave her away. And if she was found out? She would probably lose everything, everything being dignity. She would certainly lose his trust, his respect and—possibly—whatever security she was supposed now to own. It was a risk. It was a very big risk. She had never, really, taken one quite so big before. Edwin might not have her murdered, but he could very easily have her cast outside the city walls.

One thing she knew about women in her position. Birds sometimes stayed in bushes. Marie, the pretty young woman of thirty-five who had dined at the Curator's, now the Director's side at L'Arlésienne was no longer at his side. She was living in a small, cramped, dusty apartment with her grey roots growing through and little to show for her years of loyalty besides a diminishing stock of trinkets and the small, cramped, dusty apartment. Audrey visited her once and came away quite shaken. So far, as they said in the movies, she had kept her nose clean, but if she offended Edwin's curiously old-fashioned morality there was potentially a great price to pay. And old men could be fickle. She had seen that side of him too. It seemed quite appropriate to be wearing a costume that hinted of the geisha.

She hesitated. She need not go through with it. She could just melt away into the night. Problem was, she always *did* melt away into the night. And tonight she wanted to solidify. She had a score to settle. Her own honour, humble thing, was at stake. She moved forward again. She had every intention of serving it. Lightly up the grand entrance with, she fondly hoped, the right kind of small Japanese steps, she pattered. At the top she paused and took a deep breath while the doorman swung open the glass doors for her. State-of-the-art tubular steel handles, she had time to notice, just the sort of thing Patrick would approve of. He had once, in the old days, walked her around the shop called Heals and showed her Swedish cutlery which, he said, was the only stuff to buy. In the meantime, he explained, if you couldn't afford it you might as well buy your table settings at Woolworth's. She preferred the shape of the Woolworth's cutlery, finding some confusion in her mind as to which end of a perfectly designed, stainless steel Swedish knife actually did the cutting. And said so. She could still remember the pained look he gave her. But she consoled herself. He would never know that the person who misunderstood minimalism and the art of cutting meat then, was the same person who now talked to him of architectural moderns like Aldo Rossi, Mark Mack and Adele Naude as if they were old friends. And who came from Japan. Japan encapsulating all things cool and rarefied and desirable nowadays. She certainly intended to talk to him about such people—if she could effect it.

The invitation was removed from her hand smoothly enough, the smile from the flunky as he waved her graciously through showed no hint of suspicion. 'I'm in,' she said to herself, over and over again. 'I've done it . . .' Even if it was standing in somebody else's shoes.

Madame Koi paused for a moment and looked around her, smiling and nodding at the press of guests as they made their way towards the Reception Hall. A tray of drinks stood on an artistic creation that might or might not have been a trolley. She remembered the Delphine Bolle fiasco and passed it by.

On the wall straight ahead of her was a vast projected image of Isambard Kingdom Brunel standing by a table with his hands elegantly indicating the plans for the Great Western Railway. The Horsley portrait. He was looking down at her, straight into her eyes. 'Sod off,' she said to him, under her breath. She knew quite enough about him to understand that he would disapprove wholeheartedly of what she was doing. Women should be restful creatures and not go about trying to assert themselves. To be strident, and to be female, in Isambard's blinkered world, was sin.

Some hero. Her determination increased as she looked up at that deceptively quiet pose, that deceptively dignified expression. The man had dogged her for long enough. She showed him the tip of her little pink tongue and, feeling very pleased with herself, off she glided without giving him a second glance.

But Madame Koi realised that she was a little premature in her pleasure. For she had quite forgotten one little problem. And that little problem was, Other Japanese. Of whom—since Japan was booming economically and next in line for this exhibition—there were quite a few attending the function. And much as small girls at birthday parties will eye each other's frocks, say little and think much, so did the eyes of the

Japanese ladies look Madame Koi up and down, blink a bit, look her up and down again, and not know quite what to make of her.

Of course, to Western eyes, Madame Koi's appearance was—if exotic—convincing. But to the eyes of her putative compatriots, it was, quite simply, weird. Indigenous Retro had not come to the *beau monde* of Japan. If you wanted to do retro in Japanese circles, you did it Western style. You had a quiff like Elvis or sequinned denim like Dolly Parton. You did not wear a mixture of Geisha and Imperial Empress Goes Walkabout. But it did have one advantage. Only the boldest of the Japanese contingent were likely to be brave—or impolite—enough to remark on what they saw. But as Madame Koi muttered to herself as she entered the door marked *Femmes*—it only needed one. And—sure enough—here she bloody-well-bugger-it was . . .

The woman bending over and washing her hands stared at Madame Koi in the mirror and made as if to speak. Madame Koi smiled and bent her knees a fraction before disappearing into a cubicle. She did not come out until she was sure she was safe. Just what she needed, a proper Japanese woman trying to engage her in conversation in Japanese. Eventually the tap was turned off, there was the shush of a towel being thrown into the basket, and the door closed. Alone at last. Madame Koi emerged. She washed her hands, smoothed her wig, adjusted the lines of heavy make-up around her eyes, sent up a prayer to whoever might be on hand to receive it, and prepared to go back into the fray. Then she swung open the door with an air of confidence she was beginning not to feel. There were far too many Japanese guests out there to trip

400

her up. And how right she was. For she immediately fell over the feet of her previous companion from the Ladies' Powder Room, who stood, as those strange people who travel down escalators will stand, at the bottom of them, transfixed and right in her way.

The woman gave a little yelp and rubbed her foot. The man she stood with—presumably her husband—looked from his wife to Madame Koi as if wondering what to do next. They both blinked at Madame Koi who made little noises to indicate her embarrassment. She made little noises largely because—for a moment—she could do nothing else. And then a very familiar voice, from somewhere in front of her and therefore from behind her assumed companions, said in English, 'My dear Madame Kencho, are you all right?' Madame Kencho made noises of approval and greeting that were definitely genuinely Japanese in origin. The familiar English voice, with its delicate hint of accent, returned the approval in a very familiar, definitely, genuinely English-worded way. And then Madame Koi heard another voice, also very familiar, and not at all convincing in her opinion, say in Japanese, and with feeling, '*Sumimasen, sumimasen*, Madame . . .'

It was hers.

*   *   *

She heard it only faintly because the familiar, definitely genuinely English voice was still reverberating around in her head. '*Sumimasen, sumimasen,*' she said again, weakly. And waited for the God of Wrath to have his way. For the voice was, of course, Edwin's. Speaking English, presumably, because it was expected.

Madame Kencho turned to Madame Koi, who had suddenly discovered what it meant to be rooted to the spot, and directed a smiling and totally incomprehensible stream of definitely genuinely Japanese at her. The gestures that helped deliver it were obviously meant to be reassuring. The expectation of full understanding and something in return, was anything but. Madame Koi could only nod and bow with what she assumed was suitable subservience. But the woman had obviously ended whatever it was she was saying with a question. And waited.

Madame Koi smiled, shrugged and giggled. Which did not seem to hit the required spot. So, with sweetly apologetic mien, she began to back away. No such luck. The all too familiar voice said, still in English, 'Please do not leave on our account, Madame . . . ?'

She looked up and directly into the eyes of first, Monsieur Edwin Bonnard, and then his good—if on the square side—lady wife. She scarcely dared look. She then realised what was required of her by all the parties. She bowed slightly and said, in just about the silliest voice ever, 'Madame Koi.' She bowed again, glad to look away. 'I am very pleased to meet you.' She extended a hand and immediately snatched it away again. She had forgotten to remove her turquoise ring.

During the awkward silence that followed she noticed two things. One was that Madame Bonnard, rigid in black lace so that she looked as if someone had thrown a mourning tablecloth over a double coffin, did not look—quite—as frail and doolally as Edwin had led her to think. Madame B. might not be in the pink but she was a far cry from having one foot in the grave . . . Two was that Edwin was unmistakably giving her—Madame Koi—the approving eye. This produced a strange mixture of emotions in her twin personae—mainly jealousy for Audrey waiting back in the apartment, but also a little wicked, pleasurable amusement for Madame Koi. A very odd experience to be both cheated upon, and the cheater. Unique, probably. There was something else, too. Something about the wifely way Madame Bonnard had her mottled old hand with its too many rings hooked so very comfortably through her husband's arm. It gave both of her, the one waiting at home and the one here in fancy dress, a kick in the ribs. She looked up, stared straight into Monsieur Edwin Bonnard's appreciative eyes, and—on a whim—she winked.

Then she bowed once more and melted away into the throng leaving behind the charming picture of four sets of lips all making a silent 'Oh'.

Once out of sight she slumped. It shook her more than she might have expected, seeing the two of them together and so intimately. Knowing someone has a wife, even seeing photographs of them together, is not the same as being in the presence of the living, breathing flesh that is legitimate two-made-one. Beneath her pale mask Madame Koi felt herself redden at the way that plump and mottled wifely hand held on to her husband as if she had every right. Which, of course, she did. When Audrey and Edwin linked arms in the few semi-public places that might allow such behaviour, there was always an edginess about it. She knew that cement between people. It was strong, it was the rights of both propriety and property. She knew it because she had felt it once, and only once, while she was with Patrick. The absolute public right to be seen together in your own clothes. Before he dumped her, of course.

Come on, Aud, she told herself. Do not dwell. Move on. She approached one of the grand, open doorways that led to a terrace, which in turn led to the first link bridge which led to the new extension and the exhibition. There were several bridges linking the tall tower with the much shorter grandeur of Claude Perrault's East Front. Personally Audrey thought the seventeenth century looked a bit huffy alongside the upstart Babylonians, Patrick's ziggurat-style bridges, but at least the terrace leading to the first of them allowed her to breathe some of the evening air and recover herself a little.

She was in a dangerous state—inclined to go back inside—find Edwin and Mrs bloody Edwin—and announce herself. See how he liked having two of them perched one each on an arm . . . See where leering gets you, she could say . . . Except, except—back came the spectre of Delphine Bolle. That achieved nothing. Only a victory of sorts for Madame. And perhaps she had already taken enough from her. She stood there for a while breathing deeply, trying to relax, closing her eyes. But then—when she opened them again—and as if on cue—across the terrace's shadowy space she saw Patrick.

Absurdly he was standing by a tub containing some exotic kind of bush, in direct line to where she must go if she was to enter the exhibition. No violins played, no great finger came pointing at him through the deepening night sky. It was all very ordinary. He was nodding in grave concentration with an expensively dressed couple whom Audrey recognised as the American Van Crees. Mrs Van Cree was a lady who lunched. Though she never lunched with Audrey, of course. Mrs Van Cree had a great deal of money and liked to spend it on what she called 'Cultural atonement for being Americans abroad'. Which included, according to Edwin whom it greatly amused, never learning a foreign language. Why should you? thought Audrey, watching the diamonds flash. She was a redoubtable woman.

From the way she moved and her facial expression and her waving hands it was clear that Mrs Van Cree was in admiring mood and the object of her admiration was Patrick. Schmoozing the creator, it was called, and the creator, his knuckle to his chin, his expression concerned and rapt, responded wholeheartedly. Every time. Audrey had seen enough of it even in her peripheral life. No doubt they would all dine together later. Back came that flickering old flame again. For—just like Edwin—Patrick also had a wife hanging on his arm. But to Audrey Wapshott's expert eye, he did not look entirely relaxed about it and nor did horrible Peggy. Indeed, Peggy Boxer As Was looked distinctly anxious—and definitely timid and strangely windswept. She kept staring about her as if a ghost was about to walk in. Oh, it really was too, too much. All these allowable, amenable wives. If she was married to Edwin nowadays, for example, she'd kick up so hard he'd never look at another woman again as long as he lived. Not that she would marry him now, even if he asked her, she decided, in a comfortably muddled way.

Patrick. Who—and who was she kidding when she tried to pretend—looked irritatingly, maddeningly—wonderful. No. Be fair. Who looked—well—sexy. Well—sexy and desirable. She—dammit—wanted him. All over again. Like it was rotten-well yesterday. And Peggy Boxer As Was, as usual, was right in the way. Madame Koi could hardly lead him off and conduct the conversation—and anything else that might happen—while the Boxer female was pulling so hard on his arm it might come off. I am not in the least jealous, she told herself, straining to study the twitching little figure beside him—wearing red, such a harsh colour, kept her figure though, thought babies were supposed to thicken you, bit on the stringy side now—

Behind her someone spoke French, in a voice so English and clipped that she nearly laughed. The strangled very English voice now addressed an ill-assorted group of men and women. They could only be the Press.

'Mr Rennie and Mr Parker will do their press interviews immediately after the President's opening speech, in approximately one hour's time. We have an interview room behind the exhibition halls—Chamber Three—just up there—on the left.'

Madame Koi looked to see where Just Up There might be.

'It is set aside for you. Later we will bring in the interior designers who will also be happy to take your questions. After that we will go up to the Panoramic Dining Room and you can fire your shot at me . . . Mr Rennie has yet to arrive. He is currently being interviewed by the BBC.' The voice said BBC with some relief. It knew where it was with that.

'Ah,' thought Madame Koi. 'Ah-ha . . .'

Rennie, she knew from her catalogue, was the other design star in the firmament. Once they were whisked off and caught up in the whole circus of the thing, Patrick would be lost to her. Therefore, if she was to achieve being alone with him, it was now, or never. Now or Never.

*   *   *

Nearby a man was talking in Franco-English to a serious, dignified-looking group of men—probably the EU contingent—and he was explaining that for inclement weather the retractable PVC roof slid into place as easily as the hood of a Rolls-Royce convertible. Later they would see a demonstration. 'And if you will come this way,' he added, striding off across the terrace, 'I will show you the clever use of those ancient Babylonian principles of his . . . And, if we can find him, we might be able to have a word or two before the big interview takes place . . .'

She watched them go, saw that they did not notice Patrick who was still standing by the potted plant in earnest conversation with the adoring Van Crees, straightened her back, became Madame Koi again and slipped her way across to them. She thought they might hear her heart beating, or feel the heat of her. The sight of Patrick becoming closer and closer and closer, made her feel a little sick. But if she was frightened, she was also suddenly determined. She had her own form of designs on him. Nothing must stop her now.

407

Patrick looked up as she approached. Peggy Boxer As Was looked up immediately afterwards. The Van Crees stopped talking, open-mouthed. Madame Koi gave a little, apologetic smile—she was getting good at them—and slid her hand up through the crook of Patrick's other, free arm.

'Now, Monsieur Parker,' she said, in her best Japanese-accented English, which did not sound at all convincing to her, 'I have to take you away to the Press Room. You will excuse us?'

She nodded first at Peggy, then at the Van Crees, and moved him away before anything else could be said. She looked back once. Peggy, looking even more anxious and uncertain, stood there in her bright red outfit which, at that moment, both Madame Koi and Audrey were pleased to see, did little for the sudden wanness of her face.

'Do not worry, Madame Parker,' said Madame Koi, most kindly. 'I will bring him back to you safely—in a little while . . .'

And she left the three of them eyeing each other uneasily. After all, thought Madame Koi, one could quite see the Van Clees' point of view. Who would want to be left with Peggy Boxer to talk to? As Was.

13

Architecture Today

It was a good photo opportunity. Apsu knew exactly why her bursary donor agreed to taking her around the exhibition before the official opening. It looked good for him. The British press took photographs of the two of them. 'A Big Smile from the New Generation'—she could guess the headlines. 'What do you think of it, Apsu?' he asked, smiling with those even white teeth of his.

Around them the cameras were clicking, notebooks were waving, small microphones hung on the air. The Sunday Colour Supplement Rush. She sketched a line in the air. 'It should be like this, and this . . .'

Patrick kept smiling. 'You are young,' he said.

'You are old,' she replied.

'Well?' he said. 'Don't hang back. Tell me what you really think. I really want to know.'

'I think,' she said, quite loudly, 'that it is too damned Butch.'

He laughed. Perhaps even flirtatiously.

So she added, 'I think the Babylonians would have taken you outside the city walls and fed you to the crows if you built this in their name.'

Bang goes the job he offered me, she thought. But it was worth it.

'If you go on like this,' her tutors said, when she returned, 'you will be unemployable.'

'Of course I won't,' she said, more bravely

409

than she felt. 'I'm going to build good things. People will want them. You'll see.'

The one thing she knew for sure, and which made her brave, was that the bursary could not be taken away from her no matter—almost— what. So long as she did not burn the college down . . . Though looking at the building, it could certainly do with it. The marble pillars of Grand Imperialism. Never, ever, again if she had anything to do with it in future. And she would.

After Paris, Patrick Parker never spoke to her in any willing form again. Except when he was forced to, on the platform, as she was handed the College Gold Medal. 'Congratulations,' he said, in a voice that meant 'Rot in Hell, you ungrateful little bastard.'

Audrey decided to drop the accent which was growing tiresome. Happily Patrick did not seem to notice. As they stood at the entrance to the first tier of the bridge and looked along its glass path, underlit and ethereal in the night, she told him how clever she thought the concept. He was so rapt by the sudden sight of his work and by her words, and still so bruised from the encounter with his Bursary Student that morning, she could have started speaking Swahili and he would not have noticed.

To refocus his attention, she pinched him. On the back of his hand. Which was so unexpected he found it—well—almost erotic.

'It is very fine, very strong, but feminine, too,' she said, thinking that just about covered all possibilities. She kept her arm tight through his, her bosom pressing into him. 'So regular. Like the webbing of a spider.'

He brought himself back into the world of speech. What did stupid little Bursary Students know? He nodded into his thinker's knuckles again. 'A good metaphor,' he said seriously. 'Delightful.'

How she longed to say, *you've changed your tune* . . . But no. 'We must hurry.' She raced him along.

'You think it is successful?' he asked. Rhetorically, obviously.

'Very fine,' she repeated. 'Very.'

'Feminine?' he sounded worried.

'Very sexy.' She gave her little *Sayonara* giggle again.

What a sensitive woman, he thought.

Madame Koi kept her arm firmly in place. She had him now and by *tofu* she wasn't going to let him go. 'I mean, gentle on the eye,' she said, and picked up speed. The little beaded dragon shoes were a shuffling blur as they raced along. 'It makes you want to get right into it—to experience it from within. Like a woman.'

She giggled very foolishly again and surprised herself. Ancient Knowledge.

Patrick pressed his thinker's knuckles firmly against his lips. Less from any Rodinesque requirement than the need to control any sounds emanating. That's more like it, he thought.

The bridge's glow had a greenish tinge that was not, entirely, flattering. 'It would perhaps have been kinder to make the lighting *rose.*'

He stopped, stricken.

She pulled him onward again. 'But that is just a whim—who wants to light up such an august institution like a bordello? He certainly would not

411

approve.' She pointed at the wall with its hologram of Brunel. 'Something of a hero of yours, I think,' and she hurried on.

'Madame . . . ?' he said cautiously. 'I am sorry I don't know—'

She noticed that his flat Midlands accent had now been completely replaced by a carefully modulated English Received.

'You are from Coventry originally, I think?' she said. 'Ah yes. Godiva's city. The Naked Lady. I know it well. And yet you have no trace of an accent . . . Why is that?'

A man who was interested in the world might question how a curiously dressed Japanese woman came to know Coventry and its Naked Lady so well and to distinguish such things. She waited for him to ask. He did not. In general, for Patrick, how other people lived and what motivated them was not his concern. How they related to him was. And this Japanese woman was relating to him just fine.

'I have been in London for many years,' he said shortly. 'I scarcely remember Coventry.'

'David Hockney has been living in California for about the same . . .' she said crisply. 'He still talks in Yorkshire but then I suppose if one is insecure about one's breeding . . .'

'Do you know David Hockney, then?' He was impressed. An Englishman more well-known than him.

'I know everyone,' she said.

She speeded up. His stertorous breathing was music. He's taken the bait, she thought. He's taken it. She was busily scanning signs for Chamber Three as they climbed higher and higher up the ziggurat. It was—she knew—a crazy, brave design by any standards—the rising levels gentle enough, the views stunning from each of the ascending ramps. She liked it. But she was not convinced it looked right here. Presumably Babylonian terrain was rather different from the centre of Paris. She was getting puffed. Fortunately so was he.

'No elevators,' she said.

'Spoils the line,' he gasped. 'You can always come through the main building if you are disabled.'

'Doesn't that stigmatise them?'

Patrick ignored this. He knew the methods of the disabled lobby very well. A change of subject was required. 'Who did you say you represented?'

'*Nexus Tokyo*. It was founded by Isozaki.' She gave him a quick look. 'The great Isozaki who transformed modern Tokyo—'

'I know, I know,' said Patrick peevishly. 'I have worked with him. I am often in Japan.'

'I know. I can see that from this design,' she said. 'The ziggurat is perhaps a homage—one would not care to say copy—to Santos. Adele Naude Santos? You know her work. The estate complexes?'

Patrick nodded even more peevishly.

'And you admire it?'

'Of course I admire it. Those housing developments, that tight space she worked with—magnificent.'

'And when we look at your bridge we see that you have taken the common Santos elements—the organic handling of light as an essential element for moulding spaces—and we see that you have reversed them.'

'We do?' He shook his head. 'I mean, I have?'

'We certainly do. You certainly have. The underlighting you have placed under the glass

413

walkways is so bold—whereas she is so subtle . . .
You are not interested in subtle, Mr Parker, are
you?'

Her elbow immediately came out of her sleeve.
She quickly covered it as Patrick found himself—
incredibly—peeping at a bloody *elbow*.

'Now wait a minute—' he said. He *was* interested
in subtle. Very much.

She brushed his words aside. 'Now—let's get on
to the interview room and while we do so you can
explain to me about the Babylonian Principle and
the influence of Mr Brunel . . . And also—I think
your wife is very much older than you?'

'My wife? Well no. I think she's the same—'

'You only think,' Madame Koi stopped and
tapped his arm again. Any more of this, she
thought, and he'd be quite justified in throwing me
off his bloody bridge. But he showed remarkable
fortitude. 'I think we should stick to my
professional life,' he said.

Is there a difference? she wondered. 'Surely you
should know the age of your wife . . . ?'

'She is—the same—'

'Then she looks a great deal older. Do you still
sleep with her?'

'Of course—' he said indignantly.

'Our readers,' she said comfortably, 'want to
know everything, everything.'

'Brunel—' he said firmly, 'has been a great
influence on my work and my thinking and—'

'And you must even now be working on your design
for the Queen's Millennium Bridge. Across the
Thames? In Brunel's footsteps?'

Patrick stared at her.

There was something altogether *delicious* about

414

the way he frowned, she thought. All broody and moody. Like an old-fashioned film star—if she could remember who. She sent up a silent thank-you to *Architecture Today*. 'And do you think you will win?'

'None of this is official,' he said.

'No,' she agreed. 'But we all know that it is your heart's desire and we all know that a bridge is to be commissioned. You have been tipped by the pundits, Mr Parker.' She then winked.

A very faint light, accompanied by a far-off little bell, floated into his subconscious. Something was not entirely right here . . .

Madame Koi observed how his colour now changed to quite a deep shade of rose. 'I am quietly confident,' he said. 'It has always been my one great sorrow that I have never put a bridge across my own, native, great river.'

Yuk, thought Madame Koi. 'Your wife, Mr Parker? She supports you? She is your arbiter? Or does she merely wash your socks?'

The rose deepened, the eyes flashed. He looked dangerous and exciting and angered by the impertinence. Madame Koi nearly laughed with excitement herself.

'Oh, you must not mind what I ask. In Japan,' she said airily, 'we can discard our wives, or our husbands, with impunity if they do not please us in bed any more. Shinto, you know.'

She hoped he was not, like some modern creative types, into exotic religions. And she apologised, in her head, to any Shinto god who might happen to be listening. But—needs must and the devil was surely driving her. In the distance she could see the men in suits looking anxious. 'I was interested in your interest in Appelles,' she said, Japanese-shuffling and kimono-wiggling him onwards. Her energy came from adrenalin but it couldn't last for ever and she was nearly passing out with both mental and physical exertion. Patrick, too, puffed along behind her. There was something in the gradient of a ziggurat bridge taken at a lick that did not sit well with a man of his years. 'You approve of Appelles?' he puffed.

'*Hai*,' she said. And looked at him in a way that suggested there was truth behind the myth about Japanese women knowing how to treat a man. 'Alexander's artist in residence. Alexander would only be painted by Appelles, and Appelles would only paint him if Alexander gave him his beautiful mistress. Which he did. All to the artist, the artist is all.'

'Well, that's not the *only* thing about him,' said Patrick grudgingly.

I'll bet it's pretty high up on the list, she thought.

'Do you have a mistress, Mr Parker?'

'No,' he said. Patrick did not think that one of the juniors in the practice whom he occasionally saw for dinner and sex constituted the grandeur of the title. 'No,' he said again. 'I have not.'

'You should have,' said Madame Koi sweetly. 'It is good for a man. It keeps him young and vital.' He began to wish—despite the pure beauties of the ziggurat—that they had used the lift in the main building.

'And are you somebody's mistress?' he said.

'Of course,' she replied. 'And for the duration of my being with you now, I am yours. We are like that in Japan, we women. We are generous.'

There really was nothing, absolutely nothing, to

416

say to that except 'How generous?' He felt he had better not risk it. They charged on. Quite where to at this stage he was unsure. Something about Chamber Three.

They reached the top of the last curve of the ziggurat—nearer to the sky. Surrounding them was the city; pale blue dusky light, stars just beginning to glimmer, river sounds and traffic sounds drifting up to them. She would rather have turned the clock back and stood there gazing at it all as she once was—young, silly and in love, but that was never going to happen. So she might as well enjoy this little charade and get on with it. The momentum was too precious to be lost. She turned away from the dusky city and saw a neon sign in the distance with an arrow pointing towards Chamber Three. It directed them through the first of the exhibition rooms. In they went, nodding at the men in peaked caps who nodded back and picked their teeth. Patrick was very hot and shiny though it was not unattractive. Madame Koi dabbed delicately at her cheek with her fingertip—she was shiny too. It would be most interesting when they took their clothes off.

*　　　*　　　*

Room One was a shrine to all things Brunel. Models of ships, a plaster cast of his hand, his measuring tools. She bowed her head at this most prettily. There was a statuette of Isambard, in Parian ware, showing him holding his quadrant as if it were the dagger of fate and with his sleeves rolled up over his elbows. 'Ah, the Great Man in all his glory,' she said, and touched one of the jutting

417

elbows with her finger end. A peaked cap moved forward. 'Sorry,' she said. 'Irresistible.' She turned to Patrick and gave a little flutter of her eyelids. 'How lucky you men were then—how lucky you still are—with your bodies.' She gave his elbow a gentle, lingering squeeze. 'In Japan at that time they were considered . . .' She leaned towards him and lowered her voice. 'Very intimate areas. On a woman. If a woman allowed a man to see up her sleeve—it was as if—in the West —she had invited him to look up her skirt.'

Patrick felt it necessary to change the subject.

They looked at bold drawings made by Brunel, exquisite in their detail—the Italianate pumping station at Starcross with its chimney disguised as a Venetian campanile (how Madame Koi giggled at it), the Gaz engine which cost him ten years of fruitless labour, a timber trestle viaduct built in Cornwall as a temporary measure and still there nearly one hundred years later. Even the little almost-doodles he made of king and queen trusses for use in the Stroud Valley bridges were framed and hung and made to look grand. Madame Koi admired the framing very much. Patrick was not at all sure if she was joking or not.

Then there were models of many designs—some contemporary like the fragile miniature of Chepstow Bridge made by Isambard's own hand— some newly made like the massive model of the *Great Eastern*, his biggest ship, his biggest success, that the Design and Engineering faculty had constructed entirely from recycled cardboard. This towered over the room and even Madame Koi gasped inelegantly when she saw it. Patrick was entranced.

'Oh,' he said, and ran his hands over a swag of chains fixed to the wall nearby. It was Madame Koi's turn to feel—somewhat warm—watching those familiar hands trace the massive links.

'The originals, wouldn't you say?' said Madame Koi. 'From the stern checking drum.'

'Yes,' he said a little testily. 'I do know that.'

She could not resist touching the metal too. 'Oh,' she said, 'but the links are as thick as a man's thigh—' She touched his briefly. 'And high as his calf—nothing cardboard about *them*.'

'No,' agreed Patrick. He loosened his tie.

*   *   *

At the far end of the room, set out on the floor, lay two lengths of railway line—

'Ah!' said Madame Koi, 'the famous track beds. The Gauge War. They've got the four-foot-eight-inch gauge and the seven-foot beside it. Quite a difference—yes? Your Mr Brunel's Sacred Cow.'

'The four-foot-eight-inch gauge preferred by Brunel's rival, Stephenson,' she read aloud from the plaque. 'Preferred by everybody actually,' said Madame Koi sharply. 'Except your old Isambard.'

'It was a Great Design Revolution,' said Patrick firmly. 'Brunel was never wrong.'

He could have sworn he heard her mutter, 'My arse.' In curiously familiar tones.

Next to the four-foot gauge lay a length of Isambard's massive seven-foot replacement gauge *as preferred by Mr Brunel*.

'Here we have the triumph of the intellect over the puerile,' announced Patrick. 'Stephenson had no conscience about human train travellers being

419

shaken to hell and back by such an inadequate gauge.'

'Nonsense,' she said briskly. 'It was just another case of Brunel's self-deception and godlike condescension. And quite unnecessary. It didn't make the slightest bit of difference what gauge was used for the comfort factor.'

Patrick was about to defend his hero until Madame Koi did something quite peculiar with her knees—moving them sideways in a strangely seductive gesture—and then bent down. 'But still . . .' she said as she ran her hands over the seven-foot gauge. 'It is so big and strong and thrusting that—' She smiled up at him. 'You could hardly blame him . . .'

'There's Chamber Three,' he said suddenly, in a voice that seemed slightly high.

'So there is,' she said.

She smiled that affecting smile again and he helped her up. By the elbow. Intimate, he thought, and squeezed it just a little.

She noticed, said nothing, except, 'Chamber Three. In we go then.'

As she opened the door he reached up and slid back the slot above the handle to reveal the word *Engagé*. So did she. Their hands met. Both of them smiled. And in they went.

14

The Brunel Strip

Apsu pondered the problem of being young and female in her chosen profession. Which was—though she was laughed at when she said it—the design and building of bridges. Well . . . it would be . . . one day. It was not going to be easy. There were still people who thought they had better not invest in her because she would one day stop building and make babies, and that her vision for the future was necessarily clouded by the problem of which sort of nappy to use for them. Not that anyone would dream of saying such a thing to Apsu. To her they said that civil engineering was as open to women nowadays as it was to men. But this was only theory. So far no woman had had sole responsibility for the design of a bridge. Except, of course, back in the mists of time, when the placing of stones or the plaiting of grass or hemp or agave or the mud-plastering of bent reeds was considered women's work. Back in those days, she thought, everyone knew how to build bridges. In the best way possible to get to the other side.

What she saw as she looked about her increased her determination. All the British Development Corporations so far set up to help the regeneration of the inner cities had ruined their efforts with poor design—there was talk of competitions—there was talk of a woman being among those chosen to be part of the team in the proposed London Docklands Development—

but when it came to it, Apsu doubted the woman would be in the forefront.* [Author's note: She wasn't.]

The room was about ten metres square and quite plain, with a long white chamois sofa next to the low window that looked out over Paris. There were three straight-backed chairs behind a plain white desk at the far end of the room, and multi-coloured metal stacking chairs around the edges. At the windows there were pale grey blinds. It was all very cool, very Rennie. There was also a water machine that made little bubbling noises. Evidently, since no sounds penetrated beyond this, the room was virtually soundproof. 'Perfect,' she said again. She turned the lamps on low and pulled the blinds down one by one. Patrick took off his jacket and threw it nonchalantly over his shoulder, to show how casual he was. Madame Koi thought he might be sorry for having done that, later.

Patrick was staring very fixedly at the water machine. State of the art. He knew every inch of it. Somehow it seemed to offer safety. Whatever was happening, and something definitely was happening, it would certainly be a very strange interview. But then, *Nexus Tokyo* was known to reflect the wilder world of design. Influential though, certainly influential.

Madame Koi shuffled her way to the sofa and sat down, straight-backed and formal.

'I have a proposal,' she said.

It did not matter what happened in this room, she decided, nor what he thought, nor what he did. And that was the point. Once she had cared and now she would show herself that she did not. He could spit in her eye and walk away and it would not matter one jot . . . But she knew him well enough. He would not. She chose *Nexus Tokyo* because it was one of the world's most prestigious international design magazines. And because she knew he would probably float upside-down in a vat of rancid butter to get his blessed Babylonian ziggurats featured.

'Would you like to come and sit here?' she said. 'Otherwise we shall be shouting at each other. I'd like you closer.'

He had indeed moved further away from her and nearer to the water machine. It bubbled away at him softly.

'Proposal?' said Patrick.

'Yes, Mr Parker, a proposal.'

'Call me Patrick,' he said.

'Very good,' she laughed. 'And you must call me Koi-Koi.'

*   *   *

What Madame Koi—Koi-Koi—suggested as her proposal was quite extraordinary. Patrick found himself focusing really hard on the water dispenser throughout the telling of it. It was like something out of the sixties, an Event, a Happening, the sort of thing they all thought was so cool when they were young and green and nine parts stoned. But he had clocked up half a century now and it didn't seem to go with the dignity of age. On the other hand—

Isambard himself, of course, would be whizzing in his grave—but Patrick would put up a stout defence of him. You *bet* he would. For the Koi-Koi woman had suggested that it would be interesting and entertaining (you could say that again) to run a piece deconstructing his hero Brunel. And—for the sheer hell of it—why didn't they have some fun along the way? When she offered a man some fun, she implied, it was seldom refused. Patrick saw the point. He listened to her suggestion in a kind of embarrassed wonder. For Madame Koi proposed that, during the interview, every time she managed to undermine one of Patrick's testimonials to his hero Brunel, Patrick would remove an article of clothing. Every time he managed to counter her sophistry and win the point for Brunel, she would remove an article of clothing. She called it the Brunel Strip.

'Brunel's reputation is unassailable,' he said.

'Shoes and socks count as one,' she said laughing. 'Do you agree?'

He smiled, folded his arms and nodded.

'Good,' she said. 'Then let battle commence.'

*   *   *

They settled themselves at each end of the sofa and Madame Koi began.

'Isambard Kingdom Brunel was invited, as you know, to design a bridge at Balmoral for the newly married Queen. For her and her beloved Albert to drive out of their private grounds in their carriage and pass across on to the public thoroughfare. Yes?'

Patrick nodded. 'And very fine it is too.'

Madame Koi coughed with irritation. 'Queen Victoria was a happy young woman in love, both with her country and her husband—and she was

424

very feminine. She wanted something light and pretty and decorative. What he built for her—wagging his patronising finger and saying I Know Best—was a single span, wrought-iron, plate-girdered *box*.'

'It was modern. It was a little revolution,' Patrick said, feeling quite comfortable in his clothes.

'It was slightly cambered—a little too cambered for the carriage—and very springy.' She tapped his arm playfully. '*Very* springy, Patrick. Too springy for Her Majesty, you remember. Every time she travelled across it wobbled so much she thought it was going to fall down. She had palpitations. Mr Brunel would not budge. That is what he designed for her, and that is what she got.'

'Your point?' asked Patrick comfortably. 'I hope you are not suggesting that a man should compromise his design principles just because he has the patronage of the Royal House of Hanover and Brunswick?'

She smiled, pityingly. 'He misjudged his client. Even a whore knows that you can't ignore the client's wishes entirely. And certainly not if the client happens to be the Queen of England. That is not clever—that is arrogance.' She licked her lips and looked him straight in the eye, and pouted. 'I believe,' she said sweetly, 'that *faux pas* is worthy of a shoe and a sock at the very least.'

Patrick was amused enough to oblige her by removing both his shoes and both his socks. After all, he would not be removing much more.

'Look,' he said comfortably, 'Brunel was a genius. He showed the way when everyone else was taking that desiccated Ruskin's line. He overruled the old-fashioned ideas and produced a little gem of modernity. Geniuses do not fail. They forge. Even with that little bridge he was merely showing the way forward, rather than looking back—' He wriggled his bare toes at her as if to say with them, QED.

'But surely,' she said, leaning forward and speaking in a strangely husky voice that went to somewhere around the centre of him, 'a man of real genius would know how to compromise?'

'Our job is to influence, not to stand still.'

'Sometimes,' she said, 'you get there faster by taking little steps.'

'Hah!' said Patrick.

She remembered: he always said that when he was lost for a reply. Good.

He crossed his legs defiantly. His feet looked white and familiar and just a little silly poking out from under his dark blue trousers. She leaned down and ran her fingertips over them. His toes moved involuntarily. 'Sweet,' she said.

Patrick shivered. 'Little steps?' he said. 'You were saying?'

'Quite simply, Patrick, your Mr Brunel cut off his nose to spite his face. Because he didn't please the Queen she never used him again. End of Patronage. Very silly, very stubborn man.'

'Hah!' he said again.

'Never again was there a Royal Commission. Imagine what that meant in those days of Royal Patronage and Empire and the highest watermark of British Industrialisation. With Prince Albert at the forefront. And Brunel turns his back on it. No further commissions for England's greatest living designer? How could that be?'

'That could be, my dear girl, because Victoria and

426

Albert were the Hausfrau and her Herr. He saw through them.'

It was the 'dear girl' that did it. She'd have those trousers off him or die in the attempt. She smiled and shifted a little further down the length of the sofa so that she was more lying back than sitting up. She put one arm behind her head, Maya-style—and an elbow popped out. Patrick, she saw, was now very confused about the sexual nature of elbows.

'I think this is what happened,' she said. Then she paused and ran her fingers up and down her funny bone, which had an interesting effect on her own erectile tissue and, from the look of him, on Patrick's too. They both—clearly—were Up For It.

She said, suddenly snappish, making Patrick jump. 'Now. Pay attention.'

Patrick said, quite crossly, 'I am.' He was, providing he stopped watching those little sliding fingers.

'I think,' she said, 'the Queen and Prince Albert drove out of the Balmoral Estate on to the bridge. First, she did not like the heavy, masculine look of it, given the light and decorative quality of the Gothic Revival, and, second, when they drove across it—it wobbled. That is recorded in the State papers. So there are two things wrong. First she does not like the look of it, and second she does not feel safe travelling on it. So they go back into the Castle and up to the boudoir and she bursts into tears. She's probably pregnant because she always was. And she asks Albert how he could possibly have misread her desires so . . . As for that scruffy, self-opinionated little man, Brunel, We (the royal We) will never use him again. Understood?

427

And Albert, a little shaken at his usually docile wife's reaction, agrees quickly enough. So Isambard Kingdom, and perhaps the nation, loses out just because he will not compromise for a queen—and, of course, a woman. That's him out in the cold.'

'That is the job of genius,' said Patrick. 'Confrontation. One stands up for one's beliefs and one will not budge. It moves things forward.'

'It also causes wars,' she said crisply. 'A little compromise now and again is no bad thing.'

He was not going to let her get away with that. Brunel's honour was at stake. She was now pressing her knee into the side of his knee with—interesting results. But—temporarily—Brunel won.

'What about the Great Exhibition of 1851?' he said smugly. 'He was at the very heart of the committee that set it up.' Patrick folded his arms and jutted his chin in a gesture reminiscent of his mother.

Madame Koi—reverting to Audrey Wapshott for a moment—very nearly forgot herself and said so. But Madame Koi swiftly stepped in and disaster was averted. 'That was self-aggrandisement,' she said. 'He designed a most awful brick and domed building which no one liked and when Paxton came along with his creation of glass and metal, the wonderful Crystal Palace, Brunel acknowledged it was better than his idea, that it was more beautiful, but he still tried to get his ugly old thing built. He even put it in writing that he was going to.'

Patrick's jaw was still bowsprit. She reached out and with the very tip of her finger pushed it back into place. Then she leaned into the cushions behind her and folded her arms and said sternly,

'Remove your tie.'

'Now wait a minute,' he said. 'I've just proved that Brunel went on to do something major for the Crown after all.'

'Oh, no, you haven't. That was *before* the Balmoral Bridge, silly. And it never got built. There was nothing afterwards, nothing at all.' She smiled. 'Tie off, please, and you can remove your belt as well—for arguing.'

'But—'

'Careful,' she said in that peculiarly husky voice, 'or I'll have your trousers, too.'

'I think,' he said, enjoying it all despite himself, 'that it's time I took an item or two off you. And what you must understand, my little Koi-Koi,' (his little Koi-Koi went a fetching shade of peony) 'is that Brunel was a ground-breaker. Bridges that he built to last for twenty or thirty years stood for a hundred. He cocked a snook—'

'Pardon?' she said quickly, leaning forward, pressing his thigh for a moment with her fingertips. 'Cocked?' she pouted.

No, thought Patrick. No. No. No. I *will* defend him. 'You just have to hand it to Isambard, and therefore to me, that his bridges were splendid creations and finely built. Now. Off, off, off.'

'Very well,' she said. 'I will.'

And without further ado she leaned forward and unhooked the back of her mock *obi*. Its heavy silk slithered to the floor. Followed, one after the other, by her little dragon shoes. And there were her toes, too, only with perfect crimson nails, and a clear desire to make up to his own, less spectacular set. 'I give you those for free, also,' she said softly.

Patrick took a deep breath. He tried to calm

himself with pictures of Brunel's achievements but it was like being told not to think of hippopotamuses—you couldn't think of anything else. He pictured the Boxford Tunnel. Oh dear God, no, that was long and dark and to be entered. Chepstow Bridge then? But that was all about trusses—King Truss, Queen Truss: Truss, Truss, Truss . . . The SS *Great Eastern*? Good God, no— not that—for it was built with screw and paddle- wheel. As for the bridge at Maidenhead with its wide and sensual curving egress—he must not think about it, he must not, he must not, he must not . . .

A vague, creeping sense that something very ridiculous was happening inched its way around him, but he was here in his professional capacity, and professional he would be . . . For now.

'I see myself in a long line of bridge builders that Isambard set free. We make structures on a par with the Colossus. Grand markers in history which exist because of the very nature of the architecture and engineering that produced the structure. In short Brunel showed that his bridges, in particular, were of themselves. Just as Jackson Pollock and Franz Kline said that the paint and the canvas are the reality and not a vehicle for a narrative visual conjuring trick—and just as Gabo sculpted truth to materials and form—'

Madame Koi seemed to stifle a yawn at this point. 'What made you want to be a builder yourself?' she asked. And closed her eyes.

He told her all about being born into a firebombed city. How it made a deep impression on him. That it was as if some Muse guided him.

She yawned again. And wrote a note or two on

430

her pad. As she wrote she said, 'Your mother was a great support, I think.'

'She was,' said Patrick. He tried very hard not to picture his mother at this moment, for obvious reasons. 'She encouraged me to be myself.' He thought she muttered, 'You can say that again' into her notebook. 'I'm sorry?' he said.

She ignored the question. 'And your father?'

'Absolutely not. Just a ticket collector at the railway. Nothing.'

Audrey, who re-emerged, nearly threw the pad at him. Madame Koi was more polite. 'Sometimes we don't know where we get our influences from until we ask ourselves.'

'Not my dad,' said Patrick. 'Definitely.'

She yawned again.

It really was very off-putting. 'You should go to bed earlier,' he said waspishly.

'I did,' she said. 'That's why I'm tired. It was a— very—active night. And you?'

Patrick blushed. Patrick had also had a very active night, but not of that variety. Patrick had sat up in his hotel bed with Peggy by his side and she had been wondering—nearly all night it seemed to him—what she should wear the next day and whether Audrey Wapshott would be there. What was left of the night he then spent calming her down after he said, innocently enough, that he hoped she would be there, that he would like to see her again, see what she was getting up to—that he had a very soft spot for her. He only realised Peggy was upset when the bed started shaking.

Which meant that Peggy arrived here tonight looking windswept and acting like a hunted animal. How odd it all was since Audrey was so very long

431

ago.

'You cannot deny,' he said, desperately, 'that Brunel brought modernism into industrial design.'

'You mean, away with the painting of cathedrals so that we may see the shape of the stones . . .'

'Without him there could have been no Aare Bridge at Aarburg, for example—'

'Ah yes,' said Madame Koi. Her eyes were shining now, and she rubbed her foot hard against his. 'The Aare. Maillart and his transverse frames set into the—mmm—haunch—of the arch. So sexy, these terms, are they not?' She leaned forward. 'And if I am not mistaken,' she said in a low and rather wonderful voice, 'that was how he *stiffened* the platform, was it not?' She put her fingers to her mouth again and sucked the very ends of them delicately. 'I am,' she said, 'very warm. I would like to remove my robe. Have you nothing more to say on his behalf? Shall we talk, for example, about structure?'

He took her notebook from her and dropped it on the floor. 'Well, I think women's bodies are wonders,' he said, gallantly. 'Perhaps the finest structures in the world.'

Oh please, she thought. But she smiled encouragingly. 'Isn't it true to say that bridges reflect your sexuality? All that outward and upward thrust—yes? I mean,' she said, 'in the matter of your bridges. You build them Big, Mr Parker. You like them monumental.'

'Call me Patrick,' he said. He stroked her arm. Goosebumps rose. He went on doing so. 'And you are right. There is so much sky to thrust up to, there is so much water to span, so many banks to abut . . . Brunel certainly knew that.'

She retrieved her notebook and wrote something down. He wanted to know what it was. She laughed and said it was confidential. What she had actually written down was 'Bugger Brunel', which relieved her feelings. She smiled again, this time as if she was seeking his confidence. 'Mr Parker—Patrick— women have not traditionally built bridges. I wonder if you have a theory as to why this might be?'

Oh, he had been caught by this sort of thing before. Strident women. Those short-haired androgynous types. He sorted through his brain to find a useful suggestion. One that would not offend. Then, thankfully, he noticed her cute little beaded shoes. The perfect example.

'You will find,' he said, picking one up and tapping a beaded dragon playfully, 'that women are more dexterous than muscular. They have an eye for detail. Bridges are large, awkward, brawny— often disturbing things—and use hard, masculine materials. Women understandably shy away from them for the gentler forms of design. And of course, there is a place for that too—'

'Of course,' she said, and wrote again. This time he did not ask, which was just as well as she had written, 'Patrick Parker you do talk shit.' She really wanted those trousers.

'You know that he bankrupted several companies he used in the building of his designs?' she said.

'Who?'

'I have a list of them here—' He waved the notepad away. 'And he did it for no good reason except that old pig-headedness again. Money due to one of the engineers on the GWR, for example, was never paid to them. It was allocated and all

433

Brunel had to do was write the cheque—and he never did. He kept nit-picking. They pleaded. He remained immutable. Out of business they went, and at least one man died broken-hearted.'

'Hah!' said Patrick.

She got the trousers.

She got the shirt with her defence, quite correct, of the valuelessness of the seven-foot gauge over the four-foot gauge for the railway. Brunel said it would make a smoother ride, and it did not. It also cost vast and unnecessary sums of investors' money to convert.

Which only left him his—somewhat sketchy— underpants.

He, however, fought back.

'And his Great Bridge of Clifton,' she began confidently, 'with its vast span—how long was it now? So very, very big . . .'

'Nine hundred and sixteen feet,' said Patrick firmly.

'In metres?' she said.

'He worked in feet and inches.'

'Ah yes. He won the commission by saying that he would make a bridge that spanned nine hundred or so feet—much longer than his rival Telford's. But when it came to be built the span was modified and made smaller anyway. He brought it down to six hundred after all.'

'Six hundred and thirty,' said Patrick. 'And I don't think any of this is fair.'

'Fair, fair?' she said, laughing wickedly. 'How would you like to be promised nine hundred feet and only get six, Mr Parker?'

He wanted that robe.

'The point is, my lovely Koi-Koi' (she quite liked

434

the way he said this, kind of commanding), 'that he *could* have made it the original nine hundred-plus but Telford—in his umbrage at not getting the commission—withdrew some of the funds. So Brunel was forced to cede all that—*length.*' He reached over and pulled the cherry blossoms apart. She let him and she sighed. Even quasi-geishas do not wear anything next to their skin.

Underpants. They had to go.

'And was it,' she said, running her fingers up and down his leg, 'was it fair that Mr Brunel opposed any legislation to regulate engineering techniques? So that when Robert Stephenson's bridge over the Dee collapsed—where as you know he had been experimenting in the use of cast-iron beams—' She went on stroking his leg. A familiar leg, a leg that looked almost exactly the same as it looked thirty years ago (except the knees were a bit balder)—quite a desirable leg, really. A little trickle of sweat ran down between her breasts. Patrick watched its course, fascinated. 'Your Isambard would not condemn Stephenson's use of untried and untested methods, would he? No. Despite the loss of life he supported Stephenson—on the grounds that imposing any condemnation or legislation would "embarrass and shackle the progress of improvements of tomorrow by recording and registering as law the prejudices and errors of today . . ." In other words, Mr Parker, nothing must get in the way of progress—his progress—genius—of his genius—and that included a few expendable rail travellers . . .'

She paused.

She smiled again.

Very charmingly.

Though it proved to be the charm of a snake.

'Isambard Kingdom Brunel stood up at that tribunal and faced husbandless women, fatherless children, bereaved mothers and the whole phalanx of those left desperately grieving behind—and his message was as follows: "The cause of great building never comes cheap and included in the reckoning there are always human lives."'

'Like any woman,' he said, 'you bring the emotive into the calculation.'

'No. No. I bring reason. I bring humanity. Your Mr Brunel was saying that death must be part of the engineer's calculations. In the name of progress. Just as it was calculated in by the Egyptians, the Carthaginians—and your favourites —the Babylonians. Just as it was calculated in when they flew to the moon. All's fair for the cause.'

'What cause would that be?' asked Patrick, irritably.

'Heroics,' she said dreamily. 'Glory. Which is exactly what you aim for yourself.'

'Hah,' he said.

She blinked at him, sleepily, like an exotic cat.

Then she held out her hand.

'Underpants, Patrick, please.'

'I win,' she said, tapping her earrings. She wriggled towards him. 'And now—for pleasure, I think.'

'We can soon see to that,' he said.

He lowered his voice and began stroking the nape of her neck. She prayed the wig would stay in place. He seemed not to notice it and—almost—she did not care if he did. She was twenty and under his spell again.

'Do you,' he breathed into her ear, 'know the meaning of the word "quirks"? In architecture?'

Oh bloody well bugger it. That old line again. In the past he was always using it on her, and always forgetting he had done so. Ah well—Water under the Bridge, she thought, and pouting her cherry red lips, she said, 'Quirks?'

'In   architecture,'   he   said,   'a   quirk—or quirks—has a very specific meaning, a very specific meaning . . .'

'Yes?' she said demurely. 'Would you like to tell me what that is?'

'It means an acute hollow between the convex moulding and the soffit.' He reached out and touched the curve of her neck and shoulder. 'And this is a perfect, living example.'

'Ah,' she said, nodding sagely. 'I thought that's what it meant.' And she repeated 'moulding' and 'soffit' as softly and as non-committally as if the words were pillow talk. She was wondering—quite idly—if she was going to go through with it. She looked down at her discarded embroidered shoes, such silly pretty things, sewn by little dexterous feminine fingers, were they? The dragons were definitely wild and roaring now.

'You know,' she said, 'it is thought, in Japan, that the reason no women build bridges is because bridges   represent—the—er—male.   They   are considered to be manifestations . . .'

They both looked downwards to where she pointed, apologising as she did so to the entire Japanese nation for the further absurd and whopping falsehood she was about to lay at their door . . .

'. . . of that.'

The water dispenser seemed to bubble over, its ripe noise bouncing off the discreetly painted walls.

437

'I am in your hands,' he said, quite hopefully.

'And you know,' she said, 'that it is likely that the reason our *shinkansen*—the bullet train—is so called is that it comes from the same idea. Bullets being very—mmm—masculine, penetrating things, you know. Women in Japan are content to ride them, too, rather than design them.'

'And you?' he said.

'Certainly,' she said. 'I will be your abutment.'

At which she put her wriggly little fingers over her mouth and giggled again. With final, private and heartfelt apologies to the whole of Japanese womanhood.

*   *   *

Something has healed, she thought, pleased. The gap of pain was sealed over. She was just beginning to wonder if that was not enough without any further consummation—when the thought became lost in a series of interesting noises coming from just beyond the locked door. Sounds not unlike the approach of a very modern orchestra in the process of cranking up the timpani. And they grew louder, and louder, and louder.

So much for soundproofing, Patrick thought idly, stretching, wondering where to begin. And then he sat bolt upright. Reason dawned. What the bloody hell was it?

Audrey wondered likewise.

What was it that crashed and cacophoned outside the door? Well, well.

Never underestimate the efficiencies of timing employed in the singularly good art of French Corporate Catering.

15

Tokyo Cinders

So Apsu sits in an office and she designs for a firm of babyware manufacturers: she thinks up interesting new shapes for baby buggies, baby car seats, babywalkers, babyslings, swings, bouncers and cots. She keeps her head down, she earns good money, and she rents cheaply part of a decrepit old warehouse on a short lease because it is waiting to be transformed into chic and minimalist riverside apartments. When she looks out through its grimy, Dickensian windows, she sees a big glass-fronted building on the other side of the water, which is where Patrick and his partners create their ideas. If she had played the game, as her mother and father say to her woefully (for they have learned to speak the vernacular over the years too), she could have been in there—and laughing now.

At night, on her own, with Mozart playing, or sometimes Dire Straits, she designs and draws and dreams. One day, one day, the world will change. And she will be ready for it.

Almost at the same moment as Koi-Koi and Patrick heard the curiously orchestral noise, it ceased. To be followed by a rattling and a knocking and a general raising of human sounds that all led to a final understanding that Someone Was Trying To Get In. And, from the determination of the sounds they would soon succeed.

Patrick was the first to leap up with the unfortunate result that he landed a little too forcibly and awkwardly on one of his feet, and twisted it. Audrey, for it was now most definitely she, with beating heart held hard to her wig and said, 'Shame.'

Patrick howled and clutched his damaged foot. She said, 'You always did have weak ankles . . .'

He looked at her with understandable surprise. So far as he knew he had never had that reported in any newspaper. But to Patrick the faint interest he felt at the odd notion of this Japanese woman knowing about the weakness of his ankles, was as nothing to the strong likelihood he was experiencing at the prospect of his being found in a French museum with his trousers down. Off, even. He might feel the Absolute Rightness of Banishing Bourgeois Sentiment—but it was quite possible that not everyone would see it that way. And certainly—Oh my God, Peggy—not his wife.

The sound at the door increased . . .

It occurred to him that this would not look good, either, for the Queen's Millennium Bridge Project. Being divorced for this kind of thing would certainly not help. The Queen of England was a little short on sympathy for indulgers in marital hanky-panky and it was rumoured that she deeply regretted the fading of Court Etiquette banning the Monarch from having anything to do with divorcees. As one journalistic wag remarked, presumably, despite the Queen of England's regrets, it had to remain faded or she would never see any of her family again.

As for Peggy—if last night was anything to go by

he had been nurturing a jealous wife in his bosom. She was all Coventry, that one, and would easily be fooled into talking to the tabloids if the unthinkable happened. And the tabloids were never happier than when they could knock Johnny Foreigner. And Johnny Foreigner had been commissioning most of Patrick's major works for the past thirty years, so to get both him and the French in one go would be irresistible. Mix Japan up in it, too, and they'd reckon to have achieved a bullseye. Despite the pain he began to dress and as he struggled to don his underpants without standing on his damaged foot he wondered, again, how she could possibly know about that particular weakness. Mark Mack told him Japanese women were special. Perhaps, in some mystical manner, she had spotted the way his joints were put together? They were known to be spiritual—and—inscrutable—mysterious. Which is what made them so exotic and alluring . . . He'd never know now—shame, he thought.

He was just about mid-leg with the underwear when the door behind him finally swung open. He looked across at Madame Koi. Somehow she had managed to get herself quite well covered, if a little askew, and was even now doing up the belt that held her strange garment in place. Her hair, too, looked oddly lopsided and her make-up had gone rather patchy. Not, after all, the porcelain seductress. But at least she was decent. He felt sad. He did not want their meeting to end like this.

'Will we meet again?' he asked her as he stumbled and struggled. She pushed her wig about a bit and said, 'One day, perhaps.' And gave him another of those smiles.

'Your phone number?' he said, desperate as a juvenile.

But it was too late.

Bursts of laughter told him that several people had entered the room. The rattling, chinking, clanking timpani continued. He turned round to see a row— yes—a row of those state-of-the-art trolleys again— being wheeled by impeccable young men in grey zip-up suits who looked as if they had just landed from Mars. And were on laughing gas.

Behind them, wheeling a different style of trolley (he knew them so well) all perfectly arranged with canapés, came two elegant, long-legged young women in white, their black hair coiled on their heads in a peak giving them a remarkable resemblance to Mrs Whippy. But the whole effect of their cool superiority was also spoiled by the fact that they had tried—and very obviously failed—to stop laughing. And pointing. As were the young men. The bottles, the glasses, the plates of canapés fairly tinkled and jangled with hilarity.

With great dignity Patrick turned away and replaced the remainder of his clothes. The catering staff went about their business at the far end of the room, saying nothing, laughing much. Then Madame Koi was at his side—she tucked something into his pocket before helping him into his jacket. She then smoothed his hair and planted a dainty kiss on his cheek. All he had to worry about now was his tie and his shoes. He bent down to these latter, and when he straightened up again—she was gone. Nothing remained in the room to say she had ever been there but the sofa with its roughened pile, her pencil and a slowly closing door. She had even remembered to take her notebook. Cool or what?

He felt a pang. A very strange pang. And he made a rush for it—she could not go—he did not know why he felt she could not go—but feel it he did. He stepped out to catch up with her, forgot about his ankle, groaned in pain, and limped and hobbled instead. Something tapped against his hip as he tried to make his painful way to the door. He patted his jacket pocket. Strange shape. He took it out. It was a beaded shoe, its dragon gently roaring at him. He reached the door just as several people from the outside also reached it.

'Patrick,' shouted a masculine voice. It was Rennie, his partner. Reality. 'Where the hell have you been? We've been scouring the place.'

Behind him he saw Peggy, very pink in the face, anxious and angry. Guiltily he stuffed the shoe back in his pocket and stood back to let them enter.

'Time for our interview with *Nexus Tokyo*,' Rennie said.

He ushered in the Japanese man to whom he had been speaking earlier. The Japanese man—on catching his eye—bowed. He held both a small recording machine and notebook. He did not look remotely like Madame Koi.

'Patrick,' said Peggy, in a voice that made him wince. 'You left me completely alone for nearly an hour.'

Had it really been that long?

She looked him up and down. He did not appear exactly as he had appeared when she last saw him. Indeed, he looked distinctly different. 'What *have* you been doing?' she said, more curious than hysterical now.

Well—yes—what had he been doing? With a

sudden brainwave he said, 'Oh—I've sprained my ankle—quite badly—' He lifted it up to show a suitable swelling and bruise—not really a sprain as such—more of a rick—but it added credence.

Peggy, if she thought anything odd of it, knew that it was neither the time nor the place. She went over to him and smoothed down his hair. It reminded him of his mother, long ago and far away—suddenly he rather wanted to be back in that land. He let his wife steer him towards the rumpled sofa. Was it his imagination or did it feel still warm?

'Ice,' called Peggy to the caterers, who were by now pretending to be getting on with things at the other end of the room. A bucket of ice was produced, together with a large, pale grey napkin, which Peggy expertly wrapped around several melting chunks and held to the ankle. The caterers smirked.

Peggy knelt there. 'I thought you might have met up with Audrey,' she muttered.

'*Audrey*?' he said.

'Audrey,' she said. 'Wapshott?' And gave the ankle a twitch. Patrick nearly shot off the couch.

'I've been stuck in here with a Japanese journalist as you very well know. What's Audrey Wapshott got to do with anything?'

'She lives in Paris.'

'She can live in bloody Timbuktu as far as I'm concerned.'

Peggy was more gentle with him after that.

But while she was relieved, Patrick felt a curious mixture of humiliation, sadness, and loss. Of course, the Koi woman was quite wrong about Isambard—but at least she had something to say for herself. He looked at Peggy as she knelt at his

444

feet. She had never learned anything about bridges.

'Peggy?' he said.

She looked up.

'What was Isambard Kingdom Brunel's gauge size?'

She shook her head and went back to tending him.

Throughout the press conference as he tried to keep his mind focused, his ankle throbbed and the shoe in his pocket dug uncomfortably, erotically, into his ribs.

*   *   *

Audrey moved swiftly, shuffling barefoot, through the crowd. Two bare feet and a shoe in her hand. The assembled guests were more relaxed now, loosened up by the champagne, more inclined to stare. All eyes seemed to be upon her as she made her way towards the entrance. Unsurprising, really, since apart from a somewhat wonky, and very odd, appearance, to be barefooted was *wild*. She looked neither to the right nor the left but made directly for the grand doors, holding out a beaded shoe as if it were an offering. Probably, decided the throng, she was one of the mime artists from the square below—or a more distinguished performance artist. Difficult to tell. Watching her also, and with a little amused regret, was Edwin Bonnard—a bit tipsy, he assumed—if only he were a few years younger . . . Madame Bonnard clung to the crook of his arm. The outing had tired her very much. It was unlikely she would attend such a party again. But she had rallied sufficiently to put one in the eye of that accursed Englishwoman—and the revenge was sweet.

As Audrey reached the grand doors, two attendants pulled them wide for her and she exited, laughing now, out into the night, the dusk departed into bright, bright stars. The doors swung to behind her, their shiny modern handles reflecting her gaudy dress. The grand staircase, bathed in blue moonlight, was empty, and she descended—light-footedly running towards the street and hailing a taxi. As it pulled up in front of her she dropped her notebook down the grating of a drain. And that was that.

The taxi driver wanted to know if she had enjoyed herself. She said that she had. The taxi driver wanted to know if she had seen anyone famous? Gérard Depardieu, perhaps? No, she had not, she said, but there were certainly other actors about and she had seen one or two of those.

In the sky shimmered a huge, sinister hologram of Isambard Kingdom Brunel. Audrey, looking up at it from the cab window, thought that he looked down on her with a distinctly sour expression. 'Feeling's mutual,' she said. Before telling the driver to step on it. She shivered, that feeling again, as if someone had walked over her grave. If only, she thought, sitting back and relaxing at last, if only the caterers had come along even a quarter of an hour later. After all, Patrick had never taken very long in the past.

When Audrey reached home she bathed, hid everything away just in case Edwin changed his mind and came to call, put on her nightdress and robe and went and sat out on her balcony. In the distance, high in the sky, the Brunel hologram wavered and wobbled. Below her in the streets the

446

town went rushing on, going about its late-hour business, ordinary, unremarkable, as she had seen it most nights for nearly thirty years. But now it had changed. Along with the mythology of Brunel, she had removed the mythology of Patrick Parker. And she didn't know if it was better or worse. Would it have been better to continue believing that he was special, a genius, a star in the firmament that she was privileged to have pleasured? Or was it better to know the truth as she now knew it, to see through the myth to the mortal? A talent, a huge talent, but as much a weak and flawed man as she was a weak and flawed woman. Florence was not the only one to blame for Patrick's unloving spirit, Little Audrey Wapshott was, too.

It made the last thirty years a waste of bloody time. She need never have broken her heart for Patrick at all. She need never have mourned him. And she need never have thought that to be rejected by one so wonderful meant that her life was over. That she was unworthy. You only get one hero in a lifetime, she remembered thinking all those years ago, and when you have known such a one . . . If I had been wiser then, she told herself, I would have rejected Edwin at the station, or at the first sign of My Last Duchess—gone home to England, taken my French examination, passed it probably, got a good job, settled down, married a respectable man, had two children and lived quite contentedly. Never thinking of Patrick again. Just as, come to think of it, she never thought about William the train steward. She had turned Patrick into an immortal, and she had therefore paid the price. But tonight, at least, she felt she had earned some of it back.

In London Apsu sat in her large, draughty,
skeletal loft in the soon-to-be-thriving industrial
area of the easterly Thames, and played around
on her computer. Her dexterous little feminine
fingertips found it easy to negotiate the
keyboard and she seldom had to go back over
her virtual drawing of a bridge to rectify a
mistake. I must, she thought, have faith. She
had written the word SPECTACULAR up on one
wall, in large red-lipsticked letters. It was her
goad.

Hanging above it, the only framed pictures in
the room, were two reproductions of details of
paintings—the first Michelangelo's Sistine God
and Adam—the fingers about to touch—the
moment before man—and it would seem to be
only man—connects with the world, and claims it
as his own. The other, much enlarged, is a detail
from a Rembrandt drawing of a mother
encouraging her child in its first steps. The
Rembrandt detail is of the two sets of hands
holding on to each other as if there is nothing else
in the world that matters beyond this first
moment of daring, the step alone, the act of faith.
The artist has used red chalk and the
enlargement shows that his emphasis, his pressure
point, was that linking of the pairs of hands. That
was the connection upon which Rembrandt
placed the whole dynamic of the drawing.

The girl who sits experimenting with her
virtual drawing holds on to the simple, small
idea, which intellect, pride, greed, hubris and

448

desire for grandeur and glory make repeated attempts to pull from her. The simple, small idea comes from this: her grandmother lives on one side of the water, and there are places her grandmother wants to visit on the other side. At the moment her grandmother either has to walk a considerable distance (not too good for my old feet, my dear), or she must catch a bus to get to the other side (if there ever *are* any).

'It would', she says frequently to her granddaughter, 'be very useful if I could just walk over to the other side on a nice bridge.'

FOUR

AFTERMATH

1

Some Years Later—At Home and Abroad

Game: Spot the Missing Person

> Erasmus Bridge: Rotterdam, the Netherlands
> [Designed by] Ben van Berkel/ Dept. of Public
> Works of the City of Rotterdam
> Heading in Matthew Wells' book illustrating
> *30 Bridges*

> Erasmus Bridge: Rotterdam, the Netherlands
> Since its completion in 1996 the bridge has rarely
> escaped headlines. Its designers, Ben van Berkel
> and *Caroline Bos*, referring to their creation as
> 'the baby blue monster' . . .
> From text describing the same bridge in Lucy
> Blakstad's book *Bridge: The Architecture of
> Connection*

'Why do you never ask me anything?' said Patrick.
  'About what?' said Peggy.
  'About anything,' said Patrick.
  'I just did,' she said.
  'About what?' he asked.
  'Exactly,' she replied.
  Since Paris Peggy was not so compliant. Paris shook her to the core. Not only did Patrick leave her alone with the Van Crees—but the Van Crees immediately tried to engage her in conversation concerning his designs, about which she knew absolutely nothing beyond the fact that he had

done them, they were big, he was famous for them, and they stayed up.

To make matters worse the Van Crees then drifted away to be replaced by a couple, who spoke no English, only French, of which she knew but two words, those being Yes and No—and certainly not the polite word for Toilet. She had never learned what the Van Crees knew how to do, which was drift off at parties when they were bored, and she felt that Patrick had let her down badly by leaving her alone for so long. Usually, if she was invited to functions at all, she sat at the side of him while he did his interviews or whatever it was, and he would occasionally take her hand, or look at her fondly, or even let them ask her what she thought of the latest project to which she, naturally enough, would only reply—*could* only reply—that it was another very Big and very Wonderful thing. That stayed up.

Patrick's lost hour had never been fully explained. And there were rumours . . . The only reason she knew there were rumours was because—when they arrived back in London—Isambard and Polly were full of sly nudges and irritating whispers. Apparently it had been over all the papers—their sort of papers—well, her sort of papers too but she kept it to herself—that the design team of this Parisian project was British (hurray), co-ordinated by Lord Buckland (hurray, hurray—a British aristocrat—the Brits knowing how to keep their aristos and not chop off their heads) and flanked by Giles Rennie and Patrick Parker (hurray, hurray), that the exhibition was about a very British man (Isambard Kingdom Brunel—hurray), despite the French trying to say he wasn't (boo), who should have been honoured by the British rather than the

French (shame, shame)—and it was rumoured that a mysterious Japanese woman (ooh, *éxotique*) had been disturbed, semi-clad, with one of the naked (shock, horror) British designers.

No one was quite sure which of the two men it was, but it was rumoured very strongly—because, it was hinted, the other might not like undressed women—that it was Patrick Parker. This was just as tasty in a way because Patrick Parker was always going off somewhere and building a bridge that wasn't English. And getting medals. Foreign Medals. And he was always complaining that he never got asked to build bridges in his own native land (paid for by the British Taxpayer, no doubt)— just who does he think he is?—and now he was behaving like Johnny Foreigner as well.

Patrick laughed it off. Peggy knew that laugh— Isambard Junior laughed like that when he was caught playing hooky and Polly laughed like that when she was caught pinching lipstick from Woolworth's. So Peggy was not convinced. And Peggy brooded. And when Peggy brooded she ended up distraught. Peggy felt sure that Audrey Wapshott—as she still was apparently—was somewhere at the bottom of all this. No man could have been with someone for so long and then just forgotten all about them. Patrick had not married her because he loved her better than Audrey, but because she was pregnant. He probably still had feelings for his old love and he was very well aware—as Peggy was well aware—that Audrey was At Large in Paris. Of course he *would* say it never occurred to him until Peggy mentioned it but she didn't believe him for one minute. They might even have had a secret rendezvous. Florence rang up (fortunately Patrick was away at the time) and *told* her that Audrey looked wonderful at Dolly Wapshott's funeral and *that she had been asking after him*. Who knows if it didn't begin then? Florence hinted as much. Said she thought Patrick would be very interested to see how well Audrey had turned out. And should she pass on the address? Or just the telephone number? Peggy said both, but they never arrived. It was quite likely she sent them straight to Patrick. Florence had never taken to her and goodness knew Peggy had tried. Oh yes, Oh dear, yes, if she ever sat down and thought about it all, Peggy was convinced that Audrey Wapshott was somewhere at the heart of the matter.

*   *   *

Patrick was much disturbed after Paris, too. He did not know what to do. He tried to trace this Madame Koi—and indeed, for several weeks after his strange meeting with her he placed advertisements in the Parisian papers to see if they had any luck with finding her. But they did not. *Nexus Tokyo* denied all knowledge of her, so she was an impostor. But somehow that made it even more exotic. Wild. It was a long time since he had done anything even remotely unconventional. He was one of the world's leading designers, and, he *ought* to be a little on the dangerous side. Sir Ronald's advice was all very well and Peggy was a very good wife and organiser—but it never went near the soul with her, and Tokyo Cinders did. She stood up to him—and she would have lain down for him. What more, he asked himself as he looked at his poor, miserable Peggy, could a Man of

456

Destiny want?

Fortunately no one ever corroborated the rumours about who it was they found with his trousers down, and Patrick, of course, denied them. Members of the Louvre's catering staff were interviewed and bribed but since they did not know which of the two British designers was which (they all look the same, English Suits) they were—thank God—not much use. He thought about employing a private detective but that seemed absurd. She was probably safely back in Japan by now—and tantalising someone else. In the end there was nothing more to be done. He argued to himself that if French journalists—desperate French journalists —could not find her, he was hardly likely to do any better. Anyway—he thought sadly—he didn't know much about women, but he knew this. If one of the breed wants something, and it involves a man, she'll get it. So she couldn't have wanted him. And that was that. He put the shoe away at the back of one of his plan chests. But he was never *quite* unaware of its presence.

* * *

Audrey was never *quite* the same with Edwin again, either. Or perhaps, she thought, she was not the same with her life. She, too, kept the other shoe. The Cinderella touch cost her an arm and a leg at the costumiers (one shoe, madam, would be understandable—but to lose *two* . . .) And they were made by Verrier . . . She asked about the dexterous little fingertips and was told coldly that some of the best beadwork was done by Verrier's men workers. She paid the enormous bill with a

457

smile, deciding it was worth it. Objects become symbols. She placed the shoe on the dressing table where she could see it every day because it made her smile.

Edwin Bonnard noticed it and asked about it, she said it was a little nonsense that had taken her fancy in the Flea Market. He had the vaguest feeling he had seen something like it before. He picked it up and turning it around in his hands said, 'It's exquisite,' he said. 'I've an idea I've seen this before somewhere—can't think—'

'Really?' said Audrey in a not altogether gentle voice. She had not quite forgiven him for being potentially unfaithful to her with herself.

'Where did you say you found it?'

'Les Halles,' she said, and went on painting her toenails.

'I like that dark red,' he said softly, coming towards her. It was one of the activities he liked to watch her perform, which she knew perfectly well.

'Careful,' she said, and tapped him away with her hand. 'I don't want to smudge it.'

She was more like that with him nowadays. When he pointed out some of her brusquenesses she just laughed and said that she was behaving more like a proper, stricter mistress than she used to. That was all.

He ran his fingers over the beadwork. 'Pity you haven't got the pair to it,' he said. 'It's exquisite.'

She concentrated on painting her little toe, always awkward, and without looking up said, 'Oh I may be able to lay my hands on it. When I'm ready.'

'Really?' he said, and studied the dragon. 'You know—I'm sure I've seen this—'

'Perhaps,' said Audrey, keeping her hand steady, her eyes on her toes, 'you saw something similar on a little foot at the Brunel Opening?' She wiggled her toes.

He looked slightly ashamed. 'It really was the last time for Simone. It had to be done. If you are jealous—don't be.'

She considered Madame Bonnard, *Simone*, and the way she walked with her hand holding on to her husband's arm. Then she considered herself and Patrick nearly naked on that couch together. She waited to see what she felt. And then she looked up, brush poised, and said. 'No. I was once. But I am not any more. I don't want to marry you after all.'

'Good,' said Edwin. But he said it with a pleasing hint of disappointment.

*   *   *

In a royal palace, in a white and gold drawing room, with two corgis and a walnut desk between the regal occupant and the awkwardly besuited men with slightly too-long hair sitting opposite her, the Monarch holds meetings at which she has been apprised, over several months and well in advance, of various building schemes proposed to celebrate the coming of the New Millennium. Those that wish to use the name of the Royal Firm must first be approved by Her Majesty. Fair dos.

Today the Monarch is being advised not of the institutional schemes, nor of the purely governmental schemes, not the PPP schemes or those of local boroughs. She is being advised of the one scheme that will be perfectly co-ordinated, the

459

one scheme of all of them that will be stage-managed by the Royal Firm—redoubtable men in perfect grey suits (with perfectly neat haircuts)—who can manage a State Funeral and a Coronation while balancing on their heads if they have to. This Millennium project will also bear the Queen's name, but the Grand Opening, when it happens, will be filmed and shown on worldwide television. Something of a coup by the BBC who intend to make a film of the entire process from paper drawing to final cutting of the ribbon by the Queenly hand. The Royal Academy, *collegium ars gravitas,* has already agreed to host an exhibition of the best proposals, from which the final choice will be announced. The people (for this is The People's Millennium and the project will be the Queen's Bridge and the Queen belongs to her people) will also have the opportunity to say which of the offerings they choose. They are—oh horrors—to be consulted.

The awkward men who are here today are experts and they have come to lay before their Monarch's feet, so to speak, the jewels of possibility. In theory her Majesty will make the final choice. In practice, think the experts, they will make it for her. As far as they are concerned it is a foregone conclusion. The Parker Partnership will surely be the selected. But still, the democratic process must be seen to be done. Royalty is above being lobbied. Advised, but never lobbied. Already the Monarch reminds herself to keep calm and count to ten as these grey little experts (anti-royalists to a man, thinks her Majesty, who can smell such things; anti-royalists to a man until they come into her girdle of awe) go about their tawdry business. She pats a corgi's head to soothe herself. 'Next,' she says disdainfully to a drawing that is held up for her inspection. It looks like the water slide the grandchildren begged to have installed at Sandringham.

For the men in grey suits the one comforting aspect of this nerve-racking meeting today is that that wisest of all Firms, the Royal One, has allotted plenty of time. If the Royal Choice is but putative and manipulable, the Millennium itself is not. There may no longer be an Empire but it will be good to show the world how well it could be organised if there were. Still smarting from the Isambard Kingdom Brunel show across the English Channel put on by those supercilious French, the British wish to show the world that they have truly great, purely home-grown geniuses of design—and that they know what to do with them. After all Patrick Parker has built so little in his homeland. They must redress this if they are not to look more foolish and reactionary than they do already. They can only entice Parker to the drawing table if they offer him something big. He has indicated that he wants this project badly, now they must make it happen. He is also, and not a day too soon, to be properly honoured by Her Majesty. Though he does not yet know this. Neither does the Queen.

They will need all their powers of diplomacy. Her Majesty has the pragmatism of the good *hausfrau* in her blood, as well as a line of haughty kings. Like her great-great-grandmother before her, if she does not like a thing, in private at least, she will say so. It behoves those who serve her in private not to let her become displeased. One does not become God's Anointed by lying down and taking it.

Delicately they begin to talk in general terms, for

461

Her Majesty is led to believe that she is a good conversationalist and likes to keep abreast. With a royal wrinkling of her nose and the ghost of a twinkle in her eyes, she says of the Parisian exhibition, 'They've certainly put up a most futuristic connecting building over there, haven't they? The Louvre extension? That ziggurat thingie. Monstrous. But I expect it's the sort of thing Mr Brunel would like. The bridge he built at our Scottish Estate, Balmoral, is never, ever spoken about in the family and it is said that my great-great-grandmother always closed her eyes when she travelled across it. If I have to choose a bridge I think I would prefer not to have one which required me to keep my eyes closed. Not in my back yard.'

The twinkle increases. Since Her Majesty's particular backyard at this precise moment is the centre, the very heart, of London—the increased twinkle is not surprising.

'No, indeed, Ma'am,' says the older of the two men whom, she suddenly notices, does not wear any socks with his slip-on, tassel-laced, shoes. How very beatnik, she thinks. Out loud she says, 'If Our name is on it then We've got to *like* the thing— haven't We?'

'Yes indeed, Ma'am.'

Both men pray that Her Majesty is not quite so on the ball as it is said, otherwise she will remember that the design she has just decried was created by the winner (not that the competition has actually been launched yet) of this Millennium Project. The Project, of course, is a *bridge*. Therefore no better designer could be chosen than Patrick Parker. Neither of them, either, feels it

462

would be sensible to point out to their Monarch that the ziggurat bridge connection is considered one of the finest pieces of new architecture to be erected in Paris or anywhere. Once Patrick Parker is honoured it will help. Such awards give the Royals, everybody, confidence—it gives their man a pedigree.

Meanwhile form must be adhered to. They put before Her Majesty a host of bridges—some that look like cascades of water, some that look as if they are fish picked clean to their bones, bridges that (in her opinion) look as if they have undergone a military attack, bridges that seem to defy gravity and are coloured in shocking colours—green, orange, mauve. Many look awkward, wayward, unsafe. She sees submissions for some of the world's individual leading designers of bridges, British by birth or British by adoption, and she sees submissions from conglomerates. Towards the end of the range of submissions, she sees a drawing and schedule entitled—but only in brackets: (Working Title: *Grandmother's solution for getting to the other side: build a bridge*). She likes this. It makes her smile. 'This is very straightforward,' she says. 'And it has buildings. Shops. It seems to me very sensible when space in My Capital is at such a premium.'

'Mmm,' say the men in grey suits. They put it to one side and cover it quickly with a drawing of something with shining metal cable stays that looks like a large, unruly violin. They bring out The Parker Design. Her Majesty inspects it as it is laid before her on her desk.

'It is based, Ma'am,' says the Beatnik type, 'on your Coronation arches from nineteen-fifty-three.'

'I know when my own Coronation was,' the

Monarch snaps. Immediately she tacks on a gracious smile. But patience is wearing thin. She puts on her spectacles and peers at the drawing. Had she ridden under arches of these dimensions, she would have been entirely dwarfed. She pushes it to one side and gimlet sharp, pushes aside the violin and returns to 'Grandmother's Solution'. It must be put in the exhibition. By Royal Command. The men in suits bow in acknowledgement. The Queen, like her corgis, is growing restless. She must find a suitably dismissive statement. So she says, 'One does not get out to the shops *enough* . . .' And with that she gives the slightest droop of her head. The meeting is over.

The job is done, she has had her say, and she makes a note on her pad for her Private Secretary to check the final list of exhibitors at the Royal Academy. 'If "Grandmother's Solution" is not included,' she writes playfully, perhaps even wistfully thinking about those bare, white ankles, 'then Chop Off Their Heads.'

And that is it as far as the Monarch is concerned. It is just another bit of the jigsaw of duty for her. The selection of an historic, new bridge. Another stone in the fabric of the nation's existence. In a few year's time she will choose an outfit to wear which, in its own way will have been just as carefully constructed and chosen (she will therefore not arrive crumpled, the wind will not show her knickers, buttons will remain firmly done up over her broad bosom), and the fabric will be warm or light depending upon the season. She will be collected in a big, black, shiny car, and driven to a place where one of these drawings she has in front of her now will be made fact. Concrete and steel, wood and brick, glass and high-grade plastic. The Bridge. Her Bridge. May it please Her Majesty.

*   *   *

To the young woman with the fiercely concentrating look, who does not feel the cold in that loft of hers because she is burning with the future and its possibilities, it is the structure, not the name of its creator, that counts. And what it is there for, and for whom. The daughter of immigrants dreams . . . As the applause begins and the Queen starts her speech and the gulls wheel above her, and the boats sound their horns on the crowded water, she thinks of her grandmother. That is all.

*   *   *

Gradually Patrick's memory of Madame Koi fades. He is far too busy with his new project and as he forms the Meccano he suddenly remembers his father's dexterous hands. He says something of this when he telephones his mother. She is, he can tell, very offended. Women, he thinks, are a very peculiar breed. Which makes him think fleetingly of that Japanese woman again. But only fleetingly. He still keeps the shoe. Somewhere.

*   *   *

Audrey has received a letter from Lilly, or rather a letter written by Lilly's new carer. Lilly has had a little stroke and she is now in a Residential Home. Which she likes. The carer writes, at Lilly's instruction, that Florence Parker, coming along the street when Lilly was being wheeled to the shops one day, said that it was no more than she deserved for her sinful ways. Lilly says that she tried to spit in the woman's eye, but she could only dribble. Which made her laugh.

Audrey, who has not forgotten Madame Koi, not at all, picks up the shoe and sits thinking, turning the beaded dragon over and over again in her hands. There is no need for her to keep its secret any more. Edwin has gone to where he cannot be hurt. He was hoping to make it to the Millennium. But he was a few years too early. Madame Bonnard still lives. Just.

2

Time to Go Home

I think there is a question of whether this
[Millennium] bridge is actually bridging the two
communities, the poor south to the rich north. I
think the rich north will benefit more from the
poor south.
  Zedi (civil engineer, trained in Zambia,
  moved to London in 1979)

After a suitable period of mourning the desire to
move on became strong and Audrey returned to
England. She was, like any sensible Pompadour,
well set up: the owner of her Parisian apartment
which she immediately instructed an agent to let;
the owner of a handsome seafront property in
Brighton which she immediately put on the market;
the beneficiary of a series of offshore investments
which—true to his word—were placed by Edwin to
maximum effect and made over to her in his will; a
few good pieces of jewellery including a delightful
diamond crocodile brooch that had once belonged
to Mrs Simpson (Audrey's mother and father now
being dead she freely owns something connected
to That Dreadful Woman); and the crowning
pleasure, the small pastel by Pierre Bonnard which
she takes with her wherever she goes, tucked into
the bottom of her travelling case, wrapped in silk.
In the same case, wrapped in pale blue tissue
paper, she keeps the dragon shoe. Both seemed to
symbolise something. The bourgeois and the

467

exotic. The best and the worst of her, perhaps.

Her accountant, once Edwin's, suggested that now was a good time for Audrey to put the painting into a New York auction—but she said, looking directly into his eyes so that he blushed, which was very satisfying, that she would keep the painting. She thought that over the years she had sold enough of herself, one way or another. Yes?

On arrival in England she booked herself two rooms in their favourite Bloomsbury hotel. It was a good place to stay for a while to acclimatise herself. Underlying the grief for Edwin and the sadness for losing Paris, was relief. She no longer lived in that world. That world, she knew, no longer existed. She was Audrey Wapshott of England and about to please herself.

Personally, she decided, as she looked out over the drabbish Bloomsbury street, I feel I have earned my keep and deserve a comfortable, early retirement. She had burnt *her* bridges—after mending them—and that was satisfactory. She shivered, remembering her visit to Madame Bonnard made on the day before she left for England. The sweet, dough-faced nun who glided ahead of her, wimple rippling like wings, said at the door, 'She has moments, Madame, she has moments. Pray God that she has one for you . . .'

And into God Knew What moment she went.

At least the room was cheerful. Blue and white gingham, blue and white rug on the floor, bedcover of white with a blue cross-stitched border. The blue and white matched the pallor of the woman's face as it looked up from the pillow. The jaw, once so square and formidable, was now sunken, and the hands that lay lightly on the white and blue coverlet were shrunken and veined.

'Madame?' said Audrey.

The eyes, still dark, still seeing, though rheumy, focused on her. They registered a flicker of surprise. Both women stared at each other for a long time. Audrey listened to the bell tolling the half hour and to the woman's deep breathing.

Odd how quite suddenly the right words arrived. 'Madame. I ask your forgiveness . . .'

The eyes looked her up and down. They were not kind. There was another long pause before the woman drew a deeper breath than the rest and said, 'Mad'moiselle. I grant it to you.'

On the plain wooden chest at the side of the bed were three framed photographs, incongruous in the ornateness of their silver frames; one of Edwin and Madame Bonnard on their wedding day; and one each of their children at the age of twenty-one. Audrey pointed to the photographs of the children. Madame Bonnard was clearly having a moment, for she understood, and shook her head slightly. Then she did that purely French shrug, which Audrey had never—quite—mastered and which Madame Bonnard could manage even while lying on her deathbed. She shrugged and it was clear that it meant, 'What use is anything at the end?'

Audrey bent and kissed the cold brow, and left.

Behind her Madame Bonnard tutted. It was not the way things were done. Mistresses did not kiss widows on the brow. At best they kissed their hands.

That was the bridge, built and burnt in a minute, though the pallid image would linger.

*   *   *

469

Audrey's life was unremarkable. Of course, she had done some remarkable things but she was— unremarkable. Staid now. And glad to be. She planned a good book, a nice warm room, the occasional dinner with a friend. In this final stage she would suit herself. But the news of Lilly disturbed her. The memory of Patrick disturbed her. She knew that a woman did not keep a single shoe for several years without there being a Big Reason—beyond whimsical sentimentality—for doing so.

Once settled in the hotel and to pass the time she reacquainted herself with the new London, including sailing down the Thames to the building site of the Dome near Greenwich. On the way the guide pointed out the site for the new Millennium Bridge. The Queen's Millennium Bridge it would be called. Big name for Big Project.

The tour boat journeyed down the river and slowly back up again. Time to notice things. All the way along she could see fine apartments, glinting, metallic, harsh—shocking the soft, dark brickwork. There were people—The People—sitting out on little balconies with glasses of wine, looking down at the oily, grey water which Dickens had cast as one of the darkest characters in London. When she left for Paris all those years ago those places had either been working warehouses or boarded up and crumbling. No one would have seen beauty in them. Now they were desirable investment properties. Chic. It used to be one of her favourite words.

The new bridge would connect these Chic People to The People. Patrick's Bridge. It was bound to be

Patrick's. He would be sixty in the year of the Millennium. The age at which—he had said to her, years ago—all serious creators should die. Did he still believe it? When he designed the ziggurat and was interviewed about it (not by Madame Koi) he said that a Millennium Bridge would probably be his swansong—his epitaph. The one thing on which he had set his heart. She wondered if she envied him the focus of his life. Hers had been utterly random.

Back in Bloomsbury she grew restless. She visited the British Museum but the Elgin Marbles, newly housed, reminded her painfully of how gauche she once was. Something must happen soon, she told herself, something to make a balance of it all. And then, God Bless Her, Florence Parker went and died, the death was announced in *The Times* and Audrey decided that the moment had finally arrived.

She opened her travel case, removed the little beaded shoe and unfolded it from its pale blue tissue paper. She looked at it, fondled it, smiled at it, slipped it on to her foot, removed it, re-wrapped it, and then tucked it into a black leather handbag. To await further action.

That night of the barricades, when she took the beautiful boy to her bed, he read to her from Verlaine's poems. Later she bought her own copy and when Edwin found it, and raised an eyebrow, she told him that she much preferred them to the likes of horrible old Robert Browning and his Duchesses. She could quote 'Aquarelle' which she loved:

Voici des fruits, des fleurs, des feuilles et
des branches,
Et puis voici mon cœur, qui ne bat que pour
vous . . .

It made Edwin laugh. *'Oh là là!'* he said, 'she has a brain . . .' She said nothing, thought much, about this remark. If she had a brain it was hers to own, his to ponder. Had she not later wept on his doorstep in the fear that she had overstepped the mark and lost him? So she kept her preference for Verlaine to herself. If she stood on her balcony in the evening she might remember, and whisper to herself,

Il pleure dans mon cœur
Comme il pleut sur la ville:
Quelle est cette langueur
Qui pénètre mon cœur?

And think of Patrick. But now this ridiculous shoe brought comfort, for the shoe symbolised more than a good joke, more than a getting even, it symbolised her own regeneration. She was looking forward to Florence Parker's funeral, very much indeed.

3

Family Matters

I suppose it is almost like being a child, isn't it?
Making a bridge and constructing something that
goes over somewhere, over water . . . we know
we're not supposed to be there, really.
  Canon Andrew (sub-dean, Southwark
  Cathedral)

On the afternoon of his Nana's funeral Isambard
Parker, in London, flopped back on the slightly
greasy settee and flicked channels. Isambard
ignored the telephone. He knew who it was and he
knew what they wanted and he was not going to do
anything he did not choose to do. From quite an
early age he had worked out what was required of
him, avoided doing it, and enjoyed the family
frustration such perversity produced. If he did not
know anything else he knew that he was not going
to be like his father. Not in any way, shape or form.
Which got right up his famous father's nose.

  If he built anything at all—and he was toying with
the idea—it would—so far as his father was
concerned—be A Bloody Outrage. Isambard,
amused, knew this because he asked his father to
help him design it. To the eternal question 'What
are you going to do for the rest of your life?'
Isambard merely told him that he wanted to open a
cannabis café, because they were the things of the
future, he had found a site. His father, quite
predictably, shot his lid and said it was A Bloody

Outrage. It was almost as sweet as the time Isambard ripped the drawing table from his bedroom wall and threw it into the garden.

True, his father happened to be passing beneath his window at the time, which was unfortunate. 'You might have killed me,' Patrick yelled at him.

To which Isambard, feeling very shaken but he wasn't going to tell his dad, replied that if it had happened it would have been an act of Extreme Fate because Patrick was so seldom there that the likelihood of hitting him in the garden with anything would have been miraculous.

Oh no. Isambard Kingdom Parker had no reason to go up to Coventry for his Nana's funeral. His Nana was dead, so she wouldn't know, and he was too old to play the 'supportive son to the famous dad' role. He'd done that all his life, the clean and brushed son, holding hands with his clean and brushed sister, posing for the cameras for the Sunday supplements and looking up admiringly at whatever it was his youthful, dynamic father had just finished. Squirming with embarrassment and not knowing why.

And then in his teens he did know why. By naming his son after—in his opinion—England's greatest builder of bridges I. K. Brunel, his father thought he had founded a new dynasty. In the press interviews, of which there were many given the drama of his son's name, Patrick said he was sure that little Isambard Parker would follow in his father's footsteps. But he never did anything practical about it. He never invited Isambard to sit with him and draw, he never invited Isambard to come on site with him, he never even showed him the basic draughtsman's skills. The few times he did complete a little drawing of an idea it was either lost long before his father came home, or if he showed it to him he said, 'No—this bit wouldn't work, and that elevation is misdrawn,' or similar. The only thing his father did to include him in his life was to summon him and Polly when the cameras were out. As Isambard grew up he watched his father change from Patrick Parker iconoclastic Whizz Kid, to Patrick Parker International Man of Vision—and now (he watched only from the sidelines) finally into Sir Patrick Parker Distinguished Member of the Design Establishment.

It was around the final stage of The International Man of Vision (when it was announced that Patrick would do something amazing—apparently—for the Louvre) that Isambard gave up. He refused to pose with his mother and father and sister for a press photograph that was later captioned 'Ziggurat Man' and when he went up to university he grew his hair long and he wore ripped jeans and he told his Head of Department that he would not be coming back the following term. When his Head of Department brought up the subject of his being The Man of Vision's son, Isambard flicked his hair, turned his back and walked out. It felt good to go. Like a burden slipping from his shoulders.

His mother alternately wept and went cold-eyed, cajoled and shouted, but his father refused to speak to him. This was not altogether a noticeable punishment since his father seldom spoke to him anyway. When he did resume speaking again it was to say contemptuously, 'No wonder you couldn't stay the course. What do you expect if you choose a bloody geography degree?'

475

The pity of it was that Isambard really liked geography. But he was not going to tell his father that. 'Cool, Dad,' he said, and walked away.

The telephone finally ceased. Been going all the previous evening and then off and on all morning. He stretched and yawned on the greasy settee. Thank God for that. At the other end of it, Isambard knew, sat his sister Polly. Furious. Furious because she was the one left nursing their mother. Furious because he would not ease everybody's mind and travel up to Coventry to be with his father. And furious just because she always was. Furious. He could scarcely remember a time when Polly wasn't angry as hell.

Anyway, it must all be over up there now. Nan would be buried and his father would be on his own and sorting things out. Good. He was glad his mother had flu. Serve his father right. 'Patrick Parker's Muse dies' made Isambard feel sick. That he could turn even Nan's funeral into a Parkerfest. Her fault though. It was always My Famous Son and what My Famous Son wants comes first . . .

The continuation of their mother—you children should be quiet, you children should be grateful, you children should be proud. Isambard wondered what his grandfather had been like. He did not remember him at all—not surprising—and if he ever asked about him no one was interested. But Isambard had a model of a signal box, made by his grandfather. It was beautiful and perfect and he found it in the shed with a lot of other old junk. No one else wanted it so Isambard took it home. Polly had a tendency to drama and said that she wanted one, too. She cried and carried on as she always had, ever since she was born. Real little attention grabber. To shut her up his father had said he would make her another—but he never did. He was too busy being Great. Then as now. Isambard prayed to whichever god might do the trick, that his father would not win the competition for this Millenium thing, the Queen's Bridge. It meant so much to him. If he lost it perhaps he would then understand what it was to feel irrelevant. He did not deserve the happiness that he had never given to others. The telephone rang again. Isambard put his hands over his ears. 'Bugger off, Polly,' he said. And turned up the volume on the television.

*   *   *

Polly puts down the phone and turns to her mother.

'I'm not trying Izzy again,' she says. 'And you should stop worrying about Dad. Don't ring him any more either. He's not a baby. He's been round the world on his own, he's built his bloody bridges on his own—surely he can handle Nana's funeral without falling apart.'

'Take my temperature again.'

'It won't have come down since the last time.'

'I could be up there tonight. Otherwise he'll be sleeping in that house all alone.'

Polly shoves the thermometer into her mother's mouth. 'Wouldn't be the first time he's slept up there without us. He never used to let us stay in the house with him anyway so I don't see why you're worrying now.'

'Polly—' she says.

'Don't try to talk or you might bite it—then where would poor Daddy be if Mummy swallowed the mercury?'

All Peggy could do was look at her daughter with a mixture of fear and reproach. Something she had done for the last few years, ever since Polly experienced her Damascene moment of understanding: which was that in the great, turning wheel of the Parkers' life, she was irrelevant. Isambard was not irrelevant, until he decided to make himself so by dangling razor blades from his ears and trashing his room. But Polly was always irrelevant. Even her name was significantly insignificant. At least Isambard was called Something. Even if that was as far as it went. At least Isambard was *supposed* to have a role. Even if he let them down. When Polly took a doll apart to see what made it work (it had a voice that said 'Wash Me', 'Feed Me', 'Change Me') she was told off for being destructive, she was puzzled. Very quietly she went and put it back together again.

'Good gracious,' was all her mother said when she saw it. 'Good gracious.'

But no one could be bothered to answer Polly's question, which was, 'How do you find out about how things work unless you take them apart?'

Then it happened. One morning she woke to the smells and sounds of her mother's cooking and baking in the kitchen below. It was her birthday. But when she went downstairs she was told to make herself useful as this was the day her father had invited some Important People to lunch. Polly's birthday took second place to that. When she asked where her birthday present was, her mother, flustered and anxious, said that she Just Hadn't Had Time. The whole was compounded the following year when Polly asked to see her birth

478

certificate. Her father had not registered her birth for weeks. When she asked why there was such a delay she was told that her father had been too busy. From that day forward Polly decided that she Just Did Not Have Time either. She would look at her mother brushing her father's hair to tidy it before sending him out into the world, or constructing a dish for him to tempt his demanding palate, and she would curl her lip and continue to be Bloody Awful.

Hence her mother's expression of fear and reproach now. Peggy did not quite know what she had done wrong for Polly, but she knew that she had done something. Patrick simply thought his daughter ill-behaved. All he asked of her was that she was respectful and quiet, which was not very much, in his opinion.

Well, well, thinks Polly as she takes the thermometer out of her mother's mouth after the prescribed two minutes, he deserved no better. Neither of them did. He wouldn't like this, he wouldn't like this at all. He had *never* had to organise anything apart from his work. And now he was practically arranging a state funeral with the press and all.

'One hundred and two,' she says, with cheerful satisfaction. 'You're not going anywhere.'

'Oh!'

'I mean it. I want to get back to work, Mum. And if you go on like this you'll have a relapse and then I'll just have to leave you to it and then when Dad gets back *he'll* have to do the nursing bit . . . Can you imagine how much he would *love* that?'

That went home all right, Polly was pleased to see. She'd learned how to manipulate this lot.

Mrs Parker, mother and wife, was suddenly quite still and quite silent. Given her Coventry origins it did not occur to her that a nurse could be hired. If you were ill you stayed in bed at home and family nursed you. To be nursed by Patrick was a very terrible thought. He would never forgive her. Problem was, Polly was not really much good as a nurse either. She was not, really, much good at anything of a domestic nature, something which quite surprised her mother. No. Polly's life revolved around her flat in Peckham and her horse and her boat. She earned a lot of money in the City, which was nice, and she no longer tried to take things apart to see how they were made or to ask all those eternal questions about how buildings stayed up, which was a blessing. The down side was that if you asked Polly to come over and cook a meal (as they did once when Peggy sprained her wrist falling on the ice) she came over with greasy takeaways. Her joke to her Dad, being 'Take it away—or leave it—'

He was not amused.

As she rattled the thermometer back into its glass Polly felt divided on the subject of her mother's illness. On the one hand she wanted her to get better so that she could go back to her enjoyable life—on the other she wanted her to linger on so that her father really suffered. Their father couldn't shit without their mother, was what Polly and Isambard used to say. In the end the darkness won.

'How he must be hating coping up there all alone,' she said to Peggy. 'But you've just *got* to stay in bed until you are better. And that—' she rubbed her hands '—is that.'

480

It is after this conversation, when Polly has gone downstairs to watch a bit of television, that Peggy Boxer As Was thinks she will telephone Patrick again. She is a little fuzzy about their previous conversation—he wants his post sent on—she remembers that—there's an important letter he's waiting for—but there seemed to be something else—about Florence. About not liking her? She felt so ill she couldn't quite work it out. Perhaps she was a little short-tempered? It is the influenza. She will apologise.

She dials.

*   *   *

The decision has been made. The envelope containing the letter of congratulations with its Royal Coat of Arms has been delivered. The chosen will not know if they have been chosen until they open that envelope.

The young woman in the scruffy Dickensian loft who has just begun to make a name for herself in the world of serious design and who is more or less unremarkable-looking, having gone through orange hair and piercings, travels back across London in the dusk. All she wants to do is to reach home, make herself a cup of herbal tea (she still adheres to some of the ways of the old country, Grandmother's recipes), and relax with her shoes off. Everything else can wait. She gives her all when she is working and it takes it out of her. Today she has been interviewing passers-by with her small tape recorder. She is meticulous about discovering what people really want and need. Most of the interviewees she encountered were out and about

481

doing their shopping. She asks them what they think they would like from a bridge. Their answers confirm her own assumptions—but she is careful always to back these up with research. Now she knows she was right. Good. Grandmother's footsteps.

She walks through the door to her apartment, which is also her studio, and which looks out on the river but from the south side, and she bends to pick up the post. She takes it through to the kitchen area and puts it down. Tea first. She slips off her shoes.

After the Funeral

The accepted way of looking at bridges at any
one time merely represents the most dominant
viewpoint, which has overruled other
interpretations, and the rules we apply when
assessing structures are adjusted to the
continually shifting themes of design.
  Matthew Wells, *30 Bridges*

Patrick stood in the bleak hallway. If he had ever
thought he could stage-manage the occasion of his
mother's funeral, he knew better now. Most of
what happened once they were out of the church
and in the damp sunshine was a blur of confusion.
Most of what happened when they were inside the
church was a blur of confusion, too. Faces
twitching, eyes looking downwards, shuffling feet
on the gravel, no one wanting to look at him except
Father Bryan who seemed incapable of not doing
so. Now he knew the man really was mad. If he said
once back at the house how marvellous, marvellous
the occasion was, he said it half a dozen times. And
it certainly said something for the power of
suggestion because after a while everyone seemed
to believe that it had been—marvellous. Beautiful,
was what the despondent women from the
Mothers' Union called it, Florence's companions in
bitter bane. The secular doyens and doyennes of
the church who cleaned it and beflowered it and
lived their lives by its rotas took it all with

ponderous solemnity, as did the librarian who hid the books that she felt should not appear on the shelves. By the time they all left he felt that he had been to Hell and Back, twice.

'I never want to go through that again,' he said to Audrey as he closed the door on the last of them. And she, quite rightly, pointed out that unless Florence had a second coming it was unlikely. At which they both laughed. Which was highly inappropriate but a blessed relief after all that mournfulness.

'Lilly,' he said. 'How on earth did she hear about it?'

Audrey said she had probably read about it in the paper.

'If that woman can *read* it would be a miracle,' he said irritably. 'My poor mother.'

Audrey knew that what he meant was, 'Poor me.'

They stood in the depressing hallway, under the dingy light, and he smiled at her. She smiled at him. 'I'm glad you came,' he said. Despite the low-wattage bulb, or maybe because of it, she looked much younger than he might have expected.

'I don't have to go yet,' she said, when he asked. 'I'll stay.'

'Good,' he said, meaning it. 'Now for a serious drink and a chance to talk . . . I'm not going anywhere either.' He opened the kitchen door, she followed him. 'And if I have to accept one more person's condolences . . .' He ran his hands through his hair (thinner now, she noticed, but still a good colour) and picked up a bottle. 'A drink and a chance to be alone . . .'

And then the telephone rang.

Which obviously amused Audrey highly. 'Oh Sir

Patrick! Saved by the bell,' she crowed, and laughed and laughed. 'Or you never know what we might have got up to after all these years.'

He did not feel saved at all. He felt interrupted. Audrey was a completely different person from the one he'd known all those years ago. Sophisticated. Alluring even, despite her years (and he could talk). He liked her. He liked being with her. They went back a long way and he was looking forward to spending some time with her—perhaps closely with her. And having a decent glass of something. And now the bloody telephone.

It was his wife.

'Ah,' he said. 'Peggy.'

Behind him the laughter ceased.

'Who was that?'

'What?'

'Laughing.'

'Well—the funniest thing. Guess who came to the funeral?'

'I'm not much in the mood for guessing games.' As if she did not know. 'Who?'

'Little Audrey.'

There was a silence.

'Audrey. Audrey Wapshott. Remember her?'

'I certainly do. What's she doing still there?'

'Oh—we were talking about old times.'

'What about them?'

'We used to be quite good friends. From childhood. Our mothers ...'

'I know, I know,' said Peggy sharply. 'I remember.'

'Do you?' he said, surprised. Anything that took place more than a few years ago and that did not directly include his world of design he found hard

485

to retain. Not enough room in the head for small stuff like that. Even Paris, which he would have liked to remember in every detail, and occasionally tried to, had faded.

Peggy said, 'I'm coming up.'

'No need,' he said quickly.

'I thought you wanted me there. I thought you wanted me to bring you your post . . .' This last, she realised, sounded very lame. 'I thought you didn't know how you were going to cope on your own.'

He was about to say, 'But I'm not on my own,' but even he realised that this would not be sensible.

'Let me speak to Polly,' he said.

'There's no need—'

'Now,' he added, commandingly.

Polly was summoned.

'Your mother does not need to come up here,' he said, very firmly. 'I am coping very well, everyone is helping and being very kind, and I do not need her.'

'Just as well,' said Polly laconically. 'Because she's in no shape.'

'Good,' said her father. 'You keep her that way.'

Polly felt this was not quite the right way to put it but the end result was the same. She was sorry to hear that her father was coping but—well—she had done her best . . .

Patrick put down the receiver.

Polly put down the receiver.

*   *   *

Polly turned to her mother, who was last seen reclining, still pink and feverish, in her bed. Polly was surprised, therefore, to see her upright, pulling out drawers and slapping a holdall onto the tumbled bedclothes.

'You are to stay put, Mother,' said Polly. 'Dad's asked me to make sure of it.'

'You and whose army?' said Peggy. As if she didn't know exactly, bell, book and candle, the kind of relationship Patrick and Audrey used to have— and not just in childhood either. 'Get the office on the line, please. I want a car. Now.'

'I think you might be delirious,' said her daughter.

With a strength that no member of the family had ever seen, let alone experienced, Peggy pushed her daughter out of the way and picked up the telephone herself.

'Car,' she said. 'To Sir Patrick Parker's place. Now. Going to Coventry. Yup. Co-ven-try . . . I know the time. But I want it here now—or sooner.'

The receiver was replaced. Into the holdall went an odd assortment of garments, in Polly's opinion—a disgusting, black see-through nightie, a suspender belt, and an assortment of frilly horrors among them. And when her mother, staggering a little from the exertion, emerged from the en-suite ten minutes later she wore, below her ghastly face—that looked, so thought her daughter, like a rouged phantom—a leather mini-skirt and crocheted top that left very little to the imagination.

'I really don't think—' said Polly.

But the doorbell rang.

'Best you don't, then,' said her mother, staggering off on the spindliest of high heels, and down the stairs, with the bag bumping along behind her. The door closed. And frail Peggy Boxer As Was was gone.

* * *

'Who was that?' Audrey asked disingenuously.

He had better come clean. After all, they were adults. He sat himself down a little gingerly on the front-room sofa. He was half expecting his mother to pop her head around the door. He handed Audrey a whisky. Quite a large one. 'Did you know,' he said firmly, 'that I married Peggy Boxer?'

'As Was?' she said, and she nodded.

It was all she could do not to chuck her whisky at him. How could he possibly think that she would not know? How could he possibly have forgotten lying in bed beside her as he explained? *Did she know?* Indeed. She smiled at him sweetly. The smile of a serpent. He looked relieved. 'I wasn't sure if you knew or not,' he said, with some relief.

'Yes,' she said, 'I did know that.'

'She doesn't—really—understand me,' he said.

Audrey burst out laughing again.

He looked hurt and retreated back along the leatherette. 'No,' he said, hurt, 'she doesn't.'

She pulled herself together. 'Sorry,' she said, 'it's the emotion of seeing you. And you have two fine children. A boy and a girl.'

Patrick was touched. He felt emotional—if that was the right word—seeing her, too. 'Oh yes. Two children. And they *certainly* don't understand me.'

She put out her hand to reassure him.

'You always understood me,' he said, a slight peevishness creeping into his voice. 'You were always interested in what I did. I liked that . . .' he added, wistfully.

Not only brilliant in the forgetful department, she

488

thought, smiling away at him, but bloody brilliant in the area of creative hypocrisy, too.

'Oh, Audrey,' he said (it was partly the emotions of the day, partly the whisky—and partly . . .) 'You knew me so well . . . There is—I think—perhaps—unfinished business between us?'

She closed her eyes and gritted her teeth. In the deepening dusk it was hard to see her expression but it was clearly one of strong emotion. Little shoe, she thought softly, soon, but not yet. She kept her handbag right by her and a tiny piece of pale blue tissue paper peeked out.

After a moment she opened her eyes again and said quite firmly, 'It's only now that I realise how well I *did* know you.'

He slid back towards her again.

She smiled encouragingly. 'And you are right. We do have unfinished business.' She ran her fingertips over his cheek and gave him an encouraging smile. How much she had loved him.

He was encouraged. 'I want—' he said.

Outside in the street a couple stomped by, laughing. It was a raw, alien sound in that room.

'All I want,' he murmured, 'is to relax with you. Go to bed with you. Like we used to . . .'

And she was tempted, very tempted. There was absolutely nothing in the world to stop them now.

'Actually,' she said, standing up, 'what I want at the moment is a bit of a walk.'

Delayed gratification. She knew about that, too. She'd delayed hers by over thirty years.

*   *   *

It is the same for a jewel thief who can only wear

489

the stolen ruby at night when there is no one to see, or for the purloiner of a Great Painting who can only hang it in their cellar and enjoy it alone . . . Peggy Boxer As Was had never, really, felt Patrick was hers. She had stolen him. He was her ruby, her Great Painting—what her mother called the Feather in Her Cap. But always, somewhere in the back of her mind, she was aware of Audrey Wapshott. And she always feared that one day she would come back and claim what she considered still to be hers. Florence had told her often enough. Audrey would never forgive her. Audrey would have her revenge.

And now it was true. She had heard that laugh, and she had heard the faintest hint of guilt in her husband's voice. He who could do no wrong was about to. The laugh was Audrey's all right, but it was not the laugh of one who is polite, cold, distant, separated by the past—it was reckless, amused . . .

She had never felt more ill, nor more determined. In the car she goaded the driver to go faster as if she were travelling in some eighteenth-century coach with four greys and a snapping, jingling harness. She always had a penchant for romantic novels (not that she told Patrick) and had been quite relieved after Barbara Cartland died to see a very pink portrait of the novelist, called post-modern, in the Royal College's Graduate show. So she couldn't be all bad. Not that any of that mattered now. All that mattered now was to get to Coventry and save her marriage. 'Drive faster,' she shouted again. If it wasn't a harness jingling it must be her teeth. 'Go on—faster,' she yelled to the driver. 'Faster, faster, faster . . .'

The driver immediately braked and slowed and pulled into a lay-by. He turned. He smiled. He said, 'Lady Parker, your husband would not welcome it if both of us were to be found at dawn tomorrow spread all over the A40 . . .'

'He might,' said Peggy miserably.

He started up the car again and they drove the next fifty miles or so in silence. Silence, all save for the chewing of Peggy Boxer As Was's once impeccable nails. As were.

*   *   *

During their walk, as Audrey reacquainted herself with familiar places, she asked Patrick if he did not feel nostalgic. Perhaps a little sad. Patrick said that the whole of Coventry made him sad and that he never wanted to come here again. They had even asked him, he told her, to redesign the Town Hall. And had offered him the keys of the city for it. As if he would.

'You wouldn't even come to visit Florence's last resting place?' she asked.

'I don't feel anything for her,' he said helplessly.

'Do you feel anything for me?'

He stared at her. 'I don't know,' he said.

She was thinking of some of her favourite bridges. The Pont Neuf in Paris, the Rialto, the Ponte Vecchio, the tragic bridge of Mostar, Brooklyn, Ironbridge, the perfection of the Punt da Suransuns at Viamala, the broken twelfth-century bridge of St Benezet in Avignon, the Campo Volantin in Bilbao—she had not realised that she knew of so many—or that she cared about them. She fell in love with Patrick at Ironbridge, and

491

Edwin, in his last months of life, proposed marriage to her on the Pont Neuf. Bridges were powerful things. 'I saw a poster once,' she said, 'about an exhibition of town planning.'

'Oh really?' he said, politely.

'The poster,' she said, 'was from some design exhibition somewhere—and it said, "Ask not what kind of a bridge to build, but whether you need one."'

Patrick stared at her. 'Are you mad?' he said. 'If there is a void to be crossed, there is a bridge to be built.'

She walked him to his father's grave. It was dark now and she felt it was time.

'Lilly will be buried next to him,' she said.

'What about my mother?'

Audrey smiled. 'I have arranged it.'

He said nothing.

'And you will make them a monument. Lilly and George.'

Then he laughed, and it was not the whisky.

'I don't do little things like that,' he said. 'I don't know how.'

'You will,' she said.

But he shook his head. 'I thought you understood,' he said bleakly. He suddenly felt very empty. And old.

They walked back to the house in silence.

In the kitchen they sat at the table.

'A drink?' he said.

'How about', said Audrey ironically, 'a nice cup of tea?'

'Yes,' said Patrick.

He waited for her to say that she would do the honours. But she did not. There was nothing else

492

for it. Audrey sat at the kitchen table while Patrick made a pot of tea, staring about him until the kettle boiled.

It was still, very much, his mother's domain. Draped over the scrubbed wooden table was the ancient and worn oilcloth—an oilcloth in that peculiarly unappetising shade of dull green that is never seen in nature and made even more dull by years of wiping. Florence's colour.

He was not very certain of the tea-making procedure but she looked away at each mistake—at the unwarmed pot into which he shovelled four heaped spoons of loose-leaf, at the small amount of boiling water that followed them, at the uncovered pot, sitting on the chill of the old wooden draining board in the back door's draught . . . She kept her mouth shut. It was not her job. He gazed at her and then back at his watch. They waited for five minutes during which time he took the lid off the pot three times and stirred it vigorously, peering in as if the steamy depth would yield up secrets.

'How much longer?' he asked.

'For what?'

'The tea. To brew?'

'Depends how you like it,' she said, quite indifferently, and tapped the waiting cups and saucers.

'How do you like it?' he asked.

'As it comes,' she said.

At which point he gave up and poured. Tea grouts floated on the top of the orangey-brown liquid.

'Lovely,' she said. In a voice that suggested she was looking at six-day-old Kattomeat. 'Lovely.' And she thought—he can build ten thousand bridges and they'll all stay up—but he can't make a cup of tea. Just as he could not turn a heel.

And he thought—well she should have offered to help—I'm a bridge builder not a bloody caterer—

They both smiled at each other a little uneasily.

She pushed the scummy tea away from her. Her handbag, so potent with its little piece of pale blue tissue peeking out, was on the table between them. Right there on Florence's old green cloth. He did the same, pausing to collect two glasses from the draining board and the whisky from the pantry. He poured them each a tot.

'Do you love anyone, Patrick?' she asked. 'I mean, we buried your mother today and you seem—well—'

'I have a lot on my mind,' he said, the whisky relaxing him. 'I'm waiting for a letter.' Love, he thought. I love my work.

Then he asked, 'Have you seen the Sistine Chapel?' In such a way that she nearly said, 'Is the Pope a Catholic?' But years of diplomacy forbore. 'Oh once or twice,' fairly calmly.

He nodded. 'Michelangelo understood how it is to be what I am. He has a poem called something like *"Costei pur si delibra"*—they gave me a copy when I picked up my medal.'

'Woman without boundaries . . .?' she said, half to herself.

He was surprised. 'You know Italian?'

'*Poco,*' she said sharply, keeping her hands firmly around her glass in case she really did throw it this time. '*Continuare . . .*'

'He likens his art to "This savage woman, by no strictures bound, who has ruled that I'm to burn, die, suffer, though the sins she scolds weigh but an ounce or two . . ." '

'Patrick,' she said, 'You have never burned for anything.'

'I'm burning now,' he said. 'For the Millennium Bridge.' Whisky and Brunel made a powerful dynamic. 'My darling.'

She knew that the endearment was not for her.

'We all have one great moment in us, and that will be mine,' he said.

'You have just buried your mother, Patrick,' she said. 'Don't you feel anything?'

He looked at her, dry-eyed, shrugged, and said nothing.

'Your great moment won't be the building of another bloody-well-bugger-it *bridge*,' she said, so viciously that it made him jump. 'Your great moment will be when you shed a genuine tear.'

'I can't do a gravestone, Aud. I can't. It's just too trivial.'

'Well just you *memento mori*, Patrick, that's all I can say.'

*   *   *

He refilled their glasses. They were both wondering what to do next when into the stillness and the calm came the sound of the front-door knocker thundering through the house as if Mephistopheles himself had arrived to claim his prize of one damned soul. Or 'This savage woman by no strictures bound . . .' And Patrick thought—surely not—it couldn't be—did he hear the frenzied tones of his wife . . . ?

5

The Godiva Principle

There is no Mostarian who has not made love
near the Old Bridge.
Jasna

And then came 9 November 1993. General
Slobodan Praljak, a man from Mostar, a theatre
director, was the commander of the Croat forces.
Their tanks fired 68 shells of 100mm calibre at
the bridge in two days . . . After the 68th shell the
old bridge could hold no more. It gave in to
shelling at 10.16 a.m. With a horrible crash the
gracious white arch collapsed into the Neretva
River. Centuries collapsed, a friend of mine
wrote. Our lives collapsed.
Lucy Blakstad, *Bridge: The Architecture of
Connection*

It took some calming down, the situation. On
opening the door and expecting to find nothing
more than some well-wishers, or religious
doorsteppers, or someone arriving with late
condolences, Patrick had the breath barged out of
him as Peggy Boxer As Was flew past him, along
the passage and up the stairs . . . He assumed she
needed the bathroom but he heard her opening
and shutting the bedroom doors. Wrenching and
slamming would be nearer the descriptive truth of
it . . . Unlike her—he thought idly—she was usually
so quiet.

496

On the step stood the driver, Johnson, whom Patrick knew well. They had often used him. He looked agitated. Patrick asked why. It was Johnson's opinion that Lady Parker was very unwell—that the flu was causing a serious malfunction—that a doctor would do the trick. And then Johnson, looking quite nervous, retreated.

'On the account, then,' called Patrick, as normally as he could under the circumstances, and he waved the man into the car before turning back. The last door upstairs was flung open and then slammed before Peggy came whipping down the stairs again—dressed, he noticed for the first time, in an odd assortment of clothes. Plainly she was very ill indeed.

'You'd better come and sit down,' he said, quite at a loss to do more.

'Where is she?' hissed his wife.

'Who?'

'You know who . . . *her . . .*'

He thought for a moment. There could only be one explanation. Florence. His wife had become demented. 'Why, in the churchyard,' he answered soothingly.

'Liar!' yelled his wife. Her face ran with sweat, white and glistening; she looked dangerous. Delirious.

Patrick wondered if he should slap her. Round the face or on the back—or somewhere . . . 'She is at rest,' he said. 'It is all over.'

'She'll never be at rest, that one,' shrieked his wife. 'Never.'

Johnson was right. No wonder he'd backed off. Patrick felt helpless in the face of what was clear, mental derangement. He stood there, involuntarily blocking her way down the passage to the kitchen. 'Perhaps you should get into bed?' he said nervously.

'After she's been in there?'

'Well—there are other bedrooms,' said Patrick, not unreasonably. 'I could put you in my old bed—that's made up—if the other one puts you off . . .'

Peggy then went several shades of increasingly pale, shiny beige.

'You are not well,' he said, and advanced to hold her.

But Peggy Boxer had seen *Gaslight*. She knew what could happen when a husband said that to his wife.

'You are not committing me to any loonie bin,' she said.

He stood there completely at sea. What the hell was one to do with a deranged wife? And then, like an angel of mercy, the door of the kitchen opened and out came Audrey. At which point, Peggy Boxer fainted away.

'I think she must be taking something,' said Patrick, as they helped the semi-conscious figure towards a kitchen chair.

'She feels very hot,' said Audrey.

'Can't think why,' said Patrick, staring grimly at the open scrap of crochet she wore.

But Audrey had taken the dishcloth from the sink and was wiping Peggy's face and neck, which seemed to revive her. She made a noise and sat up, blinking. At which point, Audrey took her hot head and thrust it down between her knees. The head attempted to bob up again, Audrey pushed it harder. There was some snuffling and a considerable amount of lively movement. 'Give her a drink,' she said. And nodded towards the whisky bottle.

While Patrick poured whisky down his wife's throat (she who never took much more than a small glass of wine), Audrey sat opposite her and watched the woman's distress. It was not a pretty sight. The fear and anger on Peggy Boxer's face as she glowered across the table at her was very disturbing. And Patrick, who a moment ago was reasonably relaxed and friendly, now looked on his wife with loathing. Fascinating, thought Audrey, and So Sad.

Peggy suddenly snapped into lucid, secretarial mode. 'I've brought your post. There's one with a crest on it.' She got up and tottered out of the room and down the hallway, coughing and spluttering and quite clearly not well. Audrey looked at Patrick who had put his hand to his mouth and closed his eyes, clearly enraptured at the prospect of the letter with the crest, unmoved and unconcerned about helping his sick wife.

Amazing, thought Audrey.

Absolutely amazing.

To think that it could have been me.

*   *   *

About halfway through her second cup of herbal tea, just as she began to feel really relaxed, the young woman in the London apartment overlooking the river (south side) remembered her post. Wearily she got up from her chair and returned to the kitchen to collect it. There was one envelope, long and cream-coloured and expensive, that had a crest on it. She sat down again, sipped her drink, turned the envelope over and over in her free hand and began to run her thumb along its length. The result of the competition. She tried to breathe evenly. Before she opened it she told herself that she was young, that there would be other bridges, that she could not expect . . . But none of it stopped the hope in her heart as she pulled out the creamy white letter.

*　　*　　*

Peggy returned with a handful of letters, coughed over them, handed them to Patrick, and sank back into her chair as if she had just climbed the Eiger. In flu sufferers' terms, thought Audrey, she probably had.

Peggy whispered across the table, 'Have you?' she rolled her eyes ceilingwards.

'What?' asked Audrey, kindly.

'You know,' said Peggy, in a painful whisper. 'Been together—upstairs?'

Patrick coughed very loudly. And sat down heavily next to his wife. 'What rubbish,' he said. 'It's the flu talking. And anyway, you attach an importance to such things that is honestly not there.'

'Thank you,' said Audrey.

'I don't mean—' he said.

'What do you mean?' asked his wife.

Audrey decided enough was enough. Here she was in this miserable kitchen, which had seen such misery, God knows, and here was more misery. There was no fun attached to it any more, nothing playful, it was just about damaged lives. With her free hand she picked up the whisky bottle and slowly and deliberately recharged all their glasses.

'To Godiva,' she said. And drank.

Both looked perplexed.

'Someone whom you, Patrick, used to refer to as That Silly Woman.'

'Yes,' said Patrick, distractedly. 'I did. And she was.' He sorted through the post. Then he picked out a letter, the one with the crest, and was about to open it. 'Ah,' he said, kissing it, 'my acceptance. At last. Good.'

The creamy envelope crackled in his eager hands.

'Just a minute,' said Audrey. 'Wait, please.'

Patrick looked up irritably. Out came the lower lip, and the jaw. 'What?' he said. His hand hovered, he was aching to take out the paper and read and *know* . . . His life meant nothing without the commission for this bridge, this important landmark to posterity which would bear his name. '*What?*'

Audrey removed from her handbag the pale-blue-tissue-wrapped shoe. She pushed it, dragon face first, across the old green oilcloth towards Patrick.

'From Madame Koi,' she said. 'Of Paris. It seems you haven't always thought the importance attached to—going upstairs—was insignificant. You looked for her hard enough.' She pushed the dragon further towards him. 'I believe you have the other abutment?'

His gaze rose from the rustling paper and its all too familiar contents, to her, and then back again. A jumble of thoughts racketed through his head. Paris? Madame Koi? Tokyo Cinders? Did Audrey know her? Worse—did Audrey *know* . . . .? He made a little swallowing noise as he picked up the shoe and ran his fingers delicately over the beadwork.

'Oh how lovely,' said Peggy, and coughed all over it.

Patrick stared at what was in his hand as if it was the serpent itself. He knew that dragon. He could practically feel its heat. His face was—quite unreadable. He did not know what emotion to put there. 'How did you come to have this . . .?' he asked. But, really, he knew. There was something, a bell, that rang in his head. Ankles. Weak ankles. And other vague things. He gazed from the shoe to Audrey and back again. No, no, no, he mouthed silently.

Yes, yes, yes, she mouthed back. Then she stood up, very slowly, removed her handbag from Florence's dull, green, unnatural oilcloth, tucked it over her arm, put her little fingertips to her mouth, wiggled them, giggled once from behind them in a way that was all to familiar to him—and then turned with a very sweet smile to Peggy. 'We have only been discussing a little business,' she said. 'No more than that.' And she squeezed Peggy Boxer As Was's hand.

Peggy's mouth made a perfect circle. But nothing came out of it.

'Patrick is going to make a nice little monument for his father's grave. Aren't you, Patrick? With appropriate wording about what gifts he gave to him, his grateful son.'

He shook his head as if to say, she was fooling herself.

But she went on standing there, waiting, her finger ends tapping at the shoe.

Eventually she said, 'Think hard about what you consider trivial, Patrick, and remember—little

502

acorns sometimes grow into big, unruly oak trees.' She adopted a voice from her youth, The Radio Doctor: 'You know, sometimes, Patrick, we don't know what we've got until we lose it. Remember Shakespeare? Have you read Shakespeare, Patrick? "How sharper than a serpent's tooth it is, to have a thankless child . . ." I was thinking of George. I was also thinking that the reverse is true. Sometimes you don't know how lucky you are that you have lost something until you find it again.' She laughed. Not very nicely.

Patrick and Peggy both looked confused now.

'And Euripides, Patrick. Do you know Euripides? *Rhesus 1*? Just a fragmentary play but good—very good.'

He shook his head. 'I'm not very up on the Greeks,' he said, still fingering the envelope with longing.

'Well, Euripides suggests that you "Slight not what's near through aiming at what's far"—which seems the perfect epitaph for your father and Lilly's grave.'

'Lilly's?' said Peggy Boxer. 'Who's Lilly?' She was staring from one to the other of them and back at the shoe as if she was witnessing Armageddon.

'Patrick?' said Audrey, tapping the shoe all the harder.

It took a little while.

But then he nodded. The unopened envelope weighing heavy in his hand.

'I'll do it,' he said.

'Good,' she said. 'I thought you would.'

'Do what?' asked Peggy. But neither paid her the slightest attention. She mopped at her glowing face mournfully. 'I always knew it would end like this,' she said.

'Not an ending, Peggy,' said Audrey. 'A beginning.'

She picked up her whisky glass. 'Let's all drink to Brunel,' she said. 'Whose reputation is—apparently—unassailable.' And she drained her glass to the very last drop.

But Patrick was too busy reading his letter to notice.

While he read, she saw that a small tear had begun to trickle down his cheek. She pushed the shoe further towards him and very quietly, she left.

Zaha Hadid's Living Bridge
Enlightenment thinking saw inhabited bridges fall out of fashion and now the few remaining examples in Europe are thought of as quaint tourist attractions. But the appeal of inhabited bridges did not die away completely. In 1996 an initiative in London investigated the possibility of revitalising the idea. A site was chosen at the heart of the City and from a short list, Zaha Hadid's bold design was selected as one of two joint winners by visitors to London's best-ever-attended paying architecture exhibition.

Hadid's structure combines valuable commercial space with structural lightness, three lightweight pedestrian walkways, and cantilevered glass volumes in which the bridge's inhabited space can be found. A daring proposal.

Perhaps the greatest surprise is that the public liked her design so much.

Hadid succeeded in capturing imaginations with a design that Prince Charles would certainly abhor.

So far the developers who sponsored the competition have shown no signs of proceeding with Hadid's proposal.

Lucy Blakstad, *Bridge: The Architecture of Connection*

BIBLIOGRAPHY

Blakstad, Lucy, *Bridge: The Architecture of Connection*, August Media, 2002

Buchanan, Angus, *Brunel*, Hambledon and London Ltd, 2002

Ghirardo, Diane, *Architecture After Modernism*, Thames and Hudson, 1996

Pevsner, Nikolaus, *An Outline of European Architecture*, Penguin, 1943

Richardson, Kenneth, *Twentieth Century Coventry*, Macmillan, 1972

Vaughan, Adrian, *Isambard Kingdom Brunel: Engineering Knight Errant*, John Murray, 1993

Watkin, David, *English Architecture*, Thames and Hudson, 2001

Wells, Matthew, *30 Bridges*, Lawrence King Publishing, 2002

ACKNOWLEDGEMENTS

Particular thanks to Clare Reihill for being such a great editor: Coventry City Council for their help in piecing together a picture of that town: The RIBA for their endless kindness in answering my stream of questions.

Acknowledgements to the Estate of T. S. Eliot for the quotation from 'The Dry Salvages' from *Four Quartets*; to Lucy Blakstad for quotations from *Bridge: The Architecture of Connection*; to Frank Delaney for the quotation from *James Joyce's Odyssey*; and to Matthew Wells for quotations from *30 Bridges*.

1 2 3 4 5 6 7 8 9 10 11 12 13 14 15 16 17 18 19 20 21 22 23
24 25 26 27 28 29 30 31 32 33 34 35 36 37 38 39 40 41 42 43
44 45 46 47 48 49 50 51 52 53 54 55 56 57 58 59 60 61 62 63
64 65 66 67 68 69 70 71 72 73 74 75 76 77 78 79 80 81 82 83
84 85 86 87 88 89 90 91 92 93 94 95 96 97 98 99 100

101 102 103 104 105 106 107 108 109 110 111 112 113 114 115
116 117 118 119 120 121 122 123 124 125 126 127 128 129 130
131 132 133 134 135 136 137 138 139 140 141 142 143 144 145
146 147 148 149 150 151 152 153 154 155 156 157 158 159 160
161 162 163 164 165 166 167 168 169 170 171 712 173 174 175
176 177 178 179 180 181 182 183 184 185 186 187 188 189 190
191 192 193 194 195 196 197 198 199 200

201 202 203 204 205 206 207 208 209 210 211 212 213 214 215
216 217 218 219 220 221 222 223 224 225 226 227 228 229 230
231 232 233 234 235 236 237 238 239 240 241 242 243 244 245
246 247 248 249 250 251 252 253 254 255 256 257 258 259 260
261 262 263 264 265 266 267 268 269 270 271 272 273 274 275
276 277 278 279 280 281 282 283 284 285 286 287 288 289 290
291 292 293 294 295 296 297 298 299 300

301 302 303 304 305 306 307 308 309 310 311 312 313 314 315
316 317 318 319 320 321 322 323 324 325 326 327 328 329 330
331 332 333 334 335 336 337 338 339 340 341 342 343 344 345
346 347 348 349 350 351 352 353 354 355 356 357 358 359 360
361 362 363 364 365 366 367 368 369 370 371 372 373 374 375
376 377 378 379 380 381 382 383 384 385 386 387 388 389 390
391 392 393 394 395 396 397 398 399 400

401 402 403 404 405 406 407 408 409 410 411 412 413 414 415
416 417 418 419 420 421 422 423 424 425 426 427 428 429 430
431 432 433 434 435 436 437 438 439 440 441 442 443 444 445
446 447 448 449 450 451 452 453 454 455 456 457 458 459 460
461 462 463 464 465 466 467 468 469 470 471 472 473 474 475
476 477 478 479 480 481 482 483 484 485 486 487 488 489 490
491 492 493 494 495 496 497 498 499 500

M/c 3209

901 902 903 904 905 906 907 908 909 910 911 912 913 914 915
916 917 918 919 920 921 922 923 924 925 926 927 928 929 930
931 932 933 934 935 936 937 938 939 940 941 942 943 944 945
946 947 948 949 950 951 952 953 954 955 956 957 958 959 960
961 962 963 964 965 966 967 968 969 970 971 972 973 974 975
976 977 978 979 980 981 982 983 984 985 986 987 988 989 990
991 992 993 994 995 996 997 998 999 1000

M/c 3318

1431 1432 1433 1434 1435 1436 1437 1438 1439 1440 1441 1442 1443 1444 1445
1446 1447 1448 1449 1450 1451 1452 1453 1454 1455 1456 1457 1458 1459 1460
1461 1462 1463 1464 1465 1466 1467 1468 1469 1470 1471 1472 1473 1474 1475
1476 1477 1478 1479 1480 1481 1482 1483 1484 1485 1486 1487 1488 1489 1490
1491 1492 1493 1494 1495 1496 1497 1498 1499 1500

M/c 3318A